W9-AMO-047

Date: 9/30/20

LP FIC ARMSTRONG
Armstrong, Kelley,
Alone in the wild

ALONE IN THE WILD

ALONE IN THE WILD

A ROCKTON NOVEL

KELLEY ARMSTRONG

WHEELER PUBLISHING
A part of Gale, a Cengage Company

Copyright © 2020 by KLA Fricke Inc.
A Casey Duncan Novel #5.
Wheeler Publishing, a part of Gale, a Cengage Company.

Wheeler Publishing Large Print Hardcover.
The text of this Large Print edition is unabridged.
Other aspects of the book may vary from the original edition.
Set in 16 pt. Plantin.

LIBRARY OF CONGRESS CIP DATA ON FILE.
CATALOGUING IN PUBLICATION FOR THIS BOOK
IS AVAILABLE FROM THE LIBRARY OF CONGRESS

ISBN-13: 978-1-4328-7849-8 (hardcover alk. paper)

Published in 2020 by arrangement with St. Martin's Publishing Group

Printed in Mexico
Print Number: 01   Print Year: 2020

For Jeff

For Jeff

ONE

I wake buried under a hundred and forty pounds of dog. Storm knows she's not allowed on the bed, so I lie there, brain slowly churning, until I remember I'm not *in* bed. I'm on the ground. Cold, hard winter ground — the floor of a tent that is definitely not big enough for two adults and a Newfoundland dog. Which tells me one adult is gone.

I lift my head. Sure enough, there's no sign of Dalton. I peer at the glow of sunrise seeping through the canvas. I've slept in. It's December in the Yukon, when dawn means it's about . . . I lift my watch. Yep, 10 A.M.

I groan. Storm echoes it as she tries to stand, an impossible feat within the confines of this tent.

"Where's Eric?" I ask.

Shockingly, the dog doesn't answer. I blink back the fog of a night that started with

7

tequila and ended with . . . Well, it ended strenuously enough to explain why I'm still in bed at ten, though apparently my partner had no trouble rising early.

We'd left Storm outside last night. That wasn't cruel. It's hovering around the freezing mark, positively balmy for this time of year. Storm has her thick coat and her companion, a wolf-dog named Raoul. We'd brought them on our weekend getaway both for company and for training, Storm as a tracker and Raoul as hunter. Raoul's master doesn't hunt. Not animals, at least.

If Storm is in the tent with the flap closed, that means Dalton let her in. It also means he's taken Raoul. I rub my eyes and spot a note pinned to the tent flap.

When I push Storm, she grunts and shifts enough for me to scrabble over her and pluck off the note.

Hunting. Back for lunch. Coffee in thermos. Don't wander.

The note is the model of reticent efficiency, and I would say that fits our sheriff to a tee, but I've also read his near-poetic academic and philosophical musings, ones that shouldn't come from anyone without a Ph.D., much less a guy with zero formal schooling. That is also our sheriff. Two sides to the same coin. Only I get to see the second one.

I find not only coffee but breakfast in a dog-proof pouch at the end of the bed. Scrambled eggs with venison sausage, and bannock with . . . I lift the hard bread, still warm from the fire, oozing gooey brown dots. Bannock with chocolate chips. I laugh and take a bite. I won't say I'm a bannock fan, but chocolate makes everything better.

I happily munch the bannock and wash it down with coffee. I don't toss any scraps to Storm. Honestly, at her size, she'd never even taste them. Instead, she gets one of my sausages. As for the "don't wander" part of Dalton's note, I'm interpreting that as a suggestion rather than the imperative it seems. Oh, naturally he hopes I'll take it as a command, but he knows better than to expect that. He means for me to stay close, and I will. I'm not about to stay in the tent for two more hours, though.

When I finish breakfast, I open the flap, and Storm clambers out to romp in the snow. She's fourteen months old, which means she's outwardly a full-grown dog, but inside she's still a pup. At thirty-two, I understand the feeling. Or, I should say, I've regained the feeling after sixteen months in Rockton. Before that, while I remember a girl endlessly on the move, endlessly into mischief, that girl vanished when I was eighteen, shoved into hiding by the kind of mistake that banishes one's carefree inner child. Out here, I've found her again . . . at least, when I'm not on duty as Detective Casey Butler.

Dalton and I are on vacation, which means we're taking an entire two days off. Down south, we'd call that a weekend. Up here, with a police force of three, we take time off where we can find it.

Things have been slow in Rockton. The holidays are approaching, and it's as if people decided to cut us slack as a seasonal gift. No assaults. No robberies. No murders. In a town of under two hundred people, the last should be obvious, but this is Rockton. Murder capital of the world, someone used to say. That someone knew exactly what she was talking about, having turned out to be a killer herself.

Rockton is special. For better or worse. Mostly better, but the crime rate is one of those "worse" parts. We can't expect otherwise, really. We are a town of fugitives. Everyone here is running from something. Some are victims, on the run from ex-partners, stalkers, anyone who might want them dead through no fault of their own. This is the true purpose of Rockton — a refuge for those fleeing persecution. It's also home to white-collar criminals, whose misdeeds pay our bills. Then there are those whose mistakes — often violent ones — brought them to Rockton under expensively bought cover stories given even to Dalton. So it's no surprise that we have a murder rate.

For now, it's quiet, and has been for six months. Which means Dalton and I can take an actual weekend off.

Storm and I play in the snow for about an hour before I realize that I should have stoked the fire first. While Dalton had left it blazing for me, he's obviously been gone awhile, and by the time Storm and I collapse, exhausted, the fire is down to embers. I add another log, but it's not going to take. We need kindling.

That's life up here. Constant work just to survive. Heat doesn't come at the flick of a switch. Food isn't the nearest fast-food joint away. Water isn't a simple matter of turning on a faucet. In Rockton, we simulate modern living as best we can — there are restaurants in town, and water does come from taps through a pump system — but everyone needs to work to put food in that grocery, to fill the water tanks when the stream runs low. One quickly develops a healthy respect for our pioneer ancestors.

Storm and I head out to gather kindling. Soon, though, I realize that new-fallen snow is going to complicate the task. Even if I unearth sticks, they won't be dry. That's fine — the best source of winter kindling is dead trees. I'm maybe a few hundred feet from the camp when I find a brown-needled pine that's been crowded out by sturdier siblings.

I start breaking off twigs. Storm dances about, her second wind gale-force strong. When I throw a stick, she chases it, only to notice I'm still snapping off branches. She shoots me a sullen scowl.

"I'm not Eric," I say. "I play fetch properly."

More scowling. Then she flings herself to the ground with a flounce and a sigh.

"Fine," I say with a laugh. "Once and only once."

I take another branch and hold it over my head. She stays where she is, watching me, refusing to fall for this again. I throw it, and she doesn't move until I take off after the branch. Then she bolts up and runs for it. I'm one pace ahead, Storm right on my heels. She veers to pass me, and I throw myself down in a home-plate slide. I grab the stick, flip onto my back, and fist-pump it in the air . . . giving me two seconds of victory before I have a Newfoundland on my face for the second time this morning.

Sputtering and laughing, I shove her off. Then, punctuating my own noise, I hear something that makes me go still. Storm lumbers off with the stick as I rise slowly, listening.

It wasn't what it sounded like. Couldn't be.

The noise comes again, a plaintive wail, like a baby's cry.

Storm catches it. She stops and pivots, ears perking. She glances at me as if to say, *What* is *that?*

"I don't know," I answer, as much for myself.

The morning has gone quiet again, and I'm straining to listen and figure out what it really was. I mentally run through my list of "animals that aren't hibernating right now." I've heard a similar sound from a bear cub, but it's the wrong season for that. We have cougars — a female who wandered north of their usual territory and now has grown cubs. The cry didn't sound right for a big cat. Not a wolf or a feral dog, either.

Bird? That seems most likely, and I've decided that must have been what it was when the noise comes again, and it is not like a bird at all.

A fox? They make some truly bloodcurdling sounds. There's a vixen who lives near our house in Rockton, and I've heard her scream and bolted upright, certain someone was being murdered horribly right outside our window.

I'm still standing there pondering when I catch a glimpse of running black fur and realize it's my dog.

"Storm!" I shout as I bolt after her.

She stops, and I exhale in relief. This spring, I had to shoot a young cougar she chased. Thus ensued six months of special training to be sure no wild animal would ever lead her off again.

I jog to catch up.

"We'll go check it out," I say, and she may not understand the words, but I only need to take a step toward the sound for her to bark with joy.

I motion for her to heel, and she does. Dalton and I have spent countless hours training her, and it's paid off. She's not only blossoming into a first-rate tracker, but she's more obedient than I'd dared hope. That's a necessity when your dog is bigger than you.

Storm stays at my side. When a tree prevents that, she falls behind me, as she's been taught.

The wail comes again. It's weak enough that if the forest weren't winter-quiet, I'd miss it. It sounds so much like a baby that I have to pause and ask myself "Why couldn't it be?"

There are people living out here besides us. Rockton has been around since the fifties, and over the years, residents have relocated into the wilderness for various reasons. Their term ran out in Rockton, and they didn't want to go home. Or they disagreed with the politics — as the town became less an asylum for the innocent and more a pay-to-play escape for the desperate — but they still needed the refuge of the forest. Most of these are what we call settlers. True pioneers of the north, some in communities and some living independently, as Dalton's parents did. Then there are the hostiles, and that is . . . a complicated subject that becomes more complicated the longer I'm here and the deeper I dig.

When I arrived, I was told that hostiles were residents who'd left and reverted to something primitive and dangerous. I'm no longer convinced that all of them chose that reversion. But that's a topic for another time. What matters now is that people do live out here, so I might very well be hearing a human infant.

I slow to a walk, straining for the sounds of others. If I hear any, I will retreat posthaste. Even settlers can be aggressive if we wander into their campsites.

Yet I hear only the occasional cry of what, increasingly, I can't imagine as anything except a baby. Then Storm whines. I glance down at her, and she stops. Parks her butt in the snow and gives me a look that asks if we must continue. She follows it with a glance over her shoulder, in the direction of our camp, in case I don't understand what she wants.

She senses danger ahead. No, I suppose that's melodramatic. To be precise, she smells strangers, and she has learned, unfortunately, that not all strangers are kind. Something in the scent of whatever lies ahead worries her.

I motion for her to sit and stay, and she glowers at me. With a grunt, she lifts and then lowers her hindquarters. I'm as trained in Storm's language as she is in mine, and this odd movement tells me that she will sit and stay, but she'd rather come with me.

I hesitate. I've learned the hard way that my dog might be the most valuable commodity I own out here. Never mind how well she's trained; one look at her size gets a settler's mind turning, considering how she could be used, as protection or as a beast of burden.

Taking her with me is a risk. So is leaving her here, commanded to stay, prey for any human or beast who happens upon her.

I nod and motion for her to stay behind me. She doesn't like that but communicates her disapproval only with a chuff. Then she's right on my heels.

After another half dozen steps, there is no doubt that I am hearing a baby. The weak and plaintive cry comes from right in front of me. Yet I see nothing.

I blink hard. I'm in an open area scattered with saplings, not big enough to hide someone clutching a child. The cry comes from right in the middle of an empty clearing, where I see nothing.

Storm whines. When I motion for her to stay behind me, she whines louder, taking on a note of irritation now. She's asking nicely, but she really, really wants the release command. I won't give it. This could be a trap, someone . . .

Someone what? Hiding a recording of a crying child under the snow?

Under the . . .

I tear into the clearing. The heap ahead

looks like a buried log, and it's too large to be a baby, but that's definitely where the sound comes from. As I run, the snow deepens, with no tree canopy to block it, and I'm staggering forward in snow to my knees. I plow through, and I'm almost at the heap when my leg strikes something, and I stumble. In righting myself, I uncover a boot.

In two more steps, I'm beside the heap. The cries have stopped, and my heart stops with them. I claw at the snow. My fingers hit fabric. A woman's body. I can see that in a glance, and again, I don't stop for a better look. She is still and she is cold, and I cannot help her.

I keep digging, but there's just the woman, and for a horrible moment, I imagine the baby trapped beneath her. Then, at a whimper, I realize the sound comes from under her jacket. I tear at it, the fabric frozen and stiff.

Blood. I see blood under the snow. I wrestle the jacket open, and there is the baby, clutched to the dead woman's chest.

TWO

I yank the child free so fast that the momentum knocks me backward. I land on Storm, and my arms reflexively tighten around the baby.

Crushing it.

No, no, no . . .

I struggle upright as I loosen my grip . . . so much I almost drop the baby. I squeeze my eyes shut and shudder. I'm not easily rattled. I've hung off a cliff, fingers slipping, and only thought *Damn, this isn't good.* But here I am freaked out. I know nothing about babies — *nothing* — and I've just dug one out from under the snow, from the arms of the child's dead mother, and . . . and . . .

Focus, damn it! Focus!

Deep hyperventilating breaths. Then I gasp. I'm holding a baby that has been exposed to subzero temperatures. Buried under the snow with its dead mother. There is no *time* to catch my breath.

19

Clutching the baby, I look around. I spot the nearest object — a fallen tree. I race over, sit, make as much of a lap as I can, and settle the baby on it.

Baby. It's a baby. Not a toddler. Not even a child old enough to crawl. This is an infant so tiny . . .

I suck in a breath. Focus, focus, focus.

It's so small. I don't have nieces or nephews. Don't have close friends with children. I cannot even guess how young this baby might be. I only know that it is tiny and it is fragile, and for once in my life, I feel huge. Massive and clumsy. Even with my gloves off, my fingers fumble with the swaddling.

I'm not sure what "swaddling" should look like, but it's the word that pops to mind. The baby has been wrapped tight in a cocooning cloth. Animal hide, tanned to butter softness.

As I'm unwrapping the baby, I stop. It's freezing out here, and I'm *un*wrapping it? But I have to, don't I? To check for frostbite? Warm it up?

The panic surges on a wave of indecision. Run the baby back to our tent and unwrap it there. No, unwrap it here, quickly, and make sure it's fine.

The baby makes a noise, too weak now to be called a cry. The child's eyes are screwed shut. They haven't opened since I picked it up.

A bitter wind whips past, and I instinctively clutch the baby to my chest. That wind — and my reaction — answer my question. Get to the tent, to shelter. It's only a few hundred feet away.

I open my jacket, and as I do, I curse myself for being a spoiled brat. Last winter, I'd fumbled around in oversize outerwear, and I'd grumbled about it, and the next time Dalton did a supply run, he returned with a new jacket and snowsuit for me. Naturally, he bought me a sleek, down-filled parka that fits perfectly, meaning I have to hold the baby against my sweater, jacket stretched only partway across. A quick second thought, and I turn my coat around, leaving an air pocket at the top.

The whole time I'm fussing, Storm whines, which only fuels my panic. Her anxiety feels like a lack of trust. That's only me projecting, but I snap at her to be quiet. Guilt surges as she ducks her head, and I pat it quickly, murmuring an apology, knowing this is what she really wants: reassurance. I'm freaking out, and that's freaking her out, and she needs to know everything is okay.

Once the baby is secured, I start from the

clearing. Storm woofs, and I turn to see her staring at the woman's body.

Shouldn't we do something about that?

Yes. Yes, I should. I am a homicide detective, and that woman is dead, blood soaking the snow. I should at least see what killed her. But I have this baby, and it needs me more than she does. I look up, noting treetop patterns and the sun's position and distant landmarks so I can find this spot again.

Then I take off.

There is a fresh surge of panic as I leave the clearing and realize that, having been lured by the baby's cries, I'd paid no attention to my surroundings. Why the hell didn't I pay attention —

Snow, you idiot. You walked through fresh snow.

The path back to our campsite is as clear as a bread-crumb trail. It might meander, and yes, a voice inside screams that I need a direct route, but this is the safe one. I take off at a lope . . . until I stumble and realize, with horror, that if I fall, I'll land on the baby. Slower then. Step by step. The baby is breathing — *was* breathing . . .

No, none of that. There isn't time to stop and check. I've left room for it to breathe, and if it managed to survive under a blanket

22

of snow, swaddled beneath its mother's jacket, then it will live through this. As long as it wasn't already too far gone —

Enough of *that.*

I tramp through the snow for what seems like miles. Finally, I see our campsite marker high above my head, and I divert to a more direct route. The closer I get, the faster I go. When I jog across big boot prints and smaller paw prints, I stop short.

Dalton. I've been in such a blind rush that I've completely forgotten I'm not alone out here, and I nearly collapse with relief at the reminder. I don't care whether Dalton knows the first thing about babies. He's here. I am not alone.

"Eric?"

No answer. I call louder as I continue toward the campsite. I shout for Dalton. I call for Raoul. I whistle, and Storm bounds ahead, as if this means her co-parent and pack mate are back. They aren't. The camp is still and silent, and I realize the boot and paw prints are from earlier.

I check my watch to see it's not yet noon. I curse under my breath and keep going into the tent. When Storm tries to follow, a sharp "no" stops her. She whines, but only once, token protest before she collapses outside, the tent swaying as she leans against it.

I left this morning without rolling up our sleeping blankets. I brush the hides flat as quickly as I can. Then I lay the baby on them.

The infant lies there, eyes shut, body still. It hasn't moved since I left the clearing. I knew that, but I'd ignored the warning, telling myself it'd fallen asleep in relief at being found. As little as I know about babies, I realize this is ridiculous. This is a cold, frightened, hungry infant. When someone came, it should have been screaming, making its needs known now that someone finally arrived to fill them.

I lay a trembling hand on the baby's still-swaddled chest. I don't feel anything, but I'm not sure I would with the way my fingers are shaking. I check the side of its neck, and as soon as my cold fingers touch warm skin, the baby gives the faintest start.

Alive.

I fumble to unwrap the swaddling hides. The tiny body gives a convulsive shudder, and I resist the urge to re-swaddle it. The tent isn't warm, but it's sheltered, and I need to get a better look at the child.

It is naked under the cloths. A baby girl with black fuzz for hair, her face scrunched up as tight as her fists. I take a deep breath, push aside emotion, and begin an assessment of her condition. That isn't easy. I realize how cold her hands and feet are, and I panic. I notice her shallow breathing and shivering, and I panic. I see her sunken eyes, and I panic. But I keep assessing.

Dehydration. Mild hypothermia. Possible frostbite.

Her breathing is clear and steady. Heartbeat is strong and steady. Body is plump and well nourished. These findings calm and reassure me, and then I can turn my attention to the problems.

Triage. Frostbite, then hypothermia, then dehydration.

I wrap her loosely in her blankets and add a thick hide one. Then I systematically warm her hands and feet, first against my bare skin and then under my armpits. Warm, do not rub. My hands against her button nose and tiny ears as my breath warms those.

Now to replenish body fluids. I can tell she is dehydrated, but I can't determine severity.

She needs liquid. That's the main thing. I don't have any food for her. I tamp down panic at the thought that I have nothing even resembling milk. Water. Focus on getting her water.

I hurry out to grab the canteen. Then I

stop. Dalton will have it, because I won't need it at camp, where I can melt snow.

Melt snow.

I snatch up the pot and stuff it to overflowing with snow and spin to the fire . . .

The fire is dead.

Of course it is. That's why I'd left in the first place: to gather kindling, which I abandoned back in the clearing where I found the baby. I've been gone long enough that the fire is reduced to ash. It'll take forever to get it going enough to melt water.

Stay calm. Stay focused. I am surrounded by water in partly frozen form. I can do this.

I empty the pot. Grab a handful of snow. Squeeze it in my fist, and watch the water run into the pot. Grab another . . . and see black streaks on my hand. It's probably soot, but it looks like dirt, and that reminds me that my hands are not clean.

Sterilize. That comes from deep memory, a single babysitting class taken with friends, before I realized I was not babysitter material.

Then how are you going to look after an infant?

I can do this. Clean my hands first.

With what? I showered before I came. It's one weekend with backpacks — we have no room for anything we don't absolutely need.

And this is an emergency. Am I going to let a baby die of dehydration rather than risk letting her ingest a few specks of dirt?

I wash my hands in the snow as best I can. Then I'm squeezing out water when Storm, sticking close and anxious, gives a happy bark. At a whistle, she takes off, and I nearly collapse with relief.

"Eric!" I shout. "I need help!"

He comes running so fast the poor dogs race to keep up. He bursts into the camp, as if expecting to see me wrestling a newly woken grizzly. He has a rifle over his shoulder, and he's carrying a brace of spruce grouse, which he throws into the snow as he runs toward me.

"Fire," I say. "I need the fire going. Now. I have to boil water."

"You're hurt? Or Storm?" He wheels to look at the dog bounding up behind him.

"Baby," I say, barely able to get the word out, my heart thumps so fast. "I found a baby."

"A baby what?"

The infant lets out a weak cry, and Dalton goes still.

His head turns toward the tent as he asks in a low voice, "What is that?" and I realize he doesn't recognize the sound. Or if he does, it only sparks a very old memory. His

27

younger brother, Jacob, might very well be the only infant he's ever seen. Dalton was raised in Rockton, where there are no children.

Before I can answer, he's crouched and opening the unzipped tent flap.

THREE

Dalton gingerly peels back the tent flap. He peers inside.

Then he jerks back. "It's a baby."

"That's what I said."

He rises, looking stunned. "Where . . . ?"

"I found her with her mother, under the snow. Both of them — the mother and her child. The mother's dead, and I don't know how long the baby was out there, and I've warmed her up, but she's dehydrated, and I let the fire go out, and now I can't boil water to make it sterile and —"

He cuts off my babble with a kiss, gloved hands on either side of my face. Not what I expect, and it startles me, which I suppose is the point. His lips press against mine, warm, the ice on his beard melting against my chin, and it's like slapping someone who is hysterical. Well, no, it's a much nicer way to do it.

I'm startled at first, and then all I feel and

smell and see is him, and the panic evaporates. Tears spring to my eyes. As he breaks the kiss, he brushes the tears away and says, "Everything's okay. You've got this."

I nod. "I-I don't know much . . . anything really about . . ."

"It's more than I do." He smiles, and then that vanishes, as if he realizes that might not be what I need to hear right now.

"We have this," he says. "We can hold off on sterilizing the water. If she's dehydrated, just use what you have."

He returns to the tent, and I follow with my bit of melted snow. When the dogs crowd in, he waves them back. Storm herds Raoul off, like a big older sister taking charge. He's seven months old, a wolf and Australian shepherd cross, heavier on the wolf, which means he understands pack hierarchy.

After the dogs move, Dalton reopens the tent. Then he stops, and his breath catches.

"Fuck," he whispers. "Are they supposed to be that . . . small?" There's an odd note in his voice, part wonder and part terror, and when I nudge, he moves aside, letting me go in. Then he stays there, holding the flap open.

"I'm going to need your help with this," I say.

He nods, rubbing a hand over his mouth as he eases into the tent. He's still a meter away from the baby, but he moves as if he might somehow crush her from a distance.

"Pick her up, please," I say. "I have to get this water into her."

He inches closer. His arms move toward the baby. Then he stops. Repositions his arms, mentally trying to figure out how to do this.

"You won't break her," I say.

"Are you sure?" He gives me a smile, but worry lurks behind it. He looks back at her. "How do I . . . ?"

"One hand behind her back. The other supporting her head. She's too young to hold it up on her own. She's also too young to escape."

"Got it."

He still makes a few pantomime attempts, reconfiguring his hands in the air before he actually touches the baby. It's an awkward lift, and when she wriggles, he freezes. I lunge before he drops her. He doesn't, of course. He just tightens his grip a little and looks down at her and . . .

There are experiences I've heard women talk about that I have never had. Never even imagined, to be honest. Hearing about them, I'd inwardly roll my eyes, because if I never felt a thing, then clearly this thing does not exist. Or, as I've learned, I just never experienced it until I met Dalton. That thing they write poetry and songs and cheesy Valentine's cards about. Being in love. Being with someone that you can no longer imagine being without.

When Dalton holds that baby, I get another of those experiences. My insides just . . . I don't even know what. I feel things that I don't particularly want to feel at this moment, may not *ever* want to feel, considering this might be the one thing I can't give him.

I see Dalton holding the baby, and then he looks over at me with this little smile that . . .

Nope, not thinking about that. Tuck it away. Lock it up tight.

"Am I doing it right?" he asks.

"Yep," I say, a little brusquely. "Now I need to get the water into her. I don't know how old she is, but she definitely isn't weaned yet. She'll want something to suck on, but unless you have a clean rubber glove hidden in our packs . . ."

"Yeah, no."

I inhale. "It probably wouldn't do any good. Suckling requires strength, and she's weak. And I need to stop talking." I take a deep breath. "From wild panic to overana-lyzing."

"The situation isn't critical. We're only an hour's fast walk from town. We just need to get a little water into her."

He shifts her, getting more confident in his hold. Then he stops. "She's so . . ."

"Small?"

He laughs, but it holds a touch of nervous-ness. "Yeah, we covered that, didn't we. I just can't believe . . ." He swallows. "All right. I'm going to try to open her mouth so you can drip water in. Just a few drops into the back of her throat, and I'll make sure she swallows it."

"Done this before, have you?"

Another laugh, still nervous. "With a two-hundred-pound man. Years ago. Guy who ran away and passed out from dehydration. I had to get fluids into him before I hauled him to town for a saline drip. This is a little trickier. She won't need as much water, though."

"True."

He puts a finger to the baby's lips. Dalton isn't a huge guy. About six feet tall. Maybe one-seventy, lean and fit, as he needs to be for life out here. That fingertip, though, seems like a giant's, bigger than the baby's pursed lips. He prods, and her mouth opens.

"Now let's just hope I don't get bit." He wriggles his finger in and then stops. "Though I guess that would require teeth. How young do you think she is?"

"Babies can be born with teeth, but they usually fall out. They don't get more until they're at least six months. She's well below that. Maybe a month?"

"Fuck." He takes a deep breath. "Okay, here goes, I'll prop —"

Her eyes fly open, and he freezes, as if he's been caught doing something he shouldn't. She looks up at him, and it is indeed a picture-perfect scene, as she stares up at Dalton, and his expression goes from frozen shock to wonder.

I want to capture it . . . and I want to forget it. I want to pretend I don't see that look in his eyes, don't see his smile.

"Hey, there," he says, and the baby doesn't cry, doesn't even look concerned. She just stares at him.

"Water," I say, and I feel like a selfish bitch for spoiling the moment, but I can't help it. I need to shatter it, and I hate myself a little for that.

"Right." He wriggles his finger into the baby's mouth. She starts to suck on it, and he laughs again, no nerves now, just a rumbling laugh that comes from deep in his chest.

"Reminds me of a marten I found, when I was a kid," he says.

"A baby marten?"

He shrugs. "I had a bad habit of bringing home orphaned animals. My mom . . ." He trails off, and I realize it's the first time I've heard him use that word. When he speaks of Katherine Dalton, he says "my mother." That isn't who he means here. He means Amy O'Keefe, his birth mother. The parents he never talks about. The ones he can't talk about without a hitch in his words, a trailing-off, a sudden switch of subject. He lived with his parents and his brother out here until he was nine and the Daltons "rescued" him, from a situation he did not need rescuing from.

"Your mom . . ." I prod, because I must. Every time this door creaks open, I grab for it before it slams shut again.

"Water," he says, and I try not to deflate.

I lift the pot, and then realize there's no way in hell I can "drip" it from this suddenly huge pot into her tiny mouth.

"Take out one of our shirts," he says. "Dip a corner in and squeeze it into her mouth."

I'm not sure that's sanitary, but I settle for taking a clean shirt of mine, one fresh from the laundry. As I dip it in, I say, "Is this how you fed the marten?"

"Nah, it's how I fed birds. For the marten, I'd put food on my finger and hope she didn't chew it off." He looks at the baby. "You gonna chew it off, kid?"

"No teeth, remember?"

"These gums feel hard enough to do the job."

I've relaxed now. He's talking about rescuing orphaned animals, comparing them to the baby, and that eases tension from my shoulders. That's what he sees this as — the rescue of an orphaned creature. Not picking up a baby and being overwhelmed with some deeper instinct that says "I want this."

That would be silly, I guess. But we all have our sensitive spots, and this is one of mine: the fact that I cannot provide a child should he decide that's what he wants. It's an issue I never had to worry about because I did not foresee myself in a relationship where the question might arise. Now I do.

I wet the shirt and trickle water in the baby's mouth. I'm being careful to have it close enough, so we can see how much she gets, and suddenly she clamps down on the fabric itself. She sucks hard and then makes such a face that we both laugh.

"Not what you expected, huh?" I say.

36

Her gaze turns my way. I seem to recall that, at this age, babies can't see more than shapes, but she's definitely looking. Processing. I swear I can see that in her dark blue eyes. Every move, every noise, every passing blurry shape is a cause for deep consideration, her brain analyzing and trying to interpret.

I dip the fabric into the pot and press it to her lips. She opens them and sucks. Makes that same face, distaste and displeasure, like a rich old lady expecting champagne and being served ginger ale. She fusses. Bleats. But when nothing better comes, she takes the shirt again and sucks on it.

When she's finished, she fixes us with a look of bitter accusation.

"Sorry," I say. "We'll do better next time."

We aren't what she wants, though. Not what she needs.

I think of the woman in the clearing, the woman under the snow.

"We should get her back to Rockton," I say. "Can you do that by yourself?"

"What?"

"Her mother. I have to . . ." I look at the baby. "I need to get what I can from the scene."

"Scene?" He adjusts his position, making the baby comfortable in the crook of his arm. "You think she was murdered."

"Possibly. I know that isn't my crime to solve, but this baby didn't come from nowhere. She has family. She needs to go back to them."

I know that, better than anyone, because of the man sitting beside me. The Daltons found a boy in the forest, and they ignored the fact that he was well fed and properly clothed and healthy. Ignored the fact that he already knew how to read and write. They decided he was a savage in need of rescue. There is no gentle way to put it. They stole Dalton from his parents, from his brother, from the forest.

"She needs to get back to them," I repeat, and Dalton's hand finds mine, his fingers squeezing as he says, "She does."

"So to do that —" I begin.

"We have to check out the body."

"I have to check it. You need to take her."

He passes me the baby and starts rolling the sleeping blankets.

"I'm not leaving you out here alone," he says, and before I can protest, he continues. "Yes, you can find the way back. Yes, you have a gun. Yes, I could leave you with both dogs. But an hour or two will make no difference if she's wrapped well. She survived for longer under the snow."

"Yes but —"

"Maybe I should stay and check the body," he says, tying the blankets under his backpack. "I know what to look for, and I'm better than you at tracking, especially with the snowfall. I might also be able to tell if she's from a settlement or she's a lone settler or even where she comes from." He settles onto his haunches. "Yeah, that makes sense. I'll check the body. You take the baby."

I only glower at him. He grins, leans forward, and smacks a kiss on my cheek. "Yep, I'm not sure which is the scarier prospect. We'll both go check the scene first. Wrap her up properly, and I'll break camp."

FOUR

We're heading back to the clearing. Dalton has the baby snuggled under his parka, left undone just enough to be sure she's breathing. I'm in the lead, the dogs trotting along beside me, confused but calm, sensing we have this under control.

When we reach the deeper snow, it's slow going with the heavy pack on my back. It's not as bad as it sounds, though. On a trip into Whitehorse, I made an amazing discovery: backpacks are not unisex.

I had always worn a regular backpack, and if someone had offered me a "girl" one, I'd have been offended and amused, like when I saw an ad for a women's pen. Except, as I discovered, a women's backpack is a perfectly logical invention. The normal ones distribute the load across the shoulders, but women carry weight better at their hips. My new backpack utilized that, and I no longer felt like the ninety-pound weakling struggling to carry a backpack half the size of Dalton's.

We follow my boot prints into the clearing. A woman died here, and we need to disturb the scene as little as possible. At the clearing edge, I tie Raoul to a tree and command Storm to stay with him.

I return to the spot where I unwrapped the baby, and I set my backpack in the depression I'd already created. Then I unzip Dalton's jacket and carefully remove the baby. She fusses at being pulled away from her warm cocoon. I check her, and then put her back with Dalton, and she promptly quiets.

"The body's over here," I say.

Dalton follows, staying in my footsteps. The woman lies where I left her, untouched, which is a relief. I'd realized too late that I should have re-covered her with snow to stifle the smell from scavengers. But I suppose being frozen muffled her scent well enough.

I was so panicked earlier that I hadn't taken more than a cursory glance at the woman. Now I hunker onto my haunches for a closer examination. She's older than I thought, my initial observation tainted by the expectation that this would be a young mother.

I might be wrong on the age, too. This is a hard life for those who've chosen it. Still, the woman's hair is liberally streaked with gray, and I can't imagine she's younger than mid-thirties. Still young enough to have a child, of course.

She's a settler, not a hostile. In my experience so far, it's been easy to tell the difference. A settler looks like someone who stepped from a magazine article on the Klondike Gold Rush. Sometimes it's the classic version, circa 1898, complete with shabby clothing and beards to their belly buttons. Other times, they resemble modern miners, people who choose to spend part of their year here because there is indeed gold in these hills and streams.

Hostiles look as if they stepped from an entirely different magazine article, one about a newly discovered tribe. At least, that's the first impression. On closer inspection, it's more like they've compiled the most cringeworthy and stereotypical "savage" cosplay outfit imaginable. Filed teeth. Primitive tattoos. Ritual scarring. Painted faces. Tattered clothing. Zero sanitation.

This woman might be in need of a long shower, a good haircut, and a visit to the dentist, but she isn't a hostile. Her clothing is well crafted. Her hair is gathered into a rough braid. And she has only a smear of dirt on her face, otherwise as clean as I'd be if we spent a week in this winter-frozen forest, with no easy access to bathing.

She lies on her side, legs drawn up as if she'd gone fetal to protect the baby. Blood soaks the snow around her head and legs, hidden under a cleansing fresh layer. I can't estimate quantity of blood loss by quantity of red snow. I mentally add that to my research list, also known as "the list of things I never thought I'd have to know because I'm a homicide cop, damn it."

That's not a complaint. Just a wry admission that my job down south had been very limited, with experts for everything beyond my immediate scope. Up here, I'm not just a homicide detective. Not just a general detective. Not even detective plus basic law enforcement. I am all that . . . and a crime-scene tech, ballistics expert, forensic anthropologist, arson investigator, cold-case expert, even assistant coroner. If it touches on any area of crime solving, it's mine.

Down south, I'd been known as a keener, using my vacation time to attend conferences for areas of crime-scene investigation usually handled by experts. I'd been proud of my extracurricular expertise. Then I came to Rockton, and it was like studying French for two semesters and taking a job in northern Quebec.

Finding the woman's wounds is tricky. Her chest is clean, and there hadn't been any blood on the baby or her blanket. I clear snow from the woman's legs, but she's wearing light tan trousers, and they're only splattered with dark spots that might or might not be blood.

"I'm going to roll her over," I say. "How's the baby?"

"Sound asleep."

I glance up sharply at that, and he says, "I can feel her heartbeat, Casey. She's only sleeping. Keep going." I ease the woman onto her stomach. I still don't see any sign that bullets or blades pierced her thick parka. I peel the coat off . . . and there's still no blood. Her shirt is tan, light enough that I would notice blood. I don't.

As I ease back, I see a smear of blood on her neck. My gaze moves up to her hat. It's reminiscent of a Russian *ushanka,* with a tanned-hide exterior, fur lining, and ear flaps. I untie the straps. When I try to pull it off, it resists. I have to peel it from the back and her hair sticks to it. Wet hair that froze solid. I run a strand through my fingertips and see red. A blow to the base of the skull.

I shine my flashlight to see her hair is

plastered over an ugly cut. I palpate the spot. Her skull doesn't feel dented or damaged. A scalp wound bleeds a lot, and that's what soaked the ground around her head.

I look at the imprint her body has left. When I picture the body lying not in snow but on pavement, I envision a blood pool radiating from thigh level.

Checking her legs more carefully, I find what I'm looking for: a dark patch on her inner thigh. I picture her position again and see her lying on her side, legs pulled up but parted.

I finger the dark patch and find a hole the size of a bullet. Shot in the leg. Did she fall then? Or run a little more? Not far before the bullet lodged in the femoral artery. She dropped, lying on her side, cradling the baby as blood ran into the snow.

Hit in the head. *Then* shot?

I check the scalp again, thinking it might be a bullet graze. No, it's a tear, as if from a tool. Yes, she was indeed hit in the head and then shot.

I'm contemplating this puzzle when the baby fusses. That slams home the reminder that this dead body is not simply a puzzle. It's the child's mother. Her dead mother.

As cops, we catch a lot of flak for what seems like dispassionate disinterest in the human aspect of our work. That's unfair and untrue. We learn to distance ourselves so we *can* view a corpse as a mystery. Otherwise, we remember that we're looking at a life snuffed out, and we get stuck there.

I take a moment to think about this woman, because that helps, too. Place her in context. Mother of an infant. Baby wrapped under her jacket when she's attacked. Her killer leaving them both to die. I can't tell if she bled out or died of hypothermia. Either way, she'd been abandoned by a killer heartless enough to let an infant die a slow and horrible death.

I carefully remove the dead woman's shirt. Two shirts, actually. Layering for the weather. She's naked under that. No bra, obviously — brassieres are hardly a priority out here. That does make me stop to consider. Something seems wrong, but I'm no expert on this, and I won't jump to any conclusion, won't even suggest the possibility I see. There's also something else that pulls my attention away from that.

Scars.

At first, they look like regular scars. Old ones. I have more than my share, the permanent reminders of the attack that changed my life. When you are accustomed to seeing scars across your entire body, they become

46

like freckles for those who have them —
you're slow to notice them on others.

These aren't the sort of scars I bear.
There's a pattern here. Raised bumps of
scars form a mantle across her chest and
shoulders. That's the best way I can describe
it. A mantle. Three chains of parallel scars
that start on one shoulder, swoop down just
over her breasts, and then cross to the other
shoulder.

Ritualized scarring.

"There's a tattoo, too," Dalton says.

I see it then, on her upper arm. What
seems at first a modern circlet tattoo around
her biceps, but on closer inspection is rough
and primitive. Another one encircles her
other arm.

I remember something and move to the
smear of dirt on her chin. Under it, I see
three raised, round scars. The dirt seems
deliberately smeared on. Not painting
herself with it, but covering those scars with
the only kind of makeup the wilderness allows.

"A hostile?" I murmur. Then I look at the
dirt compared to her tidy clothing and
general state of cleanliness. "*Former* hostile."

A hostile turned settler. A former hostile
with an infant baby. Murdered in the snow.

Both of them left to die.

I turn to Dalton. "Should I take her back to Rockton?"

"If it'll help, sure. I can make a stretcher. Get Storm to pull it."

"I mean *should* I. I'd like to. I need to take a closer look, and I need April's help. But is it right to take her?"

He nods, understanding. "I'd say so. If she has people, they wouldn't have found her under that snow. Taking her back will help you find the baby's family. Seems proper to me."

FIVE

We have the woman on a stretcher, which is really just poles with our sleeping blankets between them. We've crafted a makeshift harness for Storm. She's fine with that. We've been training her to pull because, well, it's the Yukon. That's what dogs do up here.

Storm finds the pulling easy, the stretcher gliding along the snow. If the dead body bothers her, she's gotten over it. Or maybe because we're moving the woman, she feels as if we're helping her. Our biggest problem is Raoul, who wants to pull . . . using his teeth. What seems like strong wolf blood in him might also be husky. Plenty of those up here, and they were one breed Rockton had back when they allowed pets. We'll have to get him in a harness this winter for some early training.

We're nearing the town when Will Anders comes running, and I tense. Our deputy running to intercept us is never a good sign.

"What's wrong?" I call.

"You're back early, that's what's wrong. Is everything . . . ?" He spots the stretcher and slows.

Raoul trots along at Anders's side as our deputy walks over for a closer look. Raoul isn't the most sociable canine, but he has his favorites, which for him means "people he allows to touch him." Anders absently pats the young dog as he walks to the stretcher.

"Wounded settler?" he asks. "April's off today, but I can run and get her to the clinic."

"This one is beyond my sister's help," I say.

"Dead?" There's a long moment of silence before he says, "Not enough murders for you lately, Case, so you're bringing home dead bodies?"

"Ha ha."

Anders bends beside the stopped stretcher. In college, he'd been premed before he decided to serve his country as an army medic. They soon switched him to military police — he has a knack for conflict resolution — but he still has the basic medical training, and his gaze sweeps over the woman, assessing.

50

"Hostile markings. I'm guessing that's your interest — a subject to study." He rises and undoes Storm's harness, giving her a rub as he sets her free. Then he looks at Dalton. "Making the pup work, boss? Guess you need to hit the gym a little more, huh?"

Anders flexes a biceps . . . which would be far more impressive if he weren't wearing a thick parka. Will Anders is a big guy, a couple of inches taller than Dalton and wider, too, the quarterback to Dalton's running-back build.

Anders is grabbing the harness when the baby fusses under Dalton's jacket.

"What . . . ?" Anders says, staring at the moving lump under Dalton's coat. "Please tell me that's another puppy, because I'm still stinging from being overlooked for that one." He hooks a gloved thumb at Raoul. "I call dibs."

"I don't think you want dibs this time," I say.

Dalton undoes his jacket just as the baby lets out a wail.

"Holy shit." Anders turns to me. "Either you guys have seriously graduated from orphaned wolf pups, or you are a *master* at pregnancy-hiding."

"She was hers," I say, motioning at the dead woman. "She's dehydrated and

51

starving."

Anders looks at the woman. "Uh, not to question your medical expertise . . ."

"I mean the baby," I say with a roll of my eyes. "She needs food and medical attention, so we really need to stop talking and get to town."

Dalton conceals the baby again and cuts along the back path to the clinic while I accompany Anders and the dogs into town. When we enter, a few people run over. Then they see the body and relax, as they realize I haven't brought our sheriff home on a stretcher.

There are plenty of people in Rockton who'll mutter, after a few beers, about how much better life would be without the hardass sheriff breathing down their necks. They're like teens whining about strict parents, though. They might complain, but they sure as hell don't want to wake up one day and find Mom and Dad gone. God knows who they'd get in their place.

I field questions, of course. We live in an isolated town of less than two hundred people. Everyone's eager for news, for any change to routine, especially in the middle of winter. That would explain the holiday decorations, too. This is my second Christmas here, and as I learned from last year, this place goes a little nuts at the holidays, to stave off going a little nuts in general as the days get darker and the temperature plummets.

While Anders pulls the stretcher, we pass residents adding to the decorations. Heaven forbid a single wooden porch should lack evergreen boughs woven through each railing baluster. Or any door should lack an intricately crafted wreath. Or any lintel should lack ivy with bright red cranberries. Every tree has been decorated, and that's saying something in a town filled with evergreens. That's still not enough, and people have decorated all the perimeter trees, too. Making holiday ornaments is an all-year craft for some.

I can grumble, but that's more eye-rolling than actual complaint, and even the eye-rolling covers the fact that I secretly love the way Rockton embraces the holidays. My parents celebrated Christmas — my mother wanted her daughters fully assimilated, and any of her own Chinese or Filipino family traditions were ignored. We were Canadians, and we would act Canadian, which apparently meant "Christian" at the holidays, even if we never attended church of any kind.

Neither of my parents was all that keen on Christmas, though. It seemed like more chore than delight for them. An unwanted distraction from their careers. We did all the basics: set up a tree, put out stockings for Santa, exchanged gifts and then had a holiday meal. But the tree went up Christmas Eve and was taken down Boxing Day. There were no concerts or parties. My parents didn't have time for that. Well, no, *they* attended holiday parties — I remember them dressed up, April babysitting me — but only because the social events were necessary evils for career networking.

In Rockton we celebrate all the winter traditions, and that sounds very inclusive of us, but honestly, I think it's just an excuse for more parties. If that leads to a greater understanding of different traditions and faiths, it's a bonus. There are no churches in Rockton, but only because we don't have space for buildings that'll be used once a week. Services are held at the community center, with the various groups agreeing to a schedule.

If there's an overriding theme to our winter celebrations, it's solstice. That makes sense up here, where we are enslaved by sun and season. Next week is winter solstice, the longest night of the year. The party will last for every minute of it, as we celebrate the return of the sun, knowing each day following will be longer, until summer solstice, when the town will party from 4 A.M. sunrise to midnight sundown. When you live without TV and social media, you exploit every excuse for a celebration.

My mood lifts on seeing the decorations. With Rockton's wooden buildings and Wild West flair, there's nostalgia there, too, even for someone who doesn't consider herself particularly nostalgic. Squint past the modern clothing, and you can imagine a town from times past, bedecked in its holiday finest, everyone's step lighter, their smiles wider.

Those smiles dim when they see the dead body on the stretcher, but even then, it's simple curiosity. We are indeed, in so many ways, the Wild West town we resemble, where violence and death are as much a part of life as decorating for the holidays.

I head to April's house, beside the clinic. Like Dalton, Anders, and myself, she gets a small one-and-a-half-story chalet to herself. That's the perk of being essential services. Rockton could build one for each resident — we certainly have the land — but the larger the town is, the more likely it is to be spotted by planes. We use both structural and technological camouflage to prevent that, but we still need to keep our footprint as small as possible.

Anders takes both dogs to Raoul's owner, Mathias, who'll look after Storm while we're busy with this problem. I rap on my sister's door. I almost hope that she doesn't answer. Or that, if she does, she has company. It's her day off, and it'd be nice if she wasn't spending it home alone, but with April, that's like saying it'd be nice if the temperature hit thirty Celsius today. It just ain't happening.

No, that isn't entirely true. It would have been when she first arrived. Now, there is a chance she'll be out, not exactly socializing but at least interacting. Inviting someone into her home is too much. She's been known to haul the toilet tank onto her back porch for pickup to avoid having anyone come inside.

April opens the door as I'm reaching for a second knock.

"What are you doing back?" she says.

"Nice to see you, too, April."

Her brows crease, as if she's trying to figure out why it would be nice to see her. Isabel — a former psychologist — believes my sister is on the autism spectrum, undiagnosed because my parents refused to see anything "wrong" with their brilliant older daughter. They had enough trouble dealing with their rebellious younger one. To them, a diagnosis of even mild autism would have meant April was intellectually imperfect, and so they instead let her struggle through life, a gifted neurosurgeon and neuroscientist unable to form all but the most tenuous of personal relationships, lonely and alone and never knowing why. My parents screwed up my life in so many ways, but compared to what they did to my sister, I got off easy.

When we raised the possibility of autism with April, I'd been terrified she'd see it as sibling envy — me trying to knock down my brilliant older sister. I'd been convinced otherwise by a joint coalition of Isabel, Kenny, and Dalton . . . and they'd been right, which is humiliating to admit, proving how little I know my sister. Too much familiarity and too little actual understanding, a lifetime of trying to get to know her and, when I couldn't, creating her wholesale.

April was fine with the diagnosis. She treated it the way I would have: like a physical ailment. *Here's the problem, and now that we know what it is, let's tackle that.* Relief, I think, at giving it a name.

"I brought you a body," I say.

Her frown deepens, and she's looking for some alternate meaning in this. A sign that I'm joking.

"I found a murdered woman in the forest," I say.

Now she relaxes, and I get the April I know well, rolling her eyes at her feckless little sister. "Really? You don't have to make the world's problems your own, Casey."

"You know me. Can't relax. Always looking for work. If I don't have it, I make some." I pause. "Which does not mean I *made* this dead body. That would be wrong."

A pause. Then, "That's a joke, isn't it?"

I clap her on the arm as I propel her back into the house. "Yes, April. It's a joke." I pull shut the door before she can protest. "Don't worry — I'm not coming in for tea. I found something else, which I'd rather not broadcast."

Six

After I explain, we head out April's back door and across her yard to the clinic's rear entrance. As we do, she says, "I hope you're not thinking of adopting this child, Casey."

I tense so fast my spine crackles. "No, I'm not stealing someone's baby, April."

"The mother is dead. That is not stealing."

"Presumably the father is alive, and potentially other family, which I'm going to find."

"Good. This isn't a stray puppy."

My teeth barely part enough for me to say, "I'm aware of that," but one of my sister's cognitive challenges is interpreting body language, so she ignores that and continues.

"There is no place in your life for a baby, Casey. I realize you're comfortable here, and you've settled into a long-term relationship with Eric, but this is not a situation for motherhood."

"I found a baby with a dead mother. Buried under the snow. Alone and in distress. I brought her back to Rockton so she doesn't *die,* not to fill a hole in my life."

"There is no hole in your life. You have Eric, and you have Storm, and you have Rockton and your job. You are happier and more satisfied than I have ever known you to be."

I answer slowly, keeping my tone even. "I appreciate the fact that you recognize I'm happy, April. And there *isn't* a baby-size hole in my life. I just happened to find a child, whom I intend to return to her family. Just because I'm a woman in a happy romantic relationship doesn't mean my ovaries go into hyperdrive seeing a baby."

"Good."

I push open the back door of the clinic with a little more force than necessary. I tell myself that April isn't being patronizing. I've spent my life dealing with this from her, and I'm trying to understand that she doesn't mean it the way it sounds.

Yet it's also a constant reminder that my sister put me into my box when we were young, and nothing I've done since then has — or possibly ever will — let me escape it. I'm reckless. I'm impulsive. I'm thoughtless, rushing headlong into every bad decision life offers. My sole consolation is that anyone who knows me would laugh at all those descriptors.

Inside, Dalton and Anders have the baby on the examining table. As soon as I see that, I barrel into the room and snatch her up.

"You can't leave her on that," I say. "What if she rolls off?"

"She can't even lift her head, Casey," Anders says.

"Which doesn't mean she can't wriggle. Or slide."

He snickers. "Slide off a flat surface?"

"You are both correct," April says. "It is almost certainly safe, given the child's lack of mobility, but a slippery metal table still doesn't seem like the safest place to set a baby." She aims a look at Anders.

"Hey, I'm not the one who put her there," Anders says. "And Eric literally just unwrapped her as you two came in."

April nods at Dalton, as if to say that if *he* did it, then it's fine. The first time they met, she referred to him as my fuck toy, and I'm not sure what was more shocking, the word coming from my very proper sister or the sentiment coming from my very straitlaced sister. In the last six months, she's done a complete about-face, and now, if Dalton does something, then it's the right thing to do. I'm totally on board with her *not* treating my lover like trash, but I can't help wishing I could get a little of that approval thrown my way.

"Eric?" she says. "It's a bit chilly in here for the baby. Could you . . . ?" She looks over to see he's already starting the fire, and she nods, pleased that her trust is so well placed. Anders and I exchange a look.

I hold the baby until the fire's blazing and the chill is leaving the room. Then I lay her on the exam table.

"Would you take over?" I ask Dalton. "I need to find something for her to eat."

"Yes," April says, not looking up from her examination of the baby. "We'll need formula and bottles. Also diapers, for the inevitable after-products of feeding. Tell the general store to put together a box of all their infant supplies."

Anders, Dalton, and I all look at one another.

"Uh," I say. "We don't carry infant supplies. We don't . . . have any infants."

"In case you haven't noticed that in the past six months," Anders murmurs.

April shoots us both a glare of annoyance. "Yes, I have noticed there are currently no babies, but I'm sure there are supplies in storage for them."

"There aren't," I say. "We don't ever have babies here. Or children. Or even teenagers."

She glances at Dalton.

"Yeah," he says. "I was special. But Casey's right. We don't allow anyone under eighteen, and there's a reason why we have a shitload of condoms and diaphragms and every other method of contraception. We're not equipped to handle childbirth or children."

April flutters a hand at me. "Just get . . . whatever."

As I hurry through town, I'm trying to figure out what I *can* get. Milk is the obvious choice. We have it in powdered form, and I know that's less than ideal, but it's that or nothing.

As I'm racking my brain for alternate foods, I keep thinking, *Oh, I can google that.* For someone raised on modern technology, it's a natural instinct. Well, unless it's a medical question, where even "I have an odd rash on my thumb" will lead to "Cancer! Death! Plague!"

Sixteen months in Rockton have not yet rerouted my neural circuits enough to keep me from reaching toward my pocket every time I have a research question. Now, instead of a cell phone, I carry a notepad, where I can write down all those questions for the next time I'm in Dawson City with internet access. This problem won't wait that long.

I need to find a resident who has had a child. That should be easy enough in a town full of people in their prime child-rearing years. Yet that is exactly what makes this not easy at all. Like Dalton said, we don't allow children. We also don't allow spouses. You come alone. You leave everything — and everyone — behind. That means that if you're deeply devoted to a partner, you won't come to Rockton. If you have kids, you won't come to Rockton. There are exceptions, I'm sure, where the danger is so great that you say goodbye to your family for two years. But single and childless is the normal.

I don't even know who has grown children. Residents reveal only what they want and invent whatever backstory fits who they choose to be while they're here.

That's when I spot the one person I know for certain has had a child.

Petra is coming out of the general store after her shift. Before I can catch up, another resident stops to talk to her. I hear them discussing art that the resident has commissioned as a Hanukkah gift. Down south, Petra had been a comic-book artist. Well, *after* she spent a decade as special ops in the United States. She's also resumed the latter job here, as a spy and — at least in one case — assassin for her grandmother, one of the town's early residents and current board members.

Until six months ago, I'd have said Petra was my closest friend in Rockton. The whole "actually a spy and assassin" part has put a damper on that. Petra and I have resumed some form of cautious relationship. We're not going to sit around braiding each other's hair but we weren't exactly doing that before either. It had been a stable, steady, comfortable friendship, and it no longer is, and I mourn that.

When Petra sees I'm waiting to speak to her, she wraps up her conversation quickly. I motion her over to a gap between the general store and the next building.

"We have a baby," I say.

Before I can explain, she says, "You're having a — ?"

"No, we found a baby abandoned in the forest. She's very, very young, and we're . . . We're a little lost. We don't exactly have baby guides in the library, and I could really use some help."

When I'd first hailed Petra, her step had lightened, and she'd smiled as she walked over. Now the remains of that smile freeze before sliding away.

"I . . ." She swallows. "I can't really . . ."

"Was that a lie?" I say. "About your daughter?"

Confusion flashes, and then anger. "Of course not. What kind of person would make up . . ."

She trails off because she realizes the answer to that. A child's death is exactly the kind of tragic backstory anyone with her training *might* give. I have no idea specifically what she used to do. "Special ops" is as much as she'll say, but if she's done any spy or interrogation work, she knows only a stone-cold bitch wouldn't have been affected by the story of her daughter, so I must question it.

"No," she says, quieter now. "I would hope you'd know I wouldn't make up something like that, but yes, I get it. Anything I know about babies, I'll happily pass along, though I'll warn that my ex was the expert parent. I meant that if you're looking for someone to care for this baby?" She manages a wry smile. "I'll stick to dog-sitting."

"I understand. If you can pop by the clinic and give us anything — maybe some sense

66

of how old the baby is — that'd be great. Right now, though, we need food. She's not rolling over or lifting her head yet, and as little as I know about babies, I realize that means she's still on an all-liquid diet."

"Damn, she really is young. Okay, well, I guess milk will have to do until you can get into Dawson for formula. We'll need to rig up something to use as a bottle. Let's go into the store. I have a couple of ideas —"

"You have a baby?" a voice says.

I glance over my shoulder and wince. "Does this look like a private conversation, Jen?"

"Fuck, yeah. Why do you think I'm eavesdropping?"

I used to joke that I always wanted a nemesis. I mean, it sounds cool, and I'm not the type of person who makes enemies easily. Neither friends nor enemies. In Rockton, I have more of the former than ever. I also have my first nemesis, and she's standing right in front of me.

"Jen . . ." I say.

"You know, Detective, everyone keeps talking about how smart you are. Not as smart as your sister, but still fucking brilliant. Yet I really have to wonder sometimes. You brought a baby into town, and you think you can keep that a secret? This entire town is going to *hear* exactly what you're hiding within . . . Oh, I'll bet two hours. Petra, you want in?"

"You know what I want to lay bets on, Jen?" Petra says. "How long you can go without insulting Casey. I'll give *that* two hours, though I might be granting you too much credit."

"Someone has to keep our detective on her toes," Jen says. "And it sure as hell won't be you, Miss Artiste. Go draw some rainbows and flowers, think happy thoughts, and keep polishing your nicest-girl-in-town title. You can keep it."

I look at Petra, and I choke on a laugh.

"What?" Jen said.

I turn to Jen. "Yes, there's a baby. Yes, people will figure it out. But right now, that baby needs to eat, and we have to figure out what to give her and how to feed her."

"Powdered milk with an extra fifty percent water plus sugar."

We both look at Jen.

"That's why I interrupted your conversation," she says. "It was too painful listening to you both flounder. A baby needs formula, but watered down and sugared milk will do in an emergency."

"You have kids?" I say.

"God, no. I was a midwife."

Now Petra and I are staring.

"I thought you were a teacher," I say, and I'm still struggling to reconcile *that* with the woman I know. Jen certainly looks like she could have been a teacher — well groomed, late thirties, pleasant appearance — but I cannot imagine her interacting with children. I don't want to.

"You know how much a primary school teacher makes? I was a midwife on the side. Also did some day care in the summer, and I specialized in babies."

"Whoa," Petra says. "I finally know why you're here. It wasn't a real day care, was it? You were secretly conducting Satanic rituals on children."

"Oh, ha ha. That's actually not bad. You get a point for that one, blondie, but no, my kids were just fine. I like children. It's once they hit puberty that they become assholes. Now let's go get what you need."

SEVEN

By the time we return to the clinic, April has her report ready. The baby is dehydrated and had mild hypothermia but not frostbite. She appears to be healthy. April estimates she's approximately a month old. All of this is what I expected. Even the negatives — the dehydration and hypothermia — are minor and easily reversed. She does ask one question that makes me smack myself for not considering it before.

Were the blankets soiled when I found her?

The baby had been naked and wrapped in hide blankets. No diaper. My very preliminary exam on her mother's body suggested the woman had been dead for hours when I found the baby. The baby has been wrapped in the same blanket ever since. Yet there are no bowel movements in it, and no obvious sign of urination. When I sniff-test, I do smell uric acid, but only faintly. So even before her mother died, the baby hadn't eaten in a while. Is that significant? Maybe not, but it's something for me to remember. It also means she's very, very hungry now. Hungry enough to gobble down our make-shift formula without complaint.

Dalton feeds her. When he's done and Jen says, "Now you need to burp her," he hands her to me, and I awkwardly pat her back until Jen says, "Burp her, not jump-start her." She takes the baby. "You really don't have any idea what you're doing, do you?"

"No," April says. "It isn't a skill Casey needs when she cannot have children."

Silence falls. Dalton's opening his mouth when Anders says, "And that's no one's business except Casey's, but thanks for broadcasting it, April. I'm sure your sister appreciates that."

April turns on him in genuine bafflement. "I was stating a medical fact. It's hardly Casey's fault —"

"It's okay," I say. "Yes, these aren't skills I possess, so I appreciate Jen's help."

Anders and Dalton quickly change the subject, but I feel the weight of Jen's gaze, and even if I can't tell what she's thinking, I squirm under that.

April is right. Saying I can't have kids should be no different than saying I'm deaf in one ear or my pancreas doesn't produce insulin. It's a medical issue, beyond my control.

I've heard people admit that being unable to have kids makes them feel less like a woman. That's not me at all. I just feel . . . I feel as if an opportunity has been snatched from me, this thing I wasn't sure I wanted, but I would like to have had the option. I don't, and that stings, and it's stung more in the past few hours than I ever imagined it could.

I let Jen handle the burping while I talk to April about the baby's mother. I might not be able to burp the baby properly, but here's something I *can* do for her. I am a detective, and if her mother holds any clues to tell me where this baby belongs, I'm getting them from her.

We've put Jen in charge of the baby. I cannot believe I'm saying that. I'm definitely not comfortable with it, but we don't have a lot of options. Dalton and I need to be with April for the autopsy, and Anders has a town to manage.

Also, whatever my issues with Jen, I wouldn't leave the baby with her if I didn't have to admit she could be trusted, at least in something this important.

Once the baby is out of the exam area, we

bring in her mother's body and put it on the same table. I undress her and fold her clothing into paper bags that I write on with a marker. Dalton takes notes as I dictate my initial observations while April waits.

I take pictures, too. We have a digital camera and a laptop for me to download the photographs, blow them up, analyze them . . . Crime solving in Rockton might make me feel like I'm working in Sherlock Holmes's time, but I do have access to some modern tech. We generate a base level of solar power for food storage and the restaurant kitchens, and I can tap into that, but I don't use it more than necessary, especially in winter, when the sun is at a premium.

When I undressed the woman in that clearing, I'd made observations that I need to follow up on before April begins her autopsy. So I tell her what I noticed. She listens and frowns and then nods and checks.

"Your observations are correct," she says when she finishes. "This woman is not the infant's mother."

"Fuck," Dalton exhales.

"Seconded," I murmur.

When I'd first removed the dead woman's shirt, what caught my attention was her breasts. I might not know much about

73

babies, but I've worked alongside breast-feeding mothers, and I understand the basic physiological changes that go along with breastfeeding. This woman . . . well, she looks like I'd expect of a middle-aged woman with a D-cup bosom. In short, her breasts are not buoyed by mother's milk. That could mean she was unable to breast-feed, which is why I hadn't mentioned my suspicion to Dalton. It threw a huge monkey wrench into this scenario, and I wanted to be sure. Now I am.

"This woman has never given birth," April says.

"She could have a child without breast-feeding," I explain to Dalton. "But April is talking about her pubic bones. During pregnancy, they separate. The ligaments tear, which you'd see in a recent birth. There's none of that. Long-term, that heals, but it leaves pitting, which I learned from that forensic anthropology text you got me. That's why April believes this woman has *never* had a child."

"So she isn't the baby's mother," Dalton says. "I don't even know where to go with that."

"I do," I say. "Because I've been consider-ing it since I got a good look at her. Unfor-

tunately, that path goes in a million directions."

"I believe a million is overstating the matter," April says.

"It's rhetorical hyperbole," I say. Before
she can argue, I continue. "The woman
could be related to the baby. She could be a
caretaker. She could have stolen it. Of
course, if she'd been caught stealing it,
whoever shot her should have taken the
baby back. If she's a relative or caretaker,
I'd expect the parents to be combing the
woods looking for her, and we didn't hear
anything."

"Does it matter how this woman obtained
the child?" April asks, and her tone makes it
sound like an accusation but I'm learning
not to jump on the defensive.

"It does," I say. "Because if she knows the
baby, then her body may provide clues to
the baby's home. If she doesn't know
her . . ."

I don't finish. This woman is my only link
to the baby's origins. If she has no relationship to the child — if they aren't from the
same family or settlement — then I wouldn't
even know where to begin. It's like dropping a naked baby on a church doorstep. I
need something to work with, and this
woman is all I have right now.

I will find my clues here. Pretend I really am living in the nineteenth century and channel my inner Sherlock Holmes to tease out the threads leading to a connection that will, ultimately, take this woman and — I hope — the baby home. For that, my best clues might be contained in the literal threads that surround her: the woman's clothing. I force myself to set that aside for now and focus on what her body tells us instead.

This woman was not born in the wilderness. There are fillings in her teeth and the dents of old ear piercings. She also has a mark that may be a belly button piercing.

I take photos of the ritual scarring and tattooing. Both seem unfinished, and the scars are old. She hasn't been a hostile in a while. My mind automatically seizes on this and wants to start extrapolating potential information on the nature of hostiles. But that's not what this is about. File it for later. Focus on the clues for this woman as an individual, not as a general exemplar.

She's lost the tips of two toes to frostbite. The bottoms of her feet are callused and thick-soled. I also note that one of her wrists is slightly crooked, and April confirms that the bone has been broken and healed poorly. That could have taken place with the hostiles or afterward — medicine outside Rockton is primitive, and the fact that it healed at all shows she had basic medical care.

On to cause of death. April confirms it wasn't the blow to the back of her head. That's ugly, and it left a mark on the bone, but it wouldn't have been incapacitating. The wound on her leg is indeed a bullet hole. A pellet hole, to be exact, from a shotgun. We find a buckshot pellet. There's only one, which suggests the gun was fired from a distance. That's not how you use buckshot — if you're hunting large game with a shotgun at a distance, you'd use a slug and, arguably, you should be using a rifle, but out here, people take the weapons and ammo they can get. At that range, a buckshot pellet isn't usually fatal, but if you hit the right spot — like the femoral artery — it can be.

Struck by a blow to the back of the head. Puts on her hat afterward. No time to treat the injury? Trying to get somewhere first? Then she's shot. I don't see any signs that she'd attempted to treat that or even stop the bleeding.

Mental confusion from the head blow? Shock? Hypothermia? She'd been escaping someone in the forest, possibly at night, snow falling.

I remember her position, fetal on her side, protecting the baby.

I'm just going to lie down for a minute. Rest. That's a classic sign of hypothermia. Someone accustomed to life out here would know better, but add the blow to the head with the baby clutched to her breast, and she had good reason to succumb.

Running. Fleeing. Lost. Exhausted. Drop and curl up . . . and bleed out in the snow, too befuddled from a head injury to tend to your injured leg.

The woman's stomach has food in it. Not much, suggesting she hadn't recently eaten. There's nothing for me to analyze there. I don't know what I'd be looking for anyway — *ah-ha, she ate hare, and from the semi-digested bits, I can tell it was a specific subtype, found only on Bear Skull Mountain.* Yeah, no. She isn't starving, but neither had she just eaten before her death. That's all I need.

Speaking of eating, that makes me realize the dead woman didn't have any supplies on her. No backpack. Nothing to feed the baby either. Does that suggest she fled unexpectedly? She was properly dressed, so it wasn't as if she grabbed the baby and ran out into the snow.

I check her clothing pockets. Only her

parka has them, and I find a knife in an interior one.

Clothing next. The most interesting piece had been around her ankle — her sole jewelry. A braided leather anklet inscribed with "Hope. Dream. Love." The letters have been burned in with painstaking care. The leather edges show faint wear. It's not new, but it isn't old either.

Most of the woman's clothing is basic in its construction. It shows a knowledge of tanning and sewing at a journeyman level. It's sturdy, and it does the job. Her jacket and boots are different. They're serious craftsmanship. The parka is done in the Inuit style — caribou with the fur inside, the hollow hairs adding extra insulation. The hood is framed in ermine. Her boots are also caribou, and her socks are mink. Warm and luxurious. All three have decorative flairs not found on her clothing. The jacket buttons are polished stones. The laces on the boots and jacket end in bone carvings of fox heads — gorgeous work that I didn't even notice until now.

Her outerwear must be trade goods. With that, I have my first solid clue. Someone made her parka and boots. Someone with enough talent that others will recognize the workmanship.

The first person I'd normally ask is Jacob, Dalton's brother, who still lives in the forest. He's away, though, on a hunting expedition with Nicole, a Rockton resident. I'm hoping it's more than a hunting trip, but either way, he's not nearby. My second point of contact would be former Rockton sheriff Tyrone Cypher. Yet his winter camp is a few hours away, and he might not be there.

We'll start with option three: the First Settlement. I'd much rather deal with Jacob or Cypher, but I will admit that someone in the settlement is more likely to recognize the workmanship. It might even come from there — after Rockton, they're the largest community in the area.

Once April finishes the autopsy, I go into the waiting room to check on the baby. Jen starts passing her to me.

I lift my hands. "I can hold her if you have to do something, but I need to go talk to Phil." I take the baby and pull her into a cuddle. Then I stop. "What's that . . ." I sniff again and look at Jen.

"Why do you think I was handing her to you?" she says. "I'm about to teach you a valuable baby-care lesson. You can thank me later."

Dalton walks in. "We need to —"

I hand him the baby. "She wants you."

His brows arch, but he takes her. Then his nose wrinkles.

"Jen's going to teach you how to change a diaper," I say. "I'd love to help, but I need to talk to Phil."

I hurry out the door before he can argue.

EIGHT

Phil isn't at his house. I'll admit to some relief at discovering that, even if it means I have to go find him. When he arrived — or was exiled here as our new town council rep — he'd stayed in his house as much as April stayed in hers.

Well, no, my sister spends most of her days in the clinic, where she interacts with residents, whether she wants to or not. Phil just stayed in his house. Waiting for a call from the council, I suspect, to tell him all was forgiven and he could come home. To his credit, when he realized that wasn't happening, he stepped out and into his role.

It's in Phil's best interests to take a more active part in town life. Which does not mean he's hanging holiday decorations or mulling cider for the weekly wassailing party. Phil is a corporate man. The kind of guy who was born with a cell phone in one hand, a clipboard in the other, and both eyes on the corporate ladder. He's young — thirty — and ambitious as hell. Which makes Rockton his actual hell.

If there's a ladder here, Dalton is ensconced at the top. With a weak sheriff, Phil might have been able to muscle through and crown himself King of Rockton. Phil knows better than to even try it with Dalton, which proves he has some brains to go with that ego and ambition.

Phil is slowly carving out his place, and it's the one he's most comfortable with. A managerial position in a town that really *could* use a manager. So, if Phil's not home, then I'm most likely to find him managing. In the kitchens, analyzing production. In the shops, checking inventory levels. Or simply walking about town, making note of who is chatting on a porch when they're supposed to be working.

I'm directed to the woodshed, where he was seen an hour ago. He's made some adjustments to the winter-supply system, decreasing free allotments of heating wood while also decreasing the cost for extra. There's been grumbling, but his theory is sound. If people get x logs per week free, then they burn x logs, whether they need them or not. This way, they're encouraged to dress warmer or use extra blankets or even socialize more in the common areas, but if they really do want more home heat, the additional fee is reasonable.

These are the aspects of life in Rockton that Dalton just doesn't have the time — or the inclination — to manage. It's a matter of fine-tuning the overall system to balance conservation, labor, and resident happiness. Phil might see this as a hobby to occupy him while he waits for his release papers, but he really is helping.

"He came, he saw, he left again," Kenny says when I walk into the small carpentry shop next to the lumber shed. Kenny grabs his crutches and leads me outside.

Kenny is our local carpenter. He used to also be our lead militia, and while we haven't taken that title away, he's only recently resumed patrols. Six months ago, he took a bullet for Storm. That bullet didn't paralyze him, but he still needs crutches and leg braces. Will he always need them? That's impossible even for my neurosurgeon sister to say. In six months, Kenny has graduated from bed to crutches. He's working on regaining full mobility while understanding that may never come.

Outside the carpentry shed, he calls, "Sebastian!" The thump of splitting lumber stops, and a moment later, our youngest —

and possibly most dangerous — resident appears. Sebastian is a clinically diagnosed sociopath who murdered his parents at the age of eleven and spent the next seven years locked up. Which probably means we shouldn't be giving him an ax and sending him out to the woodpile alone. But Sebastian is . . . an interesting case.

"Hey, Casey," he says as he jogs over, ax in hand. "You're back early. Everything okay?"

"Pretty much. Mathias give you the day off?"

"Nah, I took it. He's in a mood. I decided to chop wood and stay out of his way before we kill each other." His eyes glint at that, almost self-deprecating recognition that — as we both know — this is an entirely valid concern, given the parties involved. "He'll be glad to have Raoul back, though. He spent all morning snapping about how glad he is not to have that 'mongrel' underfoot, which means he misses him."

"Well, Raoul is home, and I'm looking for Phil. Was he here?"

"Yep, he came to check the woodpiles. He left about twenty minutes ago. Said he was heading to the Roc to go over the alcohol inventory with Isabel. You want me to run grab him?"

"I've got it. Thanks."

As Sebastian jogs back to his chopping, Kenny says, "He's a good kid. Really good."

I make a noncommittal noise. Of course, Kenny has no idea what Sebastian is or why he's here. That's on a need-to-know basis, and the only ones who need to know are myself, Dalton, and Mathias. And Sebastian is, in his way, a good kid. At least he's trying to be, and in Rockton, that's what counts.

Sebastian knows what he is, and he's spent years in therapy for it. He's continuing his rehabilitation here with Mathias, the town butcher who used to be a psychiatrist specializing in psychopathy and sociopathy . . . and who may be an expert on the subject in more than just a professional sense.

It's Rockton. Everyone has a story. Everyone has shadows in their past. It's what they do here that matters. Sebastian is a model citizen. Others are not, and they don't have his excuse of mental illness.

Up here, what you were before — and what you are at heart — is not nearly as important as what you choose to be. At least for now, Sebastian chooses this path, and we'll let him have it, while we stand watch in case that changes.

I head to the Roc. It's one of two bars, which may seem unwise in such a small town. Northern communities often struggle with substance-abuse issues. Long cold winters. Limited entertainment options. The isolation and subsequent cabin fever. Rockton deals with that by regulating alcohol even more tightly than other commodities. Part of regulating it is having two bars. Two places to enjoy a social drink while being monitored by staff who will cut you off fast, because if you start a drunken brawl, both you and your server will spend a week on chopping duty.

There are also two bars because the Roc serves dual purpose as a brothel. Yes, brothel. Right now we have a hundred and forty men and thirty-two women. I'm still not convinced that "brothel" is the way to handle that disparity, but I'm a lot more willing to concede the possibility than I was when I first moved in.

It isn't a perfect solution. It leads to an expectation that, if *some* women take credits for sex, maybe they *all* will, if the price is high enough. I dealt with my share of offers when I first arrived, and in the early days of my relationship with Dalton, plenty of residents suspected I hooked up with him just to put a very big barrier between myself and the male population.

However, I will admit that Isabel regulates the sex trade as tightly as she does the booze. Part of that regulation is making damned sure every woman who does it wants to do it, is safe doing it, and can say no to any client. And woe to the man who asks twice once he's gotten that no.

At this time of day, the Roc is closed. It'll open at five, and Isabel's "girls" won't be on duty until nine. That's a recent development, as Isabel tries to make the Roc more accessible to female patrons. I'd pointed out the unfairness of having half of the bars virtually off-limits to female patrons. Isabel saw my point, and we negotiated the non-brothel early-bird hours.

I open the doors and walk into the Roc, which looks like a Wild West saloon. I'll admit that part of the "female-friendly" schedule changes are totally selfish on my part. The Red Lion can be stuffy. The Roc is a place where you can grab a drink and park yourself at any table and be welcomed into the conversation.

Right now, the inside is dim and cool and smells of pine shavings. The shavings cover the floor, both for atmosphere and easy cleaning at night's end, shavings swept up in the morning and fed back into that evening's fire as kindling. We are conservation kings in Rockton. Also, the shavings smell nice and add to that old-time saloon atmosphere.

I walk behind the bar to the most secure door in Rockton: the liquor safe. It's closed, and I raise my hand to knock just as a noise sounds from overhead. The very distinctive sound of bedsprings squeaking . . . along with other distinctive sounds that often accompany that one.

I could leave and come back in an hour. That would be the right thing to do. My business with Phil isn't urgent. Not as urgent as his current business. However . . . Well, really, this is just too much fun to resist.

I take a jug of iced tea from the underfloor cooler, pour a glass, and wait. The sounds subside after just enough time for me to finish my drink. Then I head upstairs, calling, "Isabel?"

I reach the top of the steps. "Isabel? It's Casey. I'm looking for Phil, and I was told he was here —"

The door at the end opens, and a woman steps out dressed in a wrapper. Isabel Radcliffe. Former therapist. Current bar and brothel owner. And while I'd love to claim the title of most powerful woman in Rockton for myself, I have to concede it to her. She controls the booze and the sex, and that makes her the queen.

Isabel is forty-six years old and quite possibly the most glamorous woman I have ever met. She's full-figured and attractive, but it's more than that. It's confidence and style, and she oozes both. Brilliant. Manipulative. A sheer force of nature, one I have butted heads with since I arrived, which doesn't stop me from now considering her one of my closest friends. Nor does it stop the head-butting. We'd hate to lose that.

"I found Phil, didn't I?" I say as she pads barefoot down the hall.

Her smile answers for her. It's wicked, and it's very, very pleased with herself, and I can't help laughing. She's had her eye on Phil since he arrived, which I'd been glad to see. She'd spent the last year in mourning for a lover — claiming she was over him, while not so much as glancing at another man. This is a welcome turn of events.

I'm about to comment when footsteps sound behind me. As Dalton comes up the stairs, I say to Isabel, "So, was he worth the chase?"

"Definitely," she says, leaning against the wall. "I'll admit I was concerned about that. He's very pretty, and too often, men use that as an excuse for lackluster sex. Women do, too, I presume. So it's a relief to get a partner who is both pretty and proficient." She glances at Dalton. "Am I right, Sheriff?"

Dalton arches his brows.

"Just say yes," I say.

"Considering I don't know what she's talking about, that seems unwise," he says.

Isabel smiles. "Oh, believe me, it's wise. Unless you want to say that Casey here is lovely to look at but terribly dull to bed."

Dalton looks at me and jerks a thumb toward the closed door down the hall. "Phil?"

"Yes," I say. "And Isabel assures us he's both pretty and good in bed."

"Just what I wanted to hear." He strides down the hall and bangs his fist on the door. "Phil? Get your pants on. We need to talk."

"Don't keep him long, please," Isabel says as she heads downstairs. "Twenty minutes would be optimal."

I shake my head and join Dalton as the door opens. Phil is fully dressed, as if he'd just been talking inventory with Isabel because the bedroom is a more comfortable place to do business. His fly is down, though, and the back of his hair stands on end.

"Zip up," Dalton says as he walks past.

91

Phil does and then spots his glasses on the nightstand and grabs them, which is a shame, because I was going to try confirming my suspicion that the lenses are plain glass. Phil reminds me of those stock-photo pictures of young businessmen, where they stick glasses on a male model and take a picture of him with a stack of files, as if every corporate department is filled with guys who look like this.

"I was just . . ." Phil begins, struggling for an excuse.

"Taking Isabel's inventory?" I say.

He actually blushes. It's kinda cute. He's stammering an excuse when Dalton says, "No one cares if you're sleeping with Isabel."

"Well, yes," I say. "I can think of a few women — and men — who'll be disappointed that you've chosen a partner. But *we* don't care. It's a long cold winter, and Isabel is a good choice to make it a little warmer."

"Yeah," Dalton says. "Up here relationships can get complicated. Expectations start low and soar fast. Isabel's a safe bet. It'll be straight sex. No danger of attachment."

Phil checks his glasses for smudges and then puts them on. "Yes, of course. That was my thought. As much as I admire Isabel, you don't need to worry about me forming any undue attachment."

"I meant there's no danger of *her* forming one."

Phil goes still, and the look on his face . . . I could say something, smooth over Dalton's bluntness. Once upon a time, I would have. Now, well, Phil will get over it, and if this makes him work harder to win Isabel's favor, she'll appreciate that.

"So, we're back early," I say.

"Yes, that's right," Phil says, adjusting his glasses. "You are. What happened?"

"We have a baby."

Phil blinks. "You're having . . ."

"Already have one. She's at the clinic."

More blinking. Dalton's lips twitch as he leans against the wall to enjoy the fun.

"She . . . ?" Phil says. "You had a . . . baby?"

"No, *we* have a baby. Rockton does."

"I . . ." Phil sits on the bed. "I don't . . . understand."

"I found an infant," I say. "She was with a woman who I presumed was her mother. That woman was dead. The baby was buried under the snow with the body. There was no one around, so I had to bring her back. She's at the clinic."

It takes a moment for his brain to assimilate this new information. Then he says, "We are not equipped to handle a baby, Casey."

"No shit," Dalton says. "That's why we're talking to you. We need supplies."

I hold up my hand. "We are well aware that this isn't an abandoned puppy. We aren't adopting her. First thing tomorrow, we're heading out to find her family. Given the vastness of this wilderness — and the fact it's winter — that might take a while. It's not like we can go on TV and announce we found a child. The plan is to go to the First Settlement. If they can't help, we'll need baby supplies while we continue looking for her family. So this visit is partly to ask —"

"Inform," Dalton says.

"Yes, *inform* you that we may be making an unexpected supply run. That's a given. The 'ask' part was me suggesting that we use the run to treat residents to some extras for the holidays, since we'd be going to Dawson and only bringing back diapers, formula, and whatever."

"It's been a shitty year, and they deserve a good holiday," Dalton says. "So we're requisitioning —"

"*Asking* for extra funds to do that. We'll

even say you suggested it, if you'd like. You can be Santa this year."

"Thank you," Phil says dryly, but I know I've spun this the right way. Phil is a shrewd businessman, and this is a wise investment toward cementing his local reputation.

I continue, "We also need you to speak to the council. Tell them we have a baby. Explain the situation. Give them no opportunity to later rap our knuckles for covering this up. Even they can't argue that we should have left an infant in the forest."

"Agreed."

"We want that done right away, because we know past situations have fostered an environment of mistrust, and we want to be totally aboveboard with this."

"Uh-huh. Which is an excuse for contacting them quickly, when what you really want is . . ."

I smile at him. "You're a quick study. We appreciate that. Yes, informing them of the baby is the excuse. What I really want is to tell them about the dead woman and see if there's any chance they can identify her. She's almost certainly a former Rockton resident. We can't send them a photo, of course — not until we get to Dawson and have internet access — but we'll give you a full description. If she's in their files, we may be able to figure out which settlement she's associated with. Or which settlement's residents she might know from her time in Rockton. Impress on the council that identifying this woman could return the baby to her parents. Otherwise . . ." I shrug. "Maybe you'd like a tiny roomie?"

"No," he says quickly. "Thank you for asking. I will write up a full description of this woman . . ."

I hand him my notes. He takes the page.

"If you learn anything, let us know," I say. "Otherwise, we'll be off for the First Settlement before dawn."

He grabs his jacket from a chair by the bed.

"It's not that big a rush," I say. "I think Isabel wanted to speak to you first. I'll send her up."

Dalton and I head downstairs, to where Isabel is at the bar, writing something.

"He's all yours," I say. "Better hurry, though. It's almost five."

She holds up what she'd been writing. It's a sign.

The Roc will open at 6 PM today, so as not to interfere with the wassail party.

"You're so considerate," I say.

She hands me the sign. "Hang it, and lock the door, please."

NINE

As much as we'd love to head out again, chasing answers, it's already dark. The investigation will need to wait until morning. I stop by the wassail party long enough to announce that there is a baby in town. Residents will hear her, so they need to know she's here and why. I say that I understand people may want to see her, but she's very young and we don't know the full state of her health and immune system and must restrict contact to caregivers only.

After that, Dalton and I pick up Storm and then have an early dinner, while taking the baby for a couple of hours to give Jen time to eat. Overnight, she'll stay with Jen.

Because the Roc opened late, Isabel extends the pre-brothel hours, and at nine, we're there with Anders and April, with Storm gnawing a bone under the table. It's been a long day. Tomorrow will be another long one. We can afford an hour off to enjoy a mug of mulled alcoholic beverage and kettle corn, the festive snack of the evening.

By the time Dalton is two-thirds done with his cider, I'm on his lap. I did not put myself there. I'm not quite sure how I arrived there, either, which may suggest I've imbibed more alcohol than I intended.

Isabel stops by to refill the popcorn bowl and smirks at us, Dalton with his arms tight around me, his head on my shoulder, nuzzling my neck. If he's doing that in public . . .

"Exactly how much rum is in this cider?" I ask.

"In general?" Anders says. "Or in ours?" He lifts his mug. "I do believe Iz was feeling generous tonight."

"It does seem . . ." April stares into her barely touched drink. "Strong."

"I owe you for earlier," Isabel says to me. She waves at Dalton. "Enjoy."

"This isn't a gift," I say as I firmly move Dalton's hands to my waist. "It's payback."

"We don't ever get to see our sheriff drunk," Isabel says as she refills his mug before I can stop her. "It's adorable."

"It kinda is," Anders says as she leaves. "However . . ." He looks around the Roc, at residents watching their hard-ass sheriff nuzzling his girlfriend.

"Not a good look?" I say.

"He's fine," April says. "There's nothing wrong with mild acts of public affection."

"Nah," Dalton says, straightening. "There is when it's the sheriff slobbering on his detective. And, yeah, you don't need to talk about me in the third person. I've had more than I should, but I'm not that drunk."

"Also, for the record," I say, "there was no actual slobbering. You're just very cuddly. As Will said, it is adorable but . . ."

I slide off his lap. He lets me go with reluctance and a last squeeze before saying, "Yeah, time to cut me off."

"Unless you want the rest of your cider to-go."

The slow smile that crosses Dalton's face has Anders making gagging noises. April stops him with a sharp rap on the arm, which proves that her drink is indeed strong. Dalton gets to his feet.

"I'll grab take-out cups," he says.

"I thought we weren't allowed take-out alcohol," April says.

"Eric is special," Anders says.

I give Storm a pat under the table as I watch Dalton cross to the bar. He's walking steadily, no sign of inebriation in his gait or his stance. It's still very obvious that he's tipsy. Normally, even here socially, he carries himself with a certain stiffness. Tenser. Harder. Gaze constantly scanning for trouble, the set of his jaw warning that a wrong move could land the miscreant in the water trough outside.

Tonight he's the guy I see at home. Relaxed. Calm. Happy. A slight bounce in his step and the ghost of a smile on his lips. He looks younger, too, and this is one of the reasons he doesn't drink more than one beer in public. When he relaxes, the walls come down, his guard dropping, and people suddenly remember he's only thirty-two, and they start to wonder why he holds so much power, or why a glare from him can have them straightening in their seat, their hearts beating faster.

Isabel fills two bottles with hot mulled cider, leaving them uncapped, steam rolling out. Someone cracks a joke about Dalton getting special privileges, and there's a moment where I can tell Dalton's ready to joke back, the corners of his eyes crinkling. Then he remembers himself and sobers. "You want my job? Privileges come with that, and I don't think you want this" — he raises the bottles — "that badly."

The resident should leave it at that, but Dalton isn't the only one who's had too much, and this guy is new, not yet accustomed to how things work in Rockton. He grins and hooks a thumb at me. "If she's one of those privileges, I'll take it."

Silence drops so fast it ripples through the entire bar, those too far to hear the exchange noticing the hush and following it. A buzz of anticipation follows. A sense of schadenfreude that tells me that this guy has not made friends, no one even taking pity on him by leaping up to pull him back.

"*She* is our detective," Dalton says, his voice tight with warning.

The man chuckles and thumps Dalton on the shoulder. "No offense, Sheriff. I'm just saying you're a lucky guy. Hot booze. Hot chick. Gotta love a position with perks."

Dalton reaches over and dumps the contents of one bottle down the guy's shirt.

"Huh," Dalton says as the guy lets out a high-pitched shriek. "You're right. It *is* hot." He looks at Isabel. "You heat it up a little extra for me?"

"I wouldn't want your drink getting cold on the walk home."

Dalton grabs the front of the guy's shirt. "Special treatment from the barkeep? *That's* a perk. Detective Butler? *That's* a person. Learn the difference."

"You — you burned —"

"First degree, if that. Lucky for you, the

doc's sitting right there."

Anders rises. "I'll get this one, April." He puts an arm around the man's shoulders, and the guy flinches, but Anders only gives him a friendly squeeze. "We'll have a nice chat, too, while I'm looking at that burn."

They nearly bump into Kenny, who's just come into the Roc. He looks from Anders to the burned guy. Then he sees Dalton and nods, as if this is all the explanation he needs.

I wave Kenny to our table. "Perfect timing. We were about to abandon my sister."

If it were anyone else, April would say that she'd been leaving. For Kenny, she'll stick around.

Isabel holds out a fresh bottle of cider. Dalton takes it before I can, and he motions me to the door. Storm follows at our heels.

We're outside and away from the Roc before I snatch one of the bottles and take a long draw from it.

My eyes water, and I gasp. "I think she made these even stronger than the ones we got inside."

I take another gulp, and Dalton laughs at that. His gloves go around my hips, and he hoists me onto the railing of a shop, dark and closed for the day. Then he pushes

102

between my knees, and I get a long, cider-sweet kiss.

Storm sees what's happening, sighs, and plunks down to wait, the model of patience. Dalton sips a far more cautious drink from his bottle. Hesitates. Gulps a larger swig.

I laugh and put my arms around his neck, bottle dangling from one hand.

"Having a good night, Sheriff?" I ask.

"It started off good. It's getting better." Another gulp. Another kiss. He blinks, forcing his eyes to focus, and I have to laugh at that.

"You are such a lightweight," I say.

"I'm not the only one."

"Hey, I shoot tequila. Straight."

"Yeah, Miss Two-Shots Max. You like to look like a badass, but I definitely saw some wobbling as we left the Roc."

"Which is one of the reasons we left." I hoist my bottle. "If I'm having more, I'm having it with just you."

"Ditto."

As he kisses me, his gaze shunts to the side, and he gives a start. Then he chokes on a laugh. I look to see . . .

It looks like a person standing there. It's actually a dummy, sitting on a wooden chair. A very homemade dummy, constructed of stuffed trousers stuck into boots

103

and an equally stuffed red flannel shirt. The head is cotton stuffed into a nylon and painted with a red smile and round eyes. More cotton forms a beard. On the figure's head is an old red knit hat.

"Is that supposed to be Santa Claus?" Dalton asks.

I shudder. "Reminds me of the mall Santas my parents made me sit with. We had to get a duty photo every year to send to family — one of me sitting on the knee of some very sketchy Santas. April got out of it, naturally."

He scoops me up.

"No!" I say. "Don't you dare —"

He turns at the last second and plunks onto Santa's lap, crushing the poor dummy. Then he settles me onto his own lap and tugs the knit cap onto his head.

"So, little girl, what do you want for Christmas?"

"Oh God, now I really am scarred for life." I shudder. "Wrong, wrong, so wrong."

He tosses the hat aside and leans back, arms tightening around me. "I'll ask the question like this, then. What do you want for Christmas this year?"

I twist to look up at him and smile. "I do believe I have everything I want."

He goes as red at the Santa's flannel shirt.

"You're cute when you blush." I lean over to kiss him. "Still true, though. If we make that extra trip to Dawson, I'll come up with a completely frivolous wish list for you, but you'll owe me a list, too. As for what I want tonight —"

The sudden wail of a baby sounds in the distance. We look at each other.

"Not that," I say.

"Definitely not that."

We dissolve into tipsy giggles. Then I say, "Gotta admit, you looked damn good holding a baby. It suited you."

His head tilts, and I know he's catching the note in my voice. A wistful one that says this isn't a hint that I want a child, but maybe a hint that I'm suddenly feeling the loss of that possibility.

"I might look good in a Speedo bathing suit, too," he says. "Doesn't mean I should have one."

I giggle, making me glad he's the only one here. It's definitely not a homicide-detective-worthy sound.

Dalton continues. "Now, if you said you wanted me in a Speedo, I'd get one in a heartbeat. I'm not opposed to them. Just not sure it'd suit me. Not sure it *wouldn't* suit me either. The truth is that I've never given it much thought one way or another.

I could wear one if you wanted me to. Now. Later. Or I could go my entire life without ever wearing one, and that'd be fine, too. Which is exactly how I feel about a baby."

He adjusts me on his lap. "I said the same thing the first time you mentioned the issue, and that hasn't changed. I don't have strong feelings either way. I know you probably can't have a baby. We could try and see what happens. Or we can decide that's too stressful and find a way to adopt. Or we can say we're fine like this, you and me. This ball is one hundred percent in your court, Casey. I'm good with whatever you want."

"And if that changes? If you realize you want — or don't want — kids? Would you tell me?"

"Absolutely," he says, and kisses me.

TEN

We tumble into the house, having consumed about half our cider on the way. Hey, we wouldn't want it getting cold.

The door isn't even shut yet before we're kissing. Dalton doesn't lock it. He never does. That's a show of trust . . . and also a warning. Just try breaking into his house.

Storm knows what's coming and retreats to the kitchen. Dalton scoops me up and carries me into the living room, where the fire burns low. I have him undressed before we reach the bearskin carpet. I may make a few comments about how good he'd look in a Speedo. Totally true. He has a swimmer's lean muscled body, and I thoroughly admire it while he stokes the fire.

We aren't in any hurry. We can't leave for the First Settlement until close to dawn, so we take our time in the firelight. Afterward, he's lying on his back on the rug, and I'm stretched out on top of him, tracing my finger through a sheen of sweat on his chest.

"Definitely getting you a Speedo for Christmas," I say.

He chuckles. "Good luck with that in Dawson. Not much call for them there. Not much use for one either, at this time of year."

"I'll stoke the fire so you can wear it indoors."

He's about to reply when someone bangs at the door. It's loud and insistent enough that we can't just be quiet and wait for them to go away. Dalton starts reaching for his jeans. Then he stops, muttering, "Fuck it," and grabs a blanket from the pile. He swoops it out, letting it fall over us, and then calls "Come in!" as he adjusts the blanket to cover everything it should cover.

The door opens. Footsteps sound. Then the howl of a baby, followed by Jen's voice. "Yeah, I'd scream, too, kid. No one wants to see that. You guys do have a bed upstairs, don't you?"

"The fact we're not dressing to answer the door suggests we're expecting this to be a short visit," Dalton says.

"Oh, it will be. I'm just dropping off your kid. Hope you were done, because this is going to put a damper on things." She holds out the baby, who obliges with a howl.

"What's wrong with her?" I say, sliding off Dalton, blanket to my chest.

"Huh. I don't know. Maybe . . . the screaming? She won't settle. She's fed. Changed. Ready for bed and furious. She's making it very clear that Auntie Jen isn't who she wants."

"Well, I don't think she's looking for us, either. She wants her parents."

"Close enough." She holds the baby out again.

I motion for her to turn around, and she says, "Neither of you has anything I haven't seen before but fine."

Once she's turned, I yank on my under-shirt and panties, and Dalton pulls on his jeans. Then I take the baby, who peers at me, head swaying as if trying to focus. Her lower lip trembles. When she lets out a cry, it's not the howl from before, but she's clearly gearing up for it. I pass her to Dalton.

"Me?" he says. "She doesn't want —"

I move his hands, so the baby is pressed against his chest, as she was on the way to Rockton. She fusses for a moment and then settles against him.

"I think she likes you," Jen says.

"It's my smell," he says. "I carried her back to town."

109

"Whew. 'Cause otherwise, that kid is already developing a shitty taste in men." She pats the baby's back. "Wait until you're a teenager for that."

Jen off-loads a pack from her back. "All the supplies."

"Whoa, wait," I say. "We need to leave first thing in the morning, which means we need a good night's sleep."

"Didn't look like you were sleeping when I got here."

"Actually, we were just about to."

"And now you can. She'll drift off, for a while at least. Either you take her or *no one* in town gets to sleep tonight. My neighbors were already trooping over, accusing me of beating the poor thing. She's in a strange place, and she's scared, and the people she knows best are you two."

"Fine, but come by at nine and pick her up."

"Take her with you."

"Uh, no. We're heading into the winter forest in search of her family."

"Exactly why she should go along. As for the 'winter forest,' she was born there. You guys brought her back, bundled up and happy. She's a month old. That's all she wants. Food. Warmth. Security. Pack her into Eric's parka again and off you go."

"We're taking the snowmobiles."

"Even better. You know how to get a kid to sleep down south? Take her for a car ride. The vibration and the steady noise are kiddie Ambien."

When I open my mouth to protest, she says, "I'm not trying to get out of looking after your kid, Casey. I have my monthly janitorial shift tomorrow. I would gladly — ecstatically — give that up to babysit. But she's already separated from her family, and you guys rescued her, and her tiny brain may not know much, but it knows she's safe with you. If you do find her parents, what are you going to do? Say 'Wait right here and we'll bring her tomorrow'? Her parents must be going nuts. They'll follow you back. Depending on who they are, that might not be safe for Rockton."

I look at Dalton. She's right, in all of it.

"Fine," Dalton says. "Just stay and help us set her up for bed. Tell us what we need to do. Feeding schedule, whatever."

She agrees, and we set up a fur-lined box for the baby in our bedroom as Storm snuffles her.

"The pup has to stay downstairs," Jen says. "As friendly as she is, this is a very tiny kiddo."

"I know," I say. " 'Oh, look, they're

111

cuddling' can become 'Why is the baby turning blue?' in a heartbeat."

Jen snorts a laugh. "Exactly. Also, you need a temporary name for her."

"We —"

She lifts a hand. "I've done that for you, too. It's Abby."

My gaze shunts to Dalton, who has gone still, and anger surges in me.

"That's not —" I begin, but Jen's already leaving.

When she's gone, I turn to Dalton. "We don't need to call her that. We don't need to call her anything."

He tucks the baby in, quiet as the front door closes behind Jen. Then he says, his voice low, "No, Abby is fine," and he pulls a thin blanket up and touches the baby's face before going to settle Storm downstairs.

The baby wakes twice for feeding and once for a soiled diaper and once just because, apparently, she's had enough sleep. By five we give up and start breakfast.

Dalton has not yet referred to her as "Abby," and I won't until he does. While Sebastian is young at nineteen, he isn't the youngest person to come to Rockton. That would be Abbygail. An eighteen-year-old street kid with a history of drug use and sex-trade work, she'd escaped to Rockton and turned her life around, only to be brutally murdered in the case that brought me here. By the time I arrived, she was missing, presumed dead. Everyone still held out hope until that was shattered with the discovery that her death had been even worse than "lost in the woods, succumbed to the environment." It was the human environment here that killed her.

In suggesting we call the baby Abby, I fear Jen wasn't honoring the memory of the much-loved girl. At worst, it was incredibly cruel, even for Jen, and I'd hope she would never stoop that low.

To Dalton, the death of Abbygail is his greatest failure as a sheriff. She went from hating the sight of him to idolizing him, first as a mentor and then as more. That last part was the problem. When she kissed him after her twenty-first birthday party, he rejected her, horrified. She fled Rockton and died in the forest. Or so it seemed. But her killers had exploited her crush and sent her a note, apparently from Dalton, telling her to meet him in the forest to talk. She went, and she never came back.

Jen had been the one to tell me about the kiss. She made it sound as if Dalton took advantage of Abbygail's hero worship. When

I learned the truth, I'd confronted her, and she'd shrugged it off, as if she'd known all along and just been stirring up trouble.

So what was Jen's intention calling the baby Abby? Acknowledging that he'd done all he could for the young woman and that her loss haunted him still? Or rubbing his face in his failure? I hope it's the former, but all that matters now is Dalton's reaction, and the fact that he's even considering it gives me hope. It tells me maybe he's ready to honor Abbygail's memory instead of running from it.

Before we leave, we stop at Phil's. He's spoken to the council. They have nothing to say about the baby. They don't recognize the description of the dead woman, though I'm not sure how hard they'd try. On that count, all they're saying is that, while I am free to investigate her death as a way to reunite the child with her family, please remember that I am Rockton law enforcement, and the key word in that phrase is "Rockton." The death of a settler, while tragic, falls outside my purview.

"I told them that your responsibilities here have been light leading into the holidays," Phil says. "Also, such an investigation helps hone your skills and foster better relations with our neighbors."

Unless I accuse one of them of murder.

I don't say that. I know Phil is trying for a head pat by defending me, and I give him one, figuratively at least. Then we're off.

Dalton and I share a snowmobile, leaving the other in case Anders needs it. We take turns driving, the other sitting on the back with the baby bundled in their parka. Jen was right that the baby would sleep most of the time. We stop for feedings and changes and cuddles, because the last seems to complete the trifecta of awake-baby needs. When we can't figure out why she's fussing, we bounce her and talk to her and dance her on our knees. That seems to do the trick.

We can't take the snowmobile all the way to the First Settlement. The trails leading into it aren't wide enough, intentionally. Rockton has horses, ATVs, and snowmobiles. The settlements have none of these, and so for them, wide paths only increase the chance that outsiders will find them . . . or that folks from Rockton will mistake it for a rolled-out welcome mat. So we hide the sled off the path and cover it with a tarp and snow. Then we head in on foot.

Rockton began as a refuge for the persecuted, no criminals permitted. That ideology lasted as long as the accounting books balanced. With each major shift in priorities, a group would leave. The First Settlement was founded in the sixties. Fifty years have passed since, and they're on the third generation, with only two original Rockton residents left, including the town leader, Edwin. As the original settlers die out, their town's connection with ours fades.

The relationship has never been friendly, but it has always been one of mutual disinterest. Live and let live. Dalton fears that will change when Edwin is gone. The younger settlers see Rockton as weak and wealthy. We have those horses and snowmobiles and ATVs, and we are soft, living in relative luxury. We've already seen signs of trouble.

While Edwin lives, we are trying to build bridges. While we might be a handful of shepherds protecting a fat flock, we have all the guns we need to repel an attack . . . and soak the ground with their blood. We don't want that, so we work on building that bridge while making sure the younger settlers see what they are up against.

The problem is that Edwin is an aging lion, well aware of the hungry eyes on his throne. This is not a time he can show weakness by getting chummy with Rockton — the king of the jungle conversing with the gazelle. He must instead play the sly fox who always gets the better end of any deal.

The subtle tug-of-war exhausts Dalton. Our sheriff has no fear of usurpation and no patience for politicking. His personal history with the First Settlement doesn't help. He remembers the men who eyed his mother and talked about her like that new resident spoke about me last night, as if she were a potential trade good. When the male settlers give me the same looks, it doesn't foster good relations. I'm less bothered by it than he is, as I suspect his mother was less bothered than his father. Women expect this. It doesn't mean we tolerate it, but it is a fact of our lives.

As we approach the settlement, Dalton hears someone outside it and hails them with a "Hello!" We know better than to sneak up — or give anyone an excuse to *say* we snuck up. It's one of the men, second generation, maybe in his early forties. He's hauling wood on a toboggan, and when he sees us, he nods and then keeps going, letting us follow him to the village.

I don't try to talk to the man. I've learned my lesson in this. What seems common courtesy is seen as timidity, as if I'm making nervous conversation.

When the man doesn't speak, we don't either, not until we're entering the village and Dalton says, "We'd like to talk to Edwin." The man nods and keeps walking, and we stop there, on the edge of the village.

ELEVEN

The First Settlement is also the largest. It's still a quarter the size of Rockton, with fifteen cabins. On my first visit, I'd counted ten, but there were five more deeper in, like a suburb to the main village. Even the central cabins are sparsely spaced. Protection isn't really an issue out here, and it helps to have that extra room for gardens and privacy.

As we're waiting, a shriek sounds, deep in the village. Dalton's head jerks up, his eyes following the sound. A moment later, a door opens and a man appears, dragging a child by the arm.

"You want to play outside?" the man booms. "Fine. Go to the woodpile and start hauling logs. Come back in when that" — he points at the small heap beside their cabin — "is as tall as you."

The boy is no more than six. He wails his protest, but the door slams shut. My arms instinctively close around the baby under my parka. Dalton strides forward, and I jog after him, torn between not wanting to cause trouble and seeing the child, shivering and sniveling, barely dressed for the cold.

Dalton crouches beside the boy, who sits in the snow, softly crying. Dalton pulls off his hat and puts it on the boy's head. Then he wraps his scarf around the child and whispers something to him. The boy nods and rises, pointing. Dalton strides off, the boy tagging along behind. They disappear behind trees, only to return a moment later, their arms stacked with wood.

Dalton may have no head for politics, but I give him too little credit if I expected him to go after the boy's father, all fire and fury. This is the boy's life. Crying in the snow will not help. Nor will having strangers fix his problems. I watch Dalton haul logs with the boy, and I cradle the baby under my parka and I think, more than I want to, about things I'd rather not.

Another door opens, and Edwin calls to me. As I walk over, the old man's gaze shunts to Dalton helping the boy. He says nothing. He just ushers me inside and shuts the door behind me.

The cabin is blazing hot, the fire roaring.

I unzip my parka and remove the baby from the makeshift papoose.

"You'd better not tell me that's yours," Edwin says. "Or time is passing even faster than I feared."

"I found her in the snow."

His brows rise into his hairline, and he looks at me, as if trying to tell whether I've misused a word. We're speaking in Mandarin. Mine is about the equivalent of a five-year-old's, so it wouldn't be the first time I misspoke. I'd much rather use English, but I know to indulge Edwin in this. My Chinese blood elevates me in his eyes. He's an old man, proud of his heritage, dismissive of those who don't share it.

Edwin settles onto his chair. He isn't large, and age has made him smaller still. He's healthy, though, and his mind is fully functional. He's a former lawyer, which makes this old fox particularly crafty . . . though that might be my own prejudice as a cop.

"Found her in the snow?" he says finally.

I nod.

"Well, she isn't ours," he says. "No one here has had a child in five years. Nor do we want her, if that's what you're asking."

"It isn't."

I hope I don't look relieved when he says

she isn't theirs. I keep thinking of that boy and his father, and I do not want her to be a child of this settlement. That's unfair, I know. As I said, it's a harsh life, and there is no room for soft parenting. Still, my hands clutch the baby a little tighter.

A rap sounds at the door.

"Come in, Eric," Edwin calls in English. When Dalton enters, he says, "Done playing with Jamie?"

Dalton grunts.

Edwin continues. "I'll see that you get your hat and scarf back before you go. And I'll speak to his father."

Dalton nods, and at that, the matter is dropped.

"So, Casey tells me you found this baby," Edwin says, "and you're looking for her people. As much as it pains me to say this, if she was found in the snow . . ."

He glances toward the door. "It's the beginning of winter. All signs point toward a long and cold one. Our practice of contraception, if I may be indelicate, is limited to less-than-foolproof methods. We advocate keen attention to monthly cycles, and children must be born before late summer. We would certainly never abandon a winter baby, but in the forest, between the hostiles and the nomads . . ." He shrugs. "There is,

I fear, a reason why the child was left alone in the snow."

"Under other circumstances, I'd agree," I say. "However, she wasn't alone. We found her with a dead woman who was not her mother."

His eyes glitter. "That is intriguing."

"Yeah," Dalton says. "I know your English seems perfect, but I think the word you want is 'tragic.'"

Edwin only shoots him a withering look. He turns to me and says, "Explain," in Mandarin, a clear slight to Dalton. When I answer, it's in English.

"The woman had been murdered," I say. "She died holding the infant, but our doctor says she's not the mother. The baby was wrapped only in skins, so I have no clues to her identity. I do have some to the woman's, though, which I hope will lead me in the direction I need to go."

I hand the baby to Dalton, then open my pack and pull out a decorated portion of the woman's parka that I cut off for easy transport.

I pass him the piece. I have the ankle bracelet, too, but I want to show him this first. When I do, he gives a slow nod as he runs the fabric through his fingers.

"You recognize the handiwork?" I say.

He hands it back. "If I say I do not, will you accept that the baby is abandoned?"

"We aren't looking for an excuse to keep a baby, Edwin."

"Perhaps. But I *am* looking for an excuse to stop you from returning this child to her family."

"Why?"

"Because you would make a good mother. You are young, strong, intelligent. Eric would make a good father. He is young and strong."

Dalton snorts, not missing the adjective Edwin has skipped.

Edwin only smiles and looks at me, with a wave at Dalton. "See how happy that baby is with Eric? How easily he holds it? How he helped young Jamie? He is a natural father. That's rare. You should take advantage of it."

"By stealing a baby so Eric will be stuck with me?" I say. "Not exactly my recipe for a happy family."

"Oh, I'm sure he would be very happy to be stuck with you. Wouldn't you, Eric?"

Dalton only rolls his eyes, and I say, "I'm not taking this baby from her family. If you know who they are —"

"I do, which is why I am suggesting you forget them. The child was abandoned.

124

Found with a dead woman, who probably *is* her mother. Your doctor was clearly wrong. The child is motherless and alone. You should take her."

"So which is it? The baby was abandoned? Or orphaned?"

He shrugs. "Both. The mother is dead. The father and any other family are obviously not combing the forest looking for her. The child is better off with you."

Dalton tenses. Edwin looks at him, and it's a keen look, a piercing one. I know what's coming next. I feel the subject shifting, and I open my mouth to stop it, but Edwin says, "You don't think you were better off in Rockton, Eric?"

"No," Dalton says tightly. "I don't."

"But Gene Dalton thought you were. Snatched you up and kept you, and you made no attempt to leave. You must have thought it was better. An easy life for a boy. So much easier than in the forest."

Dalton's holding himself so rigid he barely gets the words out. "I did try to escape."

"Eventually, you gave up, though. Resigned yourself to the easier life. Such a hardship."

"My parents didn't come for me," he says. "They obviously thought I was better where I was."

Edwin's laugh is sharp. "So that's what made you stop. A child's pride. The boy sulking in the corner and telling himself his mother and father had abandoned him? Do you really think they didn't risk their *lives* trying to get you back?"

"So you agree then?" Dalton says, his voice low. "That taking me was wrong, and yet here you are, telling us to take *this* child?"

We stand on a precipice. One where I see the answers to Dalton's past below. I can get them from Edwin. Dalton can get them, too. Yet to take that step means accepting the plummet that must go with it. His relationship with the Daltons is already precarious. If he learns that they didn't just naively "rescue" him from the forest but deliberately kept his birth parents away, he'd need to sever all ties with them.

In redirecting the conversation, Dalton has stepped back from that precipice. He doesn't want answers beyond what Edwin has already given. He isn't ready for them.

I can't tell whether this retreat from truth diminishes Dalton in Edwin's regard. It doesn't matter. Dalton will do what he needs to protect himself until he's ready for more, and no one can judge a person for those choices. They are what keep us sane.

What keep us moving forward.

"This is not the same thing," Edwin says. "Your parents were young and naive, but they were good parents, and their sons came first. You were not mistreated or neglected in any way. In fact, I personally worried whether they were properly preparing you boys for this life. It is one thing to teach hunting and foraging and trading skills. But we need more out here. We need a harshness and a ruthlessness that your parents lacked, and therefore could not pass on to you. If your father saw Jamie tossed out of his warm cabin, he'd have gone after the boy's father. You check that impulse. You make sure he is warm, and you help, but you do not let him shirk his duties. You would never say his parents don't deserve to keep him. This baby is different. Her people . . ." His lips curl. "Her people make Jamie's dad look like father of the year."

My breath catches, but I push it back and force myself to say, "Their worthiness as parents isn't for us to decide."

"Is it not? Down south they have child services. When I was a lawyer, my firm took on many cases of parents fighting to have their children returned. I refused to work on them. While there were cases of injustice, the children I saw were better off. I'm sure you saw the same in policing."

He isn't looking for a thoughtful, long-winded response, and that's the only one I could give. Yes, I saw children taken from bad situations, who blossomed and thrived in foster care. Those are the success stories, and there were plenty of them, but there were others, too. Parents who screwed up and lost their kids and didn't get a second chance. Kids volleyed from institution to foster care and back, who fled to find their birth parents, because however tough that life had been, it was better than the alternative.

"Tell us where we can find the parents," I say. "We'll take it from there."

His lips tighten. "She would be better off—"

"We will take it from there," I say, enunciating each word, my gaze locked with his. "Either you trust us to do that or you don't."

"You'll have to wait until spring anyway," he says. "They're nomadic. Traders. It's an extended family. The parents aren't from Rockton. I've heard they were criminals who fled to the Yukon ahead of the law. I certainly believe it. While I would prefer not to trade with them, they bring items we cannot get otherwise. They travel all the way to Dawson for them. I don't know where they overwinter, but they'll be back in spring."

The baby starts to fuss in Dalton's arms. I reach for the pack and fill a makeshift bottle with warm milk from a thermos. Dalton takes it, and the baby quiets.

"You *are* a natural mother, Casey," Edwin says. "Like Eric is a natural father. You didn't even stop to think what she might want."

"So this family of traders," I say. "They make goods like this?" I lifted the fabric.

"They do."

"And it was on the dead woman. Not the baby. Which doesn't mean the child comes from them."

"One of their women was pregnant when they were here last. I say 'woman,' but she was barely more than a girl. As for the baby's father, let's just say goods aren't the only thing that family sells."

He motions to the fabric. "This woman who died. My guess is that she stole the baby. She must trade with them regularly, and she knew what kind of life that child would have — particularly a girl — so she stole her." He meets my gaze. "To honor her sacrifice, you should keep the baby."

I snort a laugh. "Yeah, no."

He shrugs. "It was worth a try." The old man rises. "Now, let's get your hat and scarf back, Eric. I'll also have you speak to Jamie's mother, Casey. He's our youngest resident, and she may have advice for the baby."

TWELVE

Jamie's mother seems like a kind woman, if not the sort who's likely to challenge her spouse. Edwin sends the father on an errand, and we settle into the small cabin, Dalton playing with the boy while I talk to his mother. She cuddles the baby and coos over her, and we discuss the challenges of caring for an infant in the forest. Or it's a challenge for me. For her, it's called "life." She's third generation herself, twenty-two years old, her son already five, which makes me wonder just how old this baby's mother is, if Edwin called *her* "little more than a girl."

Afterward, Dalton and I leave. We don't talk for a while — we want to be farther from the settlement before we do. I'm about to speak when Dalton raises a finger and wraps one arm around the baby-bundle under his jacket as he lifts his gun and scans what seems to be a silent forest. Then I catch the squeak of a boot on snow.

I pull out my weapon.

Dalton calls, "You have five seconds to show yourselves."

He doesn't finish the threat. He could say "Or I start firing" but then he'd need to, and that's a waste of ammo.

"Five, four, three . . ." He wheels, gun aimed, and I hear a sharp intake of breath, though I see nothing in the lengthening shadows.

"You settlers love playing this game, don't you?" he says. "Let's test Eric Dalton. See how good a tracker he really is." He wags the gun toward where it's pointing. "There's one of you." He moves it to the left. "Two." Then back around behind him. "Three. Please tell me there's a prize, 'cause there's never a prize, and I'm starting to feel discouraged."

"The prize is you saw us before we put an arrow in you," a voice says.

Dalton grunts. "Guess so. Still, I'd like an actual prize. Okay, kid, step out where I can see you, and let's have a civil conversation."

"Kid?" There's clear affront in the voice, but the young man who steps out isn't any older than Sebastian.

Dalton shrugs. "Compared to me, you are, though you're older than your two companions."

The young man glances around, seeing no sign of his companions. "How can you tell that?"

"Because they let you speak while they cower behind the trees like children."

That brings the other two out. I can't say for certain whether they are indeed younger. All three are in their late teens. The one already out is dark-haired and sporting a sparse beard. The second is another boy, towheaded and smooth-cheeked. The third is a girl with straight dark hair and skin the same shade as my own. When she says, "What business did you have with my grandfather?" I'm not surprised.

"That would be between Edwin and us," I say.

She shrugs off my nonreply, as if she hadn't expected an answer. "We'd like to trade. We have furs. Caribou, fox, ermine, and mink." She passes me her mitten. It's soft suede lined with ermine. "I can make more. Jackets, too." She looks at mine. "They're prettier than that."

I reach into my pocket and tug out the embroidered piece of leather. "Like this?"

Her nose wrinkles. "Better. That crafter has spent too much time on the decoration, too little on the tanning."

"You know the work?"

She shrugs. "I've seen it. You don't want that. You want mine."

"What if I wanted both? Something from you, and something from this person. Your grandfather said it's from a family of traders, and he doesn't know where they overwinter."

"He knows," she says. "And he does you a favor not sending you to them. Your man" — she nods to Dalton — "is too rich, and you are too pretty. They'd offer to trade, and then kill him for his goods and take you."

She has her grandfather's directness, but with her, it's blunt, no coy calculation. Even when she tells me I'm pretty, it's a simple assessment, devoid of flattery.

At her words, my heart sinks. I'd hoped she'd tell me a story different from her grandfather's.

"What are you looking to trade for?" I ask.

She points at my gun, and Dalton mutters, "Of course." I could drop the conversation here. Maybe I should. But an idea sparks. Something I hadn't asked Edwin, knowing I wouldn't get a straight answer. It's too loaded a question to ask outright. This could be a sideways step into it, though.

"Do you know what this is?" I say, lifting my weapon.

Her face hardens. "I'm not an ignorant savage. It's a gun."

"I meant the type of gun. You have a rifle or two in the settlement, right?"

"We do."

"This isn't a rifle. It a handgun, intended for self-defense. It'll do a lousy job of taking down a buck — unless it's charging at you and you just want to empty the entire magazine into it. This is a semiautomatic weapon. A nine-millimeter. That means two things. It fires a lot of ammo, and it fires a very specific type. I know that's your biggest challenge up here — getting ammunition. No trader is going to carry this."

I open the weapon and show her the cartridges. Then I nod toward Dalton's weapon.

"That's a revolver. Also for self-defense. An entirely different type of ammo, though."

He opens it and shows her.

I continue. "We have a third handgun in town, for our deputy. It's a forty-five. Again, another kind of ammo. Now, first, we can't give you any of those three because they're the only handguns we have, and we keep them on us at all times." I add the last to be clear they won't find them lying around

Rockton. "We can get ammo for them. You can't. Once the magazine is empty, you'd have a lovely paperweight."

Her brow furrows, and I realize "paperweight" wouldn't mean anything to her.

"A deadweight," I amend. "Now, if you wanted to trade for a rifle, we might be able to arrange something. We don't carry ours unless we're hunting. Otherwise, they're secured in a gun safe, and even I can't get at them. We'd be willing to consider trading you a rifle but we'd need to know what caliber you have already and whether we can match it. Otherwise . . ." I shrug. "You're back to the same problem of ammo."

The girl nods. "My grandfather is very careful about that. Our rifles are all three-oh-eights."

Dalton grunts behind me. He's finally figured out where this odd line of conversation was going. I seeded in the information about our gun lockers, as a matter of security, but the main purpose is to find out what type of weapons the First Settlement has, and whether they match the one used to kill the murdered woman. While her death isn't my top priority, I'm a homicide detective; I'm not going to ignore a chance to solve it.

There'd been no way to ask Edwin this without his guessing why I was asking and tailor his response accordingly. While his granddaughter is obviously bright and shrewd, she's also young, and she doesn't sense a trap here. She's focused on her goal of getting a gun.

"I can't promise you a trade," I say, "but we might have an old —"

"We want that gun," the bearded youth says, pointing at Dalton's. These two boys have been silent until now. Dalton had called this one the leader, because he stepped out first, but it's obvious that the girl is in charge. She just wasn't foolish enough to expose herself so quickly. Having stepped out, she's done all the talking, and the boys let her, as if they're accustomed to this.

"We want a handgun, as you call it," he says. "I like his. It has bigger bullets."

The girl rolls her eyes. "Bigger only means it'll put bigger holes in our dinner. The barrels are too short, meant for shooting at close range. That's not what I want."

"I want —"

"And what are you going to trade for it?" she says. "This gun is for me."

"You do not need a gun. I will hunt for you, when you are my wife."

137

"Which is why I am never going to be your wife, Angus," she says, and Dalton snorts at that, earning a sour look from the bearded boy — Angus.

"If Felicity wants to hunt, she should," says the towheaded boy, who looks a year or so younger than the others. "She is good at it."

"Do you mean that?" Felicity retorts. "Or is it false flattery to win my approval?"

The towheaded boy stammers, searching for a response. Then he says, "You are a good hunter, and if you married me, I would let you help me hunt."

"How kind of you," Felicity says dryly. She turns to me. "The gun is for me. My grandfather says I may only have one if I barter for it myself."

"I can't promise anything, but let me see what we have, and the next time we come by, I'll speak to you."

While I'm not eager to supply the First Settlement with weapons, hers is a reasonable request. We shouldn't refuse them the means of survival for fear they'll turn those hunting tools on us. I also suspect Edwin's granddaughter would be a good ally to have among the younger generation.

The trio starts to leave. Then Felicity says something to them, and they stay where they are while she jogs back to us. When she decides we're out of earshot of the boys, she stops.

"I wanted to say thank you," she says. "For taking Harper away."

"We didn't take her," I say. "She left."

Felicity nods dismissively, as if this is the same thing. "She is Angus's little sister, so he will not appreciate me saying this, but even he would agree. She was . . . not right. Dangerous. We knew it. Angus saw it. She would do things that hurt him, and she would not care, as long as she got what she wanted. The elders never saw it. She was very, very careful."

"She was —" I'm about to say "a good actor," but Felicity won't understand that. "She was very good at being what others wanted to see."

"Yes. Sometimes, living like this, it does things to people. Makes them hard and cruel. I just wanted to say thank you." Her eyes cloud for a second as she glances at the boys. "She is gone, yes? Not coming back?"

"Almost certainly not."

Her lips set, as if that's not as clear an answer as she'd like, but she nods and says, "I hope not. For all our sakes." Then, without another word, she lopes back to the waiting boys.

THIRTEEN

When the young settlers are gone, I say to Dalton, "Were you okay with that? I didn't promise her a rifle."

"If I wasn't okay with it, I'd have said so. It's worth considering. Those boys might be vying for her hand, but they don't interrupt when she talks. That means Edwin is grooming her for leadership. She seems smart, levelheaded. Wanting to trade for her own hunting rifle is reasonable. I'd make it a hard bargain, but I wouldn't discount it."

He slows to adjust the baby, stirring from sleep. She fusses, but a few pats and rubs on her back quiet her.

Dalton resumes talking. "So, the gun that killed the woman didn't come from the First Settlement. That helps."

"It does.

"As for the baby's family, if they're as bad as Edwin and Felicity say . . ." I inhale. "I don't know what to do about that."

He takes a few more steps, and then says, his voice lower, "Yeah, you do. We both do. We wouldn't find a beaten dog in the forest and return it to abusive owners. It's a tough call, but we have to make the choice we can live with. The problem is judging . . ."

"How bad is too bad?" I say.

"Yeah."

He goes quiet after that, and I think he's going to stay that way until we reach the snowmobile. Then he straightens and says, "Main thing now is finding them. I know Edwin says they don't overwinter around here, but the baby hasn't been away from her mother for long. They must be within a day's walk."

I'm about to say that we'll have time to do that today before being stopped by the immovable obstacle of winter. Night. We can't make it before darkness falls.

Dalton has already figured this out and continues with, "We'll head back to Rockton for the night, and then tomorrow, we'll go find Jacob . . ." He trails off, cursing as he remembers his brother isn't around.

"Tyrone?" I say.

He grumbles but says, "Yeah, we'll find Ty. See what he knows about these traders."

The next morning, we take the baby to Jen's

place for the day. We expect to be coming back after talking to Cypher, so there's no reason to cart her along. Instead, we take Storm. We'd considered riding the horses, but snow fell overnight, and it's still falling the next morning. So we strap on snowshoes and head out.

Of all the "mobility tools" in Rockton, snowshoes are my least favorite. Dalton jokes that's because — as opposed to the horses, ATVs, and snowmobiles — snowshoes require actual physical effort. It's not just effort, though, it's *serious* effort, more than walking, which seems to defy the purpose of a mobility tool. Except that . . . well, if we're using snowshoes, it's because walking in boots *wouldn't* be faster or easier.

Our weekend trip had been along groomed paths. This walk will have a lot more backwoods hiking, and each step is like clomping down into knee-high mud. Snowshoes keep you on the surface, even if they're hellishly awkward to use. Or they are for me. Dalton's fine with them. He says I just need more practice. Since that means more trudging around in snowshoes, I'll stick to amateur status.

If I will grudgingly admit to one advantage to snowshoes, it's that they're excellent for hunting. They move nearly as silently as cross-country skis, and yes, I've suggested those to Dalton. He's hesitating because that's a mode of transport *he's* not accustomed to, and God forbid *he* should struggle. Admittedly, he's not sure how well they'll work in this environment. Maybe I'll ask for a cheap pair for Christmas to test them.

I might have been hired as a homicide detective, but my self-assigned secondary role is transportation chief, the chick who will ultimately bring to Rockton every possible — and possibly fun — way to traverse the wilderness. Dirt bike, dogsled, and soon, cross-country skis. Dalton doesn't appreciate my efforts nearly as much as he should, perhaps not surprising given that he's spent his career trying to convince residents that traveling outside of the town is *not* fun, not fun at all.

Since we have the snowshoes and we're heading into a game-rich area, we both carry rifles slung over our shoulders. We've also brought a makeshift harness and canvas "sled bag" for Storm to bring back any larger game.

For now, Storm is free to romp through the snow. We've shot four ptarmigan, but Dalton has those slung over his shoulder.

Down south, I'd known plenty of cops

who hunted, and some would invite me. I never accepted. I wasn't rabidly against hunting. As a nonvegetarian, I'd be hypocritical to judge anyone for killing their own meat. I just wasn't always convinced that my colleagues hunted *for* meat. Sure, they'd get some of their kill carved up, but most of that stayed at the bottom of their freezer, an excuse for the sport.

Up here, it's all about utility. Meat, fur, even the feathers to stuff pillows and jackets. Nothing is sport. Nothing is waste. That's the type of hunting I can endorse, though neither of us will pretend there isn't pleasure to be had in the thrill of a well-aimed shot.

We have a good three-hour hike ahead of us. Tyrone Cypher is wintering at a cabin he "inherited" when the former owner was killed by our resident cougar.

Cypher had been sheriff of Rockton before Gene Dalton arrived. The council decided Gene's temperament was more suited to the position, and they'd demoted Cypher to deputy. He'd stuck around for a while, but after one too many clashes with Gene, he'd stomped off into the forest, where he's still sulking. Okay, "sulking" might be a slight exaggeration. Cypher had already intended to retire into the forest when his term in Rockton was up. His temper and his pride just sent him there sooner than he planned.

Cypher is happy in the forest. His former job made him a natural for tracking and hunting game. That "former job" isn't as sheriff of Rockton. It's the career that brought him here. Tyrone Cypher was a hit man. The first time he told me that, I thought he was joking. Then I thought he was exaggerating — maybe he *once* killed a guy for money. Nope. He was a career hit man. I'd say assassin, but that conjures up an image that is 100 percent not Tyrone Cypher.

Cypher had been in Rockton when Dalton first arrived. He knows Dalton's history, which makes for an awkward relationship, especially when Cypher sees nothing wrong with needling Dalton about his "wild boy" past.

We're a couple of kilometers from the cabin when Dalton goes still. As he looks around, I lay a hand on Storm's head. When a growl ripples through her flanks, I slide my hand through her collar. She grumbles at that, offended that I don't trust her.

As Dalton scans the forest, Storm resumes that low growl. She's on high alert, her hackles up, body stiff, which means there's a predator nearby. I slide my gun out. Dalton already has his in hand. His head tilts, as if he's spotted something. He slides forward for a better view. Then he nods, backs up, and takes Storm's collar.

"Go look," he whispers, a hint of a smile on his lips. "Slow and careful. I'll direct you."

I nod at my gun.

"Keep it out," he murmurs.

It *is* a predator, then. A dangerous one. Just not the type he expects to barrel out of the forest and attack. Interesting.

I slide forward where he'd gone. It's clear, no chance of hitting branches and giving myself away. When I reach where he stopped, he motions for me to take it one more step. Then he has me crouch until my eyes are at waist level, and he directs my attention.

At first I see nothing but snow and trees. Then I catch movement. A ghostly figure, gray and white fur camouflaging with the winter forest. Brown eyes fix on me. A gray and white snout swings my way, black nose twitching as it inhales my scent. Ear pricked, swiveling when a noise comes from the side, the soft *whoosh* of snow falling from branches.

It's a wolf. A lone young male. He has his head lowered, watching me, wary but curious. If it were a pack, Dalton would scoot me out of here fast. One wolf, though, is very unlikely to attack a person, not unless the beast is sick or starving. This one is muscular and well fed. His fur ripples in the breeze, and he is one of the most beautiful things I've seen in a forest filled with beauty.

I hear wolves all the time, and I've caught glimpses of them. But this is my first actual sighting, and I stay half-crouched and watching until his own curiosity wanes and he lopes off, a silent ghost vanishing into the snowy forest.

When I return to Dalton, I'm grinning. He smiles, pleased. He's about to say something when Storm whines.

"We should take her to sniff where he was," I say. "Let her learn the scent."

"Good idea."

He keeps his hand firmly around her collar and starts into the forest, to where the wolf had been. Storm doesn't budge.

"Nervous because it's another canine?" I wonder.

"Maybe."

When he tugs her, she whines and her head whips around, gaze fixed behind us. She makes a sound that starts like a growl, but then she swallows it and whines instead.

Something moves in the thicker trees

behind us. I freeze. We'd presumed the wolf was alone, but that isn't necessarily so.

Dalton's eyes narrow. I resist the urge to watch him and turn my attention to Storm instead. Her gaze stays fixed on a single point. That's reassuring, suggesting she only smells one threat.

She's uncertain, too, about whether or not it *is* a threat. Her whine slips into a growl and then back to a whine. Her ears prick forward and then relax. Her snout wrinkles, but she doesn't bare her teeth.

I hunker to her height and look where she does. I see snow and trees. Then movement above my crouched head. Moose? Caribou? That would explain Storm's reaction. Ungulates might not be predators, but they're still dangerous. Storm surprised a doe last fall and took a good kick in the ribs as it fled.

Yet the shape has moved behind a tree, and if it were an ungulate, I'd see the hindquarters sticking out. It's at least as tall as me and can hide behind a thick tree trunk, which only describes one beast in this forest.

Human.

FOURTEEN

I glance at Dalton. He's seen what I have. He grunts, considering, his hand on his gun. Then he motions for me to hold the dog while he circles around. I aim my gun at the tree, but it's a one-handed aim, my other on the dog's collar. I flex my left hand, ready to release the collar and steady my weapon if I need to.

Dalton takes two wide steps, his snow-shoes coming down soundlessly. Another flicker of movement. My hand nearly releases Storm's collar. Then the figure steps out and says, "Eric."

I exhale. My gun lowers. Storm whines and dances, not excitement but nerves. She knows who this is, and she still isn't sure what to make of her, isn't convinced she *doesn't* pose a threat. But I know better. Dalton does, too, holstering his gun as he approaches her.

"Maryanne," he says.

I release Storm and move forward as the dog stays close enough to brush my leg. Maryanne is — or was — a hostile. I hesitate to say "was" because I'm honestly not sure of her status with them. I believe she left her group this spring. I cannot say for certain, because our relationship hasn't progressed far enough for me to ask.

Maryanne is a former resident of Rockton. That much I can say for certain. Dalton had been a teenager when she arrived. As a biologist and professor, Maryanne found peace and happiness in the wilderness, and when a group headed into the forest, she joined them.

Gene Dalton had pursued the quartet, and the militia found their camp destroyed, splattered with blood but no bodies. A year later, Dalton ran across Maryanne in the forest. When she'd been in Rockton, they'd been friends, Maryanne teaching him the science of the wilderness while he taught her the reality of it. So she very clearly knew Dalton, trusted him, liked him. And when he found her in the forest, she attacked him. He'd nearly had to kill her to escape.

Earlier this year, we'd encountered Maryanne again, still with the hostiles, but . . . I'm not sure of the analogy to use here. She was like someone buried under an avalanche

151

who had clawed her way up just enough to be heard.

That avalanche was the collapse of her own mind into madness. She'd cleared just enough of a hole in the mental confusion to hear Dalton, yet she was still at the bottom, out of his reach. The encounter, though, had been a tipping point for her. She heard a voice she recognized, and she could make out the sunlight above and start climbing toward it. And here is where the analogy fails, because in such a case, you'd eventually be able to offer the victim a hand to haul them out. Maryanne is not ready to take that hand, because what she's suffered isn't hypothermia and broken bones. Her damage goes deeper.

Some of that damage is physical — teeth filed, ritualized scarring, an ear and a couple of fingers blackened by frostbite. For a brilliant woman to start regaining her self-awareness and realize what she's done to herself? To know it isn't just a bad tattoo that can be covered up with long sleeves? And to know what those physical signs represent, proof of what she had become, the things she had done as a hostile? Maryanne is indeed still buried, under an avalanche of shame and self-loathing now, and we cannot seem to pull her out.

We've seen her a few times over the summer and fall. Her mind has cleared enough to communicate with us . . . when she chooses to. We've tried leaving supplies out for her, but that is too much like leaving food for a stray dog, and she shuns our offerings. What we want is to bring her back to Rockton. Part of that is, of course, selfish — she represents the key to understanding the hostiles. But even without that, we want to help her.

Letting Maryanne stay out here hurts no one but her. And yet, here she is, in the middle of December, with ragged boots and multiple shirts and no jacket, wearing a thin hood tied over her head. On her hands, she's tied more skins, wrapped around like extended sleeves, her fingers bare inside.

This is where my beliefs waver. Where they have always wavered. I struggled with that as a patrol officer seeing the homeless. Yes, if you choose to live on the streets, no one should be able to forcibly remove you. But at what point are you no longer making a sane choice? If I recognize signs of mental illness or drug addiction, how do I know whether you are still capable of making that choice? At what point would I be infringing on your rights if I shuttled you off to a shelter or a hospital? And at what point am

I failing as a public servant, as a human *being,* if I do not?

Maryanne is aware of her choices and her options. She stays out of shame and fear, and so, is that enough for me to say "it's her right"?

I see the same war on Dalton's face. As he approaches her, his cheek tics in a way I know well. He's holding in his frustration. What *she* sees, though, is anger in those blazing gray eyes.

She takes a step back. "Eric?"

"Hey, Maryanne," I say, giving him time to cover his reaction. "May I bring the dog over?"

She nods and smiles. It's a tight-lipped smile, as always, just as she barely opens her mouth when she speaks. Hiding her filed teeth.

I lead Storm to her, and she pushes her wrapped hands out to pet her, rubbing her back and sliding her fingers through the thick fur, warming them.

I take off my backpack. "I have extra mittens. Why don't you take —"

"No," Dalton says, so low it's more growl than word. He pulls the backpack from my hands and snaps the zipper shut. "Casey is not giving you her gloves."

Maryanne blinks. "I . . . I don't need . . ."

154

"Fuck yes, you do. How do you think you got frostbite the last time? Apparently, you kind of like it."

I have to bite back the urge to stop him. I know what he's doing, and I keep silent.

"You don't want help from us, remember?" he says. "So you're not getting Casey's extra mitts or sweater or whatever else she wants to give you. Not unless you're willing to accept real help."

She takes a slow step back.

"Yeah, that's great," Dalton says, tossing my backpack down. "Turn tail and run, like you do every time we say something you don't like. And next time we see you, it'll be your frozen corpse in the snow. Or maybe we won't find that until spring thaw. That'll be fun. Casey will blame me for not letting her give you stuff. She might even dump me for being such an insensitive ass. Imagine how we'll both feel, knowing we couldn't help you. But we can't keep doing this, Maryanne. A pair of mittens isn't going to get you through this winter. You need proper shelter. Like a cave."

Her brows rise at that, and I see a flash of the woman she was. "A cave?"

"It belonged to a friend of ours. He . . ." His voice catches before he pushes on. "He passed away this spring. I sealed it up, so all

155

his stuff is still in there. It's nice, for a cave."

"It really is," I say. "It has a couple of rooms, plenty of skins, a firepit, preserved meat and food, weapons. He was living better than most settlers."

"Yeah," Dalton says. "It's fully stocked, and it's secure. It's not exactly warm when the fire goes out, but it isn't freezing either. The temperature in a cave —"

"— is consistent year-round," she says, her voice scratchy, unaccustomed to more than a word or two at a time. "It's approximately the same as the average temperature in the region."

Dalton allows himself a smile. "You remember. Good girl."

He gets a look for that, definitely the Maryanne she used to be.

"I would like that, Eric." She speaks in that same rusty voice, faltering and hesitant.

"All right then. Let me give you directions —"

I lay my hand on his arm. "I'd like to take her to Rockton to see whether she can identify . . ."

"Shit. Yeah. Okay." We exchange a look that says, *Yes, I really do want to see if she can ID our victim, but I also want April to take a look at her, and this is a good way to go about it.* A solid reason for Maryanne to come to Rockton.

I turn to Maryanne. "We found a dead woman with a baby."

She inhales sharply. "A dead baby."

"No, the baby's fine. But the woman shows signs of having once been . . . what you were."

"A hostile. You can say the word, Casey. I knew it, and it is not wrong. That's what we — I . . ." She swallows. "It's accurate, and yes, I will look at this woman, though I'm not sure I'd be able to identify her."

"Whatever you can give will help. Will you come? Please?"

Maryanne nods.

Dalton reaches to take the dog from me. "You two go back to town. Storm and I can talk to Ty."

When I hesitate, he says, "I have Storm and two guns. I'll be fine."

"Maybe we can walk partway with —"

"We'd be heading off the path soon. I'd rather you went back while we're still on it."

He's right — that's safer, with a straight-away to Rockton. He gives me a one-armed hug and leans over as close as our snowshoes will allow. His lips press against my fore-head, and he murmurs, "I'll be fine."

He will be. Before I came, he spent most of his alone time in the forest. I nod, and he gives me another quick hug and then heads off.

"You're lucky," Maryanne murmurs as he leaves.

"Yep, I am," Dalton calls back, not turning.

I smile. Then I dig in my backpack for the extra mittens and an extra scarf, and hand them to her, and we head out.

FIFTEEN

I'm not much for initiating conversation.
I'm fine with joining it or even sustaining it,
but put me in a group and I keep quiet until
I have something to say. One on one, I'll
talk, but even then, I prefer an easy rhythm,
with room for comfortable pauses, like I get
with Dalton or Petra. I'm also fine with
someone who picks up the slack and keeps
me entertained, like Anders or Diana.

People have called me reserved, even
standoffish. They chalk it up to my Asian
ancestry — clearly, I'm playing to type.
That's bullshit. My mother had no problem
talking. It was my Scottish dad who'd been
content to listen and let her fill the silence.
I don't tell people that. If they want to cast
me into an "inscrutable Asian" stereotype,
then it keeps me from having to speak to
them.

It isn't long into the walk with Maryanne
before I'm really wishing I'd let Dalton walk

back with her. He knows Maryanne. All I can think of are the questions I want to ask, and as a scientist, she'll be the first to realize I'm treating her as a subject rather than a person.

So I offer her things, like an overexuberant puppy dropping gifts at a stranger's feet. Would you like to wear the snowshoes? No? Are you warm enough? I've got a hood, so I don't really need my hat. I'm wearing an extra sweater — would that help? Oh, I should have offered food and water. I have both. Okay, well, just let me know if you get hungry or thirsty or you need to stop for a rest . . .

It's a wonder I don't drive her off, screaming into the forest.

I do mention that I'd like our doctor to take a look at Maryanne. She tenses, and I can tell she'd like to flee, but she's a smart woman and she knows a checkup is in her best interests. When she agrees, I seize on a topic of conversation and tell her all about my sister — her name, her specialty — and that gets her interest, as a fellow scientist, but it's still awkward, as if we're both fumbling for common ground.

"Had you ever been up here before Rockton?" she asks finally. "To the Yukon, I mean?"

I shake my head, and I'm about to expand on that, but she takes over, this clearly being more than an idle question.

"I did," she says. "My parents were late-era hippies. I grew up on a tiny island in British Columbia where they taught at the one-room schoolhouse. We raised goats for milk, chickens for eggs. We grew all our own vegetables. Vacations for us meant camping someplace even more remote than our island."

Her speech isn't fluid. It stops and starts, and she struggles for words, and sometimes, her voice cracks from disuse.

"Like the Yukon," I prompt.

She nods. "We came up here a few times. For people who worshiped Mother Nature, this was our mecca. There were jamborees in the seventies, and we piled into VW vans and drove. I remember this one event where they'd hired Native Canadian locals. They showed us how to track animals, how to start fires with flints, led us through rituals that I'm sure were completely fake."

She pauses for breath, and I let the silence go on, not wanting to rush her.

After a moment, she continues, "One day, I overheard two of them. Some people at the jamboree had been talking about going into the bush permanently. Just drive north until their car ran out of gas, walk into the forest and live off the land. These locals laughed about that. Said they wouldn't survive a week. I was about eight at the time, and I told my mother, and she said the idea of running off into the forest was romantic escapism. Those campers wouldn't survive without access to modern amenities, not when the biggest complaint at the jamboree was how far people had to walk to the showers."

The path branches, and I wave her down the left side. After a few more steps, she resumes her story. "People in Rockton are like some of the ones at those jamborees. They're aghast at the portable toilets and lousy showers, but compared to backcountry camping, Rockton is a four-star wilderness resort. When I first heard rumors and whispers about Rockton, I thought it couldn't possibly be real. The chance that I could escape my situation by going to a place where I'd gladly *pay* to vacation? I also needed that escape. My husband . . ." She shakes her head. "It's an old story. I won't bore you with it."

"I wouldn't be bored."

A smile my way. "Another time. This is . . ." A deep breath. "I know you want to know what happened to me, and that's where I'm heading." Another smile. "Eventually. My point was that those Native guides said the jamboree people wouldn't survive a week in the woods, and my mother thought they meant because of the lack of amenities. What they really meant was basic survival. The four of us who left Rockton didn't wander into the forest with pie-eyed visions of Mother Nature providing what we needed. I was a biologist with backwoods experience. One of the men was an engineer turned eco-house builder, specializing in northern living. Another was a doctor who'd hiked the entire Appalachian Trail alone. The woman was a third-generation wilderness guide. We had the skills. We knew where to camp. How to camp. How to secure our food supply. But we had no idea . . ."

She takes a deep breath. "The hostiles came in the night. We didn't stand a chance. We'd heard the rumors, of course, of wild people in the forest. The others scoffed. Personally, I was fascinated by the tales — modern folklore in action, the creation of a monster to shape behavior. Fairy tales to keep us out of the forest. In not believing, we weren't prepared.

"It happened so fast. I know that's what people always say, but you don't really understand the phrase until something like that. One minute, you're sleeping, and the next . . . chaos. Shouting. Screaming. Shadows against the night. That's all they were. Shadows. They put out our fire before they attacked. I woke to Dan — the doctor — screaming like I'd never heard a person scream. They'd sliced open his stomach and . . ."

Her breathing picks up. She scoops snow with a shaking hand. Two mouthfuls. Then, in a calm monotone: "They killed the men. Then they trussed up the other woman — Lora — and me and dragged us off. After that? It's a blur. Mostly."

She starts to shiver, and I take off my jacket, though I know it isn't cold making her shake. I still put my parka around her, and she takes it, gripping it close.

"That's all I can manage for now," she whispers.

"It's enough," I say. "Thank you."

She nods.

"Would you like a story about Rockton?" I say. "I may have a few."

She manages a smile. "I'll take as many as you've got."

SIXTEEN

We're close to Rockton. I'm listening for signs of activity outside the town.

"We'll loop around —" I begin, and the bushes explode, a gray canine leaping through.

It looks like a wolf, and my hand drops to my gun. Then Raoul jumps on me with a gleeful yelp . . . and Maryanne attacks. It happens in a blink. I'm relaxing, recognizing our freckle-faced wolf-dog as he plants his forepaws on my stomach, but Maryanne sees only a wolf leaping onto me. In a blink, she has her knife out and she's attacking with an inhuman howl.

I grab Raoul and roll, shielding him. The knife slashes through my doubled-up sweaters and slices my arm. I let out a hiss of pain as Raoul whimpers under me.

"He's ours," I say quickly. "He's okay."

Silence. Gripping Raoul by the collar, I turn over to see Maryanne staring at my

165

arm. Blood drips into the snow. She looks down at the bloody knife in her hand. Then she wheels, and I know she's going to bolt. I let go of Raoul and grab her by the pant leg. The seam rips as she lunges, but I hold tight.

"Please," I say. "I'm all right. It was a mistake. I'm —"

Bushes crash. Raoul ducks and sidles up against me, still lying in the snow. He whines as Jen bursts through.

"You damned mutt," she snarls. "What the hell —"

She sees Maryanne, who is poised there, mouth open.

Jen blinks. "Fuck."

Maryanne's eyes go wide, realizing what she must look like. She lunges away again, and I'm dragged a few feet before I manage to stop, still holding her tight.

"Jen, go," I say. "Please. Maryanne, I'm sorry. It's okay. Everything's okay."

She's pulling, and I have her pant leg in both hands now, pain ripping down my injured arm. Jen's saying something, but I can't make it out. Raoul thinks it's a game and growls, dancing around us. Maryanne gives one big heave, and I'm certain that's it. She's gone, and goddamn it, why the hell is Raoul —

Maryanne stops. "Eric?" she whispers.

I follow her gaze to see a figure loping toward us. It's not Dalton, though. It's Sebastian. He skids to a stop, seeing us.

"Shit, I'm sorry. I was walking him off leash and . . ." He sees Maryanne — gets a good look at her. There's exactly two seconds of silence, and I swear I see his brain whir, lightning fast. Then he smiles and extends a hand. "Sebastian."

She blinks, and when she speaks, it's a near mumble as she tries to keep her teeth covered. "You looked a little like Eric, as a boy."

Sebastian's smile grows. "You knew Sheriff Dalton when he was younger? Cool." His voice is calm, completely unperturbed by this wild-haired woman clad in makeshift clothing.

"I'm sorry," Jen says. "Didn't mean to startle you. This damned mutt and this damned kid . . ." She glowers at Sebastian.

"Thanks for helping me get him," Sebastian says.

Jen rewards his politeness with a raised middle finger. He ignores it and takes Raoul by the collar, scolding him in French.

Sebastian looks at Maryanne. "He's mostly wolf, but he's tame. He's pretty well trained until he wants to run, and then he somehow forgets his own name."

She smiles at that, forgetting her teeth until her hand flies up to cover them, but Sebastian pretends not to notice. He has a way with people. Of course, that has something to do with being a sociopath. He's not the stereotypically suave charmer that Hollywood loves, but there's a disarming charisma to him that's hard to ignore when he switches it on.

"Sebastian?" I say. "On your way through town, could you please find my sister and ask her to meet me at my old house? Tell her to bring a first-aid kit."

"What do you need me to do?" Jen asks.

I hesitate. I want to tell her to just back off and stay out of our way after nearly sending Maryanne fleeing into the forest. But she's been quiet since then and looks almost abashed.

"Bring food and drink and clothing," I say. "Whatever you spend, we'll reimburse. Just do it as discreetly as possible." I pause, realizing who I'm speaking to. Shit. "This is very important. Don't tell anyone —"

I stop suddenly. "Wait. If you're here, where's the baby?"

"In a snowbank over there. Don't worry, she's got plenty to eat. I tied some bacon around her neck. That's okay, right?"

168

"Jen? Where's —"

"With Will at the station. We were out for a stroll when this kid lost his wolf puppy. I gave the baby to Will and came to help round up the damned mutt."

"Which was very kind of her," Sebastian says. "And has nothing to do with the fact that the reason Raoul took off is because she yelled at him for running to see the baby."

"Fuck you, brat. Keep your damn wolf on a leash or the next time I see it . . ." She catches my eye and grumbles, "Keep him on a leash."

Jen stalks off.

"She's really very nice when you get to know her," Sebastian says, and then shakes his head and mouths to Maryanne, *No, she's not.*

"I heard that!" Jen calls back.

"I didn't say a word."

"Believe me, I still heard it."

Sebastian gives Raoul a pat and says goodbye to Maryanne and they take off, zooming past Jen on their way.

"He seems like a sweet boy," Maryanne says.

I make a noncommittal noise and lead her toward town.

169

■ ■ ■ ■

As eager as I am to get Maryanne to the clinic to attempt identification of the dead woman, I know I need to take this slower. Let April examine her first at my house. I want her checked out and I want the rest of her story — whatever can help me understand hostiles, for this case and beyond. Once Maryanne sees the dead woman, though, her obligation is fulfilled and she can flee into the forest. So that will need to wait until post-examination. It's not as if I can leave town chasing new clues anyway, not while Dalton is gone.

The back door to my old house is locked. Increased tensions with both the hostiles and settlers have made it seem unwise to leave buildings with open access to the woods. For my old place, though, there's a key under the back deck, since it is technically still my lodgings, and sometimes, if work's slow, Dalton and I have been known to go on patrol and sneak in the back for an "afternoon nap."

Maryanne has said nothing since Jen and Sebastian left, and I've spent the walk stifling the urge to hold her arm to make sure she doesn't bolt. My own arm is fine.

The blade sliced the skin, nothing more. A bandage will fix it up.

I open my door and usher Maryanne through. She steps in and stops. I'm behind her, and she's blocking the entrance, but I pause, waiting. When she doesn't move, I slide past her, and I realize she's crying. She's standing just inside the door, silent tears rolling down her face.

I take off her parka. She doesn't even seem to notice. I bend and unfasten her boots, which really are little more than hides roped around her ankles. I untie the bindings and then head into the living room, saying, "I'll start the fire."

I keep an ear on the kitchen. If the door squeaks, I'll be there in a flash. Instead, tentative footsteps slide across the kitchen. I hurry to get the fire going. It's laid, needing only a match to light — at this time of year, an "afternoon nap" is a whole lot less enticing if it means setting a fire first.

I get it started in seconds; then I feed in more kindling and put the kettle on. When I turn, Maryanne stands in the middle of the room. She looks at the roaring fire, the kettle, the sofa piled with pillows, the bearskin rug, inviting in a way only a fireplace-rug-in-winter truly can be. She stares. Blinks. Then her knees give way. I

171

lunge, but I'm too slow, and she falls onto the rug. Tears stream down her face, silent at first, and then ripping out in racking sobs as she crumples, arms wrapped around her chest.

I should go to her. Hug her. Comfort her. Instead, I manage a few back pats and "It's okay" and "You're safe now," which are as awkward for her as they are for me. So I leave her to cry, and I dart around, getting things to make her comfortable. Put pillows on the floor. Grab more from behind the sofa and blankets from under it — in a place this small, you use every cranny for storage. I build a nest around her, as if she's a toddler who might fall.

Then I go into the kitchen. There's not much there. Instant coffee and tea in the cupboard. Powdered creamer and sugar. A bottle of tequila hidden under the cupboard. I bring it all. Then I check the kettle. It's barely simmering.

I don't ask Maryanne whether she wants tea, coffee, or tequila. She's crying softer now, collapsed on the rug, hugging a pillow. I drape a blanket over her. Then I pour tequila into one mug, put a tea bag in another and coffee in the third. The kettle gives one chirp, and I have it off the hanger. I fill the two mugs. Then I set them on a tray in front of her.

"Food's coming," I say. "But I have tea, coffee, and tequila."

"Tequila?"

She lifts her face from the rug. I hold the mug out.

She shakes her head, shivering. "It'll be a long time before I'll even want painkillers."

I push forward the other mugs. She accepts the coffee and rejects creamer or sugar. She sits up, blanket still over her shoulders as she wraps her hands around the mug. She leans over it, bathing in the steam.

I put the kettle back over the fire, in case she wants more. Then I look around.

"I should have a sweatshirt upstairs," I say. "And socks maybe? I'll run —"

A hard rap at the door. I open it to find Jen with a duffel bag, which she shoves at me.

"Clothing," she says. "It's mine, but it should fit. There are snacks in there, too. I'll drop off a hot meal when I bring the baby."

"Baby? I really can't —"

"If you need me to take her a while longer, I will, but she's fussy and cranky, and she wants her mommy."

"Yes," I say evenly. "Unfortunately, we

have no idea where to find her."

She snorts. "Whatever."

"She doesn't want *me,* Jen."

"Well, yeah, she'd probably rather have Daddy. Typical female, already making eyes at the big, bad sheriff. But since he's not here, you'll do."

When I start to protest, she says, "I'm not trying to get rid of her, Casey. Just take her, rock her a bit while April looks after . . . the patient, and she'll fall asleep, and you can call me to take her back. She's unsettled, and she needs sleep, and she's not getting it until she sees temporary Mom or Dad."

I pause and heft the duffel, turning toward the living room.

"And I'm sorry about spooking . . . the patient," Jen says. "She just surprised me, that's all."

When I glance over, she says, "Yeah, I'm apologizing. To her, mostly. It's like when I kicked your damn dog, I didn't think. I just reacted. I'd never have done it otherwise."

I nod. "Go ahead, and bring the baby."

SEVENTEEN

I'm getting Maryanne into the clothing when my sister arrives. April walks in, sees what we're doing, and says, "You can stop that, or we'll just be taking it all off again."

April glances at Maryanne and nods. It looks like a curt nod, but it's simple efficiency, as she strides past us to set down her bag. Maryanne could be any patient in the clinic, just another job in April's day, no greeting required.

We've fielded complaints about my sister's lack of bedside manner. I direct the residents to Dalton, who reminds them that we spent the last fucking year without a fucking doctor, and now we have a fucking multi-degree neurosurgeon, and they're complaining because she doesn't ask how they're fucking doing — which, considering she's a fucking doctor, she's going to find out anyway, isn't she? That's verbatim, although he may find an opportunity for another profanity that I've missed.

I think we should work on this with April. Dalton says no. Not a "Fuck, no" or even "Hell, no," which means he isn't adamantly opposed to a little gentle guidance, but since it's not a lack of compassion, residents should adjust their expectations instead. As Dalton says, "They want a fucking hug? Talk to Isabel's girls." He has a point. He also said, "Would they complain so much if April was a man?" Ouch.

He's right. I'm not sure I would have advocated for a softer touch if she were a man, and that stings. Especially when, as a cop, I'd been accused of not being "warm" enough, while no one ever said that to my male colleagues. It burns to realize I fell into the same trap, but it's a reminder I need sometimes. Just because I advocate for gender equality doesn't immunize me against promoting stereotypes. Even Dalton, who has never treated me differently than he would a male colleague, had an all-male militia until I arrived, and he'd never considered how that might discourage women from joining.

With Maryanne, though, I am glad of my sister's cool professionalism. As April conducts a preliminary examination, Maryanne visibly relaxes. This is familiar. It's what she

176

would have expected for a routine physical. Check heart, check eyes, check throat, check teeth . . .

April checks the last as perfunctorily as the rest, without even a moment's pause at the filed teeth. But then, after the quick assessment, she says, "Dental work will be required," and Maryanne cringes, just a little.

"There's a cavity at the back," April says. "Possibly two. We have medication to help with those if they cause pain eating. The front teeth will require caps."

"Caps . . ."

"Unless you planned to grow new ones, which I would not advise."

Maryanne snorts a laugh at this, and I relax. My sister has been attempting humor lately. That's one of the biggest hurdles with her condition — she struggles to understand jokes, and her silence marks her as humorless. She's working on that. The problem, of course, is that with her absolute deadpan delivery, people usually aren't sure she *is* kidding.

"I hadn't considered caps," Maryanne says. "That would work, I think."

"It would. I have one on my left upper lateral incisor. Casey chipped off the corner. She threw a baseball for me to catch, and her aim was atrocious."

"What?" I say. "When was this?"

"When you were three. You must remember, Casey."

"Not if I was three, I don't."

"That may explain why you never apologized."

"I'm sure I did at the time."

"No." She pauses. "You did cry. Quite a bit. I suppose that's an apology." Her tone says she's granting me the benefit of the doubt here. A lot of benefit for a lot of doubt.

"Well, I am sorry," I say. "Very sorry."

"I suppose an apology twenty-nine years late is better than none at all."

Maryanne laughs, though this, I know, is not a joke.

"April's right," I say. "Caps will fix your teeth."

"They will cover the damage," April says. "They will not 'fix' them. Nothing can be done about that. They've been filed. Intentionally. Whoever did that to her needs to be arrested, Casey. It's assault, at the very least."

"I did it to myself," Maryanne says, her voice very quiet.

April frowns. "For what purpose?"

"April . . ." I say.

178

"No, it's all right," Maryanne says. "I know you need to hear my story, Casey. Whether it's to help with this baby or the poor dead woman or the hostiles in general, you need it. I'm just not sure it will make much sense. It's like . . . a fever dream. I'd never done drugs. Well, nothing stronger than marijuana, but we didn't consider that any more a drug than alcohol. I certainly never experienced hallucinations with it."

"You wouldn't," April says. "Marijuana is not a hallucinogenic drug."

Maryanne meets my gaze and the corners of her lips quirk, as if she's figuring out my sister. She just says, calmly, "No, I suppose it isn't. But I had friends who experimented with hallucinogens. Sometimes, what they experienced wasn't so much a hallucination as a waking dream. It was real. Very real. That's what it was like for me. It was real, and I had no sense that it wasn't normal, that this wasn't who I was."

She stops. Squeezes her eyes shut and shakes her head. "No, that's not . . . That's not quite right. In the beginning . . ."

She looks at April. "I'm sorry, Doctor. You were conducting an examination. I'll wait for this."

April looks at me. I'd like Maryanne to continue — I'm afraid if she stops, she won't ever restart.

I'm still hesitating when Jen opens the door, baby in one arm, dinner in a bag over her shoulder. I tell April to continue her examination, and I take the baby, who is indeed fussing, sucking on her lower lip, as if she's a few seconds from crying.

"Is this the baby?" Maryanne says, rising. A smile spreads, a real one, her entire face lighting up as she forgets to cover her teeth. "The one who was with a former hostile?"

I nod. "The woman wasn't her mother, though."

"No, she wouldn't be. There . . ." She swallows. "There are no babies. They do not —"

She rubs her hands over her face, the move agitated, as if she's trying to scrub a memory from her mind. She stops, forcing her hands down. When she speaks, her voice is lecture-impassive. "If we become pregnant, they make sure we do not stay that way."

She catches our expressions and shakes her head. "No, not me. I had a hysterectomy a few years before I came to Rockton. I was spared . . . that."

April and I exchange a glance. Then April says, "I would like to conduct a full physical examination. Given the circumstances you were living under, there could be damage that your hysterectomy would not have prevented."

Maryanne looks at her a moment before realizing what she means. She gives a short laugh. "No, oddly, that is another thing I was spared. Children are forbidden, but so is rape. Sex must be consensual." She pauses. "Or as consensual as it can be under the circumstances." Another pause, and a wan quarter-smile. "From an academic perspective, let's just say it was as consensual as it has historically been for women. We knew the advantage of taking a mate, and we did so, and while I did not meet the love of my life, my relationships were, in some ways, healthier than the one I came here to escape. You may certainly conduct a full exam, Doctor, but rape trauma is the one thing I don't suffer from."

The baby sleeps, and Maryanne relaxes into the examination. I know from experience that bouncing back from the physical ailments is usually the easy part. The human body is a marvel of resiliency. The mind is an entirely different matter. On the surface, it has that same resiliency, yet even after we seem to be back on our mental feet, functioning and happy, the damage lingers, tucked down in the creases, impossible to scour clean.

The body repairs itself, leaving only scars where the skin can't quite smooth away the damage. The mind does the same — it reforms, it adapts, it builds bridges over the damaged parts. I can hide my physical scars with long sleeves and jeans, but I don't. They're part of who I am. Part of my history, and no cause for shame. I wish I could be as open with the mental scars. I probably never will be.

The physical damages make me look like a survivor. The psychological damage makes me feel like a victim. I know that's wrong; I just can't seem to get past the divide.

Maryanne's scars will not be badges of honor. They do show that she survived trauma that would kill most people. Yet she won't ever feel that way. When she's ready to return to civilization — be that Rockton or Halifax — she'll want help covering those signs.

In her examination, April suggests ways to conceal the rest of the physical damage. It's reassuring for Maryanne, hearing her trauma discussed in the same way a cosmetic surgeon might suggest fixing a crooked nose. April doesn't mean it to be soothing — she's ticking off the boxes that will return her patient to optimal health. Yet Maryanne *is* soothed, and that's what counts. Caps will cover her filed teeth. Plastic surgery will remove blackened tissue and make the frostbite damage less obvious.

Maryanne eats after her physical. As she does, while April makes notes, I say, "May I ask you questions?"

She smiles. "May I hold the baby afterward?"

"Certainly. I have a thousand questions, as you might imagine. But I want to begin with ones that April may be able to help me with."

My sister looks up. She says nothing, though, just resumes her note-making.

"You say that your party was attacked in the night," I begin. "The party who left Rockton with you."

"Yes."

"Were they the same people who took you away? Held you captive?"

She nods. "Yes."

"Is there any chance they weren't? I know you said it was chaotic. Is it possible you were attacked by one group and then given to another?"

I get identical looks of confusion from Maryanne and April.

Maryanne says slowly, "I'm not sure I

understand . . ."

"Is there any chance that the people who attacked your camp were not the group you later joined? Or if there were any members you never saw again?"

"It really was a blur of faces, both at the attack and later." She pauses. "Maybe if I had a better idea what you were looking for . . ."

I hesitate. As a cop, I would never share a theory with a witness. Not unless I'm trying to lead them into confessing themselves. Otherwise, it really is "leading." Tainting their testimony. So I have to stop here and analyze. What are the chances that, if I give Maryanne a theory, she'll intentionally or subconsciously shape her testimony to support or refute it, depending on her gut reaction?

She is a scientist. Whatever damage she's suffered, she's made incredible strides toward recovery. Her intelligence and self-awareness have fully returned, and I think I need to trust that.

"I'm not a psychiatrist," I say. "Or a psychologist or an anthropologist or anyone else who might know more about human evolution and behavioral changes. But I struggle with the idea that people who leave Rockton — modern humans — can revert to something that . . . primitive in a few years."

I adjust the baby to my other arm. "The theory in Rockton has always been, simply, that these people left, and because they left, they 'reverted' to a more 'primitive' form. That they were inherently more violent than the settlers, and they embraced that part of themselves when they left. I don't think that's how it works with people. I think there must be some . . . outside influence that at least escalates the process."

"You're completely right," Maryanne says. "What happens out there isn't a natural process of devolution. It's the tea."

EIGHTEEN

"The . . . tea?" That's all I can manage, and when April asks, "Who provides the tea?" I am grateful. Then I'm immediately shamed by that gratitude, because I'm only glad that *I'm* not the one asking what might be a stupid question.

"No one, right?" I say to Maryanne. "They make it themselves."

She nods. "From a root and plants. I don't know the exact ingredients. The shaman is the only one who can make them."

"Shaman?"

"That's what I'd call her now. They don't have a name for any roles. The shaman conducts rituals and makes the teas."

"Teas?" April says. "More than one?"

Maryanne hesitates. "Maybe? I always thought of it as the same tea, but in two concentrations. One is for everyday drinking and the other is for rituals. They both . . ." Maryanne rubs her face again, this time paired with a convulsive shiver. When she speaks, her voice is lower, professorial detachment evaporating. "They make everything okay."

Neither of us speaks. After a moment, Maryanne says, "May I go back?"

When I tense, she manages a wan smile. "I don't mean go back into the forest. I mean may I go back to my story. That will make this easier, and possibly more comprehensible, if such a thing is possible."

"Of course," I say. "Whatever works for you." I glance at my sister. "You don't need to be here for this."

She starts, as if from sleep. Blinks. Pauses. Then straightens, saying, "If we are discussing the effects of a potential drug, then I do believe I need to stay."

She doesn't actually need to stay, and I realize I have, inadvertently, achieved exactly the thing I'd tried to so many years ago. I have brought April something that catches her interest. Still, I have to ask Maryanne if she's okay with April staying. She is.

Maryanne continues. "I told Casey that the hostiles attacked at night. They killed the men and took the women. Two of us. We were initially separated. A classic technique: Separate, isolate, and disorientate. I woke in a cavern — too small to sit up in. I had a guard. He wouldn't speak to me. Wouldn't even look at me. They'd only bring water. I was in that cave for days, maybe a week. By the time they hauled me out, I was starving and feverish and half mad with fear and confusion. They gave me food and the tea. As soon as I drank the tea, I knew it was drugged. Everything became . . . unreal."

She shifts her position. "That's the best way to describe it. It took away the fear and the dread. When they put me back into the cave, I slept soundly. The next day, they brought me out and offered me food and more tea. I only wanted the food. That wasn't an option. Both or nothing. I refused the tea for three days, until I realized my choices were that or starvation. I drank, and they let me stay outside the cave with the group. It felt like I was in a trance. Doing as I was told earned me food and sleeping blankets and a spot by the fire. The chores were like being at camp. Gather wood. Cook. Clean. Sew. A few of the men paid me extra attention, but they didn't bother me. They were trying to get *my* attention."

"As a potential mate."

"Yes. During my more lucid periods, I'd remember to be afraid. To want to escape. The best plan, however, seemed to be to do exactly what they wanted. Just keep drinking the tea and being a good girl, and I'd get my chance. Then they brought Lora."

"The other woman who'd been taken with you."

She nods. "Lora wouldn't drink the tea. They brought her to show her how well I was doing, how much better shape I was in. I tried to persuade her to drink and bide her time, but to her, I was weak, surrendering when I should be fighting. She was a twenty-five-year-old wilderness guide, tough as nails. I was a middle-aged academic. We . . . we'd never really gotten along. She fought them every waking second and eventually, they fought back. They beat her. They gave her only enough water to survive. Then they took away her clothing. After a week, she escaped."

I raise my brows, and Maryanne nods. "Yes, they *let* her escape. I realized that later. One of the men tracked her. A week later . . ." She swallows and rubs her face. "They took me to see her. To see . . . what was left."

I tell her she doesn't need to continue, but she says, "No, this is part of the story." Another few minutes of silence before she says, "She'd collapsed. Exhaustion. Hypothermia. Starvation. She couldn't go on.

The tracker had tied her to a tree. Then he put tea beside her. Drink the tea, and he'd give her food and clothing. She didn't, and so he left her there, and I . . .."

Maryanne swallows. "I hope she just fell asleep. Died quietly. If not . . .." Another swallow, harder. "Something got her. An animal. Either it scavenged her dead body or it killed her. That's what they brought me to see, and that was a message. Drink your tea and behave, and do not even think of running, or this will happen to you."

"So you stayed?"

"I still planned to escape. I'd give it a month, even two, until they trusted me. I'd be fed and strong, and I'd have clothing and weapons, and I wouldn't end up like Lora when I ran. Then they gave me the other tea. There was no peaceful trance with that."

She looks at me. "I've never been an angry person. No matter what my husband did, I stayed calm and looked for solutions. I *had* anger, though, and that tea brought it out. It induced hallucinations and violent frenzies and . . .."

Her face reddens. "It induced *all* the impulses. It unleashed the id, and it was addictive. Not so much the drug itself as the experience. Cathartic. In my already confused state, it felt as if I'd discovered

190

something I'd been looking for all my life. Like our family friends dreaming of walking into the wilderness and reuniting with Mother Nature. I embraced it, and I'm ashamed of that now, but when it happened . . ."

She looks at me. "Most of the time, we drank the first tea, the same as you'd have your morning Earl Grey. Then there were the rituals with the other one, so you went from a sense of tranquil unreality to those wild, primal frenzies. There wasn't anything else. After a while, it became harder to focus, harder to think straight. All that mattered was surviving. Hunting, finding shelter, protecting territory, satisfying needs and urges."

She shifts position again. "When I met you and Eric in the forest that first time, I was in what you might call a down phase. We all were. In a frenzy, we'd have attacked and taken what we wanted, but in the down phase, they could think it through enough only to threaten you."

"They'd still have killed us, though," I say. "That's why they asked Eric to remove his clothing. So they wouldn't ruin it when they killed him."

She nods. "Yes. They'd have killed him and any other men in your party. They'd

191

have taken you. Young, strong men seem like an asset, but they're also competition for goods and women. A young, strong woman is the truly valuable asset."

She inhales. "I didn't recognize Eric. That's no excuse. I was still watching them do exactly what they'd done to my own party from Rockton, and I wasn't lifting a finger to stop it."

"You couldn't."

"Yes, but I wouldn't have either. In that phase, I would regret what happened, but it would never occur to me to stop it. When I did recognize Eric, though, it was like a light in the darkness. That one tiny pinprick that cut through the fog. Once I started remembering, I couldn't stop. It helped that I didn't go back to the tribe. That wasn't really a choice. Our entire hunting party had been wiped out, including our leader. I'd lost my mate a few months before, and that left me vulnerable. I had enemies, including the shaman, who was the dead leader's mate. Not returning turned out to be my salvation. My mind didn't clear overnight. Even now, sometimes I wake up, and I can't remember how I got where I am. I'm alive, though, so I'm clearly not wandering around in a daze. I think it's more like blackouts, lost memory."

"Effects of long-term drug use," April says. "My doctoral advisor had a subspecialty in hallucinogens. What you are likely looking at is something that produces effects similar to PCP. Long-term use leads to long-term effects, as with most drugs. Blackouts or loss of memory would be one of them."

"Will that stop?" Maryanne asks.

"While I believe that 'long term' implies it isn't permanent, I can't say that without further research."

"Which we will do," I add quickly. "If it isn't likely to clear up on its own, there must be treatments."

April gives me a look. Brain damage isn't something that heals like torn tissue, and she doesn't want me sounding so certain, but thankfully, she doesn't say anything. Maryanne isn't a child needing sunshine and roses, but she is fragile, and if I lean one way, it'll be toward convincing her that a normal life is possible.

It helps that I believe it. I've seen people come back from situations that I'm not sure I could have psychologically survived. Determination and optimism might not solve every issue, but it gets you a good chunk of the way there.

For all my sister's challenges, she under-

193

stands this. She would never tell Kenny that he won't walk again, and nor will she tell Maryanne her mind might never fully heal. Her glare just warns me to watch my step, because I'm such a sunshine-and-roses person myself that I might blithely lead poor Maryanne down the happy path of delusive hope. Yeah, my sister really needs to get to know me better.

With that we reach the end of what Maryanne can tell me for now. I have more questions — so many more — but she's tiring, and that trip down memory lane wasn't a joyful one. As eager as I am to take her to try identifying the dead woman, she needs a rest first and, again, I'm otherwise stalled until Dalton returns, hopefully with information on where to find the baby's parents.

NINETEEN

As Maryanne naps, so does the baby, while I make notes on Maryanne's story. As I watch the baby soundly sleeping, I marvel at my maternal skill. All those stories about babies crying constantly and moms never getting a moment to themselves, and here I am, with time to write down all my notes and then make coffee and even leaf through a novel I'd accidentally left under my old sofa. Clearly Edwin is right, and I'm a natural mother.

Yeah . . . I'm not that delusional. The baby deserves all the credit for this. I'm guessing that, at this age, they sleep a lot of the time, like Storm and Raoul did as puppies. Also, having lived in the wilderness, born in winter, the baby wouldn't be accustomed to a cushy life where Mom and Dad can jump to fulfill her every need. She's curled up with Maryanne on the sofa, snuggled deep into a soft source of body heat, and she's happy.

The baby does eventually fuss, and I take her from Maryanne, who is so deeply asleep that if the house caught fire, I'd need to haul her out. Alone in the wilderness she's probably done little more than nap for months now, staying just warm enough to doze without drifting into the endless slumber of hypothermia.

When Maryanne does wake, I summon Jen to take the baby while I finally escort Maryanne to the clinic, where I hope she can identify the dead woman.

We're at the clinic, having come in the back way. April has made sure it's empty, and I ask her to stay in the front room, in case anyone arrives. Maryanne and I walk in to find the dead woman on the examining table. Maryanne takes one look and stops midstep. I resist the urge to jump in with questions. I can see mental wheels turning, and I don't want to do anything to put on the brakes.

Maryanne walks to the table. She looks down and whispers, "I'm Ellen." She looks over at me. "That's what she said. *I'm Ellen.* I met her . . ."

Maryanne looks around, and I push over

a chair. She eyes it, this simple object that would once have been so familiar. Then she gingerly lowers herself onto it.

I pull another chair from the next room and sit in front of her.

" 'Met' isn't quite the right word," Maryanne says. "I encountered her. It was . . ." She shakes her head. "Time is difficult to judge. I remember it was warm that day. It might have been last summer. It could even have been the one before. I'm sorry I can't be more specific."

"That's fine."

"We were gathering berries. If you need the exact time of year, that could help. They were crowberries. I was with the shaman and the two other women from our group. She" — Maryanne gestures toward the dead woman — "came out of the woods. Carefully. I remember that. She made enough noise so we'd hear her, and she had her hands raised so we could see she wasn't armed. She did everything right."

"And?"

"The shaman tried to kill her. It was like the men with Eric. He'd be an asset as a worker, as a fighter, but all they see is competition. Our power, as with most patriarchal tribes, came from our mates."

"Fewer women means more opportunity

to snag a powerful man."

"Yes, and I would strongly suspect that freeing Lora was the shaman's idea. Lora was young and strong and pretty. If she'd survived, she could have taken the best mate, become the most powerful woman, possibly even become shaman. This woman" — she nods at the body — "wasn't young, but she'd still be competition. The shaman ran her off and tried to get us to hunt and kill her, as a supposed threat to the group. We were in a down phase, though, so myself and the other women pretended to give chase but didn't put much effort into it. She got away easily."

"Do you know what she wanted?"

"That's what I'm struggling to remember. She spoke to us, but while I would have understood her at the time, the memory faded quickly. What I remember isn't the conversation but the gist of it. She wanted to help us. I was confused at first, because she said something about help, and I thought *she* needed help, but that wasn't it. She wanted to help us."

"But before that, you didn't know her. She wasn't from your tribe."

Maryanne shakes her head. "She was a settler, not a hostile."

"Could you take a look at this?"

198

I rise and fold back the sheet to show the woman's — Ellen's — upper-chest scarring. Before I can say anything, Maryanne sucks in breath.

"Oh!" she says. "That's . . . Yes, that's the other group." She looks at me. "There are two tribes in this area. I don't know if there are more farther afield, but we only had contact with this other one, and as little of that as possible. It was like two wolf packs, equally matched in size, with enough territory that they didn't need to cross paths. My feeling is that the two groups had been linked at some point."

"One initial group that split," I say. "Like Rockton and the settlements."

"Yes, but that's just my presumption. It wasn't as if we sat around talking about our tribal history. I don't know if it was the drugs themselves or the result of living that way, but everything was very focused on the now. Any discussions we had were the simple exchange of information needed in the moment. *The fire is too small. We need more kindling. Hey, that's my meat.* Even things like hunts or gathering expeditions were very in the moment. *We're running low on meat, so we need to hunt. It's blueberry season, so we should pick blueberries.* When someone died, we buried him and divided

199

up his things, and rarely referred to him again."

She takes a deep breath. "And that's the very long way of saying that there were two tribes, but we didn't interact, and if there was any connection between the two, no one ever mentioned it to me."

Maryanne runs her fingertips over the woman's raised scars. "This is definitely their work. When I met her, though, I had no sense she was a hostile. If anyone had suspected she came from the other tribe, that would have been far more worrisome, being so deep into our territory."

"My guess is that she'd been a hostile and left them. She has facial markings, too, which she covered with dirt. The chest ones seem unfinished, but they aren't fresh."

"Left her tribe to become a settler. That would also explain why she'd reached out to us as a party of women. Like an ex-cult member trying to help those still drinking the Kool-Aid." A wry twist of a smile. "Or, in our case, the tea."

She steps back for a broader view of the woman. "If she did leave her tribe and stumbled onto them again, that might have explained how she died. They would have killed her. I see you've shaved part of her head. I'm guessing that was what did it? A blow to the skull?"

"Is that a common attack method for hostiles?"

A humorless chuckle. "Their murder modus operandi is 'whatever gets the job done.' They have knives, but they'd grab a rock if that was closest at hand."

"She did suffer blunt-force trauma," I say. "But cause of death was a shotgun pellet."

"Well, then that's not the hostiles. Some use bows and arrows, but no one would ever get access to a gun, much less ammunition."

So I have a name for the woman. The fact that she'd tried to help Maryanne and the others gave me some small insight into her. While she could have stolen this baby for herself, I'm leaning harder now toward other possibilities.

If the baby's mother belonged to the trading family that Edwin dislikes, then perhaps Ellen thought she was saving the child. With Maryanne and the others, rescue would have been warranted. With the child, though . . .

We were back to the problem Dalton and I discussed yesterday. At what point do you declare parents unfit? The baby is healthy, showing absolutely no signs of neglect or abuse. Yet, according to Edwin, the family prostitutes its daughters. If he's right about that, then looking after a baby girl is little different than treating your sled dogs well.

What if that is the sort of situation we find? A child who will grow up to that sort of life?

For now, I need to focus on finding the baby's parents. I hope Cypher can shed more light on that.

TWENTY

I talk to Phil about Maryanne. I'm trying to play fair with all parties, especially in light of the "Whoops, guess the council *isn't* responsible for hostiles" revelation. I'm feeling sheepish about that, and in response, I decide to be aboveboard regarding Maryanne's presence.

I explain to Phil. He responds with a shake of his head and zero questions, as if he's beyond surprise when it comes to Rockton. He'll tell the council Maryanne is here and sees no issue with that. It's a humanitarian gesture.

At one time, I'd have thought Phil incapable of understanding that concept. While he doesn't exactly trip over himself to offer her hospitality, he doesn't question giving her a house for the night, food, fresh clothing and supplies come morning.

I've brought the baby back from Jen's, and Maryanne is resting, so I've requisitioned a men's parka from the supply shop, put the baby into the front sling we fashioned yesterday, and tucked her under the jacket. We're both restless, and walking with her seemed like a fine solution, though it might suggest that I have far more experience with puppies than babies.

She doesn't sleep, but she settles in with only the occasional grunt to let me know she's there.

Walking through town means more stopping-and-greeting than actual movement, especially when I have a baby strapped to my chest. It's like walking Storm — even after a year, people still stop me to give her a pat. The baby doesn't want to be patted. She conveys that with a yowl the first time a resident's icy fingers touch her cheek.

So I take her out of town. There's a path that runs just beyond the forest edge, one that residents are allowed to use if they really feel the need to commune with nature. I can go farther, of course — perks of being law enforcement — but with the baby, I'll stick close. It's also dark. Not night yet — not even dinnertime — but dark nonetheless.

I see the glow of Dalton's flashlight first, bobbing along like fairy-fire. Then Storm gives a happy bark and thunders down the path. I drop to one knee before she bowls me over. While I pet her, she dances and whines as if we've been separated for months. Then she sticks her big nose into my parka and licks the baby. The baby's head rolls back, as if trying to see. Storm snuffles the black-fuzzed head, and the baby only grunts in surprise.

Dalton approaches with a guy half a head taller than him, a burly bulk of a man with a snow-crusted beard halfway down his chest.

As I stand, Cypher says, "Either that's a baby under your coat, kitten, or you've taken up serious snacking."

"My snacking habits are none of your concern," I say. "But yes, it is a baby."

Cypher gives me a one-armed hug, which I return. Then he peers down at the baby, who whimpers in alarm.

"Still scaring dogs and small children," Dalton says. "You might want to trim that beard." He pauses. "No, I guess at her age she can't see more than shapes. It must be the smell."

"Ha!" Cypher jabs a finger into Dalton's chest. "You're getting better at the jokes, boy. They're even close to being funny. Also, you really gotta stop letting this girl of yours wander around the woods. If she's not tripping over dead bodies, she's rescuing wolf pups and throwing bear cubs, and now she's bringing home lost babies. Must be a talent."

"I don't find the dead bodies," I say. "I make them, to liven things up."

"Hey now, that's my line."

"You make any dead bodies lately, Ty?" Dalton asks as we head for home.

"Just the kind I can throw into a stew. And, before you ask, that doesn't include people. My hit-man days are behind me . . . unless you need someone put down, and then I'll make an exception."

"For a lifetime supply of coffee creamer?" I say.

"Hell, no, kitten. I want the coffee, too. I'm a skilled tradesman. I don't come cheap." He looks over at the baby. "Mind if I hold the tyke when we get inside where it's warm?"

Dalton and I exchange a look. Cypher sees it and sputters. "What? You think I'll drop her on her head? My own girl grew up just fine. Twice as smart as her old man."

"You have a daughter?" I say.

"I do indeed. She's a lawyer down in Hawaii. Not the profession I would have chosen, but she isn't fond of mine either, so we agree to disagree. She married a few years back, and she's got herself a pair of twin babies. I haven't broken them yet."

"You've . . . seen them?" I say.

"Only once so far, but I plan to get down again this spring. Fly south with all the other snowbirds, work on my tan on Waikiki."

I stare at him.

"What?" he says. "You've never heard of these big things called airplanes? Sure, first I gotta get to Dawson, and that's a good week's walk, which is why I don't do it in the middle of winter, even if I'd appreciate that sun and sand even more."

"I never knew you had a kid," Dalton says.

"Because you never asked." Cypher throws his hands in the air. "No one asks. I'm just the crazy ex-sheriff who lives in the forest."

We're in Rockton now. People have heard us coming. More accurately, they heard Cypher. He tramps out of the forest like a Norse giant, clad in fur and snow. People clear a path all the way to the police station.

The first time Cypher walked in, they'd scattered even faster, all Dalton's bogeymen-of-the-forest stories springing to life. They've seen him enough now that they don't flee; they just retreat.

I'd lit the fire in the station before I left,

and when we walk in, Dalton swings the kettle over the flames. Then he helps me out of the parka and takes the baby.

"She have a name?" Cypher asks.

I glance at Dalton.

"Abby," he says. "Or that's what we're calling her for now."

Cypher takes Abby and dangles her in front of his face, his one hand supporting her neck. "You didn't have your name stitched on your blanket? What kind of foundling are you?"

I settle in by the fire. "How much did Eric explain?"

"Just that we'd discovered a baby and a dead woman — who isn't the mother — and we need help finding the actual mother," Dalton says as he preps the French press. "Tyrone wouldn't let me tell him more. His price for information is a one-night stay in Rockton, with access to food and a shower. I agreed, but he refused to talk to anyone except you. I think he figured if I got his information, I'd renege on the bargain." He shoots Cypher a look.

"I wasn't questioning your integrity, boy. Your voice just isn't nearly as sweet as Casey's. Now, what's going on with this tyke?"

I explain. When I tell him who Edwin

fingered as the family, he lets out a string of curses, and then stops short and puts his hands over the baby's ears before finishing.

"You know them," I say.

"Fuck, yeah."

"And they're not actually upstanding citizens."

"Fuck, no."

I rise to take the whistling kettle, but Dalton beats me to it.

"Edwin says they . . . sell their girls," I say. "Prostitute them."

"Yeah, sorry, kitten. I know you were hoping I'd say that's a load of hogwash, but it's not. I don't trade with that family unless I absolutely have to — they have some items I can't get elsewhere. And, yeah, sex might be on that list of rare commodities, but I'm sure as hell not buying it like that."

Cypher settles in, grunting as he shifts his bulk. "I don't have an aversion to such trade in general. If a woman's willing, and it's a clean transaction, well, I figure that's better than going into a bar and ending up with a woman who drank more than you realized. These particular traders offer me a girl every time, and they get the sharp side of my tongue instead. One of the girls even asked me to take her away and marry her."

He scratches his beard. "Shit. I didn't

209

know what to do. Ended up saying no, and then spent a whole lotta time feeling bad about it. It's a complicated situation. I sure as hell don't want some little girl who stays with me because I rescued her. I could take her to Dawson, but what then? Give her a few grand and abandon her? She's never lived outside these woods."

"If that ever happens again, bring her here," Dalton says.

"It's not that simple," Cypher says. "It isn't like those girls are tied to a wagon, beaten and bruised, and I'm trading with their daddy while pretending not to see them because I really need new underwear."

I snort, and he arches his brows. "You think I'm kidding about the underwear, kitten? You try making them from deer hide. Going without ain't an option. I tried that one summer. It was warm enough, but then you got the chafing and the hanging and —"

I hold up my hand. "I get the pict— Nope, sorry. I don't get any picture at all."

He chuckles. "Point is that those girls aren't being held against their will. There's three of them — sisters — and if I tried rescuing two of them, they'd scratch my damned eyes out. The third — the one who asked — wasn't looking for rescue. She just figured I'd be a good provider. If I did walk her to Dawson, she'd turn around and find her way back to her family." He waves at Dalton. "Like you did, when the Daltons brought you to Rockton."

Dalton goes still. I stiffen, looking over. He says, very softly, "I tried to get back to my parents. To my family."

"Exactly," Cypher says, blithely missing Dalton's body language. "You were better off here, but you still wanted to return to your folks out there."

Dalton's storm-gray eyes fix on Cypher. "Better off?"

Cypher waves away Dalton's words — he's ready to move on. I'm trying to decide what to do when I hear myself saying, "Why did you think that?"

Dalton's gone still again, his nostrils flaring as if he's struggling to breathe. I could withdraw the question. Maybe I should. I don't.

"Why do you think Eric was better off in Rockton?" I press. "Was something wrong with him? Was he sick? Malnourished?"

"Nothing like that. I'm sure his folks were decent kids. But they were already leaving him to fend for himself. That ain't right."

"What?" Dalton says, his face screwing up.

"Your daddy — Gene Dalton — saw you a few times out there, all by yourself. Hunting and fishing. You told him your parents had gone off to trade, and you were old enough to look after yourself. They must have taken Jakey with them. Gone for weeks, they were, leaving you alone."

"That . . . no, that never . . ." Dalton struggles for words. "That did not happen. Yes, I was old enough to go hunting or fishing. But for a morning or an afternoon. If my parents went trading, we all went. I never spoke to anyone from Rockton before Gene Dalton captured me."

Cypher frowns. "Maybe you've forgotten. Anyway, I don't know the details, and I might not have had much use for Gene Dalton, but your momma was a good woman. She wouldn't have kept you if there wasn't a problem with your folks. I wouldn't have let them keep you either."

There's a set to Cypher's jaw, one that says he's not trying to convince Dalton; he's trying to convince himself. He believed whatever tale Gene Dalton spun, and he cannot afford to second-guess now.

"Eric?" I say. "Maybe you want to take Abby home for a nap. You could check on Maryanne, too."

His lips tighten, and my gut seizes. I

212

shouldn't have asked about his parents. I should have respected Dalton's wishes and kept out of it until he was ready. When he sees my face, he squeezes my hand and leans over to whisper, "Nothing I didn't already suspect."

Before I can react, he says, "Let me take Abby and Storm for a walk. I should check on Maryanne. I'll be back in twenty minutes."

When Dalton's gone, I say to Cypher, "May I ask you a favor?"

"Sure, kitten. What is it?"

"Don't mention his family — either one, really. He has good memories of his birth parents, and what the Daltons did is confusing. I know you didn't mean anything by it, but I'd be very happy if it didn't arise in conversation again."

He looks toward the door Dalton exited. "He's upset."

I could almost laugh at his genuine surprise. He really did miss the clues, even as they'd flashed neon-bright. I remember who I'm talking to and limit my response to, "He's angry about what happened back then."

Cypher looks at me. "You can say he's upset, Casey. I'm not one of those assholes who'll give a guy flak for showing a bit of

213

emotion. If it bothers him, I won't bring it up."

"Thank you. Now, about finding this baby's family . . ."

"Yeah, that was the topic of conversation, wasn't it?" He eyes me. "As for giving the baby back, Edwin's right. Those traders went on a long supply run." He stretches his legs. "Could be spring before they get back."

"Damn. So I guess we'll just need to adopt her."

"Seems like it. I know you and Eric are busy with your jobs, but you've got a town full of folks who'll help babysit, and you'd make good parents."

"People keep telling me that," I murmur. "So this family, they must have left in the last few days. You don't think we could catch up with them?"

"They move fast."

"Huh. Weird, though, don't you think? That they'd decide to do a supply run at this time of year. You said yourself that you wouldn't travel to Dawson in winter. Too hard going."

He shrugs. "That's me."

"Yet they not only chose to leave as soon as the weather got bad . . . but they'll be away all winter, when people would be most in need of trade goods, willing to pay dearly for food and ammo."

"I didn't say they were *good* traders."

"You and Edwin have decided the baby would be better off with us. I get that. Under the circumstances . . ." I exhale. "Well, I don't know what's going to happen under the circumstances, but I'm not about to hand a baby girl back to a family who'll prostitute her when she's old enough."

"They don't really wait until they're old enough."

"And you think I'd return a child to that? All I want is to assess the situation. Maybe they abandoned the baby. Edwin thinks so. Maybe the woman who died found her in the snow. Or maybe the mother is frantically searching for her child and can be convinced to leave her family and raise Abby in a safe place. I have no idea what our next move is, but I'd like you to trust us."

He sighs. "Don't get your back up, kitten. I know you and Eric gotta do the right thing, but sometimes, doing the right thing isn't really doing the right thing, if you know what I mean. You tie yourselves into knots weighing the ethical and moral bullshit, when common sense says 'Fuck that.' If a kid has a choice between growing up with good parents who'll give her the best fucking life they can . . . and parents who'll whore her out before she's old enough for high school? Pretty sure *no one* sees much of a decision there. It just seems best to me if I say the family's long gone, and any fault for a fib falls on me. I won't lose a moment's sleep over it."

"True, but now that I know you're fibbing, I will lose a *ton* of sleep over it, wondering if I should tell Eric my suspicions, wondering if I stole a baby from a young woman needing rescue herself, wondering if —"

"Life would be a whole lot easier if you could just shut off that brain of yours. Same with Eric. Yeah, what happened to him was messy, but he's fine now, and the Daltons are down south, and his parents are dead, and he's still got Jacob, so what good does it do to dig up the past?"

I ignore that and say, "This family of traders didn't go to Dawson. So the question is whether you're going to help us get to them, or we're going to track them down on our own."

He sighs and grumbles and says, "We can talk about that over dinner. I'm hungry, and I want a shower and a proper sit-down meal in your restaurant."

TWENTY-ONE

Dalton returns with Abby and Storm just before we head out. We're putting Cypher up overnight in one of the empty apartments, and he wants to shower before dinner. He also wants clean clothing and a full line of toiletries, including beard scissors.

"You're going to dinner with us," Dalton says. "It's not a date."

Cypher doesn't respond to that. I glance over, and he's scratching his beard. When he catches my eye, he looks almost sheepish.

"So," he says, clearing his throat. "Earlier, I might have said I don't have any problem with the concept of . . . purchasing the time of . . . ladies . . ." He glances over, clearly hoping to be freed from this conversation with a nod of understanding. I frown, pretending I have no idea what he's talking about.

He clears his throat again. "Last time I

was here . . . I overheard a comment that led me to asking your deputy a question, which he confirmed."

Another look my way. Again, I offer Cypher no sign of rescue. Dalton's busy murmuring to Abby, who is awake and trying to look around.

Cypher continues, "It seems you have legalized the, uh, sex trade in Rockton. So I thought, maybe, if I cleaned myself up, one of your, uh, ladies might consider . . ."

Dalton looks over, brows raised, as if he caught just the end of that conversation.

"He's getting himself dolled up because he *is* hoping for a date," I say. "A paid one."

Cypher glowers at me.

"What?" I said. "Did I misinterpret?"

He mutters under his breath.

"You can try," I say. "But we'd need to front you credits. They don't take hides in trade. Probably best if I speak to Isabel, and she can have a word with her girls, and they can get a look at you over dinner and let her know what they think. It's entirely up to them."

"As it should be," he says. "But, well, while I'm open to possibilities, there was one lady in particular who caught my eye. That's what led to the conversation with Deputy Will. She came by to give him shit

218

about something, and he made a comment, and after she left, I confirmed the sex-trade thing. I'm presuming, from his comment, that she's one of the . . . ladies for hire."

"Ah, you already have your date picked out. I'll ask Will who —"

Before I can finish, Jen marches over. "You steal my baby, and you don't bring her back? I said her feeding time was six, and it's already ten after, and I see you just waltzing around with her, while she freezes her tiny ass off."

As she talks, Cypher steps away — quickly. I don't blame him. I'd like to escape, too. But something in the way he quickly side-steps catches my attention.

Jen sees him. "Oh, it's Grizzly Adams. Come down from the mountain, did you? You don't need to jump. I don't bite."

"I wasn't jumping, miss. I was moving downwind so you don't smell me before I get a shower. Which I was just about to do."

"I've spent the last two days changing shitty diapers. You can't smell any worse than that." Jen reaches for Abby. "Gimme."

I catch the look Cypher is giving her, and I accidentally say "Jen?" aloud, and she turns on me with a snapped, "What?"

I motion to Dalton, whose eyebrows disappear under his hat. He looks from Cypher to Jen.

"What?" Jen repeats.

"I think we'll keep the baby for now," I say. "We'll feed her, and then Petra wanted a visit. We'll leave her and Storm there over dinner. Would you mind doing us a favor, though? Tyrone's going to get cleaned up and grab dinner at the Lion, and I'm not sure we'll be done with the baby in time. It's probably best if he doesn't walk into the Lion unescorted."

"You want me to eat dinner with Grizzly Adams?" She looks over at him and shrugs. "Fine with me, but you'd better make sure he *wants* to have dinner with me. He looks ready to bolt back into the forest."

"Like I said, miss, I just don't smell too good."

"It's Jen. I haven't been a 'miss' for a long time. If you're okay eating with me, then sure, go get your shower. I'll come by in thirty minutes. Just don't make me wait. I'm hungry."

She leaves before he can answer. I call after her, "Thanks, and dinner's on us!"

"It better be," she calls back.

When she's out of earshot, I say, "That's all we're paying for, too."

Dalton watches Jen. "She's the . . . ?"

220

"Can't even get the rest out, can you?" I murmur.

"She's a little rough around the edges," Cypher says. "But I'm not exactly smooth myself." He eyes her retreating form. "You think I have a shot? I mean, if I pay, obviously."

"Here's the thing," I say. "When Will said we have sex workers, he didn't mean Jen. Yes, he may have made a smart-ass comment to her. That's because she's been known to moonlight, which is strictly prohibited. As far as I know, she hasn't done that in a while. So my advice is to have a nice dinner, see how it goes, and if she makes you an offer, I'll tell Isabel it's a special case."

"A charity case," Dalton says.

Cypher pokes him in the chest. "How about you just go back to *not* trying to be funny, boy. I don't need charity. I just need a long shower, some good soap, and clean clothing. And beard trimmers."

"Or hedge clippers," I say.

"Oh, you too, huh? I clean up just fine. As you will see."

"Actually, we won't. You get Jen all to yourself. Tell her we decided to eat in with the baby tonight. Go have your date, and try not to spend too much of our money."

We're at home with Abby and Storm. Dalton checked on Maryanne earlier, and she's fine. He sensed she'd had enough company for the day, so he had Anders take her dinner and a few supplies, and she's in for the night. Anders will keep an eye on the place and make sure no one goes nosing around. He'll also let us know if Maryanne gets skittish and bolts.

I feed Storm and then Abby while Dalton makes dinner. He's better at that. It wasn't a skill I developed at home — we had a housekeeper who cooked. That's no excuse, I know. It just always seemed like there were other things to do, and it was easier to buy takeout or cook a pot of pasta or slap together a sandwich. I *can* cook — I'm just not very good at it, and the limited ingredients here frustrate me. Dalton's never known anything else.

Tonight, he's making venison cutlets with a mushroom ragout on a bed of egg noodles. Everything is fresh — the meat hunted, the mushrooms picked and dried, the egg noodles handmade. We may not have a supermarket's worth of variety here, but the food is worthy of a posh Toronto eatery.

I'm putting Abby to bed when Dalton declares dinner ready. We eat in front of the fireplace, Storm at our feet, Dalton stretched out on the sofa, me curled up at the other end, plates on our laps, wineglasses on the side tables.

I plan to find other conversation for the meal, but as soon as we settle and I open my mouth, I hear myself saying, "I'm sorry."

He glances over, brows rising.

"Earlier with Tyrone. When he mentioned your parents, I should have dropped it, and I didn't."

He turns to me, and his head tilts, just a little, eyes piercing with a look I know well, from our earliest days. That keen scrutiny, as if he's trying to peer right into my brain and figure out what I'm thinking.

"Is that what was bothering you?" he says.

I glance over.

He sets his plate down, one knee coming up onto the sofa. "You looked freaked out when Tyrone was talking, and I thought you were just shocked by what he said. Were you honestly worried I'd be mad at you for asking?"

"It's your business, and if you wanted details, you'd ask. I shouldn't do it for you." I put my fork down. "It's not just *for you,* either. I want to know. I want to understand.

223

That isn't right."

His head tilts again. "Being concerned for me isn't right?"

"It's . . ." I flail my hands. "Complicated."

"Yeah, it is. Those relationships are complicated. Ours isn't, and if I'm making it complicated, you gotta tell me so I can stop. I sure as hell don't want you thinking you need to tread lightly or you'll piss me off. You asked the obvious question. One I should have asked myself, but . . ."

He shrugs. "It feels like picking at a scab. That scab's not healing, though. I just . . ." He exhales, a long hiss of breath between his teeth. "I just don't want to get into it."

He stops, lips parting. "Fuck, that sounds bad. It's not that I don't want to get into it with you. I don't want to get into it with myself. Best to stuff it under the bed and tell myself it doesn't matter. Except it does matter. I haven't gone to see the Daltons since you arrived, and part of that's because when we have time off, I want to be with you. But part of it is that you give me an excuse. They're my parents, and I should want to see them. Only they're *not* my parents, and unless they have a damned good excuse for what they did, I'm not eager to spend my free time with them."

He looks over at me. "They don't have a

good excuse, do they?"

"I have no way of knowing that, Eric."

"But you think the same thing I do. They lied about my situation. They made shit up to justify bringing me into Rockton."

"Gene did."

He rubs his mouth. "Yeah, and I don't know how to deal with that, because my gut says he lied to my mother, too. He presented her with a situation she wouldn't argue with. Like Edwin trying to tell us the baby had been abandoned. If that's the case, then I'm doing a shitty thing, shutting Katherine Dalton out of my life. But if it's not? If she knew, too?"

He looks at me. "If she knew too, that's gonna hurt. I need those answers. I'm not ready to march down south and get them. But you don't ever need to worry that you're going to upset me by prodding. Fuck knows, I'm the king of pushing people to face shit they don't want to face."

He lifts my plate and holds it out. "Eat."

When I hesitate, he leans in, his forehead touching mine. "I love you. You know that. Sometimes I wish there was something more to say, a higher escalation. I can't find the words to go beyond it, you know?"

I nod, still not speaking. I feel his breath on my lips, close enough to kiss, but he stays there, just breathing.

"I'm still afraid," he says, "of doing something to scare you off. I'm mostly past it, but I worry that if I dive into this, and I can't deal with it, you'll decide I'm just too fucked up to be with."

"Pretty sure my baggage is as heavy as yours."

"Yeah, but what's in your baggage has been sorted and arranged, and you open it up for a look now and then. Mine's stuffed in a suitcase full to bursting, held by triple locks, and I don't even peek inside. You shouldn't feel like I'd go ballistic if you even jangle the lock. Especially when I'm throwing yours open, riffling through it, tossing shit everywhere so I can see what you've got in there."

I laugh softly. "That is an awesome analogy."

"Thank you. Totally true, too. I love you. I don't want to lose you. You're going to need to be patient with me. Right now, my life is fucking awesome, and if there's this one suitcase under the bed that I don't want to touch, I know that isn't healthy, but I'm not ready to rip it open. You may, however, jangle the locks now and then to remind me it's there, and that I need to deal with it eventually."

I press my lips to his. It's meant to be quick, but he bears into it, pulling me against him, the kiss hungry, edged with desperation. I slide my plate onto the table and pull him to me as I fall back onto the couch.

Twenty-Two

I'm on the floor, resting on my stomach, eyeing my plate of half-eaten food.

"You know what we need?" I say. "A microwave."

Dalton snorts and pushes up. "You southerners make everything complicated." He pulls out a tray that hangs over the fire, sets our plates on it, and adjusts it over the flames. Storm lumbers over to lie closer to the fire. She doesn't even eye the plates. She knows better.

"A microwave would be faster," I say.

"But it wouldn't give the meat that nice, smoky taste. And if you were so hungry, maybe you shouldn't have insisted on sex halfway through dinner."

"Insisted?" I sputter. "I don't even remember *asking*."

"Exactly. That only makes it worse."

I pitch a pillow at him. He catches it, scoops me up, and deposits me on the sofa, then drops the pillow on my head. When I go to throw it back at him, he lifts my wineglass, and I stop.

"Thought that'd work," he says, handing me the glass as he takes away the pillow. "Don't wanna spill the wine."

He's about to settle in beside me when the baby wails. He levers up, but I put a hand on his knee.

"I've got this," I say.

I root my panties and bra out of the pile of clothing — somehow, this seems the proper line between acceptable and unacceptable attire in front of an infant who can't see more than blobs. I pull them on as I head upstairs.

By the time Abby is changed, our meal is warmed.

"You eat first," I say. "I'll handle cuddling duty."

I sit on the sofa with Abby, and she snuggles against my bare skin. Storm lies on my feet. I have Abby cradled in my arms, which apparently is the proper position for breast-feeding, because her head turns and her tiny mouth clamps down on my bra. I laugh and shift her away, murmuring "Sorry," as I sweep my hair back over my shoulder.

I look over at Dalton, and I'm about to make a comment when I see he's staring, and the look on his face . . . It's the same look I'm sure I had, watching him cradle the baby that first time, an expression of revelation and a pang of unexpected longing from some instinctive place.

He looks away quickly and says something, too gruff to make out. I slide over and kiss his beard-rough cheek. He turns to meet the kiss, hand slipping into my hair. It's a quick one, and then I'm back in my corner, watching him eat as he sneaks almost guilty glances my way.

We'll have to deal with this. With the questions Abby raises for us. But I'm no longer freaking out at the thought. For now, we have other concerns. I start by telling him Maryanne's story. He stops eating several times as I talk, chewing over my words with his dinner, but he says nothing until I'm done. Then he's done, too, and he wordlessly switches his plate for the baby so I can eat.

"Huh," he says as he bounces Abby, hand behind her head, as if this has become second nature.

"Yep," I say. "Huh, indeed. Thank God I didn't tell anyone else about my 'council is responsible for the hostiles' theory. You should have seen the look I got when I asked Maryanne whether anyone else could be involved. I felt like Brent with his crazy conspiracy theories."

I pull my legs up, sitting sideways and cross-legged as I dangle one hand to pet Storm. "For the record, I knew I was being paranoid suspecting the council."

"Yeah," Dalton says. "Because they are *never* behind the weird shit that happens here. It's not like they're bringing in killers without warning us or setting spies among us or planting a goddamn secret agent to assassinate liabilities."

"Petra will love 'secret agent.' She might want a badge."

He snorts. "Nice job of ignoring my point, Detective. You never blamed the council. You only floated the possibility. Your primary suspicion was simply that the hostiles didn't just devolve into fucking savages after a year or two in the wild. Now we know your main hypothesis is correct. The hostiles aren't residents-gone-wild. They're a cult."

My brows shoot up.

Shades fall over his eyes — the pride of a brilliant man who realizes he can misunderstand concepts those from "down south" take for granted. It only lasts a second, though, before he relaxes as he remembers who he's with.

"Yeah," he says. "That might not be the

right word. We had someone up here, a few years back, escaping a cult, so I did some reading. Maybe not as much as I should have."

"The fact that you did *any* research to help understand a resident's situation puts you head and shoulders above most of us, Eric. And my look didn't mean you had the wrong idea. It was surprise that you had the right one."

When he chuckles, I say, "Sorry, that came out wrong. I'm not surprised that *you* had a good idea. I'm surprised because I hadn't thought of it that way. While I never dealt with cults down south, I did attend a seminar on them. Most times, you have a charismatic person recruiting easy targets — people who want to get rich or feel loved and accepted, depending on what your cult is selling. They're always selling something. The hostiles don't fit that."

"Yeah, crappy analogy."

"No, it's not, because the basic idea still works. People who leave Rockton *are* seeking something. A more natural way of life and a stronger community. Most of all, though, they're looking for a new *experience.* That's what Maryanne wanted. The hostiles aren't willing recruits, though. Sure, I suppose it's possible someone could be attracted to that lifestyle, but mostly, they're being brainwashed. That's where the cult analogy works best."

"It starts with the tea," Dalton says. "A group of settlers, maybe with some experience in drugs, looking for *that* kind of back-to-nature experience. Rockton got a lot of that in the early years. People grew their own marijuana, their own mushrooms. Neither was particularly conducive to productivity, though."

I smile. "No, I suppose not. But yes, back to nature can mean plant-based methods of communing with the forest. Early settlers probably did experiment with what they found out there." I turn to him. "What is out there, anyway?"

"Fuck if I know. We still get residents poking around. They end up in the clinic for smoking all kinds of shit."

I laugh.

He shifts Abby to his other arm. "No one's ever found anything that'll send them on a drug trip. My guess is that whoever concocted this tea knew exactly what they were doing. They didn't just randomly throw plants into a pot."

"The inventor and their fellow settlers get into it, and everyone likes how it makes them feel. It makes them more comfortable with violence, more fixated on daily survival and less concerned with everything that gets in the way of it."

"The tea hones their survival instincts and dulls their self-awareness."

"So they don't sit around moaning about wanting a shower." I remember what Mary-anne said, about how that was the big concern with her parents' hippie friends. Scarcity of creature comforts is the thing people complain about most in Rockton. I've learned to live without a microwave and internet access, but that doesn't mean I don't feel the lack of them. That's where Dalton has the advantage.

It would be simpler if we could temporarily forget the lack of comforts. That's why we control alcohol so tightly. It's also why Rockton had a hellish problem with a homemade drug when I arrived. Drinking the hostiles' tea would be rewarding in so many ways.

I reach for my wine and sip it, thinking. "I feel like there's more to it, but we have a good starting hypothesis. We know at least some hostiles are there against their will, and we'll need to decide what to do about that. For now, in regard to Abby, we know she isn't a baby hostile, and we know the dead woman — Ellen — was a former hostile. She wasn't shot by one, though, so it seems any connection to the hostiles is only tangential. Our goal is finding Abby's family."

I tell him what Cypher did — and did not — say on that matter.

"Yeah, fucking complicated," Dalton mutters. "Everything always is. He'll tell us where to find these traders, though, especially if he gets laid tonight." He looks at me. "So Jen, huh?"

I sputter a laugh that startles Abby. She cranes her neck, looking toward the source of the noise. Dalton hands her to me, and I expect her to complain. Instead she snuggles, cheek on my bare skin, chubby legs and arms drawing in like a frog's.

I stroke her back. "Yep, Jen. Gotta give him credit for keeping his aspirations reasonable."

Dalton throws back his head and laughs, and Abby makes a chirping noise, but only snuggles more, as if she can burrow into me. I tug up a blanket.

"Isabel and Phil, Cypher and Jen . . ." I say. "Spring must be just around the corner."

"Nah, up here, it's winter that gets them. Long, cold nights." His gaze travels over me, still in my panties and bra. "Speaking of which . . ." He leans toward me. "I was kinda thinking we might spend our evening playing a game." He waggles his brows.

"Uh-huh," I say.

He leans to whisper in my ear. "I swiped Scrabble from the community center. You in?"

I grin. "Totally."

"How about you bring Abby's bed downstairs so she can hang out with us. I'll start coffee and break out the homemade Irish cream."

"And cookies?"

He smiles. "I believe I can find cookies."

It's just after eleven when a familiar pound on the door has Dalton calling, "Come in!"

A moment later, Anders steps around the corner, his hand over his eyes.

"Ha ha," Dalton says. "We're decent."

Anders walks in and looks at the Scrabble board. "You guys know how to rock an evening in, don't you?"

I lift my cookie. "We do indeed."

Anders shakes his head. "It's been, what, a little over a year, and you're already an old married couple, spending your one evening off playing Scrabble and drinking coffee."

"It's spiked coffee."

"Oooh, living it up. Better be careful. Too much of that might lead to the proper definition of couple's night in." His gaze travels over to my shirt and jeans, crumpled on the floor, and he glances back at me, realizing I'm wearing the shirt that Dalton is not. "Ah, no, Scrabble is the afterglow. Carry on, then."

He reaches down to scoop up Abby. As he does, he gets a look at my tiles. "Boss? Better block 'phone.' Casey's about to change it to 'xylophone' for a gazillion points."

I smack his leg.

"Hey," he says. "Baby on board. Careful."

Dalton alters "phone" to "telephone." I smack Anders again.

"I like you just fine, Case," Anders says. "But he's the boss. Now he owes me at least two days off for helping him win."

"He was already winning." I wave at the board. "House rules allow profanity, and he's really, really good at it."

Anders laughs. Then he hunkers down. "So, as much as I'd love to share one of those spiked coffees, I'm not interrupting your evening merely to be annoying."

"Merely," Dalton murmurs.

"Disrupting your sappy domestic bliss is always a valid side goal. However, my main purpose is to tell you that someone was skulking around your old house, where Maryanne is spending the night."

I shoot upright. "What?"

He motions me down. "It's okay. It was just Phil, who already knows she's there."

"You said 'skulking.' That implies he wasn't popping by to see if she needed extra pillows."

"Yeah, it was weird, which is why I'm here. And before you freak out, Casey, I confirmed that the doors were locked and ordered one of the guys to keep a watch on the house while I ran over here. I didn't tell him that anyone is in it — just that a resident was poking around your old place."

"Okay. So explain the skulking weirdness," I say.

"I'm getting to that. Just fending off 'Oh my god, you saw criminal activity and just walked away!' "

"I never —"

"The point?" Dalton says. "Or do I need to go investigate myself while you two squabble?"

Anders continues. "Phil was definitely skulking. Dressed in dark colors, no flashlight, hood pulled up. He was wearing one of the militia parkas instead of his completely inappropriate for the weather but terribly stylish ski jacket."

"Was he doing anything besides skulking?" I ask.

"Yep, which made it extra weird. So, I'm on patrol, and on each round, I pass the house twice. I'm literally walking by the front when he darts from behind a tree. I'm, like, seriously? Could you not wait ten seconds for the guy with the flashlight to move on? I turn off the flashlight and take it slow, but I'm not Eric Cloud-Foot. You can hear my boots crunching snow. I slip around the house, and Phil's trying the back door. Like he expects it to be open. I yell 'Hey!' and he takes off." Anders shakes his head. "The guy would starve to death as a cat burglar."

"You're sure it was Phil? You saw his face?"

"No, he had the sense to turn that away from me. But, like I said, world's worst cat burglar. He might have found new clothes and tied a scarf around his face, but he still wore the boots he had the council ship up."

That was one concession the council made, likely to counter Phil's sense that he'd been exiled here. *What? No, that'd be illegal. You're being held there as an emergency measure to fill an essential position, for which you will be well compensated. I know it was unexpected, so just tell us what you need from your condo.*

Phil's winter wear was what you'd expect from a Toronto exec whose subzero excursions were limited to the half-kilometer walk between his condo and the subway station. Phil has never confirmed his actual city of origin, but I'd lay serious money on Toronto. He has that New York Lite vibe. His boots are definitely not the bulky, rubber-soled footwear that keeps us warm and upright out here.

"What the hell is he up to?" Dalton mutters. He looks at Anders. "You okay watching the baby for an hour or so?"

"If I get a spiked coffee and one of those cookies."

"One coffee," I say. "And don't go inviting all your friends over for a party as soon as we leave."

TWENTY-THREE

Dalton pounds on Phil's door. He has to do it twice before Phil pulls it open, robe tied over his bare chest and sweatpants, feet equally bare, one hand holding his glasses as he blinks at us, as if bleary-eyed with sleep.

"Eric? Casey?" He lifts his wrist to check the time, and blinks again, as if struggling to process the fact that he's not wearing his watch.

Phil may be a shitty cat burglar, but his acting skills aren't half bad, if a little community theater.

"Why were you at Casey's old place tonight?" Dalton asks.

"What? When? I haven't been out since dinner."

"No?"

Phil finds the expression he wants, somewhere between annoyance and condescension. "No, Sheriff. I don't socialize in the evenings."

"Just the afternoons," I murmur, and his cheeks color at that. He opens his mouth, but I cut him off with, "So you haven't been out in the last few hours?"

"That's what I said."

Dalton steps forward, and Phil backs up with a snarky, "Please come in. Two A.M. is a perfectly fine time for a visit."

"It's not even midnight," Dalton says.

I ease by them and lift one of Phil's boots from the mat. It's still caked with snow.

"You thought you could put that one past a fucking detective?" Dalton says, pointing at the boot.

"I meant that I hadn't been out and walking around. Not that I hadn't stepped beyond my door. One of the shutters was banging. I couldn't see anything, though I'd like Kenny to check in the morning. I'm sure I heard a clatter."

"On the rooftop maybe?" I say. "Santa making a practice run?"

I get a cool look for that. Then his lips purse. "Are you saying someone was at the house where you're keeping Maryanne? Perhaps *that's* what I heard — someone went to the wrong perimeter house searching for her."

I'm about to call his bluff. Then I reconsider and nod. "Someone who spotted her when I brought her in. They got curious and snuck in for a closer look."

"Perhaps, but I wouldn't be so quick to write off a potential threat as mere curiosity."

"Threat?"

"She's a hostile. She makes people nervous. Remember how they tried to lynch Oliver Brady. If they know you have a hostile here, they might decide to do something about that."

"Most residents don't even know what hostiles are," Dalton says. "Hell, they see Tyrone Cypher and think that's what I mean. And Ty's in town tonight, so if they decide to form another mob, they'll just go after him. Which is fine. He can look after himself. Give his rusty occupational skills a workout."

"Tyrone Cypher has no legal authority here."

"I don't mean his skills as a former sheriff. I mean from when he was a hit man."

Phil looks at Dalton. "I realize I'm still relatively new, but I believe we may dispense with the hazing jokes. Whatever Rockton's issues, the council would not put a killer on the police force."

"Uh . . ." I say. "I know you've read my file."

"You're an exception." He pauses. "Like Deputy Anders."

"Given the track record of Rockton law enforcement, I suspect 'killing someone in cold blood' is actually a prerequisite. Except for Eric. Eric's special."

"In so many ways," Phil murmurs under his breath. "My point —"

"Your point was that you think Maryanne is in danger," Dalton says. "And it's interesting that you jump to that rather than the more mundane explanation of a bored resident. Also interesting considering *you're* the person who was trying to break into her house. Ever been diagnosed with multiple personalities?"

"Don't give him any ideas," I say.

"I wasn't. Dissociative identity disorder is exceptionally rare and experts disagree on whether it exists at all." Dalton catches my look. "We had a resident who said she had it. So I did my research. She was wrong. Had a helluva time convincing her of that, though."

"Cultists, psychopaths, multiple personalities, hit men . . . Is there anyone you haven't had here? Oh, wait. No zombies. At least not yet, right?"

"Actually . . ."

I arch my brows.

Dalton says, "Well, he wasn't *really* a zombie. But he hated it here. Wanted to go home before his two years were up. He was looking for a loophole, and he knew we can't handle residents with serious mental illnesses. Seems he'd seen a TV special raising money for . . ." His eyes roll up, accessing his files. "Collard's syndrome? Cotard's delusion? Something like that. Anyway, it's a real illness where people think they're dead and rotting. He faked that. I convinced him he was wrong, which was much easier than convincing the multiple-personality lady."

"Do I dare ask what you did?"

He shrugs. "We can't have rotting residents. That's unsanitary. So I dug a hole, cuffed him, and tossed him in."

"Whereupon he had a miraculous recovery."

"I'm a man of many talents. Especially when it comes to sniffing out bullshit." He turns to Phil. "You don't have dissociative identity disorder. And you're not a zombie. But you were spotted trying to break into Casey's old place tonight."

"No, I was not. If someone was, then I would suggest you reconsider Maryanne's stay in Rockton."

I eye him. "Would you?"

"Yes. Personally, I have no problem with it, and neither does the council. But, if she's in danger, then I would suggest you give her supplies and turn her out."

"In the middle of the night?"

He hesitates.

"How about first thing in the morning?" I say. "Before dawn."

Phil nods. "That should be acceptable."

"Really?" Dalton says. " 'Cause if you're worried about a resident attacking her, that would happen at night."

I hold up a hand against Phil's protest. "You're not half bad at this game, Phil. However, the next time you decide to play dress-up, I'd suggest changing your boots. They're very recognizable. Let's go sit down and chat, shall we?"

When he doesn't answer, Dalton and I pull off our outerwear and proceed into the living room.

Phil lowers himself to the sofa. "I don't see the point of this. Someone spotted a resident attempting to break into your old house, and that resident mistakenly identified my boots."

I sigh. "I just took off my stuff. Please don't make me go outside and find the fresh trail you made through the forest to my old house."

He goes still.

"It's winter," Dalton says. "You walked through snow and made a trail that we don't need Storm to follow. Now, if you need us to prove this, I'll go out myself while Casey warms up, but if I find that trail, you've just undone every iota of goodwill you might have built since you got here. Trust is —"

"Fine," Phil says. "It was me. I was curious about Maryanne, and I will admit I went about it the wrong way."

"Yeah, no," Dalton says. "You weren't sneaking in the back door to watch her while she sleeps."

"You weren't actually trying to break in at all," I say. "You knew that door would be locked. You stepped out from behind a tree right when Will passed by. You waited for him, so he'd see you try breaking in. You wanted us to think Maryanne was in danger. You want us to get her out of here before dawn. Why?"

I think I know the answer, but I'm still smarting from my mistake with the hostiles, and so I will hold back here.

"I . . . I just feel it's unsafe," Phil says. "Volatile elements and all that. It seems unwise. I wanted to alert you to the pos-

247

sibility of trouble."

Dalton leans back on the sofa. "Well, then, next time, just come and tell us. We're the local law. We'll decide whether there's a credible threat. I say there isn't, so Maryanne stays. In fact, I'm going to encourage her to stick around an extra day and night. Casey and I have a baby's family to locate, and Maryanne really should get more medical treatment —"

"No," Phil says. "I'm sorry, but we are not a rehabilitation facility. We can provide emergency aid, and of course we aren't going to send her into the wilderness without supplies, but she must go by dawn."

"Why don't we ask the council about that?" Dalton says. "Dawn is midmorning. We'll call them at nine and relay your concerns —"

"No, you can't . . ."

When Phil trails off, Dalton leans forward. "Can't what? Can't tell them that you spoke to us about this? You've dug yourself into a hole here, and you're still grasping at roots, trying to yank yourself out. But you're grabbing the ones that are going to snap and send you falling back into that hole with a busted leg. Slow down and think."

Phil does. Then his lips form an unspoken curse.

"Yeah," Dalton says. "You just advised us to get Maryanne out, and even if we do that, there's nothing to stop us from innocently mentioning it when we talk to the council next. Telling them that you insisted."

"The council didn't say they were fine with having Maryanne here, did they?" I say, finally working up the courage to voice the suspicions Dalton is obviously suggesting. "*They're* the threat, not random residents."

Phil's mouth opens. Then he thinks better of whatever he'd been about to say and withdraws.

I push on. "You dressed up and pretended to try breaking into Maryanne's place in hopes we'd worry and shuffle her out before . . . before what?"

He still doesn't speak. He's not denying it either, though.

"Oh, for fuck's sake," Dalton says. "Would charades help? You act out the situation, and we can guess what the problem is?"

Phil glowers . . . and says nothing.

"He wants us to guess," I say. "By now, Phil, you've realized that there are a lot of little moments during your stay here when you make a decision that sets your feet on a certain path. Like those old Choose Your Own Adventure books. Constant choices, and for some there's no turning back. This is one of those forks. If the council told you to do something about Maryanne, and you did, that would be your quicksand fate. There's no convincing us later that you were still on our side. Instead, you warned us. That's another of those paths, because if the council finds out, you've walked into more quicksand. Now you're into the smaller choices. They're subtler. They're you choosing where you're going to stand on that line between the two sides. If you decide to stop here, I understand."

Dalton grumbles under his breath.

I shoot him a look. "The main thing is that we've been warned. Of course we want more. But I understand the position you're in and the dangers of telling us more. I also hope that you understand, Phil, that by *not* telling us more, you leave us to imagine the worst. I do believe some elements of the council are working toward our common goal. But some of them are very clearly not."

He's quiet for another few moments. Then he says, "What if I don't necessarily agree? If I believe the council is indeed acting in Rockton's best interests, but that they overestimate the danger and . . . ."

He trails off, and we wait. When he speaks again, his tone is slow, measured. "Being in

Rockton, my vantage point has changed, yet I still try to balance the needs of the individuals with the needs of the whole. Ultimately, any choice must favor the whole — keeping Rockton safe and self-sufficient. However, living here, I think you two sometimes fail to see the larger picture."

"That if the town loses money, we shut down?" Dalton says. "Fuck no, we don't see that at all. That shit grows on trees, doesn't it?"

"Rockton isn't a nonprofit," I say. "No one expects that. We do think it should be a not-for-profit, though."

"This isn't the time for that discussion," Phil says. "My original point wasn't financial. By big picture, I mean security as well. We make choices to protect the whole. You both do, and the council does, and some of them are choices you'd rather not make. The difference is . . ."

Phil searches for something and then blurts, "Zombies."

I lift my brows.

He continues. "Let's say one person in your city becomes a zombie. There's a chance of treating her, but an even greater chance that she'll infect others and it'll spread. The obvious solution is to kill her. But what if this zombie is Casey? That will affect your decision. Likewise, living here, you can never be completely unbiased. Imagine you have a resident who is at high risk of going south and telling the world about Rockton. Imagine she's also a friend. If you fear the council might take drastic measures to stop her, will you inform them? What if you don't and she tells her story to the world, and Rockton ceases to exist? She lives and others don't because there's no Rockton to escape to?"

"Fine," Dalton says. "You're saying we might not be the best judge of threats because we live among the residents as individuals. Not arguing. But Maryanne isn't going to lose her mind, revert to being a hostile, and start murdering residents."

"Does the council know that? I *am* trusting your judgment, but I also see their point of view. They asked —" He takes a deep breath. "They *ordered* me to bring her to Dawson City. After you two left pursuing the baby's parents, I was to sedate her and enlist the help of residents who have a working relationship with the council."

"So the council planned to take Maryanne," I say. "And then what?"

"Get her appropriate medical and psychological treatment. I believe them when they say that. However, it's still removing her against her will. Also, I know you've taken an interest in the hostiles, Casey, and having lived here, I fully support any research that might eventually lead to the end of that particular threat. However, if I challenge the council, they'll recall me, fire me, and replace me."

"But you *want* to be recalled," I say.

"If I stay a year, I earn a quarter million on top of my salary. If I defy them, I might as well tell future employers that I spent the last eight years in Tibet with monks. That's lovely for personal growth, but on Bay Street, no one cares about your self-actualization."

He looks at us. "I'm never going to see the beauty of the north and fall in love. However, I am committed to Rockton for my own reasons. I can be an ally, but I need your protection in return."

"In other words, this meeting never happened," I say. "We get Maryanne out before dawn, so you can say we left with her before you could."

He shakes his head. "What you do with Maryanne is your own concern. However, come morning, you must report to me that she's left of her own accord, and you have no idea where she went. You cannot track her because you have a lead on the baby's parents, which is your priority." He pauses. "I trust that Tyrone Cypher's presence here means you have a lead?"

"We do."

"Then follow it."

TWENTY-FOUR

We veer past the place we gave Cypher for the night, in case we can talk to him now and save a step in the morning. But there are signs he's not alone. I stick a note under the door warning we'll return at six.

Back home, I update Anders while Dalton changes and feeds Abby. We set the alarm for five, which gives us four hours of sleep. Abby allows us almost that much, rising at four thirty, and I'll forgive her for that.

After breakfast, I take Abby so I can talk to Cypher while Dalton takes Storm to the storerooms, where he'll pack supplies for Maryanne.

When I rap on Cypher's door, it takes a while for it to open, and then Jen's there with her foot on the note.

"It's five in the fucking morning," she says.

"Five forty-five. And that note you're standing on says we'll be by at six, so I can come back in fifteen minutes if it makes a difference."

She lets out a string of profanity. I wait it out.

She glances at the bedroom. "You taking him?"

"Undetermined. However, I do need to give you this little one." I gesture at Abby, tucked under my jacket. "But, like I said, I can give you fifteen minutes."

She eyes that direction again, and I hear Cypher rising with a bleary, "Jennifer?" Then a few profanities of his own, in obvious disappointment at finding himself alone.

"Make it twenty," she says.

I leave just as Dalton passes with Storm. I tell him I'll swing by my old house and wake Maryanne.

Once she's up, I tell her there's some concern over the council's interest in her, and we're not overly worried, but it seems wise to head out before dawn. She decides on another shower as I make breakfast, and I ask if there's anything in particular she'd like us to pack, after I run through the list of what we have.

"I do have one request that you probably can't fill," she says. "I know you said there are books at the cave, and I see you're grabbing some more for me but . . . I don't suppose there are any reading glasses. I had laser surgery before I came to Rockton."

That's one of the prearrival suggestions, because we can't supply contacts or easily replace glasses.

"However," she says, "I've aged since then, and I've had trouble with my sewing lately. I tried a book last night, and I can manage it, but yes, evidently, I'm getting old."

"Considering the median age here is late thirties, reading glasses are a must," I say. "There's a stash of them in the library. I'll grab a few for you to try. Also, let me know if you want a specific type of fiction or nonfiction. If Eric grabs books, you'll end up with everything from historical romance to archaeology to biographies of obscure ancient warlords."

She smiles. "Not because he'll randomly grab a handful, but because he's read them all himself. I remember that. Especially the romance. One of the militia razzed him for reading one, and Eric said he was learning skills that guys obviously hadn't, considering he was always complaining about his three ex-wives." Her smile deepens. "Guess he did develop those relationship skills."

I return the smile. "He did indeed."

"Well, presuming you have historical romances and weren't just teasing me, I'll take some of those. Maybe fantasy, too. And mystery. Oh, and nonfiction, textbooks or whatever . . ." She waves a hand. "Honestly, you can do exactly what Eric would. Just get me a random selection of everything. I'll be like a kid in a candy store."

Despite his presumably good night, Cypher isn't any easier to deal with than he was yesterday. He does not want to tell us where to find Abby's mother, and Jen isn't helping. She hovers with the baby until she overhears the situation, and then it's "What kind of monster are you, Casey?" in far more profane language. And also "If you don't want the baby yourself, at least give her to someone who does," until I snap.

"Come on, kitten," Cypher says when I tell them off. "We're only trying to help."

"By accusing me of wanting to turn this baby over to a family who'll whore her out when she's twelve?"

"Jen didn't mean it like that."

"Yeah, actually, she did. You might want to get to know someone before you sleep with her, Ty. We're on a schedule here. I'll take Abby with us, and we'll see if we can track down Jacob and get his help finding this family. Because I will find them. I will evaluate the situation. If there is no way to resolve it, then I *will* keep this baby."

Both of them look over my shoulder. I turn to see Dalton standing there.

My cheeks heat. "I didn't mean — Obviously, I wouldn't decide on my own to . . ." I swallow. "I was only reassuring them that I wasn't trying to get rid of Abby."

Dalton glares at Cypher and Jen. "What the fuck?"

"Yes," Jen says. "We upset your princess."

"Hey," Cypher rumbles, turning a look on Jen. "I figured you were just sounding off. If you were really accusing Casey of wanting to get rid of this baby, maybe you oughta head on home, 'cause that's some world-class bullshit right there."

I expect Jen to tell him to go screw himself and storm off. Her mouth does set in a firm line. Then she says, still glowering, "Casey knows I didn't mean it. She's a bit sensitive."

"Yeah, I'd be sensitive too if you accused me of that." He turns to me. "I will take you to this trader family, kitten. I'm trying to make the situation easy for you, but that's not my place." He turns to Jen. "We'll be back before dinner. Can I ask you to join me? Or did I just blow my chances?"

Jen's eyes widen, as if she'd figured *she'd* blown *her* chances. Then she shrugs and says gruffly, "I guess so. Better be back by seven, though. I need to eat." She hesitates, considers. "If you're late, we can grab a drink."

"If I'm not late, then we'll do both. Now, you mind taking the tyke from Casey? I think we're best leaving her behind for now."

I agree. Unlike with the First Settlement, I will definitely want time to evaluate the situation before I hand Abby over.

We are gone before dawn . . . if not quite as early as we anticipated. As we're slipping into the forest, I swear I see Phil standing at his bedroom window, watching us with disapproval, as if we're teens who promised to leave the house quietly and did everything short of setting it on fire as we went.

I walk up ahead with Storm and Cypher. That gives Dalton time to talk to Maryanne. Cypher regales me with tales of life in the wilderness. He goes overboard being entertaining, as if that's an apology for earlier.

Usually Jen's insults slide past, but sometimes they cut a little too close to truth. I'm not trying to get rid of Abby, but I'm susceptible to the charge because I want to believe Jen's right — that the proper and humane thing to do is keep Abby here and give her the kind of life every child deserves.

But isn't that what Gene Dalton thought when he saw Eric? *That child deserves better . . . and I can provide it.* Classic white-savior syndrome. I see this child who comes from a place I deem less "civilized," and I will save her, and the world will throw laurels around my neck for my selflessness.

Pimping your child goes way beyond "less civilized." Few people would say, in that situation, that I should mind my own business. But if I don't confirm the situation, how different am I from Gene Dalton? Yet if I do evaluate, where do I draw my line? That I will return her if her mother agrees to come to Rockton? That I will return her if they promise — cross their fingers, hope to die — never to prostitute her?

It's not as if I haven't considered this. The problem is that I can't stop considering it. My brain is a gerbil in a wheel, squeaking endlessly and getting nowhere. Having Jen act as if I'm blithely going to hand Abby off is like slamming a sliver deeper into a festering infection.

As we walk, I watch Storm explore and let Cypher's tall tales clear my mind. Then we near Brent's . . . and my mood stumbles as I realize I'm going to a place where I lost a dear friend, where I held his hand as he died.

Dalton catches up then. He gives Maryanne's supply pack to Cypher with, "You can carry it uphill." He leans in to whisper to Cypher. "Maryanne's getting tired. She won't say it, so tell her you need a rest. Casey and I will go in first."

Cypher heads back to Maryanne as Dalton and I carry on. After a few steps, I glance over my shoulder.

"Maryanne's fine," Dalton says. "I just figured we might want to go up alone."

I squeeze his hand. "Thank you."

His hand moves around my waist. "You doing okay?" He pauses. "That's a rhetorical question — I know you're not okay, and I know you'll tell me you are. Not sure why I bother asking."

I lean my head against his shoulder. "I'll be fine. It's tough coming up here, but it's amazing that we have this place for Maryanne. I like knowing Brent's cave and his things will help someone."

"Yeah, I was thinking that, too. I also meant, though, that this morning's bullshit is bugging you. But I get the feeling you don't want to hash that through with me."

"I didn't mean —"

He bumps my shoulder. "It's fine. I get it. We're stuck in a loop we can't escape until we have additional information, which we'll get soon, I hope."

"Yes." I move behind him as we start the ascent. "Also, about earlier, when you walked in on me with Jen and Cypher."

He chokes on a laugh.

I slug him in the ass. "Not like . . . Damn it, don't put that in my head."

"I didn't say a word."

I grumble under my breath. "You knew what I meant. But what you heard me say, that I'd take Abby myself, I wasn't making a statement. I wouldn't do that without talking to you."

"I know. You were just telling Jen that she's full of shit. Which, personally, I think we should tattoo on her forehead."

"True. But I know it sounded bad, when that isn't something we've discussed."

He shrugs. "It is, though. I said the baby ball is in your court."

"I'd rather it wasn't. If it comes to that, I'd like us to discuss it. I honestly don't know what I want. I'm not considering the options because I don't want that to influence my decision about giving her back."

"We need more information."

"We do. So let's get Maryanne settled, and then we'll go get it."

TWENTY-FIVE

Maryanne is thrilled with her new lodgings. It's a cave. Literally a cave, and not the kind we see in depictions of Neolithic humans, some massive cavern that opens on ground level. This is up a mountainside, where we need to crawl through an opening that Storm no longer fits. From there, we climb down into a cavern the size of a small room. There's an even smaller one for sleeping. The main room has a natural chimney, which is what made Brent choose the spot.

It's the sort of place I'd consider a wonderful weekend adventure. A truly unique experience. But, well, it's a cave. There's a limit to how comfortable and well-appointed it can be. For Maryanne, though, it's ten times better than where she's lived for the past decade. So we settle her in and leave her happy.

We put on our snowshoes after that. Cypher wore his own homemade ones on the way to Rockton, so all three of us are outfitted. He's as proficient as Dalton and finds much amusement in me toddling after them like a two-year-old.

Cypher knows where the trading family winter camps. When the weather turns bad, they switch from traveling salespeople to pop-up store.

It is not an easy walk. I've always kept myself in good shape — it helps combat the muscle aches of my old injuries. I have never, though, been as physically fit as I've become up here. Amazing what an outdoorsman lover, an energetic dog, and a lack of couch-suitable entertainment will do for your fitness level. Yet despite all that, by the time we near the spot, I'm ready to collapse. Fortunately for my ego, Cypher is the first to say, "Now *this* is a workout," as he starts lagging behind with me, huffing and peeling off his parka.

Storm feels it, too, giving me her are-we-there-yet look. I don't suggest a rest. We'll barely make it by midday, and we already got a brief rest at Brent's. We stop to give Storm water breaks — and take long pulls at our own canteens — but nothing more.

"You don't feel this at all, do you?" I say as I move up beside Dalton.

"Feel what?" he says.

At my scowl, he grins and says, "Nah, I feel it, and I'll feel it a helluva lot more tomorrow."

"You'll be wishing you installed that hot tub," I say.

He laughs. "Fuck, yeah."

Last year, a group of residents had written a request for a hot tub. It had been posted, along with Dalton's creatively profane response. Then, a couple of months ago, we went to the hot springs outside Whitehorse, and Dalton discovered the appeal, particularly after a long day of winter work. Curious, I'd gone online and found a radio clip about a guy with a hot tub who lived off-the-grid in the Yukon wilderness. His was modeled after a hot spring — a big barrel of hot water, rather than the modern Jacuzzi-style tub with jets. So, while I may have said earlier that I wanted gift ideas from Dalton, I was totally lying. Kenny's working on a hot tub for our backyard. If other residents want one, they can commission their own. This one's ours.

Cypher tramps up to tell us we're getting close. We'd guessed that from the faint smell of smoke. When I crane my neck, I see it spiraling up a few hundred feet away.

"You'll stay back here with your pup, kitten," Cypher says.

My back must rise at that, because he lifts a hand. "Let me and Eric make the approach. Eric can put his scarf on and pull up his hood, and we'll let them think it's Jakey. They don't have much trade with him. Bad blood."

I arch my brows. "You're going to let them think Eric is the guy they don't like?"

"The bad blood is on Jacob's side. They thought he'd make a fine son-in-law, so they kept bugging him to take a freebie, and when he didn't, they sent one of the girls to follow him and climb into his sleeping blankets. From what I hear, he didn't just refuse nicely. Got himself into a right temper over it, which isn't like our Jakey at all."

True — Dalton is the brother with the temper — but I can imagine how that would have set Jacob off. After their parents died, Jacob had been on his own. As a teenager, he'd had an encounter where he'd been taken captive and sexually assaulted. Dalton doesn't know that. I'm not sure anyone does besides myself and maybe Nicole. If someone crawled into Jacob's bed after he'd made his refusal clear, he would not respond with a gentle rejection. I don't blame him.

Cypher continues. "Jacob stays away as much as he can. I haven't seen them myself much since I've opened trade with Rockton. They're a nasty bunch. Not fit to raise dogs much less . . ." He trails off and shoots me a sheepish look. "Sorry."

"I've gotten the message loud and clear," I say.

"And she doesn't need it on constant repeat," Dalton adds. "Casey's going to need to talk to these people herself. We both want to evaluate the situation."

"I understand that," Cypher says. "But if all three of us tramp in there, we'll put them on the defensive. Especially once they realize you two are from Rockton. I can pull a little sleight of hand with you, Eric. When they find out you aren't Jakey, they'll be pissy, but I am not responsible for a misunderstanding. With Casey, though, you could only pretend she's Edwin's granddaughter, and believe me, that'd be worse."

The plan seems overly complicated and makes me wonder exactly what we're dealing with here. But if it is a delicate situation, Cypher is right that all three of us shouldn't go marching in. There's also an advantage to having me and Storm hang back where we can come to their aid in case of trouble.

They continue on, and I take Storm off the path. I know not to wander far, but that rising smoke is an easy landmark. In a small clearing that's been intentionally clear-cut, I take off my snowshoes and perch on a tree trunk. I expect Storm to drop at my feet in exhaustion, but she sits, looking up at me. Looking up . . . looking down . . . looking up.

"Fine," I say with a sigh, toss my pack down and then drop onto the ground.

Storm grunts in satisfaction and curls up with me. From puppyhood, we taught her that she can't sit on laps and sofas and beds, and we'd congratulated ourselves on our forethought. While it was difficult to keep her on the floor when she was a tiny bundle of fur who only wanted to cuddle, we knew that one day she'd take up the entire sofa. The problem is that, to indulge her need for puppy cuddles, we'd get down on the ground with her. Perfectly reasonable . . . except that she came to expect that, and while she'll curl up at our feet, if she's tired and cold, she wants us to cuddle with her . . . on the snow-covered ground.

We curl up together, resting and snacking on venison jerky. I listen for trouble from the direction of the camp, but the murmured voices stay low and calm.

Once Storm has had her cuddles and her food and water, she's ready to play. I pick up a stick and say, "I am not chasing this. Just so you know."

She dances in place. I throw it. She hesitates, looking my way, then chuffs a look of disappointment at my old-lady frailties before taking off after the stick. We do that a couple of times, but it's clear I'm being judged, so I switch to hide-and-seek. This is one of her favorite games. She sits, looking the other way, while I run a twisting trail before hiding downwind.

I make this one as tricky as I can. I hop on a couple of stumps and leap off them to interrupt the trail. I even climb a tree and slip into the branches of another. When I finally hide, I pick a spot behind a bush where some small beast has crawled under and died, masking my scent. I crouch behind it, mitts over my nose, hoping Storm appreciates this.

Peering through the bush, I watch her untangle my trail. My stump jump doesn't stump *her* at all. The tree leap does, but only for a moment before she's tearing through the snow following my trail and —

Metal glints in the midday sun. I'm not even sure what I see — some instinct processes the sight before my brain fully comprehends, and I charge from my hiding spot with a "No!" as I race toward Storm.

As I do, I see the long barrel of a rifle pointing through the trees. Pointing at my dog.

I slam into Storm's side, and we skid across the snow, me sprawled over her. There is no shot. Just a grunt of surprise, and then footsteps approaching and a man's voice saying, "What the hell is that?"

I lift my head. As I do, I see his face and . . . There is still a gut instinct women have, an inner alert system that says, "Do not go home with this charming guy you met in a bar." One glance at the man with the gun makes me decide I will not tell him who I am. Maybe it's the set of his thin lips. Maybe it's a glitter in his dark eyes. Maybe it's merely a sixth sense that says beware.

"It's . . . it's a dog," I stammer, pitching my voice low. "My dog."

I stay on the ground, over Storm, my face turned down just enough to let my hood shadow my face.

The man tilts his head. "Where'd you come from, boy?"

I mentally nod in satisfaction as he makes the mistake I hoped he would when I changed my voice. I remembered the first time I met Cypher, when he mistook me for a boy. It's easy to do, with my size and build, especially if I'm wrapped in my winter wear.

Cypher also mistook me for Indigenous. I

could roll my eyes at that, but it happened even down south. I am a racial puzzle that strangers want to solve, even when I'd rather they looked at me and only saw a person.

"I'm with my dad, trapping." I lift my chin a little. "I have a right to be here. My mother's family is Tr'ondëk Hwëch'in."

His snort suggests he isn't the type to respect territorial rights.

"Get up, boy."

When I hesitate, he points the gun and growls, "I said get up. This ain't your land. Hasn't been in five hundred years, so don't pull that shit on me. You know who this land belongs to? Whoever has these." He taps his gun. "So get on up and let me see that so-called dog of yours."

I rise slowly, my hand on Storm's collar. I pat her head and murmur words of reassurance.

"That's a dog, huh?" he says, eyeing Storm.

"Yes, sir."

"Never seen one like that."

I shrug. "Dad got her for me in Dawson. He didn't know how big she'd get."

He eyes Storm. "Good for pulling sleds, I bet."

I laugh softly. "No, sir, she's no sled dog. No hunter either. Dad calls her a waste of good food, especially in the winter, but I hunt for her, so he lets me keep her."

His hand snatches my jaw. I don't see it coming until his icy fingers clamp on my chin. Storm growls, but I twist her collar, a warning for silence.

"I need to get back to my dad, sir," I say, as calmly as I can.

"Do you?" He turns my face. "You're a pretty boy, aren't you? Pretty little half-breed."

My eyes narrow at the slur, and he laughs. "Got some fire, huh?" He strokes my cheek with his callused thumb. "Such soft skin. Makes me wonder . . ."

He yanks down my hood. My hand flies up to stop him, but again he moves too fast. Then he grins, and there is no humor in that grin, no lasciviousness either. There's something deeper, hungrier, uglier. His hand vise-grips my chin, fingers digging in.

"Look at this," he says with a low whistle. His other hand rakes through my ponytail hard enough to pull out hair along with my elastic. I still don't fight. I just breathe through my mouth, keeping my temper down so I don't alarm Storm.

"Not a boy after all," he says.

He reaches for my parka zipper. I beat him to it, yanking it down as I glower up.

"Sorry to disappoint," I say as his gaze moves to my breasts, nearly invisible under my double layers.

"Nothing wrong with that," he says. "You might not be a boy, but some men like to close their eyes and pretend." He winks. "Not my style, but I don't judge. And I can see the appeal of a woman who can pass for younger, if you know what I mean."

My stomach churns at that. I've only unzipped my parka to my waist, so he can't see my shoulder holster, but the weight of the gun reassures me.

"I'm going to take my dog and go now," I say.

He throws back his head and laughs. "You really do have some spark. What part of this conversation made you think leaving was an option?"

"I would suggest you might want it to be," I say.

He reaches for me. I see that one coming, but it's too dangerous to fight. He grabs my hair. His fist wraps in it, and he throws me to the ground.

Storm lunges. I'm still gripping her collar, and she yanks me up as she lunges for the man, snarling. He raises his rifle.

"Get your dog under control, girl," he says.

I pull her to me and stay down, sitting on the ground. Storm positions herself over me.

"I said get your damned dog under —"

"What you have got there, Owen?" a woman's voice says.

TWENTY-SIX

I twist as a figure emerges from the trees. She's wrapped tight in a parka, hood pulled up, bulky boots on her feet. In her hands, she holds another rifle. When she turns to me, I see a face even harder than the man's.

She pulls down her hood to get a better look at me. She's younger than me, maybe mid-twenties. Blond hair. Wide-set blue eyes. High cheekbones. A mouth that looks like it should be pouting in some sultry ad for fifty-dollar lipstick. Pretty, in a chilly Nordic way.

I glance at the man, having not paid close attention to what he looks like until now. He's closer to my age, dark-haired, sporting a solid build with a scar cutting across his nose.

As she approaches, he gestures at me, grinning like a child showing off newfound treasure.

"Huh," the woman says. Her gaze is as

coldly assessing as his. "Where'd she come from?"

"She says she's with trappers, but I ain't seen no trappers. I think she's all by her lonesome. Just her and that thing." He motions to Storm. "She claims it's a dog."

"Huh," the woman says again. She turns that assessing look on Storm and then back to me.

"You think she'll fetch much?" the man says.

I shrug. "Not really. She expects *you* to fetch *with* her."

The man snorts a laugh.

"I don't get it," the woman says, in a low tone that warns me she doesn't appreciate being excluded. She doesn't know what playing fetch is, meaning she's from these woods, like Dalton. The man is not.

"You're asking how much you can get for me," I say. "Thank you for your interest, but I'm not for sale. Now, I'm going to take my dog —"

The woman swings behind me, lightning fast. My hand clenches, itching to feel the gun in my hand, but I've missed my chance to do that easily. As my heart picks up speed, Storm growls. I pet her and murmur that it's all right, even if I'm no longer sure it is.

"How do you feel about getting yourself a husband, girl?" the man says.

"I've got one. Also, I'm not a girl. I'm older than either of you."

"She's got a smart mouth, doesn't she?" the man says. "That'll bring the value down."

The woman snorts. "Did it bring *my* value down, Owen?"

He grins at her. "That's a different story."

"It's just a matter of finding the right buyer. Like with any goods, you turn the flaws into assets. You're not going to sell that mound of fur to someone who wants a hunting dog. And you're not going to sell this girl to a man who wants a quiet little mouse. Well, unless you cut out her tongue. Which is always an option."

I want to say they're trying to spook me. That's what Dalton and I would do, the sort of repartee that, afterward, we'd laugh about and say "Can you believe they actually took us seriously?" That could be what's happening here. They'll talk about selling me like a side of venison, and then, when they demand my coat and my snowshoes and whatever else I have of value, I'll gladly hand them over, scamper off into the woods, and consider myself lucky.

And yet . . .

Those words aren't directed at me. They pass right over my head to her partner, said in the same way she might suggest cutting my hair.

Cold nestles in my gut. I knew the man was trouble. Manageable trouble, though, like an asshole who might hassle me in the city. The woman is the bigger threat, and I realize I should have pulled my gun earlier.

Pull my gun when she was nearby? When she was close enough to run in and shoot me?

No, trying to end it sooner might very well have made it worse.

Storm keeps growling. The woman says to her partner, "Take the dog."

"And shoot it?" he says.

"If you need to," she says. "Otherwise, someone will want it, if only as dinner."

My hands wrap tight in Storm's fur. "She's fine. I can control her."

"You keep thinking you've got options here," the man says. "Like this is a business negotiation. Now hand over that dog —"

"Why not make it a business transaction?" I say. "Wouldn't that be easier? Yes, you have me dead to rights, but I'm going to be trouble. You see that already. So let's negotiate. I accept my capture. You find a . . ."

I'm struggling to say "buyer," but my lips

won't form the word. "A man who wants me. I play the scared mouse, and you get your money, and then . . . Well, then it's up to me. If he relaxes his guard, I can escape, and you've still made your money. You didn't sell false goods. He just failed to protect his purchase. You keep the money. I get the chance to escape. I'm willing to take that risk, if we can do this in a civil manner."

Owen's lips curve in a slow smile, his eyes glinting in a way that is no longer mercenary interest. "Clever girl. What do you think, Cherise?" He must be addressing his partner, but his gaze never rises from me. "I do believe we have some room to negotiate."

Storm wrenches from my hand. I'd loosened my grip, relaxing as I talked, and now she rips free and I spin, to stop her from going after Owen. But it isn't Owen she's leaping at. Cherise is raising her rifle . . . straight at me.

Storm slams into Cherise just as I hit the ground. I roll up and grab the barrel. As I do, the gun fires and I glance over at Owen because I do not forget he's holding a gun of his own. But he has it lowered, and he's leaning back, watching with amusement.

Cherise struggles with Storm, who's snapping and snarling. Not biting, though.

Never biting. The sheer weight of her is enough to put Cherise on the ground.

Cherise's hand drops to a pocket on her thigh. I grab her wrist, pin it, yank out the knife, and throw it as far as I can. Then my hand goes to Cherise's throat, as I take Storm's place.

I glance over at Owen. I'm awkwardly positioned, with him behind me. He could attack, and I'd never see it coming. Yet he's still leaning against a tree, not the least bit concerned that his partner is pinned. When he catches my eye, he winks and my stomach clenches.

I've made a mistake here. A very dangerous one. I *did* think I was being clever, offering a solution that would make them relax their guard so I could escape. But in doing so, I've sparked Owen's interest . . . and could have earned a bullet from Cherise.

I should feel shocked and sickened. Instead, rage washes over me. White-hot, all-consuming rage.

I slide the gun from under my jacket, keeping it close to my body so Owen won't see. When Cherise spots it, her eyes only narrow and meet mine in defiance.

I jam the barrel under her throat. "You didn't like my offer? Then say so. You don't need to be a bitch about it."

I'm speaking low, my words only for her, but Owen hears and his laugh rings out behind us.

"Cherise didn't like your offer because she's the clever one here," he says. "And no one takes that away from her."

"No," Cherise says, her teeth gritted. "I didn't like her offer because you were fool enough to consider it, Owen. A pretty girl shows a bit of spirit and intelligence, and you fall over yourself."

"So you were jealous? That's new. I like it."

" 'Cause you're a fucking idiot. I don't give a shit if you want to screw her. I do give a shit if your dick stops your brain from working. She wasn't going to negotiate with us. She was just buying time and keeping you from hurting her damned dog. Now, since you haven't noticed, she's got a —"

My free hand chops down on her throat, cutting her off in a strangled gurgle. I wrap my hand tight around her throat and twist toward Owen, my gun swinging on him. His eyes widen. Then he laughs. Throws back his head and laughs.

"Gun on the ground!" a voice snarls as someone crashes through the forest. "Fucking gun on the fucking ground, now!"

I do not for one second think the new-comer is talking to me. I recognize the voice, the words, even the crashing of brush.

Storm lets out a bark and races to meet Dalton.

"Back to Casey," he says after a pat on the head, and she returns to me, tossing Cherise a growl for good measure.

"Jacob?" Cherise says, and it's clear from her voice that she's trying to come up with another explanation. This man might look like Jacob, but he certainly doesn't sound like him.

"Nah," Owen says. "This is his big bro. Hey, Eric, long time."

"Not long enough," Dalton mutters. "You remember the position, Owen? I put you in it often enough. I'm sure you must remember."

"Fuck you." Spots of color touch Owen's cheeks. "This isn't Rockton."

"Yeah, it's not. But I still have the gun, and you're still a fucking idiot."

Cherise lets out a cackling laugh at that, but Dalton ignores her, his attention on Owen.

"On your hands and feet," Dalton says. "Ass in the air. I know you remember it."

"Eric?" I murmur. His gaze shoots my way, and I subtly shake my head. I've already made an enemy here in Cherise, and I don't want to make the situation worse by humiliating Owen in front of her. Dalton's gaze goes from Owen to Cherise, and he grunts, and I know he understands.

"Just put the rifle on the ground," Dalton says.

Owen does. Dalton walks over and picks it up.

"Hers is over there," I say, gesturing. Dalton nods and collects it.

Then he looks at me. "You okay?"

I don't answer, but he must see something on my face and his goes rock hard.

"What happened?" he says.

"I was playing hide-and-seek with Storm," I say. "These two are the ones who found me."

"And . . ."

I shrug. "They said something about selling me as a wilderness wife, blah, blah, blah."

A laugh sounds. It's not Dalton, who — despite my light tone — looks ready to spit bullets. Cypher strolls from the forest.

"That's your own fault, kitten," he says. "You are such a sweet and docile little thing. Can't blame them for thinking you're in need of a big, strong husband. They were just taking care of you."

"Evidently," I say.

I rise off Cherise, keeping one eye on her in case she attacks. Dalton walks over and lowers his lips to my ear. "You okay?"

"I will be," I murmur as softly as I can. "But I'd like to ease out of this."

He nods. There's nothing to be gained by getting into a pissing match with these two.

Dalton kisses the top of my head and tugs my hood back up.

"Are you shitting me?" Owen says. "The cowboy? Really?" He shakes his head. "You can do so much better, girl."

"Girl?" Dalton's brows shoot up. "She's a woman, and her name is Casey."

Owen ignores him. "What the hell do you see in Deputy Dawg here?"

Now my brows are rising, as I say, "Deputy?"

"Owen left Rockton right before my father retired."

"Eric's the sheriff now," Cypher says. "Casey here is a homicide detective. Or is that homicidal detective?"

"Depends on the situation," I say, smiling my thanks at him for continuing to lighten the mood.

"You're . . . a detective?" Owen says. "Like, a cop detective?"

"That's usually what 'homicide detective'

285

means," Cypher says. "You picked this boy for his looks, didn't you, Cherise?"

Cherise doesn't reply. She hasn't spoken, and in that silence, I feel her assessing, evaluating, and I suppress a shudder. A keen intelligence always catches my attention, but this isn't the kind that promises a challenging game of Scrabble. This promises a knife through your back when you least expect it.

Owen says, "I thought cops had laws about height and whatnot. She's such a tiny thing."

"And yet she had you and Cherise at her mercy, both of you armed, too. Size isn't everything. I'm sure Cherise tells you that all the time."

Owen only throws off the insult with a laugh. He's *not* the bright one. Nor is he particularly dangerous, much slower to take offense than his partner. I don't want to be alone with Owen, but he isn't the type to pull a knife over what's obviously just ribbing between men.

Cypher continues, "If we're done chitchatting and waving guns and trying to sell human beings, I'd suggest we go back to camp. We were just chatting with your family, Cherise. I think you'll want to be part of the conversation."

Family?

Oh, shit.

This pair didn't just happen to stumble on me close to the traders' camp. If I hadn't jumped to that conclusion sooner, it's because when I thought of this family's poor daughters forced to prostitute themselves, I had *not* pictured the woman standing in front of me.

At first, I only deliver a mental kick in the ass for my preconceptions. Then it sinks in.

These two people — this *couple* — are part of the trading family we've come to see about Abby.

I look from Cherise to Owen, and my insides freeze.

No. Please, no.

The same thoughts connect in Dalton's mind. His eyes widen, just a little. Then they harden to cold steel, and when he looks at me, his jaw is set so tight every muscle stands rigid.

I want to tell him we can stop here. Cypher's right. Jen's right, too, God help me. We need to retreat and forget this madness, and keep Abby, because if these two are her parents . . . ?

My breath comes fast and hard, and I swallow. Then I squeeze my eyes shut and push down the panic. Nothing will change if I stick around for a definitive answer. It'll just save me from second-guessing later.

Cherise and Owen never need to know we found a baby — possibly *their* baby. I don't care if that isn't my decision to make. I will make it.

As we head out, Dalton falls in beside me, leans to my ear, and says, "Yes," and my eyes mist. I squeeze his hand. "Thank you."

"No question," he murmurs. "No question at all."

TWENTY-SEVEN

We enter the traders' camp. It's more of an encampment. I'm not sure if there's actually a difference between the terms, but to me, a camp is a small and temporary arrangement. An encampment is bigger and more permanent.

They have three tents plus two igloo-like snow structures. There are sled dogs, too, which confuses Storm, who's never seen so many canines in one place. She sticks close to us, like a child hiding behind her parents on the first day of kindergarten. I let her stay there. The dogs seem friendly enough, but unless we're told she can visit, it's unwise to presume. And we aren't told anything of the sort.

Near the fire sits two young women and a man in his fifties. I don't see the matriarch, and when I look around, Cypher says, "The girls lost their ma about six months ago. We were just talking about that when Eric heard the shot and took off like one."

"I'm sorry for your loss," I say to the man.

The patriarch — I haven't been given names — shrugs and says, "Cancer. It got bad, and she decided she was done."

I hope I don't blink at that. I can't tell if he's saying she committed suicide or they helped her. I've known people who died of cancer, and I cannot imagine what it'd be like out here, with no access to doctors or painkillers. What shocks me is the way he says it, so matter-of-fact. It's like saying one of the sled dogs had to be put down . . . and not even a favorite dog at that.

None of the three daughters give any other reaction. They just wait for us to get on with the conversation. Or so it seems until I notice the youngest daughter's eyes glistening. When Cherise shoots her a sneer, the girl blinks fast and straightens. They are very clearly sisters. All blond and pretty with a similar look — tall and thin and a little bit distant.

If I'd peg Cherise at mid-twenties, I'd put the middle sister a few years younger and the youngest at maybe nineteen. When the youngest glances Cypher's way, there's trepidation and anxiety in the look. I remember what he'd said about one of the girls asking him to take her. Those looks say she's worried that he might say something and get her in trouble.

As I'm thinking this, the middle girl says to Dalton, "I knew you weren't Jacob."

Dalton turns to her. "Never said I was."

"You're nothing like him," she says. "He's . . ." She wrinkles her nose. "Skittish. Weak. I don't know how he survives out here."

"I would suggest that you don't know my brother very well. And you don't know *me* at all."

She smiles. "We could fix that."

"I'm married," he says.

She shrugs. "I don't care."

"His wife might," Cypher says. "You can ask her. She's sitting right there."

The middle sister's gaze trips over me, and she shrugs again. Then she turns to Dalton. "Offer stands." She smiles at me. "Unless you have a problem with that."

"Don't worry, Leila," Cherise purrs. "His wife is just as helpless as she seems. She'll be fine with it."

Leila's brow furrows as Owen laughs, and she scowls at him. "What's so funny?"

"Not a damn thing." He waves at Dalton. "Go for it. Please."

"It's not Casey you need to worry about," Dalton drawls. "If I'm stupid enough to

291

fuck up what I have with her, that's my problem. And I'm neither stupid nor remotely interested."

"So you say, in front of her."

"I'll say it behind her back, too. You come sneaking into *my* bed, and you'll find my brother really *is* the nice one."

Cherise and Owen laugh and the girls' father joins in. Even the youngest smiles, though she tries to hide it.

Family? Hell, no. This is a pit of vipers.

"Are we done with this bullshit?" Cypher says. "These two need to get back to Rockton, and we have trading to do. First, though, I think Casey was hoping to see the baby."

My gaze shoots to him. He pretends not to notice.

"Baby?" Cherise says.

"The new family addition. I heard one of you girls is a momma, and Casey was hoping for the chance to bounce a baby on her knee." He looks around. "You hiding the little tyke?"

The family's expressions . . . I hesitate, worried that I'm seeing what I want to see. But there isn't a single look of comprehension among them. The youngest sister frowns, as if she's misheard. The father scowls, as if Cypher is making some kind of joke. Cherise peers at Cypher, as if there's some hidden meaning to his words. Owen and Leila just look confused.

"Baby . . ." Cherise says carefully.

"Right. You know, miniature human. Demanding little critters that expect everyone to wait on them hand and foot. Are you the proud new momma?"

Cherise looks nothing short of horrified, and I restrain a shuddering sigh of relief.

"There's no baby here," the father snaps. "You think we're fool enough to have one in winter?"

"Or fool enough to have one at all," Leila says.

"I'd like a baby someday," the youngest says, her voice soft. "But not now."

I want to drop the matter here. See? There's been a terrible mistake, and these are not the parents. Yet I hear the father's words and wonder what would happen if one of the girls did give birth in winter. Edwin mentioned abandonment. That's what people used to do, whether it was a baby or an infirm relative, when winter came with no extra rations to sustain the weak.

If that is the case, then I need to know that I can stop searching. *Fine, you abandoned your baby, and now we have it and may*

293

proceed with whatever option we choose.
However, if Abby's mother is still out there,
I need to keep looking.

I'm struggling for a way to get a definitive
answer when Cypher says, "See, that's what
I was wondering. I told Casey and Eric that
if you folks did have a winter baby, you
might be willing to part with it. But since
you don't . . ."

When I realize what he's saying, I flinch.
The words have barely left his mouth before
Cherise pounces.

"You want a baby?" she says to me.

"We're not —" I begin.

"If you had one, she might be willing to
pay," Cypher says. "But since you don't —"

"We can fix that," she says. "Make us an
offer, and me and Owen will consider giving you a baby."

"Unless the problem is the cowboy,"
Owen says. "Which I'm sure it is. In that
case, I can fix it for you." He winks at me,
and I tense, my gaze shooting to Cherise.
But she only says, "For a *price* he will. I'm
not giving you free access to my man."

"Unless the problem's yours," Leila says,
"in which case, I'll help. For the right price,
of course."

"Jesus," Cypher mutters. "You want to get
in here, Missy? Offer to rent out your baby-

making body parts, too?"

The youngest shakes her head, her gaze lowered, and I shoot Cypher a look to back off her. He frowns, as if genuinely baffled.

"We aren't in the market for a baby," I say. "Ty's beating around the bush here, and I appreciate his discretion, but it's leading to a serious misunderstanding. We found a baby. A little boy, left in the woods. He seems to have been abandoned, but we want to be absolutely certain there isn't a family frantically looking for him before we send him down south for adoption."

Leila's mouth opens, and I know she's about to claim that, whoops, yes, she totally forgot about that baby she left in the forest. Cherise beats her to it with a more measured, "All right. It is . . . possible that we had a winter-born child. If we didn't say so, it's because we don't need your judgment. You have no concept of a life where horrible choices must be made."

"Like leaving a baby to die of cold?" Dalton says. "Or be ripped apart by predators? Instead of just suffocating him mercifully? Also . . ." A pointed glance around their well-stocked camp, complete with storage facilities. "I can tell you folks are hard up for supplies. I have no idea how you'll get through the winter."

Cherise glares at him. "Don't presume to understand our choices. I thought I had suffocated the child, but clearly, I was too distraught to do it properly."

Dalton's mouth opens, and I know he's going to tell her to cut the crap, but a look from me stops him. I must admit, I'm impressed by Cherise's performance. But dragging this out isn't going to help anyone.

"So you bore a son?" I say.

I'm sure I say it with complete calm, and certainly the others don't react. But by now, I've realized their father is patriarch in name only. I sense that the real power lies in a nearby grave, her position taken over by Cherise, who sees the trap in my words.

"Did you say son?" she says carefully. "A boy?"

She's gauging my reaction as carefully as I'm gauging hers, like prizefighters in the ring trying to anticipate the next blow and react accordingly.

I could gamble here. I don't need to, though. I shrug and say, "Okay, you got me. It's a girl."

She leans back. "Of course it is. I know my own child."

I take my backpack, dump the water from my canteen and hold it out. "I'll need proof."

Her face screws up.

"Proof that she's yours," I say. "Proof that you're a nursing mother."

Leila bursts out laughing. Cherise swings on her so fast, the next thing I see is blood in the snow and then Leila cupping her nose. She didn't make a sound, only glares at Cherise before dropping her eyes in submission. Cherise's gaze turns on Missy. I expect the youngest to look away fast, but she holds her sister's gaze with a level, open stare. Not challenging her, but not backing down either. Cherise snorts, and it's an animal sound, the alpha accepting that no threat is forthcoming and leaving the younger one be.

"That's enough, girls," their father says, and it is the voice of every parent who doesn't want to seem as if he's lost control of his children. The girls ignore him — they're already settling in after their scuffle.

"So the baby isn't from here," I say. "That's all I wanted to know. However, if you have any idea who she does belong to, and you're correct, we'll pay for that information."

"Two hundred dollars' worth of goods," Dalton says. "Tell us what you want, and I'll get it in Dawson or Whitehorse."

The patriarch's eyes glitter. "Alcohol.

That's liquid gold out here, especially this time of year."

"We'll take *some* alcohol," Cherise says. "Among other things. And we want a thousand dollars' worth."

"First you need to get us the information," Dalton says. "Then we need to confirm it. Then you can choose between two hundred dollars from your shopping list or four hundred from ours."

"Five hundred."

Dalton looks at me. He's not verifying the amount. With my bank account, that's pocket change. He's seeing if I have any restrictions or limitations to add.

I pet Storm and casually say, "We have a doctor in town who will examine the mother, to be sure she gave birth at the time the baby was born." Of course, there's no way to be quite that specific, but these aren't medical professionals.

I continue. "So if someone claims to be the mother in hopes of getting a reward, it'll be a waste of everyone's time. The mother must come to Rockton for the child."

In other words, I don't want this family taking the mother captive and then calling us to deliver the cash.

I add, "And if the child was abandoned,

we're fine with that. We won't judge the mother's choice, and we will make sure the baby goes to a good home."

"How much will you get for that?" Cherise says.

"Paid adoptions are illegal in Canada."

She snorts. "Their laws are not our laws. If you sell the baby —"

"We won't," Dalton says. "We may keep it or we may find a suitable home, but no cash will exchange hands. People aren't trade goods."

She rolls her eyes at our ridiculous scruples. This is a woman who was sold herself, from a very young age, probably — as I realize now — by her own mother. That practice hasn't stopped since their mother died. Cherise certainly was ready to see what she could get for me. I would like to say I can't wrap my head around that — how could you be sold yourself and then do the same to others? The truth is much more complex. Just ask anyone who was abused as a child and does the same to their own offspring.

As we finish the negotiations — which is mostly closing any loopholes for Cherise to exploit — we're preparing to leave when the father says, "I'm glad we reached an agreement here. I've always said that trade relations are important."

Dalton slowly turns but says nothing, waiting for what we both know is coming.

"We'd be a valuable trade partner for Rockton," the man says.

He means that we'd be valuable to them. I see Dalton getting ready to make some sarcastic comment, but then he tightens his jaw and slides a look my way, tossing this grenade to me.

"That's an interesting proposition," I say. "If this goes well, we could discuss it." I take off my pack and open it. "We don't have a lot of need for trade supplies in Rockton, but there's always an interest in craftsmanship. We'd love work like this."

I pull out the piece I'd cut from the dead woman's jacket. I'm not eager to open trade with this family, but if I were to hazard a guess on the artisan, I'd point at Missy. If she can create items that Rockton considers valuable, it might help her position here.

But when I show the piece, I get only blank expressions. Then Cherise says, "I don't have time for pretty sewing, but Missy might be able to do something like that."

Missy nods. "They say I do fine work, with my tanning and my crafting." She takes off her coat and passes it to me. It is indeed excellent, and I say so, but when I ask if she

300

does anything decorative, she considers and then says, "Those we trade with are looking for practical pieces. Long lasting and warm and pleasant to wear — soft furs and smooth leathers. They aren't interested in work such as that, so I haven't tried it, but I could, if you left that with me."

I say I will, though I assure her that Rockton is interested in general craftsmanship, too, and while a little decoration would be appreciated, what she's already doing would also be valuable. Far more so than the meat or hides her family would otherwise provide.

"As for this work . . ." I lift the piece, and I'm ready to ask if they recognize the workmanship, but Cypher catches my eye and I stop before linking it to the baby. We'll deal with this family if that's our only way of finding Abby's mother, but I shouldn't provide clues to set them on her trail.

I cut the piece in two and leave half with Missy, and we say our goodbyes. Storm and I walk in front, the guys behind, all of us quiet. Once we're far enough from the encampment, Cypher says, "That piece you were showing. You didn't just happen to be carrying that in your pack, did you?"

"It's from the dead woman. Edwin identified it as that family's work, and he said one of the girls was pregnant, so it all lined up."

"He lied," Dalton mutters. "Lied and sent us on a wild-goose chase."

"I think he was hoping to send us into a dead end," I say. "Tell us what we needed to conclude it was the baby of a family who shouldn't be raising one. We'd decide to keep Abby. Everyone's happy. Well, you know, except the actual *mother*." I shake my head. "Sure, I get that he thinks we'd make good parents, but what about *her*?"

"He lied because he knows where that comes from," Cypher says. "And he doesn't want you and Eric going there." He glances at Dalton. "It's from the Second Settlement."

Twenty-Eight

There are two major settlements out here, both originating from Rockton. The first and, yes, the second. No reason to get fancy with names. The first is an actual settlement. It's been in the same place since Edwin led a group from Rockton. The second is more nomadic. They build semi-permanent residences, which they abandon when the food supply shifts. They'll also move if they feel at all threatened by trappers, miners, settlers, or hostiles. The Second Settlement does minimal outside trading, and that's a two-way street of paranoia. They don't like mingling with others, and others don't like mingling with them. Secretive and eccentric. That's what I'd call them. As for Cypher's opinion:

"Batshit fucking crazy," he says as we walk. "You were telling me you think the hostiles are some kind of cult. If they are, they might have come from the Second

303

Settlement, 'cause those fuckers *are* a cult. Except they aren't the kind that recruits in shopping malls. Their doors are closed."

"But you know them?" I say.

"Once upon a time, I was an exception to the rule. And the rule itself wasn't so much a rule as a general guideline. While they didn't throw open their doors to traders, they did business with a very select number of settlers. They picked me because I was sheriff when a group of them left Rockton. I let them go and sold the council a line of bullshit about how hard I looked for them. So, when I left Rockton, they invited me to trade. But then, about five years back, they had a change in leadership, and the doors swung shut."

"Why did Edwin lie?" I say. "If they don't trade, he can't be worried about us opening a line of exchange with them."

"You know Edwin," Cypher says. "He's a crafty old bastard. He's hedging his bets here, protecting what's his. The Second Settlement doesn't hold a grudge against Rockton. If you go sniffing around . . . ?"

He shrugs. "You and Eric make a good team. That's why Edwin's reopened that connection. He might talk shit about Eric, but he trusts him. Eric's a strong leader. Tough and fair. He can be a pain in the ass to deal with, but you're not. You're the diplomat. If Edwin's opened that door for you two, the Second Settlement might, too. Edwin doesn't want that. Also, the old man's got a nasty streak. Giving you their baby would warm the cockles of his heart all winter."

I'm not sure that last part's true. Edwin might really have presumed the winter-born baby had been abandoned. It's still a shitty thing to do.

"So where do we find them?" I ask.

Dalton jerks his chin east. "That way, almost a full day's walk. Yeah, I keep tabs on them. Never talked to them. I was raised not to. They made my birth parents nervous, so we steered clear. Gene Dalton wanted nothing to do with either settlement and advised me to do the same. But I always know where to find them. They've been over there for the last few years."

"So back to town for the snowmobiles?" I ask.

Dalton shakes his head. "There aren't any trails out there. We gotta walk. Which means going back to town and gearing up for a full-on camping trip."

"Why don't I head on back to Rockton and you kids overnight at my place," Cypher says. "It's a helluva lot closer than Rockton.

If you strike out from there in the morning, you'll reach the Second Settlement by afternoon. You'll need to grab a tent to overnight on the way back, but I've got one and plenty of blankets. Take what you need from my supplies." He smiles. "That gives me permission to take what I need from yours."

Cypher leaves for Rockton, and by nightfall we're made it to his winter cabin. It used to be owned by a settler named Silas Cox. Come winter, Cypher would rent a sleeping bag in the corner. Then Cox fell victim to the local cougar, and Cypher took over the lease. When spring arrives, he'll be on the move, following game and trading, like Jacob. In winter, though, everyone wants a place to hunker down, and this is Cypher's.

Since taking possession, he's made repairs. Cox had been the kind of guy who builds a half-assed structure and stays until it rots. Cypher has filled cracks between the logs, fixed the roof, and added a sturdy food-storage compartment around back. When we get inside, we find as cozy a cabin as you could want. It's only about ten by fifteen feet, but out here, extra room means extra heating. The interior has a fireplace, an underfloor icebox, a low bed, and a table with one chair.

Before we split from Cypher, he'd asked us to check his snares. Trapping is his preferred hunting method — he doesn't use guns and has never mastered a bow. We leave Storm inside with some dried meat and head out in the dark, flashlights in hand. The snares haven't been checked in two days, and we find two snowshoe hares, a marten, and a mink. Dalton skins the marten and mink for Cypher. The meat is only eaten late in a cold, hard winter, and we presume Cypher won't want it, so we cook it up for Storm. What she doesn't eat, I'll dry in strips overnight in the fireplace and we'll take it with us for her.

I cook one of the hares for our dinner. We don't eat anything else with it. Cypher isn't a gardener, and 90 percent of his food stores are meat, so we won't raid his meager supply of dried greens, berries, nuts, and roots. We have a half dozen chocolate-peanut-butter protein bars in our packs and split one for dessert.

We're in bed by eight. That's what can happen when night falls by late afternoon, and you haven't slept more than a few hours in days. We don't sleep, though. No sex either. It's been a long and unsettling day, and even after we crawl into bed, we don't talk about it right away. We've let Storm stay in the cabin — there's plenty of room.

I curl up with Dalton, my cheek resting on his bare chest, listening to his slow breathing. Feeling the tension, too, strumming through him, and waiting for him to speak.

"What happened today . . ." he says finally. "With Owen and Cherise . . ."

"Trying to sell me?" I say, my voice light. He's on his back, and I roll on top of him, my arms crossed on his chest. "Owen came out first, and I had that situation under control, so I tried to defuse it rather than fight. I didn't expect Cherise."

I purse my lips. "Pretty sure no one expects Cherise. She is a piece of work. But I still wasn't in danger of being carted off like a side of venison. I was trying to keep things cool until . . ."

I remember, and I shiver. I don't mean to. I can't help it. Under me, Dalton goes rigid.

"What happened?" he says.

"Cherise happened," I say, again keeping my voice light. "I got a bit of a scare, but . . ."

I want to fluff it off. But after a moment, I say, "We'll need to keep an eye on her. She's smart as hell, and twice as vicious."

He nods. Says nothing, his nod tight as he

holds in whatever he's thinking, whatever he wants to say.

"Eric?" I say.

"I'm concerned about Owen," he says. "That's not underestimating Cherise. She's a fucking cobra. She's smart, though, like you said, so I get the sense she can be managed. Very, very carefully managed. With any luck, she'll decide she doesn't want to lose Rockton as a prospective trade partner. But Owen . . ."

He exhales, breath hissing through his teeth. "The way he was looking at you . . ." Dalton makes a face. "I don't mean I'm jealous. None of that territorial bullshit. Men notice you. They pay attention. You don't pay attention back. If anyone tries anything, you take care of it — you don't need me to protect you. But Owen . . . Fuck."

"You know him."

"Yeah."

"What was he in Rockton for?"

Another exhale. "That's what I want to talk to you about. If I'm hesitating, it's just . . ." He waves his hands, gesturing, and I start to roll off, but he holds my hips. "It's the usual bullshit, this part of me that wants to smooth it over, pretend it's not that bad, so I don't scare you off. I wouldn't

309

do that. You need to know. I just . . ."

Another helpless wave. "You were in the forest, playing with our dog, and a couple of psychos threatened to kidnap and *sell* you. That's fucking nuts, and it's just another day out here, and it shouldn't be. Biggest thing you should need to worry about is the wildlife. But no, it's the crazy people who want to kill you or, now apparently, sell you."

I laugh. I can't help it. It starts as a snicker, and then I'm sputtering, choking on laughter.

"It's not funny, Casey," he says.

"Oh, but it has to be, doesn't it? Otherwise, *we'll* become the crazy people." I settle in and look down at him. "We're in the Yukon wilderness. There are people here for this lifestyle, like you and me and most settlers. But there are also people with a certain level of eccentricity and, yes, crazy, who come here *because* of that. They're here to escape the norms and rules of life down south. That can be a positive thing — they want something less rigid and more natural. Or their disregard for the rules of law is the *reason* they're happier here, where they can do whatever they want. That's going to mean, overall, a high quotient of . . ."

310

"Batshit crazy, as Ty said?"

"In every possible way, the good and the bad. It's a world of extremes. It's like walking down a city street and winnowing out all the average people, the people who are happy enough going about their lives. The people who don't yearn for more, yearn for change, yearn for *different*. That's who we have here, long-term. The dissatisfied and the dreamers and the doers and, unfortunately, the dangerous — those who want to box up their superego and let their id run free. You get that down south, too. It's not as if people like Petra and Sebastian and Cherise and Mathias are some new species I never knew existed. I've met variations on all of them before. There's just a significantly higher concentration here."

"Yeah."

"As for Owen . . ." I prompt.

Dalton sighs and reaches for his canteen, taking a slug and then offering me some, which I accept.

"Owen came to Rockton five years ago. I was deputy, and it was a little more than a year before Gene retired. Owen and I are about the same age, and that caused problems. He saw me as competition."

Dalton rolls his eyes. "By that time, I'd had my bad experience with a woman, so he was welcome to them. It's not like he'd have had a problem anyway. When he showed up, they paid attention. He screwed around a bit, and then he set his sights on Isabel, which I couldn't figure out."

I sputter a laugh. "Don't let her hear you say that."

"Nah, she said it herself. I don't mean any insult. But she was fifteen years older, and he had his pick of women, and it wasn't as if he knew her well enough to fall for her. He acted like a new stallion in a herd of mares, making his way through them, and when he came to Isabel, he figured he'd have a go and then move on. I mean, *obviously* she'd be all over that, right?"

"She wasn't, was she?"

"Hell, no. Isabel might have an eye for younger men, but she's never been hard up for attention, and she's a helluva lot pickier than 'young and good-looking.' When Isabel rejected him, she figured he'd sweep up his wounded pride and stalk off. He didn't. The more she said no, the more he wanted her. Pretty soon, she complained to Gene."

"How'd that go?"

He shifts and makes a face. "I said this was shortly after my 'bad experience.' "

I know what he's talking about. When Dalton was young, he had plenty of women

312

happy to introduce him to the joys of sex. He'd been in his late teens, and they'd been five to ten years older, so everyone knew it was just fun. Then he reached his early twenties and relationships became a possibility. He wasn't interested, and if the women were, he stepped away. Then he hit the one who didn't give up so easily.

"It wasn't even one of my usual casual-but-committed relationships," he continues. "We hooked up a couple of times, and she hinted at wanting more. Seeing the warning signs, I backed out, as gently as I could."

"She didn't take 'no' for an answer."

He nods. "At first, it was like she was just trying to change my mind. But then . . . I'd come home, and she'd be in my kitchen, making dinner in her underwear. I'd be sleeping, and she'd slip into my bed. Hell, she walked into my *shower* once. Fucking scared the life out of me. First time I ever locked my doors."

"Shit."

"Yeah. It was bad. If another woman even talked to me, she'd get in their face, and it wasn't like I was trying to pick anyone up. We're talking conversations with women. Normal conversations."

"What'd you do?"

"Tried to handle it myself. When I

313

couldn't, I asked other guys for advice. They laughed. Told me I should take advantage. So I went to Gene. He didn't laugh, but he didn't see the problem either. Even my mother wasn't much better. She felt sorry for the woman, who'd obviously fallen hard for me, and said I should be more understanding. Maybe I should give her another chance. This woman is fucking up my life because she wants me back . . . so I should give in? Because, fuck yeah, that's the kind of woman I want." He shakes his head, and in his eyes, there's old hurt, old pain, old anger.

"That's bullshit," I say.

"Yep, but it happens to women all the time, doesn't it? That's what I realized. Gene was telling me that this woman wasn't a threat, wasn't actually *hurting* anyone — including me. She just liked me a lot, as if . . ." He waves his hands. "As if that's my fault, because I'm so irresistible."

I smile. "I think you are. But yes, it's bullshit, and yes, women hear that all the time. *He just likes you. You should give him a chance.*"

"Exactly. I pulled my head out of my ass and realized that when women came to us with the same problem, we didn't do jack shit. If it wasn't assault, then it was just a

314

guy trying to get sex."

"Boys will be boys."

"Right. And this is my very long way of explaining what happened with Owen and Isabel. Iz came to Gene with her complaint. Gene told her to be firmer with her refusals."

I snort a laugh.

"Yeah," Dalton says. "No one is firmer with her refusals than Isabel. So I tried to handle Owen and made an even bigger enemy in the process. I also realized this wasn't some guy being atypically aggressive with a woman. He had a past. He must. So I started digging. It was the first time I'd done that."

"And?"

"First, I checked his reason for being here. As deputy, I didn't have access to that, but I knew where to get it. I discovered that he'd come here after an attempt on his life. He'd had a fling with a married woman, and the husband went after Owen, who narrowly escaped. The man vowed to finish the job. So Owen came to Rockton."

"Uh-huh. Not exactly how it happened, is it?"

"No, and Gene should have looked at Isabel's complaint and at least wondered if there was more to Owen's story. He didn't.

So I did some research when I went to Dawson. Turned out there was no fling, but not for lack of trying on Owen's part. He was stalking this woman, and her husband went after him because the police wouldn't. I also dug up his name as the defendant in a rape case. What they used to call date rape."

"He wanted sex, and the women didn't, so he took it."

"I'm not even sure if he asked. It was a college thing. A frat party. She said he put something in her drink. He denied it and said the sex was consensual. It never went to court. She dropped the case and dropped out of college, claiming harassment from Owen and his buddies."

"I wish I could say I've never heard that story before."

"Yeah, so the fact this asshole has turned his eye on you has me worried. Just because Cherise has the upper hand in the relationship doesn't mean Owen is harmless."

"Thank you for telling me."

"I'd never *not* tell you. As much as I hate making this place any scarier than it is."

I hug him, and he pulls me into his arms as we curl up for sleep.

TWENTY-NINE

We're asleep, and I'm dreaming of Abby. Dreaming that she's lost in the woods, and I hear her crying, and I can't find her. I'm running through the forest, bottle in hand, thinking she's hungry and I need to feed her. I'm following her cries . . . and then she stops. Just stops.

I startle awake. Storm whines, and I realize she was already up. She's still lying on the floor beside me, but she has her head raised, and she's whining deep in her throat. She smells or hears something.

The cabin is silent and nearly dark, with just enough moonlight streaming in for me to see the outline of Storm's massive head. She glances my way, and I catch the gleam of her eyes. Another whine, sharper now. She rises with the huff of propelling her big body off the floor. Her nose nudges me, and I run my hand over her head as I listen for what woke her.

A whisper of movement. That's what I catch. The soft sound of a foot in snow. Then another. A noise follows. A grunt? I think of bears, but even if one woke from hibernation, the sounds are too soft for that. They're too *careful* for that. Something is outside, and it is staying as quiet as it can.

A bump startles me. It's a soft thud. Someone bracing against the wall? Trying to peer in a window?

I glance at Dalton, but he's sound asleep. If I rouse him, however gently, he'll startle awake with enough noise to scare off who-ever is out there.

We're several hours' walk from Cherise's camp, and I can't imagine she'd have let Owen follow us. But they may have tracked us after sundown.

Another bump against the wall, and I peer at the window. Storm whines again. She's rigid, staring at that wall, her tail sweeping the floor. It's not a happy wag. It's cautious, uncertain.

I slide out of bed and keep bent over beneath window level. I tug on jeans, a sweatshirt that turns out to be Dalton's, and my parka. Then I retrieve my gun.

I glance at the bed again, in hopes my moving around has brought Dalton closer to waking, but he's still dead to the world.

I head for the door. Storm follows, nails clicking. I back up and tell her to stay, adding reassuring pats. She is not reassured. When I pull on my boots, her butt bobs off the floor.

I consider. When Owen and Cherise first caught me, I'd wished Storm hadn't been there. She was a weakness they could use against me. Yet she may have saved my life. It's like Dalton with me. He'd love to tuck me away in a safe spot when danger strikes, but he knows I belong at his side, where we can look after each other. I need to start thinking the same with Storm. We trained her for work, and I have to let her do it, not play overprotective mom and tuck her away.

I give the release sign, and when she comes over, I tell her to stay close and stay quiet. As I ease open the door, she's right beside me.

We slip outside, and I pull the door shut behind us. There's a flashlight in my pocket, but I keep it there for now. I have my gun in hand instead, as I look over the snow-covered field. It's a three-quarter moon on a cloudless night, and the light reflects off the snow, lifting the glade to soft daylight.

I adjust my gun and glance at Storm. Her nose works madly, but she's still processing the danger, not ready to commit to a decision.

We start along the wall, toward the spot where I'd heard the thumps. The squeak and crunch of snow announces our approach, and there's little I can do about that except keep my gun trained and my ears tuned for the sound of flight. Nothing comes.

I reach the corner and duck before peering around with my face at a height any intruder won't expect. There's no one in sight.

I ease around the side and check the back, in case the person ducked there. Nothing.

Backing up, I look at the snow. It's trampled in a path from Cypher walking to his storage shed. I don't see any other trail.

I bend to examine the prints. They all look to be from the same set of boots, which suggests they're Cypher's, but even as a prank he'd never sneak around a cabin with two armed cops sleeping inside. I'm still bent when I see smaller prints leading from the forest and back again, and I'm leaning in for a closer look when Storm growls. I turn to find myself looking at a pale figure poised at the forest's edge.

I'm on eye level with it, and our gazes lock. I tighten my grip on the gun and rise as slowly as I can, while giving Storm the signal to stay where she is. She does, but she's growling, her hackles raised. The intruder isn't watching me now. He's looking straight at her. He takes a step our way. Then another.

Storm feints, obeying the order to stay while surging forward in warning. He stops, tilts his head, considers, and then cannot resist another careful step.

It's the lone wolf from the other day.

He's paying me no attention. I'm not the one he's here for, not the one he's curious about. He takes another step as he watches Storm. She makes a noise that starts as a growl, then switches to a whine before ending with a growl. She is curious, too, as she was with the sled dogs. Curious yet wary. She is no longer the pup who tore after a young cougar. She bears the scar from that encounter, and it has carved a path in her neural network, straight to her memories, as my scars do to mine.

I lower my hand to pet her head as I murmur reassurances. The wolf is as tall as Storm, but she's significantly heavier, all thick muscle to his wiry frame. Between her size and my gun, she is safe. If she becomes distressed, we'll withdraw into the cabin. But it is safe to satisfy her curiosity.

When I pet her, she is indeed reassured,

and she relaxes. Both the whines and the growls subside, and she eyes the wolf, taking his measure. Then she puffs up in a way that makes me smile. She pulls herself straight and tall, displaying her full size. Her tail stays high, indicating welcome but not submission. Her head lifts, and her ears relax. If she is nervous, she doesn't show it. She has assessed the wolf, declared him to be a lesser beast, and stands before him as a haughty queen, giving him permission to approach.

With Raoul, Storm is the "alpha." She's bigger and older, and so she is in charge. This wolf looks like a larger version of her pack mate, and so she will not bow to him.

The wolf continues his slow approach. When he's within a couple of feet, he stops and the silence is broken by two canines sniffing the air madly. Then he stretches his muzzle, and their noses touch. As adorable as it is, I'm tensed for trouble, the mom assessing another child, still not convinced he doesn't pose a danger to her baby.

While I have my gun, I'm also ready with my foot. I do not want to shoot a wolf for a show of dominance. I've dealt with enough stray dogs to know that a well-placed kick will allow us to retreat into the cabin.

The wolf circles Storm, sniffing her. I

instruct her to stay standing. Her head turns, though, following his progress. When he reaches her rear, he sticks his nose under her tail, and she jumps. He backs up only a second before returning, determinedly sniffing her there as he begins to whine and quake with obvious excitement. That's when I realize why this wolf has conquered his fear of humans to make his way here.

"Oh," I say, the word coming on a laugh.

They both startle.

"Sorry," I murmur.

The wolf tries sniffing under Storm's tail again, but she keeps it firmly down, and I have to chuckle at that. I also give her the release word. I'm not going to make her stand there, suffering the unwanted interest of this wolf.

She turns to sniff him. He keeps trying for her tail, but she shoulders him aside and huffs. I tense. He accepts her annoyance, though, and lets her sniff him. Greetings over, she hunkers down, an invitation to play. He races around her, and she spins, ready to give chase, but he's only trying to get behind her again.

Storm snaps and growls, and she issues the play invitation again. He seems to accept . . . and then swings behind and tries to mount her. I don't need to intercede.

Storm yanks away, grabs him by the foreleg and throws him down with a growl that very clearly says there will be none of that.

Two more invitations to play only result in two more aborted mountings. Finally she huffs her disgust at me, and I have to laugh.

"I know," I say. "You want to be friends, and he's just looking to get laid. Some guys, huh?"

It's clear that the wolf really is only interested in one thing, and he's not getting it — Storm won't let him, and I wouldn't either. She retreats behind me, and I shoo him off with a "Hie! Hie!" as I lunge in his direction.

As the wolf flees into the night, the cabin door bangs open and I hear, "Shit! Casey!"

I look around the corner to see Dalton, staring at the retreating wolf.

"Uh . . ." I say. "Did you forget something?"

He looks down.

"Yep, clothing for one thing. Please get back inside before you lose any body parts I'd really rather you kept. I was, however, referring to . . ."

I lift my gun. "What were you going to do? Punch the wolf in the nose?"

He blinks, obviously still waking up. Then he says, "Wouldn't be the first time. The

324

last one was a feral dog, though."

"Back inside," I say.

Storm and I follow Dalton. He's shivering, not surprisingly.

"Was that the same wolf?" he says.

"Yep, remember how we were talking earlier about unwanted advances and guys who don't take no for an answer? It seems Storm has a suitor."

He blinks, still bleary-eyed. "What?"

"She must be coming into estrus," I say. "I haven't seen signs, but she's old enough, and that wolf picked up a scent that said, if his advances weren't accepted right now, they might be soon."

"Shit."

"Yep. I know when we took her for her annual shots, the vet mentioned spaying, and we hadn't made a decision on that. We're going to need to."

I crouch and hug Storm, running my hands over her as she trembles in lingering excitement from the encounter.

As I pet her, I say, "Down south, spaying would be a no-brainer. No one needs more dogs. Here, though? I don't know. There could be some advantage to breeding her once. If we do want more working dogs in Rockton, we know she has good genes. On the other hand, we don't want every wolf and feral dog volunteering as puppy daddies."

"Is there some way to control her cycles?"

"Doggie birth control? I have no idea. More research for our next trip to Dawson." I give her one last pat as I stand. "At least one of us might be able to have babies, huh?"

I say it lightly, but I feel Dalton's gaze on me.

"I was kidding," I say.

"Kidding . . . and not kidding." He checks his watch. "It's after five, so I think we're up for good. If I put on the kettle for coffee, can we talk about this?"

I shrug. "Nothing to talk about, really. Yes, it's on my mind lately, for obvious reasons, but talking is just treading the same ground over and over. It doesn't get me anywhere."

He fixes me with that look, trying to extract from my brain the answers I'm not giving. Then he puts the blackened kettle directly on the fire.

"You need to teach Ty how to set that up properly," I say.

"Guy drinks instant coffee with powdered creamer. I don't think he cares whether he's heating the water right."

He backs from the fire and pulls on his sweatpants. He's still adjusting them, not looking at me, when he says, "You had so much other shit to deal with after the beating. Just getting up and around again. Then getting your strength back. Getting on the police force. All the things they said you couldn't do, and you did. This other thing was . . ."

He struggles for words. "It's an injury to a muscle you weren't sure you'd ever want to use. Except it's more than just a muscle that doesn't work. It's something they took from you, on top of all the rest, something you can't fix through sheer determination and hard work."

Tears roll down my cheeks. I don't even realize it until he reaches for me. He has put into words everything I've been feeling these last few days, and it's as if I've said them myself, but better, because I didn't have to.

Fourteen years ago, four men beat me and left me for dead. They took my mobility, leaving me with a leg injury that doctors said meant I'd never run again. They left me with scars — physical and psychological — that people said meant I'd never become a cop. They took my pride, too, and my dignity and my self-confidence.

But I triumphed because I fought back in the way that really counted. I *can* run. I *am* a cop. And while there's still psychological damage, in regaining my mobility and achieving my career goal, I won back my pride and my dignity and my self-confidence. Wherever those four thugs are now, I have a better life than they do. I'm sure of it. So I won.

Except now, as Dalton says, there's this one thing they took that I cannot regain. It didn't matter before because I never saw myself as a mother. I had an all-consuming career and no interest in long-term relationships. Being with Dalton changed both those things and nudged that old scab. Then came Abby, and seeing Dalton with her and feeling my own reaction to her has ripped that scab clear off, and it hurts. It hurts so much.

Tied up in that pain is rage. Those men *did* take something from me, something I cannot get back, and here is this life choice that I'm not even sure I want, but I should damned well have that option. I don't, and it is their fault.

I say all this to Dalton. The kettle boils and it boils, and I'm still talking, the words rushing out. Finally, there's nothing more to say, and I take the kettle and pour the coffees, brushing him off when he tries to help. I measure in the creamer with such care you'd think it was powdered gold. Then I stir, slowly and deliberately, giving myself time to recover.

"There are options," he says. "If that's what you want."

"I'm not sure it is. I have no idea right now, and no time to sit and think about it. There's no point either. If we don't find Abby's family, then she's one option, and I'd do that before I'd even try carrying a baby to term myself. If we do find her family, then I need to figure out whether what I'm feeling is just a surge of maternal instinct. Then you and I need to talk about it, either way, and . . ."

I wave my hands. "Part of me wants to consider options, and another part says that's like deciding which university to send your kid to before she's even born."

Dalton settles onto the bed with his coffee and motions for me to sit beside him. I do, and Storm moves to lie across our feet.

"So," Dalton says. "You know that the council has threatened to kick me out of Rockton. Even when they don't say it, I feel the weight of that hammer over my head. This woman, who is very smart, once told me that the best way to cope with that is to figure out a game plan. What I'd do if it happened."

"I never said it was the *best* way. Just one way."

He waves off the distinction. "The point is that my brain works like hers does. We need solid footing. I need to know that if I get kicked out, I have a plan. So I'm going to suggest that she needs the same thing. A plan for what we'd do if we ever decide we want one of those wrinkly things that screams for us to feed her and screams for us to change her shitty diaper and won't let us sleep more than three hours at a stretch."

"You make it sound so enticing."

"I know. But in spite of their unbelievably selfish behavior, I will admit that I do see an appeal to babies that I never did before. Which is not to say that I want one. If we don't find Abby's parents, then I would seriously consider it and lean toward yes. Otherwise, I'd back up to just seriously considering it, for some point in the future."

"Agreed."

"So, let's jump past Abby and jump past the soul-searching and decide on a plan of action, should the answer be yes, we want kids. How would we do that?"

I exhale. "Okay. Well, the problem, according to the doctors, isn't whether I could get pregnant but whether I could carry to term. I would try, but it's not like taking endless shots on a basketball net, waiting to sink one. Trying and failing would be . . ."

"Traumatic."

When I make a face, he shakes his head and says, "My mom — my birth mother — lost a couple of pregnancies after Jacob, and I might have been young, but I remember it was really hard on them. So that's an option, but with a limited number of trials."

I nod.

"And if those trials put you in danger, would I have the right to say stop?" he asks.

"You would."

"Good. Next option."

I go quiet for a moment. Then I say, "Adoption is the most obvious. Maybe even the best to start with, but it's not easy getting a baby. Even if we could . . ."

"You'd prefer your own. Our biological child."

I'm about to shake my head. Then I pause to consider it more. "All other things being equal, yes, I suppose I would, as selfish as that is. But I'd take another baby in a heartbeat. Having our biological child isn't that important. It's just . . ."

I squirm, and his arm slides around my waist.

I continue, "I would worry that, given your situation, even if you felt okay with

331

adoption, you might have misgivings later. What if it's a very young mother who later regretted her decision? What if the child grew up wanting answers, wanting his or her biological family? That's probably natural at some point, but I think it would be . . . difficult for you."

He opens his mouth, and I can tell he's ready to deny it. Then he pauses, like me, to consider before he says, "I would like to think I'd be fine. I do see your point, though, and it wouldn't be fair to a kid if I brought my baggage into parenthood. However, if adoption is the best option, I'd be fine. I'd make sure I was."

"The other is surrogacy," I say.

He frowns, and I explain.

"So, we rent a womb?" he says.

I sputter a laugh. "It's a little more complicated, but yes, that's the basic idea."

"Okay," he says, nodding. "So that's the plan, then, if we ever reach that stage. Try ourselves, and if that doesn't work or it endangers you, then option two is surrogacy. Option three is adoption." He looks at me. "Does that help?"

"It feels a little silly, coming up with a course of action for something we may never want, but . . ."

"It's never silly if it makes you feel better."

I lean over to kiss him. "It does. Thank you."

THIRTY

We set off after a world-class breakfast of
instant coffee, protein bars, and venison
jerky. Then we walk all morning in snowshoes, carrying provisions on our backs,
stopping only to dine on . . . water, half a
protein bar, and a slab of venison jerky. I
can grumble about the menu, but by lunch,
I'm like a starving cartoon character, spotting shy Arctic hares and seeing only their
plump bodies roasting on a spit.

Off again, and it's midafternoon before
Dalton slows to examine landmarks, like
reaching the right neighborhood and slowing the car to read street signs. Storm
whines, and we go still, listening. When we
hear the crunch of snow he calls, "Hello!"

The footsteps stop.

"I'm letting you know we're here," Dalton
says. "We're armed, and we have a dog.
That's not a threat — again, just letting you
know so we don't give you a scare. We're

restraining the dog and lowering our weapons. We'd like to speak to you, please."

Silence.

Dalton grunts, as if to say he hoped it'd be that easy but knew better. Still, he tries again with, "My name is Eric Dalton. I know the Second Settlement is out here, and we found something in the forest that we're told might belong to you. We only want to return it."

More silence. Dalton grumbles now, but I catch the faintest whisper of fabric. I touch Dalton's arm and direct his attention left, where a figure stands in shadow, watching us as cautiously as any wild beast. It's a young man, late teens, maybe twenty. He carries a bow, but it's lowered, and he's just watching, reminding me of that wolf the day before.

"Hello." I resist the urge to say we come in peace, though I doubt this young man would get the reference. "We just need to speak to someone from the Second Settlement. My name's Casey. This is Eric."

He keeps watching us with wary curiosity.

"And this is Storm," I say, nodding down. "She's a dog, not a bear." I smile. "She gets that mistake a lot."

No reaction.

"I'm holding her by the collar," I say.

335

"She's big, but she's friendly, if you want to come closer."

He doesn't move.

"May we speak to you from there?" I ask.

When he stays silent, I'm beginning to wonder if he understands English. Then he says, "Yes."

"Before we do," Dalton drawls, "I'd appreciate knowing if we need to watch for anyone jumping at our backs. I'm sure you aren't out here alone."

Silence, and even from here, I swear I see the boy considering.

Finally he says, "The others are close. They'll come if I call them."

"Fair enough," Dalton says.

"I'm going to remove my pack," I say. "I'm getting something out that I want to show you."

I take the remaining piece of Ellen's parka from my bag and hold it out. "We're told this was made by someone in the Second Settlement."

He squints. Then he eases forward, until he's about five feet away. He reaches out, and I pass him the material. He peers at it and then shakes his head as he returns it.

"It's not ours."

"You sure?" Dalton asks.

The young man's eyes flash. "I know the

336

work of my people. I don't know what you've found, but if that was what led you to think it is ours, then someone has made a mistake. Or someone is trying to cause trouble for us. We don't want the kind of trouble that comes with you."

"Me?" Dalton says. "Who am I?"

"It's not who you are. It's where you're from." His gaze travels meaningfully over Dalton's clothing. "Rockton. My people separated from yours, and we ask only to be left alone."

"And you're not missing anything?" I ask. "Missing any*one*?"

"No, we are not."

"You sure?" Dalton says again.

He gets that same flash of annoyance, stronger now. "If we were missing a person, I'd be out here hunting for him."

"Maybe you are," Dalton says.

"Then I'd be more interested when you said you found something of ours, wouldn't I? We have no quarrel with Rockton. If we had someone missing, we'd be grateful for your help. If we found one of yours, we would return him."

Despite those flashing eyes, the young man keeps his voice calm. He's well-spoken. Polite. I get a distinctly different vibe from him than I do from the First Settlement.

There's no challenge here. We're just two groups occupying the same region, and this one would rather keep those lines of separation clear. Like an introvert neighbor who thinks it's very nice that you're throwing a BBQ and hopes it goes well, but doesn't want to attend, and would politely request that you stop asking.

"You have any idea where this came from?" Dalton says, pointing at the fabric.

"No, and if I did, I would tell you."

"All right. We'll keep looking then."

The young man nods and withdraws without another word.

We watch him go. Then Dalton says, "You buy that?"

"He seems sincere, but Ty was certain he knew where it came from. That kid really doesn't want us getting closer to their settlement. I'm not ready to drop this on his say-so."

"Agreed."

We follow the young man at a distance. According to Dalton, he's heading toward the settlement. Moving quickly, too.

We start closing the gap between us. It's better to catch up with him on the outskirts, where it's too late to blow us off again, yet it's clear we aren't trying to ambush his settlement. I spot smoke rising over the trees ahead when Dalton grasps my arm. His hand drops to his gun, and I pull mine.

Dalton pivots. "Step out. There's a gun trained on each of you."

His gaze flicks in the other direction, and I turn that way, my gun rising.

Silence.

"Look," Dalton says. "I don't want to pull this shit. We're walking to your village. We talked to a kid from it, but we need more information, and he didn't seem the right person to give it. We appreciate your caution, but our guns do a helluva lot more damage than your bows, and they work a helluva lot faster. Also, you're making our dog nervous."

As if on cue, Storm growls.

"Just step out please," Dalton says. "Then we'll all lower our weapons and talk."

No answer.

"Fuck," Dalton grumbles. He turns to me and says, loud enough for them to hear, "Don't you just get tired of this shit?"

"I do."

"Do people pull this crap down south?"

"No, but we have cell phones. We can call before we show up."

"Well, that's what we need. Cell phones. Can we get a few of those?"

"Sure. First, you need a cell tower."

"Fuck."

"Or we could do it the old-fashioned way," I say. "Ring their doorbell."

"Hell, yeah." He raises his voice more. "You guys got a doorbell? No? How's this?" He raps his knuckles on the nearest tree. "Sheriff Eric Dalton, of Rockton, calling with my wife, Detective Casey Butler, also of Rockton. May we come in?"

A man appears from Dalton's direction, shaking his head. "I suppose you're trying to be funny," he says, no rancor in his voice.

"Yeah," Dalton says. "I make a better asshole than a comedian, but I'm trying a new tactic."

The man's lips quirk as he walks over. "Might want to keep working at it, but I appreciate the effort."

He's in his mid-forties, a tall, rangy man with weathered skin. He's dark-haired and round-faced, and his countenance reminds me of the young man's. A relative, I'd guess.

The other man comes into view but stops short as he sees me. "Tomas?"

"Yes?" the older man replies.

"You get a look at the girl? She's not from Rockton. She's Edwin's."

Tomas turns his gaze on me and frowns. He takes in my clothing. Then he looks at the other man. "Just because she's partly Asian does not mean she's related to the only Asian person you've met."

"I'm not," I say. "I know Edwin, but I'm no more likely to share ancestry with him than with you." I glance at Dalton. "Or with him, which would be really awkward."

Tomas chuckles. The other man's eyes stay narrowed in suspicion.

Tomas stretches his hand to me and then to Dalton. We shake it. The other man stays where he is.

"We met a young man a few minutes ago," I say to Tomas. "Maybe late teens? He bore a resemblance to you. Your son?"

"Nephew," Tomas says. "But my wife and I have been raising him the last few years. We saw you tracking him and got concerned."

"I apologize for that," I say. "We have some questions. We found a . . ." I hesitate. "A body. A woman dressed in clothing that we were told came from the Second Settlement. But your nephew didn't recognize it. He said no one's missing, and he obviously wanted to leave it at that but . . . We need to find out where she belonged. Even if she's not yours, any help would be appreciated. I understand you prefer not to have contact with Rockton."

"Eh," Tomas says with a shrug. "We're not exactly hiding behind a wall with archers and a moat. We do keep to ourselves, but we'd like to help you find this poor woman's people. That's only right."

The other man snorts and stalks off. Tomas shakes his head with a wry smile. "While not everyone here will be so helpful, they won't object to me speaking to you."

"Thank you." I take the scrap from my pocket. "The person who sent us to you had a long-standing trade relationship with your settlement, and he was convinced someone there — maybe someone who used to live there — did the craftsmanship."

"How is Tyrone?" Tomas asks, and I must look surprised, because he laughs. "Not many people have had that 'long-standing trade relationship' you mentioned. Tyrone was sheriff when my brother and I left Rockton, and I advocated for trade with him when he left himself. We had a change in leadership a few years ago and . . ." He shrugs. "Tyrone Cypher is an unusual man. He made our current leader nervous, and she decided to cut ties."

"Ty's fine, thank you," I say. "And yes, he's the only one who recognized this."

I hold out the piece. The man frowns. He takes it and examines it, his frown growing.

"You don't recognize it?" I ask.

"No, I certainly do. I was just wondering why Lane — my nephew — told you otherwise. But I shouldn't wonder really. People here can be very secretive, and my brother always had a touch of paranoia, which is how the two of us ended up in Rockton in the first place. I apologize for Lane. He didn't mean any harm. Yes, I definitely recognize this, because it's my work. Well, the leatherwork is mine. The decorating is my wife's."

He smiles, his eyes warming. "She's the artist. I just try to provide a canvas halfway worthy of her art."

"It is gorgeous work," I say.

"But you mentioned that you found it on a dead woman. No one's missing from our village. While we do trade with former members, no one has left in years and the only woman we actually trade with —"

He trails off, and he blinks. When he speaks, his throat dries up, and he has to try twice before he says, "Could you . . . describe this woman?"

"Are you familiar with the hostiles?"

He pales. Then he forces a ragged laugh. "Haven't heard that word in a very long time. We call them the wild people. But yes, it's hard to live out here and *not* know them, as much as we might wish otherwise. This woman . . ." He swallows. "You asked that for a reason, didn't you?"

"I did."

"Ellen," he murmurs.

I nod. "That was apparently her name." I take out the leather anklet she'd worn. When I pass it over, he stares at it and sways, just a little. His eyes squeeze shut, and he nods, as if to himself, and says, in a small voice, "How did it happen?"

"She was shot," I say.

He flinches. Then he says, slowly, "And this, Sheriff, is the truth of your earlier words. Why your guns are so much more dangerous than our bows. Yes, it is possible to accidentally shoot someone while hunting, but the chances of killing them are slight. We always hope that the scarcity of ammunition will decrease the use of firearms in these woods, but . . ."

His gaze rises to Dalton's, meeting it. "That will not happen while Rockton has guns and ammunition, and the willingness to trade both."

My brows rise.

Dalton says to me, "Yeah, under Tyrone, Rockton traded ammunition to help those who chose to leave. Giving them a higher chance of survival. Of course, another philosophy is that if you *don't* trade, maybe they'll see the light and come back. That's what Gene thought. By the time he left, people had found other sources of ammo, and I'm sure as hell not giving them extra."

He looks at Tomas. "I'd supply it in a matter of life or death. I'm not going to let anyone starve. But personally, I'm on your side. I'd like to see a lot fewer guns. Fuck, I'd make our own residents use bows if that didn't mean we'd be facing settlers and traders and miners with guns. Rockton hasn't supplied weapons or ammunition in years. And, though you haven't suggested it outright, we didn't kill this woman. We found her on a camping trip."

Tomas nods. "I wasn't accusing you, but thank you for clarifying. I'm guessing that's how it happened? A hunting accident?"

"It's . . . difficult to tell," I say. "The reason we're pursuing it is that she had something . . . with her. Something that may be important to someone."

I still want the chance to evaluate Abby's parents before I return her. I know I may not have that right. Yet after meeting Owen and Cherise, I will place myself in this role, judging who does and does not deserve their child back.

If I need to justify *that,* I'll do it with the

345

reminder that Ellen could have rescued Abby from abandonment. If her parents were from the Second Settlement and hid the pregnancy, they won't want their fellow settlers knowing what they did. If the Second Settlement was complicit in the abandonment, they won't want her back. Either way, the settlement might lie and take the child to save face.

When I say this, being cagey, Tomas's gaze drops to the bracelet, still in his hands.

"Not that," I say. "If anyone in the settlement knew Ellen well, we'd love the chance to speak to them. I'm trying to piece together her final days."

The corners of his lips rise in a strained smile. "You really are a detective then."

"I am."

"Well . . ." He trails off, and I can see him thinking. Considering his options.

Finally, he says, "My wife was close to Ellen. They were friends. I would appreciate the chance to speak to Nancy — my wife — first, if you don't mind. I'd like this news to come from me."

"We understand."

"I'll go into the settlement and tell people what has happened. They won't be thrilled at you being here, but with a death involved, they will understand. Many were fond of

Ellen. This will be difficult."

I nod. He starts to leave. Then he looks down at the bracelet. He stares at it a moment before clearing his throat, his expression unreadable as he says, "May I ask . . ." Another glance at the bracelet. "I'd rather not show this to anyone yet. It was . . . very personal."

Dalton and I exchange a glance. I agree, and Tomas pockets the bracelet before heading toward the village.

THIRTY-ONE

It takes a while for Tomas to return, but we expect that. We take off our snowshoes and packs, drink some water, share another protein bar, and play with Storm. Or Dalton plays with her. I lie on my back in the snow. Just making snow angels, really. Not collapsed from the exhaustion of snowshoeing all day.

When Tomas returns, he's alone, and I'm braced for "Sorry, but you can't come in," but he waves for us to follow. After a few steps, he says, "Nancy is . . . taking it hard, as you might expect. She'll speak to you, but she asks for a few minutes to gather her thoughts."

"Of course."

As we approach the village, I expect a loose cluster of buildings, like the First Settlement. Instead, there are a few small outbuildings clustered around two large ones that remind me of Indigenous long-houses.

"Communal living," I murmur. I think I've said it low enough, but Tomas hears and smiles.

"Yes. It's more economical for heating and food. Everyone works together, whether it's cooking or child-rearing." He glances to the side and his smile grows. "Speaking of child-rearing . . ."

A little girl, maybe five or six, comes racing over and throws herself into Tomas's arms. He swoops her up and swings her about as she squeals. I notice a boy a year or two older eyeing us. Tomas waves him over.

"These are my children," he says. "Becky and Miles."

"Eric," Dalton says. He shakes the boy's hand. The girl just giggles, but when I introduce myself, she shakes mine. They aren't really interested in us, though. Both pairs of eyes are fixed on our furry companion. I introduce Storm and have her sit while the children pet her.

"Can you guys do me a favor?" Tomas asks. "Your mom is busy right now, so I'd like you to stay with us. We're going to speak to the elders."

"And if you can keep Storm company

while we do that, we'd appreciate it," I say. Then to Tomas, I add, "She's very well trained, and we'll be close by."

He nods and charges the children with "watching" the dog, which really means just walking along beside her and petting her while we all enter the first longhouse.

A campfire within is the main source of light, and it takes a minute for my eyes to adjust. As I look around, I remember once going to a park with re-created Iroquois longhouses. That really is what this reminds me of. Down the center is a workspace, where women sew and children play and men whittle. Bunks line the walls, three high. Drying herbs and vegetables hang from the ceiling.

At the back sits a group that I'm guessing are the "elders," since they're talking, rather than working. The eldest is in her sixties. That makes sense, given that the Second Settlement launched in the seventies.

At the First Settlement, we're always met with a combination of curiosity and hostility, emphasis on the latter. It's saber-rattling. They want us to know how strong they are, how well defended. A pissing match that we must engage in, or we're the submissive wolf rolling over to show our unprotected belly.

In the Second Settlement, we get curiosity

tempered by caution. While Tomas's daughter ran out to see us, her brother held back, and that's what many of the adults do. They withdraw, physically and emotionally, stepping backward to let us pass, their faces blank. Even in their caution, though, there is politeness rather than aggression. *You are welcome enough here, but please don't stay long.*

Others are more like Tomas and his daughter, the friendliness outweighing any reserve. They smile, and they nod as we pass, and I do the same in return. Storm's presence lures a few of the children closer, especially when they see Tomas's kids petting her. I get her to sit a few feet from where the elders wait, and the children surge in, with adults supervising.

There is another thing I notice as we walk. Signs of . . . well, the words I consider and reject are "religion," "faith," "ritual," "belief." It's not as if I'm seeing crucifixes or dharma wheels or anything I recognize, yet my brain still identifies them as signs of a ritualized faith. There is what appears to be an altar built of stones and filled with dried grasses that add a sweet, pleasant scent to the campfire smoke. Other stones line the walls, each carved with an unfamiliar symbol. I see ones that look like stylized versions of wind and rain and snow. I also spot animal carvings, too many to be mere toys. And the sleeping berths bear more carvings, some symbols and some animals.

I struggle not to draw conclusions from what I'm seeing. Take in the data and store it for processing once I have more information.

I don't get more information on this by speaking to the elders. Well, I do . . . and I don't. It's not as if they extend a ritual greeting or ask that we all bow our heads in prayer before we speak. But there is a calm here that reminds me of a church, a hush and a peaceful contentment, and a reverence in the way Tomas addresses the elders. I may not see religion and ritual, but I feel it.

The conversation itself is a ritual I know very well. We have been presented to the leader — Myra — and she welcomes us, and we extend our greetings and explain our purpose. She expresses sadness at our news, gratitude for our attempts to find this woman's people, and promises of cooperation. It's like when I'd dealt with crimes involving an organization of any kind, social or political or business. "Yes, this is a terrible crime, and of course, we're here for anything the police need to solve it." Honest intent or empty promises? That's always the question, and if I was to hazard a guess, based on my experiences, I'd say that the Second Settlement isn't going to actively block my investigation, but they're not going out of their way to help it either. Ellen isn't theirs, and since she'd been shot — and they forbid guns — her death isn't theirs either.

The meeting lasts about fifteen minutes, and it's nothing more than a formal exchange of information and promises. As we leave the longhouse, the women at the cooking pit press food into our hands, fresh stew in beautifully carved wooden bowls and hunks of warm bread. They give some to Tomas, too, for himself and his wife, and we all thank them as we depart.

When we're out of the longhouse, Tomas quietly offers to switch bowls with us.

"In case you're at all concerned about the contents," he says. "I spent a lifetime with my paranoid brother. I would understand if you'd prefer to eat what they gave me."

We assure him we're not worried, and he passes his bread to the kids, who trail along after us with Storm.

"I'm going to ask you two to go back into the big house," he says to the kids. He looks at us. "May they take the dog?"

"Of course," I say.

The girl starts to give Storm her bread, but Tomas pulls her hand back. "Never feed an animal anything that she might not normally eat. It can upset her stomach. Ask Josie if they have bones instead. Big bones, from caribou or moose. The dog will like those better."

I motion for Storm to go with the kids, and she gives me a careful look, as if to be sure she's understanding. Then she lets them lead her back into the longhouse.

Tomas takes us to what seemed like a storage building, small and round. As we approach, I see smoke rising from it.

"As much as we believe in communal living, we also understand that sometimes, privacy is required, and in the winter, we can't just head into the forest to find it. This is our alone-hut, for individuals and" — he winks — "couples. Nancy will meet us in here."

It's a hide-covered structure, and he pulls back the flap. We have to duck to go inside. It's brighter than the longhouse, though. There's a fire and a hanging lantern. A woman sits on the floor. She's about my age. Tears streak her face, but as soon as the flap opens, she jumps up to greet us. Tomas waves her back inside. We enter, and he hangs back, as if uncertain. She tugs him in, and his face relaxes with relief. She takes one bowl from him and sets it down on the ground, and they sit, her hand entwined with his.

We introduce ourselves.

"I'm sorry for your loss," I say, and down south, that would be a cliché, but it really does say what needs to be said, *all* that can be said when talking to a stranger.

Nancy's eyes fill. Tomas grips her hand tighter, both hands wrapping around it. She sees we aren't touching our food, and says, "Eat, please. I won't, but you should. It's good stew, and the bread is even better."

We take a few mouthfuls, and both are indeed excellent. Once I've had enough to be sure my belly won't rumble, I say, "I'm not sure how much Tomas told you. I was a homicide detective down south."

She frowns and glances at Tomas.

"Nancy hasn't been down south," he says. "She was born in the Second Settlement." He quickly explains what a homicide detective is, and her brows furrow, as if she's struggling to understand the need for such a job.

I say as much, lightly joking.

She nods and says, "I know it's different down there. There are so many more people.

It's good that they have people to do that job. But Tomas said Ellen was killed by accident."

"We hope so," I say. "Right now, I'm trying to piece together her final days. She had something with her. Something I need to return. I'm sorry I can't say more than that."

Her lips curve in a wry smile. "Because whatever this thing is, it's valuable, and if you say what it is, people here might falsely claim it."

"Probably not," I say. "But we need to be extra cautious."

"We understand," Tomas says. "We'd like to do whatever we can to help Ellen."

Nancy hesitates at that, and her gaze drops, just a little, but then she nods and squeezes her husband's hand. "Yes. Anything you need. She was a dear friend."

"She didn't live here, though?"

Nancy shakes her head. "We asked her to. We . . ." She looks up at me. "I know nothing of how a detective works down south. I realize it is a job, and therefore, you might want only the details that will help you."

"Just the facts, ma'am," Tomas says, and we exchange a smile for a joke the other two won't get.

"Down south, we're on a schedule," I say. "People's taxes pay our salaries, so we need to be efficient. Brutally efficient even. Up here, it's different. Eric and I can't get home tonight anyway. As long as the settlement doesn't mind us setting up our tent nearby, we're in no rush. Here, I have the luxury of time, and I appreciate that. It gives me a chance to get a better understanding of the victim. In other words, take your time. Anything you want to explain, I'd like to hear."

"All right. If I go too far off topic, please stop me, but I . . . I would like you to understand more about us, too. It isn't as if we saw Ellen struggling to survive and closed our doors to her. We don't do that."

"I understand."

"We've helped a few of the wild people. Some in our community disagree with that. We believe in harmony with nature — the spirits of the forest and all that live in it. We hunt, of course. But we don't interfere with other predators, which includes the wild people. The question we disagree on is whether 'interference' includes helping them escape their situation."

She shifts, getting comfortable, and Tomas pushes blankets forward to let her lean on them. She smiles at him, and it is the smile of a long-married couple, instinctively understanding what the other needs and still able to appreciate these small acts of kindness.

"Ellen and I spoke often of her past," Nancy says. "I've taken her story to the elders, in hopes of convincing those who say we shouldn't interfere with the wild people. Ellen herself, though, would not speak to the elders. She was . . . conflicted on this. I'm not sure how much you know about the wild people."

"We're helping a woman who left them recently," I say. "She's a former Rockton resident. Eric knew her. He grew up there."

"Oh." Her eyes widen as she looks at Dalton. "You're the boy. The one Tyrone spoke of."

Dalton nods, his jaw set, and Nancy sees that, murmuring, "I'm sorry. I didn't mean to pry. I just remember Tyrone's stories."

"Ty has plenty of those," Dalton says. "Not all of them true, but yeah, I was born out here and . . . taken to Rockton."

She rocks back, as if stopping herself from comment. She reaches for her bowl instead and takes a spoonful of stew. Then she stops, frowns, and pulls a shotgun pellet from her mouth.

"Thought you folks didn't use guns," Dalton says.

"We don't," she says. "But sometimes we

still find pellets in the meat. When other settlers injure large game without killing them, those end up in our food."

"It's been happening more and more recently," Tomas mutters. "Someone cracked a tooth just last month."

I reach to take the pellet, but Nancy tucks it aside, as if she didn't see me reaching. I hesitate and then withdraw my hand wordlessly.

I resume our conversation. "So we know this woman, Maryanne, and her situation. She left Rockton with a party of would-be settlers, and they were set upon by the hos— wild people. The men were killed. The women were taken."

"Oh!" Nancy's hand flies to her mouth, her eyes rounding. "I'm — I'm sorry."

"That isn't how they 'recruit' around here?" I ask.

"Not Ellen's group. The wild people actually rescued her. Ellen and her husband were up here mining. They were new at it — it was only their second season. They were crossing a river swollen with spring runoff when they fell. He drowned. She made it to shore, but all their supplies were gone. She was nearly dead when the wild people took her in."

"And she stayed with them."

Nancy looks at her husband, as if unsure how much to say.

Tomas makes a face. "That's the problem. They have these teas. They're . . . like ours, but not like ours."

"I've heard about the teas. They — Wait, you said they're like yours?"

He nods. "We have two. There's the peace tea. It's . . ." He looks at me. "Have you ever smoked weed?"

"Once." I quirk a smile. "It wasn't quite my thing. Slowed me down too much."

"Right. That's what it does. Relaxes you, makes you happy and peaceful. We have a tea like that for relaxing. The same way someone might have wine with dinner. Then there's the ritual tea. There's this root that grows wild here. I have no idea what the real name is, but we call it the dream-root."

"A hallucinogen."

"Yes. We use it for ceremonies. To bridge the gap between us and nature." He lifts his hands, as if warding off comment. "Yes, I know. Between that and the peace tea, it sounds very nineteen sixties. But we have our ways here, and they don't harm any-one."

"I wasn't going to question," I say.

Tomas chuckles. "Tyrone sure did. He thought we were all a bunch of loony hip-

360

pies, dancing naked in the woods. Our ways were definitely not his."

"These teas, though," I say. "I'm told the wild people have two as well. One that makes them calm and one that causes hallucinations. Are they the same?"

"I'm no scientist — I was a truck driver down south — but from what Ellen said, I think theirs are stronger versions of ours. Much stronger. Ever tried peyote?"

I shake my head.

"I have," he says. "That's what our ritual tea is like. We drift into a dreamlike state, hence the name. What the wild people take makes them, well, wild. Increased violence. Increased sex drive. Their version of the peace tea is also stronger. Between the two brews, they seem to make the wild people stay with the group. Ellen had family down south. Parents, siblings, friends, a job. She only came to the Yukon for an adventure that was her husband's dream. She had no interest in staying long-term, let alone permanently."

Nancy nods. "But the tea made her forget the rest. Her family, her job, her life. At first, she stayed with the intention of getting well enough to travel back to the city. Then she just . . . forgot all that."

"How did she come out of it?" I ask.

Nancy glances at Tomas, uncomfortable again. This time, he isn't quite so quick to answer but rubs his beard, and looks back at his wife.

"There are . . . rules," Tomas says. "Every community has them. Ours is no different. There are laws meant to protect us, and there are laws meant to protect our way of life, to put our belief into deed."

"Religious prohibitions," I say.

He makes a face. "I wouldn't call what we practice a religion. I guess it is, but I was raised Catholic and . . ." He exhales. "Call it what you will. A friend with far more education than me said it's a belief system rather than a religion. Part of that belief system is noninterference. We don't interfere with Rockton or the First Settlement. We don't interfere with nature, either, any more than is needed for survival."

"And you don't interfere with the wild people," I say. "Or you're not supposed to. But there's some differing opinion on whether they've actually *chosen* that lifestyle. The woman we know was clearly a hostage, at least at first, and after a while, she was still hostage — to those teas. Her free will was being held hostage."

"Yes," Nancy says. "Ellen stayed by choice, but at what point was it no longer a choice? If she chose to drink the tea, and it caused her to stay, does that mean she *chose* to stay? Some here would say yes. But drinking the tea is a requirement for staying in that group. And it isn't as if she realized she was losing her free will and *chose* to keep losing it."

Tomas chuckles. "Nancy's better at explaining this. It makes my head hurt. All I know is that it doesn't seem right, leaving them out there like that, if they don't have the . . . what do we call it down south? The mental capacity to choose."

"Like seeing an addict on the street and not getting them to a shelter because they initially chose the drugs."

"Exactly."

"So, what you're trying to say . . ." I hesitate, consider their situation, and reword it. "In a case like that, someone might choose to help a person when their community says they shouldn't. If their community learned of it, they would be in trouble."

Neither speaks, but both give me a look that says I've guessed correctly.

"Okay," I say. "How Ellen extricated herself from the wild people is unimportant. You say your community has helped some of them. I'm guessing that means they've offered assistance to wild people who have voluntarily left their tribe. That is allowed. That's not interference."

Nancy nods. "If they leave on their own, we can offer food, trade goods, even shelter. Two of our members were former wild people. Ellen wanted to live on her own and, when she was ready, travel back home. She left her group the summer before last, and she hoped to return home in the spring. She was so excited . . ."

Nancy's voice catches. Tomas puts his arm around her shoulders, and she leans against it. I eat more of my now-cold stew and glance at Dalton. He's been silent, letting me handle this. When he catches my eye, he nods, and I'm not aware that I'm communicating anything to him, but after a moment, he speaks.

"When's the last time you saw her?" he asks.

Nancy starts, and it might be surprise at Dalton talking, but it's more, too. She's sinking into her grief, and we've finally reached the heart of what I really must ask her. We can't let her drift now. That's the message Dalton read in my look.

This is going to be tough, and I need help.

I need someone to push. Someone to play bad cop.

When Nancy hesitates, Dalton says, "This is important."

"I know," she says. "It was eight —" Another catch. "Eight days ago. She needed supplies."

"Like what?"

Dalton grills Nancy on specifics. It isn't easy. Speaking of Ellen in the abstract had been fine, but now Nancy must dissect what she realizes is the last time she'd ever see her friend. Tomas glances at her, concerned, but he doesn't interfere and Nancy gives no sign she needs to stop.

Ellen had came by on a supply run. She did that weekly. As a lone settler, without the time to build a permanent residence, she lived light, with only a tent and a pack. It was easier for her to trade weekly with the settlement, giving them her extra meat and furs in return for dried vegetables and other foodstuffs.

Her last visit, however, had been unscheduled. She usually stopped by on what they called "the sixth day" — Saturdays. This visit came on a Tuesday, and she'd brought an entire caribou plus three hares, hoping to trade for winter blankets and scraps of leather.

Dalton frowns. "She lived alone last winter, and this one isn't any colder."

"She said she used last year's blankets to sew summer clothing."

"Why now? It's been fucking freezing for two months."

They both flinch at the profanity, and it takes him a moment to realize it. He nods, understanding. There are people in Rockton who take exception to his language. If they're troublemakers or chronic complainers, he might even pile on a few "fucks" to annoy them. But if they are good people, like these, he holds back.

Nancy admits she doesn't know why Ellen suddenly wanted extra warm blankets. There's hesitation, suggesting she found this odd herself, but Dalton only nods, as if accepting her explanation. Then he says, his voice casual, "A caribou and three hares. She must be a really good hunter."

They say nothing, but their discomfort is palpable.

"That normal for her? Bringing so much meat, three days after her last visit?"

Silence. Dalton's gaze cuts my way, bouncing the ball over.

"I know you trade with a very limited number of people," I say. "I'm guessing Ellen was an exception because she's a former wild person. In need of help."

366

They both nod, as if grateful for the easy answer.

"What about others?" I say. "Regular settlers who need assistance?"

"It would depend," Tomas says. "We'd never turn away someone who was in desperate need, of course. We make exceptions. But only in emergencies, and then we direct them to other sources, such as the First Settlement."

"What if an accepted trade partner, like Ellen, brought you goods from someone else?"

They exchange a look.

"That would be . . . prohibited," Nancy says. "By our laws."

"Which Ellen knows. She'd never risk your friendship by openly trading on someone else's behalf. But if she says nothing . . ."

They don't answer.

Dalton surges forward, clearly ready to press the matter, but I shake my head. I consider for a minute, and then I say, "Ellen was a good friend, yes? And also a good person, it seems. If she knew of someone in need, she would trade for them and not tell you. I respect that. However, given that she is dead — possibly murdered — I need to pursue this. I'm not asking you to confirm that she was trading for a third party. But did she give you any idea what she needed those leather scraps for?"

"She said she was going to try her hand at sewing."

"Did she need a specific size of scrap?"

Nancy shakes her head. "I had scraps no bigger than my hand, and I said they were useless but she took them."

"Did she request anything else? Anything unusual?"

"Salve," she says. "For her lips, she said."

"Were they chapped?"

Nancy shakes her head.

Scraps of leather, any size. When we were diapering Abby, we used fabric scraps for extra padding. That could suggest Ellen was caring for the baby herself, but she hadn't requested anything she'd need to feed Abby. The mention of salve, however, reminds me of a colleague joking about his wife putting lip balm on her nipples during nursing. That would suggest Ellen wasn't caring for the baby herself; she was helping Abby's parents get supplies they needed.

"About that caribou," Dalton says. "Did she usually bring in game that large?"

"She said she got lucky," Tomas explains. "We didn't question."

"How did she usually hunt? With a gun?"

"Oh, no," Nancy says. "The wild people

don't have guns. They're like us. And we allowed her to hunt on our territory, which means she isn't allowed to use guns. She wouldn't anyway. She only traps and fishes." She hesitates, as if seeing the problem with that, given that Ellen brought in a caribou.

"Had the caribou been shot?" I ask, trying not to glance at where Nancy tucked away the pellet.

"She brought it partly slaughtered," Tomas says. "She kept the head. She said she wanted the antlers, but I suppose, if someone gave her the animal, it could have been shot in the head. That's what I figured. That someone traded the caribou to her, and she was trading it to us, which wouldn't break our laws. I hadn't thought of it being shot, but I suspect that's the caribou they used for the stew today."

The stew with shotgun pellets.

We run out of questions shortly after that. We know Ellen had made an unscheduled stop in the Second Settlement, trading for unusual items and using unusual payment. That supported the idea she'd been helping Abby's mother. That might also suggest Abby's parents were responsible for the caribou Ellen brought in.

They'd shot it and removed the head, so it wouldn't be obvious that someone else killed the beast. From what Tomas said, though, it wasn't the first time they discovered pellets in their meat, and that's been more common lately. Had Ellen been working with Abby's parents for a while? If so, wouldn't someone have realized the pellet-shot meat all came from her?

I might get more answers by tracking the source of the stew meat, confirming it came from that caribou. But when I ask if I can personally thank the cooks for the meal, Nancy shuts me down. Oh, she's polite about it, saying she'll pass on my appreciation, but I know when I'm being blocked. She doesn't want me speaking to them. Just like she didn't want me having that pellet. I get the latter, though — I surreptitiously scoop it up while the children bring Storm to show their mother.

We wait outside as the children say their goodbyes to the dog. While they do that, I pull the pellet from my pocket for a discreet closer look.

It's a buckshot pellet — the same kind that killed Ellen.

THIRTY-TWO

Tomas takes us to a place where we can camp for the night. As expected, there's no invitation to stay in the settlement, but we wouldn't have accepted one anyway. We do take the food they offer, along with Tomas's help locating a well-situated campsite.

The site has obviously been used before and recently, with only the lightest layer of snow over a campfire circle, log seats, and a spot cleared for tents. Tomas says it's for the teens and unmarried adults who need an escape from the close quarters of the longhouses.

As I watch Tomas leave, Dalton says, "You want to go after him," before I can ask.

"Something's up," I say, "and it's not just that shotgun pellet. I think Tomas had an affair with Ellen."

Dalton's brows shoot up. Then his face falls with, "The bracelet. Fuck." He mutters a few more curses, and I understand his disappointment. Nancy and Tomas seem like a deeply committed, loving couple, and no one wants to think a guy who has that at home will betray his wife. But I suspected it from the moment his eyes lit on that bracelet, the flash of grief as he realized who'd died. Asking us not to mention the bracelet cemented my suspicions — this isn't a polyamorous relationship, where Nancy knows what he's doing and approves.

"I'd just like to follow him," I say. "See if he takes a moment to find his game face before he heads back to his wife. You and Storm can come along, but I'd appreciate it if you hang back."

He nods, and we set out. I leave the snowshoes. The forest here is dense enough that I can jog through the light snow.

Soon I see Tomas trudging along ahead. I slow to keep out of sight and follow him for about a hundred feet. After a glance, he makes a left off the trodden path. I slip after him, tracking his jacket in the fast-falling twilight. Finally, he comes to a clearing, where he sits on a fallen tree.

Tomas pulls the bracelet from his pocket and runs his fingers over the leather. Then he clears the snow, digs a shallow hole, and lays the bracelet in it. His hand touches the discarded dirt, ready to refill the hole. After a pause he takes the bracelet out and runs his thumb over it. His head drops and his shoulders shake, racked with silent sobs.

I glance over my shoulder but see no sign of Dalton and Storm. They're there — just giving me room. I look at Tomas again. As a person, I want to leave him to his grief. As a detective, I cannot. I have a murdered woman, and now I'm looking at her secret lover . . . whose wife tried to hide a shotgun pellet that may have come from the murder weapon.

I step from the trees and say, "I'm going to need that bracelet back."

Tomas jumps. I have my gun lowered, but his gaze still goes to it and his eyes widen.

"We're alone in the forest," I say. "I'm not about to demand murder evidence without a gun in my hand." I put my hand out. "How about you give me that instead of burying it?"

"Burying?" Another widening of the eyes. Then he winces. "Burying the evidence. No, that wasn't what I was doing. It's just . . ."

"Maybe not evidence of a crime, but evidence of a secret. A lover's gift."

He nods, his gaze still down, shoulders hunched as he sits with the bracelet in his hand. "I wanted to bury it. Pretend it never happened. But that isn't fair. It isn't right.

This was . . ." His hand closes around it. "Important."

"So what were you going to do with it?"

He exhales. "I don't know. I should talk to Nancy. That's the right thing to do, and maybe I'm a coward, but I just . . ." He opens his hand again. "I shouldn't pretend it didn't happen. Nancy and I need to discuss *why* it happened. I just . . . I want to protect my family. Down south, I had girlfriends and lovers, and that's all I thought there was, for a guy like me. Then I met Nancy, and she's so much more. A friend, a partner, a lover. And now . . ." He takes a deep breath. "I just don't want Nancy to think I blame her."

"Blame your wife for you screwing around? I should hope not."

He looks up in genuine confusion. "Screwing . . . ?" A short laugh. "Of course that's what you thought. That's how these things normally go, isn't it? I wasn't having an affair with Ellen."

"But you wanted to," I say. "You gave her that."

He shakes his head. "I'm not the one who gave it to her."

There's a moment where I don't understand. As soon as I do, I feel stupid. I also feel very close-minded. My brain drew what seemed like the obvious conclusion, because it's the one that fit the norms I was raised with, and even if I'm long past that, my mind still follows that long-carved path.

I remember Tomas's pain on seeing the bracelet. I remember how he'd hesitated, coming into the tent with Nancy, how he'd hung back and made sure of his welcome before comforting her. It was behavior consistent with a man who'd cheated on his wife. It wasn't, however, what I'd expect from a man who'd *just* discovered his wife had been cheating on him.

"You knew," I say. "About Nancy and Ellen."

He forces a wry smile. "I might have barely gotten my high school diploma, but I can figure some things out just fine. I knew they were more than friends. I just . . ." He takes a deep breath. "I thought it was a fling. That bracelet means it was more. Nancy loved her and . . . . I didn't expect that."

"Finding out your wife was having a fling with a woman must have come as a shock."

That twist of a smile again. "Such a shock that I went crazy and shot Ellen? The redneck trucker so horrified by the thought that his wife prefers women that he destroys the evidence? No. I knew what Nancy was when

I married her and . . ."

His face screws up in pain as he rubs his hands over it. "Growing up, my friends called gay people fags and homos. Did I stop them? Hell, no. I chimed in, because that's what we were taught — that homosexuality was wrong. When I was twenty, a bunch of us were at a bar, and my friends went after a gay guy. We beat the shit out of him, just because we were drunk and spoiling for a fight and he seemed a perfectly fine target. After I sobered up, I realized what I'd done, and I was sick. I didn't exactly start joining gay-pride parades, though. I just stopped caring about other people's sexual orientation. Then along came Nancy, and I still didn't care, but in the wrong way, you know?"

"You married her knowing she preferred women."

He nods. "That's not acceptable here. We might be all about nature and kindness and love thy neighbor, but we must procreate, and for Nancy to say 'Sure, I'll have babies, but I'd rather be married to a woman' was not an acceptable work-around. Her parents caught her with a settler girl, and they offered her in marriage to this other guy. Nancy said she'd rather marry me. I was . . ."

He flails his hand. "I was a twenty-five-year-old man who figured he wasn't ever getting a wife because he wasn't born here. Then this eighteen-year-old girl is in trouble, and she wants to marry me, and I like her, and I know this other guy's a jerk, so I say sure. Look at me. A damn hero stepping up like that. A hero, though, would have taken her out of here. Taken her back to Rockton and let her go down south to be with someone she wanted."

The tears start again, and he looks away, bracelet still in his hands. I remember their obvious love and affection for one another, and I know they've made the best of a difficult situation. Nancy just needed more, and she'd tried to get it without hurting her husband. I don't see wrongdoing on either side. I see tragedy. The question I must ask, though, is whether one tragedy led to another. Led to murder.

I don't question Tomas further. There's no point. He knows he's a suspect. He may even realize Nancy is, and something tells me he'll protect her even more than he'll protect himself.

I tell Dalton about Nancy and Ellen. He says, "Fuck, that's a mess all around."

He's right. Everyone loses here. And for

377

what? As Tomas said, marrying a woman wouldn't have stopped Nancy from procreating, if that was so important to the settlement. They never gave her that option, though, which means that, like most of those objections, the justifications are just excuses to backfill a decision rising from ignorance rather than rational thought.

However "enlightened" the Second Settlement is, they'd still brought their prejudices with them, because those who made this law had grown up in the same world as Tomas, where it was fine to insult and beat homosexuals because they needed to be "scared" onto the right track.

The settlement elders had given Nancy an ultimatum, and she made the best of it, choosing her own husband. Tomas knew he wasn't her actual "choice," but he went along with it, driven by those old prejudices, too, the ones that doubtless whispered that if he was a good enough husband, Nancy wouldn't miss anything. Only she did. Ellen comes along, they become friends, and then more than friends . . . and Ellen winds up dead.

Tomas might have said he understood — maybe *wanted* to understand — but when he first found out, had he seen red, grabbed his forbidden shotgun, and hunted down his rival? Or did Nancy do it in a lover's quarrel? Perhaps she expected to go south with Ellen in the spring, and Ellen told her no. Or Nancy didn't *want* to go south, so Ellen threatened to tell Tomas about them.

Where does Abby fit into this? Nowhere, I realize. Nor does she need to. Ellen was helping Abby's parents. She might have been looking after the baby when she'd been shot, and with Abby hidden under Ellen's coat, her killer never realized they'd almost claimed a second life. Solving Ellen's murder may not find Abby's parents, but it is still justice for one victim I found in the snow.

The big clue here is the shotgun. I suspect that someone in the Second Settlement is cheating on the "no firearms" rule. They've gotten hold of a shotgun and been shooting their prey and then jabbing in an arrow making it look as if the beast was brought down with a bow.

Does the entire settlement know someone's breaking the law? Are they turning a blind eye because it's winter and meat equals survival?

Nancy knows what's going on, though. I'm certain of that. She knows who has a shotgun, and that's why she tucked away the pellet.

Is it Tomas's shotgun, and she's covering for him? Or has she only figured out that *someone* in the village is using a gun, and she's protecting whoever it is?

I need to find out who has that gun.

THIRTY-THREE

Dalton and I are talking around the fire when we hear running footfalls. We shine our flashlight and a voice huffs, "It's Tomas," sounding out of breath, before he appears. He bursts in and stops, panting, "Nancy's gone. I got back to the village, and went to speak to her. When I couldn't find her, I thought she was avoiding me. Miles said she'd told the kids to stay with the other women, that she needed to find Lane."

"Lane?" I say, and it takes a moment for me to remember that's his nephew. "Where is he?"

"Hunting. Lane . . . struggles with village life. His mother died when he was a boy, his father passed five years ago, and he lost his best friend the summer before last. Lane's had a rough go of it lately. He spends most of his time hunting. Nancy and I worry about him, but the elders tell us not to interfere. He's the best hunter we have."

"Because he's not using a fucking bow," Dalton mutters.

"What?" Tomas says, sounding genuinely surprised.

"Someone has been hunting with a shotgun," I say, "while pretending to use a bow. That's why you've found so many pellets in the meat. Nancy figured out it was Lane, and now that Ellen has been killed with a firearm . . ."

Tomas's eyes widen. "You think Nancy's gone after Lane. I thought . . ." He swallows. "I thought that was just an excuse to get away, that she was distraught over Ellen. Lane would never hurt Nancy, but we still need to find her. It hasn't snowed in three days, and there are too many prints for me to track. You'd mentioned your dog can do that."

"She can," I say. "But she'll need —"

He's already pulling a shirt from his pack. He manages an anxious smile. "I used to watch a lot of cop shows."

"All right then. Let's go."

Storm picks up the trail easily. According to Tomas, Nancy rarely leaves the settlement in winter. The rest of the year, she loves to walk and gather berries and nuts and greens, but in winter, she hunkers down with her needlework. It's been days since she's been beyond the perimeter, so her trail is easily followed.

It's only 10 P.M., but it's been dark for hours. All around us, the forest slumbers, and every step we take seems to echo. It also means that every noise Nancy or Lane makes will do the same, and we've been out less than twenty minutes before we hear their voices on the night breeze.

"You made a mistake," Nancy is saying, her voice low and urgent. "I understand that. This is why we don't use guns, Lane, and when we do, we make mistakes even more easily because we're unaccustomed to handling them."

"I *still* don't know what you're talking about," Lane replies.

"The gun. The one you got in a trade from those . . . those people. You've been using it to hunt. I told you that you needed to be more careful. If you wanted to do that, then you couldn't hunt on our territory, where someone could get hurt."

"And I told you I don't have a gun."

"I found pellets in the hares you brought us last week. I showed them to you."

"And I said they weren't mine. It's like the elders say — sometimes they get into our game from other hunters."

Nancy's voice rises in frustration. "I'm trying to help you, Lane. You tell me you don't have a gun? All right. Then take that gun that I'm clearly imagining and get rid of it, please. Hide it somewhere."

"I don't have —"

"Stop, Lane. Just listen to me and protect yourself. This woman from Rockton, her entire *job* is finding people who kill others. Your uncle told me all about it. She's trained to find murderers by studying blood and bullets and dead bodies. If your gun killed Ellen, she won't understand that it was a hunting accident. She'll find the gun and know it's the one that killed Ellen. Then she'll read your fingerprints on it. But if there's no gun, you're safe."

"I don't have a gun."

"Then who does?" I say as I step into the clearing, gun in hand. "Besides me."

Nancy staggers back, Tomas rushing in to catch her. His arms go around her, and he tugs her out of the way. Storm growls beside me. Through the woods, I see Dalton soundlessly slipping behind Lane.

"If this was a hunting accident, then I *will* understand that," I say. "Like your aunt said, you lack experience with firearms. But, like she also said, I can indeed connect your shotgun to you and to the pellet that killed

384

Ellen. There's no point in arguing it wasn't you. Just explain what happened. If you made a mistake, then it was only a tragic accident."

It wasn't. I'm certain of that. I might not be a forensics expert, but I know Ellen died at night. The only thing Lane had been hunting at that time was Ellen herself. Step one, though, is getting a confession to the killing.

"I don't have a gun," he says.

"Then who does? Has someone you know been giving you their game? Trading it?"

This makes no sense, but I'm giving him an out here. Dalton's behind Lane, still tucked into the dark forest, his gun drawn. I have mine out, too. Lane's face says he's two seconds from bolting, and I need to give him an explanation that will allow him to relax. Then I can get the truth.

Still, he shakes his head and says, "I don't know what you're talking about."

Nancy breaks from Tomas's arms and steps toward her nephew.

"Lane, please," she says. "I know you're scared —"

"I'm not scared," he says, jaw setting. "I don't like being accused of things I didn't do."

"Nobody is accusing you," I say. "We just

want to know what happened. Give us that, and this will be over."

"Listen to her," Nancy says, taking another step toward him.

"Nancy?" I say. "Move back, please."

She shakes her head, her gaze still on her nephew. "I know you'd never hurt me, Lane. You are a son to me, and I trust you completely."

I don't like her tone or her words. They're too much, her gaze fixed on him, her voice low and soothing, and it's exactly what I've done with dangerous suspects.

I know you don't want to hurt me. You don't want to hurt anyone. You're not that kind of person.

Words I'd said when I knew my suspect *was* that kind of person, but I was trying to defuse the situation, while my colleagues kept their guns trained on the suspect.

Half the time, the suspect called me on my bullshit. Yet I continued doing it for those where my words did nudge something deep in them, did convince them to surrender.

That is what Nancy is doing here. Except she's not a trained officer. And the fact that she's doing it tells me Lane *isn't* a sweet, harmless young man. I sneak a glance at Tomas. His face is taut, gaze fixed on his wife as he rocks forward, torn between pulling her back and not wanting to set his nephew off. His gaze cuts my way, communicating exactly what I expect — a warning and a plea.

"Nancy?" I say. "I know you're trying to help, and I know Lane would never hurt you, but I have a gun, and my dog is trained to attack. Any wrong move, however unintentional, could get both of you hurt. Just step back, and let us handle this. Lane isn't armed. He's not going to hurt himself. He's listening to us. I just need you to —"

Lane lunges, and there's nothing I can do about it except bark at him to get back, get the hell away from Nancy. He grabs Nancy and yanks her to him, and Tomas lunges toward them, but Lane already has his arm around Nancy's neck, a hunting knife in his hand.

"Why?!" Lane screams at his uncle, spittle flying.

Tomas falls back with the force of that scream, the venom in it. Even Dalton startles. Storm growls, hackles rising.

"Why do you care?" Lane screams at Tomas.

"Do you mean why do I care about you?" Tomas says. "You're my nephew, my brother's child, you're a son —"

387

"I mean her." Lane shakes Nancy. "Why do you care what I do to her? You knew what she was doing."

"I . . ." Tomas swallows, and when he says, "I'm not sure what you mean," it's obviously a lie.

"That wild woman. Your wife was . . . was . . ." He can't finish, his face choked with rage. "She betrayed you with a *woman.*"

Nancy's gaze shunts to her husband, but Tomas straightens, voice calm as he says, "That would be between my wife and myself, Lane. Yes, I knew, and I've done nothing about it, which means it is none of your concern."

"She betrayed you."

"I don't see it like that."

Lane snarls, "My father always said you were a fool. He told me about her." He shakes Nancy again. "How you married her even after she was found with another girl. You were a fool then, and you're a fool now, but you're still my uncle. You were good to me. Better than my father ever was. You were good to her, too, and we don't deserve it, but at least I appreciate it. I care about you. I won't stand by and watch you be *humiliated* by your wife."

Tomas goes still, drawing in ragged

breaths. "Lane, let her go. Please. If you really do care about me, you will let her go. I love you. I'll help you, no matter what you might have done."

"What I *might* have done?" Lane's face contorts in a sneer. "You know what I did. I did what you couldn't."

"Lane?" I say. "Stop right there. Whatever you are about to say, consider it before you do. Let Nancy go, and we can talk."

I'm not giving him a free pass. Once he speaks those words, though, he tumbles over a precipice. Admit to one murder, and it'll seem easy to commit a second.

"I don't want to stop," Lane says. "Why should I? I'm not ashamed of what I did. I —"

"Lane?" I say. "That's enough. Let Nancy go —"

"Yes, I killed that woman. Shot her and left her to die. She deserved it, and so does this filthy excuse of a —"

Dalton grabs Lane's knife arm. He'd been sneaking up from behind, Lane so intent on his confession that he never realized Dalton was with us. Now Dalton yanks Lane's arm back, the knife dropping. I run for the weapon. Tomas runs for Nancy and pulls her from the scuffle.

Dalton wrestles with Lane. I can't do

more than stand back, my gun aimed. I could threaten to shoot Lane, but he's in such a frenzy, I doubt he'd hear. I could hardly follow through either, with Dalton lost in that blur of blows.

Dalton goes down, his knee buckling under a savage kick. Lane wheels and runs, and I lunge after him, but I'm too slow — my bad leg will never let me keep up with a fit young man. I see Storm. Lane is running across the clearing, past where Storm's huge black form blends into the night. Her gaze swings on me, a question in it.

I instinctively raise my hand for her to hold her stay. Then I remember my thoughts from earlier. Storm is a working dog, and I need to use her.

"Go!" I say, pairing the command with a wave that releases her.

She's off like a shot. She isn't built for speed, though, and she has to give chase, the two of us running after Lane, oblivious to whatever is happening behind us. Storm closes her gap, as I fall behind, my bobbing flashlight beam allowing me only glimpses of them ahead.

Storm catches up, and she's right behind him, and I think she'll have no idea what to do next. Which proves, I suppose, that I really am a fretful parent, worrying about what I haven't prepared my "child" for. My "child" is a dog. A predator. No one needed to show her what to do when Cherise posed a threat to me. And no one needs to tell her what to do when she catches up to Lane. One powerful lunge, and she's on him, knocking him facedown in the snow.

It's the next part that confuses her, as it did with Cherise. She's been taught not to hurt people. Even in play, she can never snap or snarl or growl, even grab an arm with the intention of clamping down. She's *too* well trained here, those teachings overcoming instinct. She takes Lane down and then just stands on him, and looks back at me, but I'm fifty feet away. Lane flips over, shoving at her even as I shout a warning.

Lane scrambles up, and Storm knocks him down again. He slams a fist into her chest, and a snarl of rage behind us tells me Dalton is coming. Yet he's too far back, and so am I, and Storm's trying to figure out what to do, butting at Lane while he hits her.

I have to clamp my jaw shut not to call her back. I'm almost there. Lane's unarmed and —

A flash of silver.

He has a knife.

"Storm!" I scream, which is not a command, not a goddamn command at all. "Come! Storm, come!"

The knife slashes. Blood sprays onto snow, and I scream again. Then something bursts from the forest. A blur of gray. I'm only ten feet away, close enough to see what it is. The wolf.

He grabs Lane's arm. His teeth clamp down, but the young man's wearing a thick parka, and the wolf only hangs there. He bites hard enough to startle Lane into dropping the knife, though. Lane realizes there's a hundred-pound wolf hanging off his shoulder, and he screams, kicking and punching.

I'm there. Finally there. I ram the flashlight into my pocket, holster my gun, and grab Storm's collar to drag her back. I ignore Lane. I know he's my target, but there's blood in the snow, and it belongs to my dog, and that's what matters. The wolf can take Lane for all I care.

Lane and the wolf fight, battling with growls and grunts and gasps of pain. Storm whines, her body trembling as I run my hands along it. She flinches when I find the spot where the knife went in, but she doesn't stop straining to see the fight, nudging me out of the way when I block her view.

The blade sliced her left shoulder. Her fur

is wet and sticky with blood, and I tug out the flashlight for a look. It's a slice, not a stab, and as I palpate the wound, she huffs in annoyance more than pain, Mom fussing over a scraped knee when her child just wants to run back onto the playground. That reassures me even before I get a good look at what is indeed a flesh wound, a shallow slice maybe two inches long. It'll need stitches, and I'm sure as hell not letting her jump into the fight, but she's all right.

I see Dalton then. He's circling Lane and the wolf, looking for an opening. His knee gives a little when he feints too fast, telling me Lane really did give it a solid kick. The wolf and Lane are squaring off, circling each other, Dalton outside looking for a way in.

Looking for a way to get between Lane and the wolf.

Oh, hell, no.

I pull my gun. "Lane! Get on the fucking ground, and we'll take care of the wolf."

Lane's gaze darts my way.

"You heard me!" I bark. "On the ground now."

He spins and kicks at Dalton, aiming for his wounded knee, and rage fills me, the kind of rage that let me shoot Blaine Saratori, the kind that had me put a bullet through Val's head. But I learn. Each time, I

393

learn because I can never pull this trigger and *not* question afterward. With Blaine, I have every reason to question. I made a mistake. With Val, I did not, but I still suffer for it, wonder if there'd been a way to protect Dalton without killing her.

This time, there is no question. Dalton isn't in lethal danger — Lane is just really, really pissing me off, trying to literally throw Dalton to the wolves.

So I shoot, but it's aimed over them. The gunfire startles Lane, and it warns Dalton, and between the two, Lane's kick is aborted as Dalton dodges. Lane comes out running as he tears into the forest. The wolf starts to go after him, and my idiot lover leaps between them.

"No!" Dalton shouts, startling the wolf, which skids to a halt.

Dalton's bigger than Lane, and he's making himself bigger still, puffed up, gun out, shouting at the wolf. Personally, I'd let the damned beast go after the bastard, but this is why, no matter which roles we play best, the "good cop" is the guy in front of me.

The canine stands his ground but shows no sign of attacking. Storm is fine, and her attacker is gone, and the wolf himself seems all right. He approaches Storm, stiff-legged, and we let them do the sniff-greeting again.

Of course, he's hoping for a reward from his rescued damsel, but this time, as soon as he sniffs behind her, she snarls and spins away, and after one more halfhearted try, he lopes into the forest.

"Sorry!" I say. "No reward sex for you." I turn to Dalton. "And definitely none for you. What the hell was that? Coming between a confessed killer and a wolf?"

He pauses and then says, "I was worried about the wolf."

"Right answer." I lift up to peck his cheek. "Even if it's utter bullshit, and you just saw a dangerous situation and decided to play hero by leaping into the middle of it."

"I didn't actually leap in. I was looking for a way to break it up."

"Refereeing a wolf fight?" I shake my head. "I don't think the wolf would have listened. Hell, I don't think either of them would have." I look in the direction Lane went. "So I guess we're stuck tracking him."

"Is Storm okay?"

He bends to pet the dog, and I hand him the flashlight and point out the damage.

"I should stitch her," I say, "but we have surgical strips in our packs at camp. That'll do. We just need some way to mark this spot so we can pick up Lane's trail after."

Dalton digs into his pocket, and I'm about

to point out that tying a marker to a tree won't work at night. Instead he pulls out a package of surgical strips.

"The man comes prepared," I say as I take them.

"Do I get reward sex for *that*?"

"You just might. Now hold her steady while I clean the wound and plaster it shut."

THIRTY-FOUR

Once Storm's fine, we track Lane. It's easy at first. He doesn't have a flashlight or a lantern. In winter, under a three-quarter moon, the reflection off the snow is enough. However, that leads to a quandary for Lane. More open land means better light but deeper snow. His choices are clear sight or easy movement. He tries both, racing through thicker woods, and probably tripping over an obstacle or two until he veers to less dense forest, and then staggers through knee-deep snow. Eventually he finds a happy medium. He's still walking through snow, though, meaning we barely need Storm to track him.

At some point, he must realize that and he heads for the foothills. There he finds windswept rock to run across, and Storm earns her keep then. Ultimately, though, we lose him. Storm is wounded, and she's been up since her wolf suitor came to call yesterday morning. She isn't the only one flagging either. When Lane plays one too many tricks on us, we run out of the patience needed to keep Storm on target. We also run out of the will to push her when she's so obviously exhausted.

Lane has confessed to killing Ellen. He's a threat to Nancy, but . . . While I won't say that's the Second Settlement's problem, I have no jurisdiction here. The dead woman was their friend. The killer is their resident. I have no right to keep investigating. I will, if they ask for help, but I have a baby momma to find, and solving this crime doesn't get me any closer to resolving that one.

When Dalton came after me, he'd told Tomas to take Nancy home. That's where we go, and it's seven in the morning by the time we get there. It'd have been longer if we backtracked, but I'm blessed to be with a guy who doesn't need to follow his own footprints to find his way in the forest.

Tomas and Nancy haven't told the elders anything. They're waiting to talk to us, and I fear that means they want us to cover for Lane. They don't. He didn't kill Ellen in self-defense. He has no excuse and no remorse, and he followed up one cold-blooded murder by attempting another, this time against the woman who raised him.

I can blame a twisted sense of loyalty to his uncle or the homophobic teachings of his settlement, but neither is an excuse for murder. Whatever his father and the settlement taught him, Tomas and Nancy raised him in a loving and open-minded home.

We speak to the elders with Tomas and Nancy. Lane will face their judgment. They'll wait for him to return, protecting Nancy and the children, and if Lane doesn't come back, then yes, they would appreciate our help finding him.

Afterward, Tomas and Nancy ask us to join them for breakfast before we leave. The children feed Storm, who is doing an excellent impression of a fur rug, sprawled on the snow, refusing to move. Apparently, she's getting breakfast in bed, and I have no doubt she'll rouse enough to eat it. I wouldn't mind an hour of sleep myself before the long walk home, but I can also rouse myself to eat, and I know Tomas and Nancy want to talk to us.

We're barely settled into the small alone-hut when Tomas says, "I would like to ask for transportation down south. For my family."

"What?" Nancy says, startling enough that she nearly drops her breakfast bowl.

Tomas doesn't look at her. "We'll go to Whitehorse. I should still have money in an old account. It'll be enough to get us started. I'll set up Nancy and the kids someplace outside the city, where they'll be more comfortable, and I'll rent an apartment and find work in Whitehorse."

"Did I miss our discussion on this?" Nancy says. "Because I'm quite certain I'd have remembered it."

Tomas folds his hands in his lap. "I should have done this twelve years ago. Taken you away instead of marrying you and tying you down with —"

"With our *children*?" Her voice rises. "If I have ever — ever — given the impression that I consider our children anything but blessings —"

"I don't mean it like that," he says quickly. "I just . . . I made a mistake, and I want to fix it now." He looks at her. "I want to set you free."

"Set me free? Or be rid of me?"

Dalton says, "Maybe Casey and I should wait out —"

Nancy doesn't seem to hear him. "I made a mistake. Not a mistake in what happened with Ellen. Maybe I should say that was wrong, but it was something I needed. The mistake was not telling you that I needed it

400

and working out a solution together. If you want to leave, then I understand, but as for setting me free?" She meets his gaze. "You never held me captive. I could have left anytime I wanted. I didn't want to."

I slide toward the exit, Dalton following, but Nancy stops us.

"Yes, we apologize for making you bear witness to a very personal conversation," she says, "but I have a feeling if you aren't here, this won't be resolved. You are our passage south. We need to decide this before you go."

That isn't true. We'll be back. But I understand what she's saying. They've avoided this conversation for over a decade, and if we're awaiting an answer, they can't push it aside again.

"Do you want this?" Nancy asks Tomas. "If you do, then yes, we'll go south and start over in separate lives sharing our children. Because that last part is the most important. I'd never give them up, and I'd never ask you to. They are ours, whether we are together or not. But if you're offering me a way out of this marriage, the answer is no. I don't want that. If you're saying I can stay on the condition this never happens again . . ."

She meets his gaze. "I cannot promise you

401

that. I have no idea if it will or won't, and that is a very long conversation we need to have if we want to make this work. But I would *like* to make it work. You are my partner. You are my friend. You are my lover. Nothing has changed for me. With Ellen, I was answering a question about myself that I should have answered twelve years ago. And I don't know if I did. I found something I needed, but it didn't change what I already have, and I'm not sure what to make of that. I need time to work it through, if you can give me that."

Tomas nods. That's all he does. Wordlessly nods, his eyes glistening.

"You want me to stay?" she says.

Another nod, and a quiet, "Please."

"Then the question is 'do *we* stay.' And the answer . . ." She exhales. "The answer is no. Not here. Not after all this. It will be too hard for the children, and really, that's just the excuse I think we needed to go. We'll remain for the winter and then we'll decide our next step."

And now, in the midst of tragedy, I need to ask them a question unrelated to any of this. I kick myself for not doing it earlier, but it isn't as if I'd forgotten the reason we were here: to find Abby's parents.

Earlier, it'd been clear that Nancy didn't

realize Ellen had been trading goods to help Abby's mother, so I didn't see a lead there. Also, I'd suspected one of them might have murdered Ellen, so I hadn't been about to expose Abby's existence. Now, though, with Ellen's death unrelated to Abby, there's no reason not to ask.

I ask with extreme care, hoping I won't seem too callous.

Sorry your nephew murdered your friend and lover, but while I'm here, maybe you could help with this other case?

It helps, of course, that the "other case" is a lost baby. It's hard to begrudge help with that. They are both horrified and relieved. Horrified that Lane almost accidentally killed an infant . . . and relieved that the child is safely in Rockton.

"We had no idea," Nancy says. "It makes sense, now that you've told us. Yes, she'd have wanted those scraps for diapers and the balm for breastfeeding. There were other items, too, and they all fit. She was helping a woman who'd borne a winter baby."

"As she would," Tomas says softly.

Nancy's eyes glitter with tears. "Yes, she would. Absolutely. I only wish she'd told us, if only so we could help you get that baby back to her mother. She must be going mad with worry. When we find Lane, he may be able to tell us what Ellen was doing or where she was coming from when he . . . when he . . ."

She breaks off, her voice catching. Tomas reaches for her, hesitating a little, but she falls into his arms. We slip out after that, followed by Tomas's promise that they'll help us in any way they can. In return, we promise that we'll be back in a week or so, to see whether they need help finding Lane. Then we're gone.

We rest back at our campsite. We must, considering how far we need to walk. A four-hour nap before we break camp and walk until the sun starts to drop. I want to push on after that, but Dalton says no. We're less than halfway home, with no chance of making it back without more sleep. Better to find a spot and get our shelter up before it's fully dark.

We're in bed by six, asleep 1.5 seconds later. As exhausted as we are, though, we don't need twelve hours of sleep, so we're on our way again by three in the morning, our flashlights leading us through the darkness.

It's nearly noon when we reach Rockton, and I can say with absolute certainty that these were the most physically strenuous

three days of my entire life. Dalton's promise of an entire batch of fresh-baked cookies
may be the only thing that gets me through
the last ten kilometers. I'm holding him to
that, too, and washing them down with
multiple mugs of spiked coffee, followed by
an afternoon nap that may last until morning.

I reach the town perimeter and topple
face-first into the snow. Or I try to, but my
feet tangle in the snowshoes and Dalton
grabs me before I snap my ankle with my
drama-queen gesture. He lifts me over his
arms, and I struggle to get out, saying, "I'm
fine. Just being a brat."

"Too late. I'm carrying you."

I start to settle in. Then he flips me over
his shoulder, firefighter style, which is a
whole lot less flattering.

"No, no, no," I say, renewing my struggles.
"Just let me —"

"Too late."

"You can't —"

"— embarrass you by carrying you over
my shoulder through town? Yep, I believe I
can."

Storm starts dancing around us, barking,
finding her second wind. I grab the back of
Dalton's parka and yank, and I'm just goof-
ing around, but it's hard enough to make

him stagger, and apparently Storm chooses that moment to cut in front of him, and we all go down in a heap of curses and yelps and giggles.

As we untangle ourselves, a voice says, "First, you disappear for three days. Now you are napping at noon. I understand the holidays are coming, but as a taxpayer, I object."

I twist to see Mathias standing there. "Since when do you pay taxes?"

"I treat each and every person in this community with marginal respect. It is very taxing."

We untangle, and Dalton and Storm rise as I snap off my snowshoes. "What are you doing out and about?"

"There is caroling. It began at ten in the morning. After two hours, my choices were to walk in the forest or begin a quiet but relentless slaughter of the offenders. Knowing the latter would force you to work through the holidays, I chose the former. It is my gift to you."

"Thanks."

We start for the town.

Mathias falls in beside me. "Also, speaking of relentless, we must discuss this constant flow of visitors you have unleashed on our peaceful village, Casey."

"Peaceful?" Dalton says. "Where have you been living?"

"In a town where people do not wander in from the forest and make themselves at home. Your detective is the Pied Piper of the Yukon, leading people to our town with her charming manner and sunny disposition."

I look at Dalton. "You have another detective?"

"Compared to me, you *are* pretty damned charming. Not sure about sunny, but people definitely find you less intimidating than me, which just means they don't know you very well."

Dalton turns to Mathias. "Yeah, we've been doing more outreach since Casey's been here. Building relationships with the community really wasn't my strength, apparently. If you're talking about Tyrone —"

"I'd rather not really. Mr. Cypher has chosen his alias well. I do not know what to make of him, and I have decided he is a puzzle I do not care to solve. The problem is that the procession of strays does not end. I discovered only today that you had a hostile in town. A live hostile, which you promised me for study, and you whisked her in and out without a word to me."

"You requested a hostile," I say. "I chose

407

to deny that request."

"Instead, you give me other strays. A wolf and a feral boy."

"First, you *asked* for Raoul. Plenty of people wanted him, and you got him, and therefore you owed me a favor, which you repaid by taking Sebastian, who is a resident, not a stray. Also not feral."

"He spent half his life being raised by narcissists who treated him as a fashion accessory. Then he spent the other half imprisoned for their murders. He may have learned very pretty manners, but Sebastian is as feral as that half-breed dog, and I have spent six months sleeping with one eye open, wondering which will kill me first."

I could point out that Sebastian doesn't live with Mathias, but instead I shrug as we enter town. "Fine. Give me the dog. Our deputy will be thrilled to have —"

"It is too late. Raoul is accustomed to me."

"Then I'll take Sebastian back and —"

"He is accustomed to me as well. And it is my duty to monitor him, for the sake of the town. No one else is equipped or trained for such a task."

"You're just bitching for the sake of bitching, aren't you?"

"I do not *bitch*. I simply point out that you need to stem this flow of strays. You have barely removed one when another takes her place."

I stop and look at him. "What?"

"You have a visitor. She is in the town square. William attempted to show her the hospitality of the police station, but she is another of your wild things and refuses to go indoors. She is with Raoul and Sebastian. Raoul is guarding her. Sebastian is . . ." He purses his lips. "I am not certain what he is doing. Perhaps drinking in the rare beauty of this wilderness flower. Perhaps considering the myriad ways he could kill her with maximum efficiency, should she prove a threat. He may be doing both simultaneously. It is Sebastian."

I pick up my pace, breaking into a jog as I shout back, "Next time, Mathias? Cut the preamble and get to the damned point."

"That would be no fun at all," he calls after me.

THIRTY-FIVE

When Mathias says we've attracted another woman from the woods, hinting she's young and attractive, my first thought is Cherise. Yet when I draw close, I spot a small dark-haired figure, one who is younger and significantly more welcome than Cherise. It's Edwin's granddaughter, Felicity.

Sebastian is neither gaping at her nor plotting her demise. He's playing host, pulling out his charm and his manners and his high-society upbringing, telling Felicity a story complete with blazing smiles and dramatic gestures. There's no flirtation there. Yes, she's his age and pretty, but if he's noticed that, he's tucked it aside, as if it would be rude to see her as anything but a guest in need of hospitality.

As for Felicity . . .

I remember when I was thirteen, and my mother sent me to finishing school. Okay, it wasn't called "finishing school." I'm not sure those exist anymore, and I sure as hell wouldn't have attended. It was billed as weekly classes for teen girls to learn teen-girl stuff, everything from putting on makeup to protecting yourself online.

I might never have been the most feminine girl, but I was not opposed to learning the secret language of stiletto heels and smoky eyeliner. While the class offered that, it was more like a finishing school, with lessons for privileged young ladies to learn to act like privileged young ladies.

I *was* privileged. I took private lessons and flew business class — well, unless there weren't enough seats, and then my parents put April and me in economy, supposedly as a lesson so we'd grow up vowing to get the kind of careers that meant we never needed to fly coach again.

The point is that those girls should have been my people. Except I was a half-Asian tomboy from the suburbs, and they were all white, elegant, and city-bred. I felt like a gawky country girl stumbling into a debutante ball.

That's how Felicity looks sitting beside Sebastian. She follows his story stone-faced, her gaze locked on him in a look of barely concealed panic. Not so much transfixed as held captive, fearing if she moves a single

411

muscle she'll reveal herself as a teenager from a very different planet than the one this self-assured and animated boy clearly inhabits.

When Sebastian sees me, he smiles and stands with "Hey, Casey," and I swear Felicity deflates in relief.

"I was keeping Felicity company while she waited," he says. "Talking her ear off with my boring stories." He flashes a smile her way. "Sorry."

"Yes." Color rises on her cheeks. "I mean, yes, you were keeping me company. No, your stories were not boring." She flails a moment, as if struggling to find the girl I met the other day, the one who'd been equally self-assured in her natural environment. "I came to talk to you, Casey."

"And now you can," Sebastian says. "You're free of my awkward hospitality."

"Yes." Another mortified flush. "I mean, yes, she's here, and yes, you do not need to stay with me any longer. Thank you for keeping me company. It was very kind."

He grins. "My pleasure. I will leave you in Casey's capable hands."

He jogs off, and Felicity watches him go.

"How . . . old is he?" she asks tentatively.

"Nineteen. He's our youngest resident."

"Oh. I am eighteen. Angus is twenty, and

that boy seems . . . older, but he didn't look it, so I thought . . . I suppose that is how boys are, down south."

"Not exactly," I say. "Sebastian is a special case, but I'm glad he kept you company."

"He was very entertaining. His stories were funny." She takes a deep breath, throwing off any lingering discomfiture, and turns to me. "I have information you want. I would like to trade for it."

I glance around. Dalton's taken Storm to get her stitched up at the clinic, and he's left me to this.

"All right," I say. "Let's go into the police station —"

"I would prefer to stay outside."

"May we at least leave the town square? Everyone can hear our conversation here."

She nods, and we begin walking.

"You found a baby," she says. "That's why you came to my grandfather. You didn't tell me that. You should have."

"Edwin had already told us where to find the baby's parents."

"He lied."

"So we discovered," I mutter. "The clothing came from the Second Settlement, not the trading family he sent us to."

"Did you speak to the traders?"

I nod.

"And what did you think?"

"You were right. Not the sort of people I care to do business with."

"They *can* trade fairly. The problem is that we only use them when we must, and then they know how badly we need their supplies, so we pay far too much. Grandfather would prefer not to do business with them. He'd rather do business with you."

"Understandable. We'd rather do business with him."

"Good."

She slows to look up at a decorated pine towering over us. I imagine her assessing not the beauty of the object, but the relative wealth that it requires — the expenditure of both time and goods.

"It's the holidays," I say. "Time to celebrate the solstice."

She nods. "We do that as well. We do not string berries in trees, though."

"The birds will appreciate them."

She snorts. "The birds that come for those will not be good eating."

Apparently she thinks our decorated trees are luring dinner. I'm about to say not everything is about food, but fortunately, I do nothing so thoughtless. For settlers, everything *is* about food — or shelter or basic survival.

"People enjoy seeing the birds," I say simply.

"You sound like those from the Second Settlement."

I glance over at her. "I thought you didn't have contact with them."

She shrugs. "That is my grandfather's way. It is their elders' way. It is not our way." She pauses to watch a few residents race by, sliding on the packed snow and laughing like children. She shakes her head. "It is different here."

"They're just on lunch break before their afternoon shift."

"So you met the Second Settlement," she says. "What did you think of *them*?"

"Interesting."

A snort. "That is one way to put it. They have ideas. Odd ideas. They won't trade with you, though. Not the way we will."

"I got that impression."

She nods, satisfied. "My grandfather should have let you go to them. There's nothing to fear. He just worries." She looks at me. "I would like a gun."

"So you've said. But right now we're still busy trying to find this baby's parents."

"That is why I'm here. To trade. It is also why you should have told me about the baby. I know who it belongs to."

"Do you?" I say, keeping my voice calm. "Oddly, your grandfather said the same thing. Those traders also tried to claim her."

"Is it a her?" Something flickers in her eyes, gone before I can chase it. She nods. "You have been fed many lies, but I tell the truth."

"In return for a gun?"

"Yes."

I face her. "Yeah, here's the problem with that. Edwin told us the baby was from these traders, in hopes we'd keep her and avoid contact with the Second Settlement. The traders told us she was theirs, in hopes we'd pay them for her. Now you're telling us you know where she belongs, in hopes of getting a gun. See the pattern? We've spent a damned week tramping through the forest, trying to give a family back their lost baby. This doesn't benefit us at all, and everyone *else* is trying to benefit from our good deed, and I'm getting really pissed off. If you don't actually know who this baby's parents are, then I'd suggest you turn around right now and go back to the First Settlement or you are never going to see a gun from me."

She eyes me, much the way she might eye a wolf in the forest, trying to decide exactly how dangerous it is. "You're frustrated."

"How very astute of you."

416

Her lips quirk. I won't call it a smile, but it's something. She might be appreciating my directness. Or she might be amused at my show of weakness, allowing my temper to get the better of me.

"No one out here will reward you for your good deeds," she says.

"I'm not looking for —"

"A reward, I know. You want us to help or stay out of your way. Instead, we're making your task unnecessarily difficult."

"Yes."

She eyes me again, head tilting as if considering. Then she says, "It is a test. Not intentionally or overtly, but in the end, you are being tested. Do you see through the lies? How easily are you manipulated? How much can you be used? That's what everyone out here is thinking. How useful can you be to them? And you are thinking the same thing. Can the First Settlement be useful? The Second? The traders? Tyrone? Jacob?"

She lifts a hand against my protest. "Yes, Jacob is Eric's brother, and you are not trying to use him, but it is still a reciprocal relationship. Your goal is not to take advantage but to establish mutually beneficial relationships. Everyone else is doing the same. They're just less concerned about making those relationships fair. Everyone wants the best deal. You would not take advantage of Jacob. You might not even take advantage of me, because I am young. But if you could take advantage of those traders? Of course you would. Everyone wants something. No one wants to be cheated."

She's right, of course. That isn't only life up here; it's life in general. It's just more obvious here, everyone angling for an advantage over the limited resources we share.

"They are testing you," she says. "You're a good person. The question is *how* good, and can it be used against you? You ask whether I'm lying. I'd be a fool to do that, wouldn't I? It would be cheating you on our first trade. Foolish and shortsighted, like a bear trampling an entire berry patch for one meal. Better to cultivate the patch."

"And you're cultivating me."

"You know I am. There's no point in lying. Also, I don't do it. That's my grandfather's way, and it works for him. It does not work for me. If I don't want to tell you the truth, I won't answer. When I say I know where to find this baby's parents, I'm negotiating in good faith. I'll take you to them, and then you owe me a gun."

"You'll hold this child hostage for a gun."

Something flashes behind her eyes. Then her jaw sets, and she says simply, "I would like a gun. I believe finding this baby's parents is important to you, and therefore worth the price I'm asking."

If I don't want to tell you the truth, I won't answer.

I remember her expression when I said the baby was a girl. That flicker of emotion.

"You know her parents," I say.

"Did I not say that?" she snaps, annoyed at being more transparent than she intended.

"I will pay you for this information." I say. "Five hundred dollars' worth of our goods or two hundred and fifty of your choice, to be purchased in Dawson."

Her eyes harden. "That means nothing to me."

I wince. Of course. Unlike Cherise, who travels to Dawson, Felicity has never used money. "Right, sorry. Five hundred dollars would buy you five good pairs of boots or five decent parkas or five hundred cans of soup."

She tries to cover her shock, and says nonchalantly, "How many guns?"

I smile. "Nice try, but if the council caught us buying guns for you, they'd kick us out. Later, I can try to negotiate to get you *one,* but I can't promise that now. It's the five hundred in random goods or two-fifty in goods of your choice, same as I offered Cherise."

She blinks. "You offered Cherise so much for finding this baby's parents? That was . . . unwise." She says it carefully, an adult gently admonishing a child too young to know better.

"In retrospect, it probably was. Fortunately, it seems I'll be paying you instead."

"I will take your goods minus the price of a gun, which you will get me before spring or pay me double its value in additional goods."

That's fair, but I pretend to consider it before agreeing.

"The baby's mother is from the First Settlement," she says. "She is — was — a companion of mine. We'd meet up with a couple of the Second settlers around our age. My grandfather doesn't know this, and I would appreciate you not telling him."

"I won't. I'm sure he's seen it with others, though. You're two small communities with a limited number of people your own age. Down south, that'd been like the kids from neighboring small-town schools hanging out together." I smile. "It widens the dating pool."

She frowns, and I'm about to explain when she figures it out, deciphering unfamiliar words from the context.

"You mean our choices for marriage prospects," she says.

"Or just romantic relationships."

A wave of one hand, dismissing the concept. I suppose, to them, dating would be similar to wooing a hundred years ago. There's always an end goal, and that goal is finding a marriage partner.

"I sought out their young settlers for an exchange of ideas," she says. "I see advantage in that where my grandfather does not. We hunted together. We camped together. We grew close."

"You became friends."

A twist of her lips. This is a girl who sees friendship — like romance — as a frivolity for those who can afford to be frivolous, and she cannot.

"You became allies," I say, and she nods, clearly more comfortable with that. "But your friend — your *companion* — found more. She found a marriage partner."

Felicity's face darkens. "That was not supposed to happen. Intermarriage between the communities is forbidden."

I chuckle. "When it comes to romance, nothing tastes as sweet as the forbidden fruit. People have written a thousand stories about it."

"*Romeo and Juliet,*" she says, her lip curling. I must look surprised because she gives me just the faintest hint of an eye roll. "We are not savages. The first generation brought their stories, and my grandfather brought books. We all know *Romeo and Juliet.* A ridiculous tale of two foolish dolts."

I have to smile at that. "They were very young."

"I heard the story when I was younger than the characters, and my reaction was no different. Romeo is madly in love with some other girl, sees Juliet, and falls madly in love with *her.* The boy wanted to be madly in love, nothing more."

"I'm not disagreeing."

"Even Sidra said Romeo and Juliet were dolts. And then what does she do? Falls madly in love with a boy from the Second Settlement and runs away with him." Felicity harrumphs. "They might as well have committed suicide. For all I know, she died in childbirth, with no one to help her." Felicity's face stays dark, scowling, but I see the fear in her eyes. Fear and worry and hurt.

"The baby has been well fed," I say. "She'd need her mother alive for that."

She nods, the relief seeping out. Then she snaps, "Then Sidra was lucky. But what about next time? Is she going to continue breeding with him? Without any help? I could have —" Her teeth shut with a click, and she retreats into a deeper scowl. "Dolts."

"You didn't know she was pregnant," I say softly.

"How could I? She left the summer before last, and I warned her that if she went, I wouldn't . . ." Felicity swallows and doesn't finish.

"You said you wouldn't help her, but you didn't really mean that. She took you seriously and stayed away."

"I was angry. I begged her to stay. Not to give him up. I knew better than to ask that. But if she'd given me time, I could have brought Grandfather around to the idea. She didn't even give me time to *ask* him. She staged her own death, like Juliet. Can you believe that? They both did, the fools. They left bloodied clothing, and I was supposed to grieve as if she'd died." Her jaw tightens. "I didn't. That would feel like a lie. So I pretended I didn't believe she'd died, and everyone thinks I just can't handle the truth."

"She put you in a very awkward position."

"Yes, she did. Grandfather listens to me, but she didn't trust me. She thought if she asked, they'd marry her off to Angus. I've known her since we were babies, and she is . . . She was very important to me, and I was not so important to . . ."

A deep breath as she blinks back tears and straightens. "She chose him. She met him, and she chose him, and she forgot me."

It's an old story. Diana accused me of shunning her when I fell for Dalton. Of course, that ignores the fact that she dumped me with every new boyfriend since we were in high school together. Also, the entire reason I'm in Rockton is because she and her ex conspired to convince me I'd been found out for Blaine's murder.

This has, I suspect, been the complaint of friends since time immemorial. A romantic partner shouldn't replace a best friend, but they are competition for that role. In circumstances like mine, your lover is also your friend, yet it's not like simply adding a new friend to the mix, because you want plenty of alone time with this one. That leaves your best friends to the timeworn wail of "you're always with them," devolving into the desperate battle cries of "bros before hos" and "chicks before dicks."

I doubt Sidra forgot Felicity. It just feels

that way.

As much as I value my friendships, no one can ever be as close to me as Dalton. We work together, play together, live together, plan our futures together. That doesn't mean I fail to understand Felicity's hurt. I felt it myself every time Diana swanned off with a new lover, forgetting me until a hole in her social calendar needed filling.

I could give Felicity advice. But she won't want it. She needs to work this out for herself. Instead, I ask if she has any idea where to find Sidra and her partner. She doesn't know exactly where they're camping, but she has a rough idea. The region is about a half day's walk from here . . . in the direction of where we found Abby.

"May I see the baby?" she asks.

"Of course."

THIRTY-SIX

Petra has Abby while Jen naps. We pass Dalton, who strides by with a gesture that I think means he'll catch up with us, but he's moving too fast for me to be sure. I call after him that we'll be at Petra's, and he lifts a hand in acknowledgment without slowing.

When Petra opens the door to Felicity, she does a subtle shift into the young woman's line of sight, as if blocking her from seeing Abby.

"This is Felicity," I say. "She's Edwin's granddaughter. She's a friend of the baby's mom."

Petra nods, but she's still wary as she escorts us in. We find Abby in a wooden cradle that someone has painted with a carousel of wild animals.

"We're gone three days, and you guys have built her a cradle and decorated it."

"She was in a box," Petra says. "A cardboard box."

I lift a fur teddy bear from the floor and sigh, shaking my head. Abby's eyes open, and her head rolls as her lips purse in what threatens to be a wail if I don't pick her up in the next two seconds. I scoop her out of the cradle and hug her, crooning under my breath. She snuggles in and then stops, head rolling again.

"No, Eric isn't here," I say. "You have to make do with me."

"Daddy's little —" Petra begins, and then her gaze shunts to Felicity and she stops herself. This isn't our baby. She has parents, and unless they abandoned her, she's going back to them. Still, Petra's lips tighten as she assesses Felicity again.

I turn to Felicity, who hasn't said a word. I hold out Abby, and she just stands there, looking at her. Then she touches one finger to the baby's cheek.

"Does she look like your friend?" Petra asks, and there's challenge in that, as if she's going to make damned sure we aren't being misled.

"She looks like a baby," Felicity says. "My friend does not."

I smile at that. "True."

"Sidra has skin the color of mine," she says. "Her grandmother was Arab. That's what Grandfather called her. Sidra has dark hair and blue eyes. The boy — Baptiste — is French. He also has dark hair, but lighter skin and brown eyes. I see nothing that says this baby is not theirs, but they will need to confirm that, of course."

I explain the full situation, and Petra only says, "So you don't even know if your friends had a baby?"

"We'll confirm it, like Felicity says," I counter. "Now —"

Two sharp knocks at the door, and I see Dalton through the front window, something in his hands. Petra calls a welcome, and the door clicks open and then smacks into the wall, as if he has his hands full.

"You breaking down my door, Sheriff?" Petra calls as she walks into the front hall. "Ah, you come bearing gifts. You're forgiven. You will have to pay the toll, though."

"Better ask Casey. I promised her a whole batch."

He walks in with an insulated box and a thermos. Abby has her head up again, wobbling toward him.

"Someone hears you," I say. "Trade?"

He takes the baby, and I get the treats. The thermos holds spiked coffee, and the box is stuffed with chocolate chip cookies, warm from the oven.

"Oh my God," I say. "I love you."

428

"I keep my promises." He hefts Abby, talking to her. While I know it's gas, I swear she smiles up at him. "How about you, kiddo? You want a cookie? Irish coffee? Make you sleep really well tonight and let us get some rest?"

Abby coos at him.

"She has parents," Felicity says.

"Everyone does. I'm hoping that means you can help us get her back to them?"

Felicity hesitates. There's annoyance in her gaze, offended on her friend's behalf at this man who's playing with Abby as if she's his. Not unlike Petra eyeing Felicity, ready to defend my claim on the baby.

I tell Dalton about Sidra and Baptiste as I pass out cookies. Felicity examines hers and then takes a tiny bite, startling at the taste and pulling back as if poisoned.

"What is this?" she says, touching her fingertip to a gooey chocolate chip. "Fruit gone bad?"

"Does it taste bad?" I say.

"Don't say yes," Dalton says. "Or she won't let you finish that cookie. Casey is very protective of her chocolate chips."

"This is chocolate?" Felicity touches it again. "I've heard of it in books." She puts her fingertip in her mouth, tasting it and then nodding. "It's good. I just didn't know what it was." She lifts the cookie. "And this is a cookie?"

"Yep." I take a mug from Petra as she brings them. "This is coffee. Spiked with brandy. Alcohol. Which you are, by Yukon law, one year too young to drink."

"We don't drink it anyway," she says. "It is forbidden."

"Well, you can try it or we can brew you a regular cup."

She considers and then accepts a quarter cup. We sit and make plans for tracking Abby's parents. It's too late to head out today, so we'll start before dawn. Felicity will come with us. She insists before I can offer. She's making sure *her* tip is the one that leads us to Abby's parents and there's no wiggle room to claim otherwise. Or that's what she says. The truth, I suspect, is that she wants the excuse to reunite with her friend.

Stubborn pride. The kind that only hurts yourself, that stops you from having something you really want because God forbid anyone should think you want anything.

I understand that. I understand it all too well.

"You can stay in my old place," I say.

Felicity shakes her head. "I have a tent

and blankets. I will camp outside your town."

"Yeah, no," Dalton says. "First, you don't trust us to play fair with your lead, and we don't trust you not to send us on a wild-goose chase like your granddaddy did."

"I would not —"

"Second, I cannot allow anyone to camp outside our town. You are a guest here, but you're also an intruder. You'll sleep where I tell you to sleep."

"She can stay here," Petra says.

Dalton and Petra exchange a look. Petra isn't being hospitable; she wants Felicity under watch. When Dalton's gaze slips my way, I hesitate. Petra is the council's tool. She has killed for them. She has also vowed that her loyalties lie with Rockton itself over the council and even her grandmother.

At what point is a lack of trust simply caution? And at what point does it tip into pride?

You hurt me. I feel betrayed. I understand that it wasn't about me, but I want to stand my ground. Keep that door shut so you can't hurt me again.

That's what I feel, and it is exactly what I suspect Felicity does, with Sidra.

"I'll go with you tomorrow, too," Petra says when I finally agree.

"We shouldn't take the baby," Felicity says. "So we won't need you to look after her."

Petra looks at Felicity and bursts out laughing. "Yeah, kid, I'm offering to go along as the babysitter. You just keep thinking that." She turns to me. "I'm guessing you'll take Abby tonight and —"

"Her name is Abby?" Felicity says. "How do you know that?" Her expression says she's guessed the answer, and she'd better be wrong.

"We don't know what Sidra and Baptiste named her," I say. "But we needed something to call her. It doesn't mean anything."

Felicity's gaze moves to the painted cradle and the toys. Then she looks back at me.

"Yes," I say, "we have too much free time here. People wanted to do something for Ab— the baby. Sidra will be welcome to take anything they've made. Now, I think we should —"

"I'd like to go along tomorrow," Petra repeats, as if I've forgotten the request. Technically, she should ask Dalton, but her gaze is on me.

When I don't answer, she says, "Will has to stay in town. Tyrone is still here, but you'd need to pry him away from Jen. Also, with you both being gone for a few days, it's been easier on Will having Tyrone around playing backup deputy."

"We've already found Ellen's killer," I say. "This is a simple tracking mission. I'm not even sure both Eric and I need to go."

Dalton's grunt tells me I am mistaken in this.

"I have tomorrow off," Petra says. "And I'm requesting permission to accompany you. Who knows, maybe you'll find another baby along the way and need someone to look after it." She shoots an amused glance at Felicity.

She's really saying that she doesn't trust this girl. Doesn't trust we aren't being led into a trap. If I refuse the request, I'm being stubborn . . . and maybe a little petty.

"All right," I say.

"Good," Dalton says. "Now, Felicity, I'm guessing no one has given you a tour of the town?"

"No, but I don't need —"

"We insist. It's only polite. Get your stuff on, and we'll show you around."

Dalton doesn't insist on the tour to be hospitable. It's a message, one Felicity can take home to the First Settlement, like when I told her how we store our guns and how tightly they're controlled. He also shows her that, as part of the "tour."

We have guns. More than you do. And they're locked up so tight even our residents can't get at them, so don't even think about stealing any.

We introduce her to the militia and explain the twenty-four-hour armed-guard patrols. We show her the storehouses, windowless and well secured. Of course Felicity realizes what's happening. But we don't need to point out the security features — she's already looking and calculating.

At first, I'm surprised she initially declined the tour. She's Edwin's granddaughter, and this is a rare opportunity to assess our wealth and defenses. She must be curious, too. That, I realize, is where I'm mistaken. Yes, she's curious, but she's also wary, and this is why she didn't want to come inside — because she didn't want to see more.

I had a friend in elementary school who was from a less affluent part of the city. I know that private and charter schools are popular in the States, speaking to the quality of the public school system in some areas. In Canada, private schools are for the rich. My parents used to say they were for parental bragging rights. That's not entirely true, but our public school system is good enough that parents like mine rightly declared a private education unnecessary. But there are still differences between schools themselves, and this girl's parents drove her to ours.

We became friends, and one day, I got permission to bring her home. I'd been so excited to show her my house, with my big bedroom and private bath and huge yard. That wasn't showing off — I was too young to understand such a thing. I just wanted her to see my domain, the places that were uniquely mine.

When I invited her back, she refused, and an invitation to her home never came. It's only now, as an adult, that I understand. My house was a glimpse into a world of privilege. A world where you don't share your bedroom with two sisters and your bathroom with your entire family. Where you don't bother with the neighborhood playground because your yard is bigger. Where you can open the fridge and eat whatever you want because it'll be replaced as soon as it's gone.

In my house, she saw what she lacked through sheer happenstance of birth. Had I gone to her place, I'd have seen the same — except for me, it'd have been spending time with her tight-knit, loving family. If I'd experienced that, would I have stayed away, too, avoiding a very different reminder of what could be?

Felicity looks around Rockton and compares it to what she has, and it makes her uncomfortable. Ambition is healthy. Envy is pointless and potentially destructive. It leads to the dissatisfied cry of "Why?"

Why do they have this, and I do not? It isn't fair. They don't deserve it. They haven't earned it.

But Felicity quickly finds the solution to her problem. The only healthy solution to envy: What can I learn from this that will make my own life better? She begins to examine our building construction and asks questions about our sanitary system. We answer, and we continue with the tour.

Afterward, we don't invite Felicity to join us at home. Petra will take care of her. We need time to rest and be alone. We indulge in a long dinner for two. Then Dalton goes to the station for a bit of work while I take Abby. By eight, we're asleep.

THIRTY-SEVEN

The next morning, we're off by seven, walking with flashlights into the darkness. Felicity and Petra are with us. Neither says much, and I get the impression that was the state of things last night.

When we meet up with Dalton, he says to Petra, "You got that gun I dropped by?"

She hesitates only a second before nodding and opening her jacket to reveal her personal handgun. If we get into trouble and Petra pulls out an unauthorized weapon, it'll tell Felicity we're lying about our gun regulations. Petra understands this and plays along.

We take Storm with us. Abby stays behind. I do not expect that we're going to find unfit parents at the end of this journey. At worst, it might be a young couple who, with great reluctance, abandoned a winter-born child. That's horrifying to us, but it's the way Sidra was raised, and possibly Baptiste, too, and it's been the way of hunting societies since time immemorial.

If this is the situation, I'll struggle to see them as good parents for making that choice, but I must put that aside and ask instead "What if you could keep her?" *What if we gave you what you needed to make it through the winter with an infant?* If the answer is still no — that they are not ready for a child — then we'll take her.

If they want Abby, I'll still bring Sidra back to Rockton to ensure she is her mother. How much of that is healthy caution and how much is a secret hope that we can keep Abby? I don't know, and I'm afraid to analyze. I do know that I will not stand between these parents and their child.

It's late morning by the time we reach the area, about five kilometers past where we found Abby. Before Sidra left, she told Felicity that this would be a good area to live, where they had camped and hunted and fished with Baptiste and others from both settlements. Sidra framed it as an offhand conversation.

Hey, you know that spot where we all camped last summer? That'd be a good place to live, don't you think? Not that I'm planning to run away and fake my own death so I can be with my beloved or anything like that . . .

Clearly it'd been a hint. A plea even. Like giving an estranged friend your new phone number, in case they find that jacket you left at their apartment once.

If you want me, you know where to find me.

The place is a river valley with abundant game and fresh water and mountain shelter. While that sounds like a settler's paradise — and therefore, it should already be occupied — it is only one spot in a thousand just like it out here. It's just a matter of picking the one that suits you best. Like pioneers heading west and choosing their plot of land. The possibilities stretch to the horizon.

When the pioneers headed west, they each got a hundred and sixty acres. Out here, a settler can "claim" even more. There is no actual claim, of course. Anyone can hunt or fish or walk through your territory, and challenging them on it would be pointless. The territory this couple have staked out is huge, so they won't rush to find exactly the right spot to build a permanent home — perhaps one for summer and one for winter. The upshot is that we're talking a general area at least a couple of kilometers, and that's not easy to search.

We split up. Dalton assigns me Storm and Petra, and he sends us to check flat and open areas along the river. Meanwhile

Felicity knows a half dozen spots where they camped over the years, and she'll show those to Dalton.

We've been searching for over an hour when our paths cross and Dalton asks to take Storm. While he wanted her with me for protection, she's better sniffing those old campsites to see if she can pick up a scent.

Petra and I continue hunting along the river. She's been quiet, but now she says, "I heard you brought Maryanne to town."

I grunt a nonreply.

"Did you get any answers from her?" she asks. "About what the hostiles are, how they came to be?"

I bend and check what looks like a boot print in well-trampled snow.

"I know you thought the council was responsible for them," she says. "Did you find anything to support that?"

If she said it with even a hint of mockery, I wouldn't answer. But her tone sounds genuinely curious . . . with a hint of trepidation. Is that fear I'll uncover the truth? Or fear that there *is* a connection?

Her gaze shutters, giving me nothing.

I consider. Then I say, "Tea."

Her brow furrows. "What?"

I twist, still hunkered down. "The hostiles consume a narcotic and a hallucinogenic

440

tea. Same as the Second Settlement, who seem to use the latter for something that seems almost like prehistoric rituals."

"Prehistoric people consumed ritual hallucinogens, probably because the altered state made them feel as if they were seeing and communicating with their gods."

I nod. "Whatever the hostiles have added to the Second Settlement's brew makes theirs far more potent. And more dangerous. Theirs is addictive, and it affects free will — they're happy and content, and they stop thinking about their other life, eventually stop remembering they had one."

She listens, saying nothing.

I continue. "In high doses — or maybe with an added ingredient — it induces frenzies. Heightened id, lowered superego, if you took Psych 101."

A strained smile. "I did. Does that explain the violence, then?"

"Apparently." I rise. "I believe it's a natural evolution of something that began in the Second Settlement. They discover this root that makes a ritualistic tea. Someone from the settlement experiments and creates a new version and then breaks away from the group — or is kicked out — and starts their own community, which devolves into what we have today."

I wait for her to jump on the fact that I'm absolving the council, but she still seems to be processing, so I say it for her. "A natural evolution based on natural substances, with no outside influence. I still, however, hold the council responsible for allowing the devolution. Rockton has been reporting hostiles since Tyrone was sheriff. Yet the council dismissed the claims as . . ." I throw up my hands. "I don't even know what they thought people were seeing. Bears? Settlers?"

"I was told it was both," she says, unexpectedly. "That some settlers were more violent than others, and some had 'reverted' more than others — not being as 'civilized' in their dress and their mannerisms. The more extreme accounts were thought to be wild animals mistaken for humans, probably bears."

I wait for her to add a justification, a defense. Being a thousand miles away, the council understandably questioned the wild stories, like the tales of ancient sailors spotting manatees and somehow mistaking the ugly sea mammals for beautiful women. Isolation plays tricks on the mind, heightens fears and desires. To the council, Rockton's hostile sightings were no different from Bigfoot sightings. Even I will grant them that, and I expect Petra to point this out. Maybe she thinks it's obvious. Maybe now that I've acknowledged my mistake, she doesn't want to rub my face in it.

When she says nothing, I continue. "The point is that with so many sightings and encounters, they should have encouraged investigation. Better yet, they should have sent a team to investigate. What they'd have found isn't a tribe of happy former Rockton residents gone native. It was a drug-enslaved cult where at least some of the members, like Maryanne, didn't sign up voluntarily. She was from Rockton. Her whole party was — the two men the hostiles brutally murdered and the two women they took hostage. Maryanne played along, expecting the chance to escape, and instead fell under the influence of the tea. The other woman did escape — and was hunted down, tied up naked, and left to the elements and the predators and the scavengers. This is what the council allowed."

Petra looks as if she's going to be sick. I don't expect that either. She takes a deep breath before straightening with, "All right."

"All right what?" I say, a little sharply.

Silence. Then, "All right, I understand, and I agree this has been handled badly."

I wait for more. When it doesn't come,

I'm annoyed, and I don't like that. Am I spoiling for a fight? My mistake with the hostiles and the council has bruised my ego, so now I want Petra to say "I told you so" so I can light into her?

Today's hunt has me on edge, and Petra's not giving me the response I want so I'm being cranky.

Forget hostiles and the council and Petra. None of them have anything to do with returning Abby to her parents.

I find a footprint, and I focus on that. It's near the riverbank, pointing inland.

The river is mostly frozen, but temperatures haven't dropped enough for it to be a solid sheet of ice, and we're near an inlet that's running too fast to freeze. That's why the snow is so trampled — animals finding this spot and drinking. I definitely saw a boot print, though, and when I search, I locate more. Humans have used this spot for water. Possibly also for hunting. Drops of blood and scattered white fur suggest an Arctic hare was killed as it came to drink.

It's been two days since the last snowfall. These prints are even more recent, layered on top of animal ones. When I get about three meters from the river, the prints fan out, the animals and the humans going their separate ways. I can get a better view of the human ones here. Two sets, one about a men's size ten, and one a little bigger than mine. A man and a woman, both dressed in boots like what Ellen wore, thick and heavy, with no tread.

The human prints lead to the remains of a camp. A year ago, I'd have walked right through it. Now I notice the rectangle where a tent stood. I see irregular patterns in the snow where items were set down. I spot blood under a tree nearby, where game was hung and slaughtered. And there's the firepit. It's only a circular patch of packed snow, but I dig down to find embers still warm.

"A camp," Petra says, as if just realizing this.

I nod.

"What's that over there?" she says.

I twist, still crouched, as she heads toward whatever she's spotted. When I catch movement in the trees, I start to call a warning. Then I see a dark parka-like jacket on a man Dalton's size.

She's looking at something else, and as she bends for a better study, the figure moves from the trees, and it is not Dalton.

"Petra!" I call, my own gun out, rising.

She spins to her feet . . . and the figure raises a rifle.

445

"Stop!" I shout. "There is a gun pointed at your head, and there are two more people walking up behind you right now." I'm hoping I'm loud enough for Dalton to hear if he's nearby. "We are all armed. Lower your weapon —"

"Lower yours," the man says. He's young, and his voice is deep and seems steady, but I've dealt with enough situations like this to recognize that tremor, the one that says he's in a situation he's not equipped to handle. It's too easy to pull that trigger when you're afraid and angry and trying to pretend you are willing to do it. I know that better than anyone.

"Baptiste?" I say.

His shoulders jerk just enough for me to know I've guessed right.

"Where's Sidra?" I ask.

"That's my question to you," he says, in a voice that carries the accent of those raised in the Second Settlement. "What have you done with my wife?"

"Nothing," I say. "We came looking for you. We're with Felicity."

"Felicity?" Baptiste spits, and his gaze turns on me. "*She* took Sidra, didn't she? Dragging her back to that grandfather of hers. If I —"

Petra flies at him. She dives at his legs,

446

knocking him back. The gun fires. Not a rifle but a shotgun blast.

"Casey!" Dalton's voice slams through the forest.

"Gun down!" I shout, as much for Dalton as for them, to let him know I'm fine. "Put the goddamn gun —"

"I've got it," Petra says. "We're both fine, no thanks to this idiot."

"And no thanks to the idiot who jumped a kid with a shotgun," I say as I walk over.

"I didn't expect him to have his finger on the trigger."

"In the real world, people often do. We aren't all government-trained secret agents."

"I'm not . . ." Petra trails off, shaking her head.

"Not government trained?" I say.

She only rolls her eyes and holds out the shotgun. I walk past her to where pellets peppered a tree. I dig one out.

A buckshot pellet.

Just like the one that killed Ellen.

THIRTY-EIGHT

I turn to Baptiste. He's about eighteen. Brown eyes. Dark curls cut in a mop that makes him look like the puppy-cute guy in a boy band. He's trying very hard to play this cool, setting his jaw and hardening his eyes, but those eyes don't have the life experience to harden. He reminds me of every kid I questioned who got caught up in a petty crime with his friends, struggling to play it tough while two seconds from breaking down and admitting he's made a huge mistake, but he'll take the punishment, just please don't call his parents.

Dalton comes at a run, calling a warning before he bursts through, as if we wouldn't hear him. Baptiste gives a start as Storm races past.

"She's a dog," I say, patting her head. "Eric, this is —"

"You!" Baptiste spins on Felicity, who's trailing Dalton. "What did you do with

448

Sidra? Did you take Summer, too? I swear if you hurt either of them . . ."

Summer.

The baby's name is Summer.

That throws me enough that it takes a moment for me to react, and Dalton beats me to it, grabbing Baptiste's shoulder as he advances on Felicity. Even then, my brain throws up excuses. Maybe Summer is a friend. Or a pet.

Yes, Casey, they have a pet dog named Summer, and this isn't Abby's father. It's pure coincidence that their dog is also, apparently, missing.

Dalton's hand tightens on Baptiste's shoulder. "You see those guns pointed at you, kid? Those mean 'Don't move.' "

"Just like the one you had pointed at me," Petra says.

"You moved," he says.

"And could have gotten you both shot up with those pellets," I say.

Those pellets.

He was carrying a gun loaded with buckshot.

Like the weapon used to kill Ellen.

The weapon Lane swore he didn't have.

Yet Lane also swore he murdered Ellen.

A flash of Tomas saying Lane had a friend who died last year. Then Felicity saying she and Sidra hung out with two kids from the Second Settlement.

Shit.

Questions and theories ping through my brain, and I squeeze my eyes shut and push them back. Gather more data. Work this through.

"Where is Sidra?" Felicity says.

"That's what I'm asking you," Baptiste says, as they lock glowers. "You took her back to your grandfather, didn't you?"

"She's missing?" Felicity's eyes snap. "You lost your baby, and now you've lost Sidra?"

"I didn't lose —"

"Enough," Dalton says. "Felicity, go sit over there with Petra. Baptiste, you and Sidra have a baby?"

"Had," Felicity says. "Had and lost —"

Baptiste swings on her, and Dalton and I both raise our weapons, ready to order him back, but it's only a warning lunge, accompanied by a snarl.

"Felicity?" I say. "Sit and be quiet, please. Even if he provokes you."

"I'm not the one —" Baptiste begins.

"You don't get along," I say. "That appears to be an understatement. But we need answers, and we aren't getting them with you two spitting at each other like bobcats."

That is really what they look like, backing

up, glaring at one another. It reminds me of Diana and Dalton, Diana convinced he's keeping her from me, and Dalton hating the way she's treated me. The lover and the friend as rivals. It doesn't need to be that way, but sometimes it is, and as with Dalton and Diana, it goes deeper, to a fundamental personality clash that the competition only exacerbates. I suspect that's the same here — that even without Sidra in the middle, these two never got along.

I walk to Baptiste's other side, forcing him to turn away from Felicity.

"You have a baby," I say.

He nods, and I see the struggle to remain calm, not to shout that his child is missing and his wife, too, and he doesn't have time to stand around answering my questions. The fact that he's trying suggests I was right — he's not usually a hothead who threatens strangers with shotguns. He's backed into a wall and acting out of character.

Is he? If he killed Ellen, then shooting Petra *wouldn't* be "out of character."

Tuck that aside. Focus.

"A girl or a boy?" I ask.

"A girl. Summer."

"How old is she?"

"Thirty-eight days," he says, so quickly that I suspect, if given a moment, he could tell me the number of hours, too.

"What happened to Summer?" I ask.

"The wild people took her."

Petra snorts. "Is that the Yukon equivalent of 'dingoes ate my baby'?"

I give her a hard look, but she meets my gaze, her expression saying she's already decided these aren't suitable parents, based on nothing more than the fact that she doesn't want them to be.

"Evidence suggests dingoes may actually have eaten that woman's baby," Dalton says.

When I look at him, he shrugs. "I read about the case. The problem with her story was that dingoes weren't known to take children. The problem with your story, kid, is that the same applies to those you call the wild people. They don't have kids. It's against their rules. So they sure as hell aren't going to steal one."

This isn't entirely true. We know Maryanne's group prohibited children, but that doesn't mean others followed the same laws. Dalton's just putting Baptiste on the offensive, trying to break his story.

"We found evidence," Baptiste says. "The wild people came, and they took her."

"They snuck into your tent in the night?" Petra says. "Plucked her from your arms while you slept?"

452

"We did not sleep with her in our arms. Sidra's mother lost a child by accidentally suffocating her in the night, so Summer slept in a box that I built. It was evening. I was hunting, and Sidra was with the baby. She was making dinner while Summer slept in her box, right near the fire. Someone grabbed Sidra from behind. Put a sack over her head. She fought, but she was overpowered. She heard grunts of communication, like the wild people. She smelled wild people. While she was bound and blinded, they took our baby. In her place, they left one of their skulls, the sort they use to mark territory. They told Sidra not to come for Summer. The voice was low, guttural, like the wild people. They said Summer was theirs. Sidra screamed and screamed, and finally I heard her and came running. We found tracks. We tried to follow them, but they went on the ice and we could not."

"When did this happen?"

"Ten days ago. We have been searching ever since. A friend is searching, too. She used to be one of the wild people. She said she would find Summer, but we have not seen her since she left, and then, last night, Sidra disappeared."

"This friend," I say. "You said she's a wild person? Are you sure she didn't take Sum-

453

mer herself? That'd be a nice trick — steal your child, blame it on the others, and then offer to get the baby back herself."

Baptiste hesitates. I'm watching for some sign of calculation in his gaze. There are possibilities here that lay the blame for Summer's fate at his feet. Maybe he exposed her himself, pretending hostiles took her. Maybe Ellen *did* take her — rescuing her from unfit parents. If so, he'll see an opportunity here to blame Ellen, especially if he knows she's dead and can't defend herself.

I'm watching for the look that says he's considering his options. Yet when he hesitates, he only seems to be thinking through what I've said, wondering if it's possible that Ellen took their baby. Then he shakes his head.

"No," he says. "When Sidra told her the wild people took Summer, Ellen was confused. Like you said, she claimed they don't have babies. She knows of two groups in the area. Tribes, she calls them. Neither allows babies. She thought we were mistaken. Then we showed her the skull, and she said it was definitely the wild people. Her own tribe, judging by the markings. After thinking about it for a while, she said she remembered one woman who wanted a baby. Ellen wondered whether this woman might take Summer, in hopes that the tribe would let her keep her. Or maybe she wanted a baby more than she wanted to be in the tribe."

"Take Summer and flee with her," I say.

He nods. "There wouldn't be any reason for Ellen to steal Summer."

"Down south, plenty of people can't have babies and would happily pay for one."

His brow furrows. "How would Ellen get Summer down south?"

"Maybe she didn't think you should keep Summer. You and Sidra have only been on your own for a year. Adding a winter baby seems . . . unwise."

His cheeks color. "It was an accident. Ellen used to be a nurse. She said if we didn't want the baby, she'd have helped us end the pregnancy. If we did want the baby, she'd help us with that, too. It was completely up to us. We decided to have the child. The birth was easy, and Sidra's milk came in, and Summer was healthy."

All true. Abby — Summer — was indeed healthy and well cared for, and from what I learned from Tomas and Nancy, Ellen had been helping the young couple, just as she promised.

So why was Baptiste carrying the gun that

might have killed Ellen? I'm not seeing an easy answer here, and I need to set that aside. There's a bigger issue to deal with.

"Tell me about Sidra," I say. "She disappeared last night?"

Baptiste nods. "When I woke, she was gone. I didn't worry at first. She isn't sleeping well, with Summer gone. Neither of us is. She also needs to rid herself of the milk a few times a day. Ellen said that was important. She has to . . ." He struggles for the words. "Express, Ellen said. Express the milk, even if it goes to waste, so she'll keep producing it for when Summer comes back to us. It's painful — the milk — so Sidra often gets up in the night. I've told her to just do it in the tent, where it's warm, but I think she liked the excuse to . . ."

Baptiste looks away. "It hasn't been easy for us, with Summer gone. Sidra thinks I blame her because she was with Summer when it happened."

"Do you?" That's Petra, challenge in her voice.

Baptiste snaps, "Of course not. Sidra was ambushed. Maybe it's my fault. I ran as soon as I heard her screaming, but it wasn't fast enough to catch whoever took Summer. Sidra says she doesn't blame me, and I say I don't blame *her,* but . . . It's been dif-

456

ficult. I think she's found excuses to spend time away from me, and that hasn't made things easier. When I woke and found her gone, I didn't want to run after her. I . . ." He trails off.

"You wanted time away, too," Petra says. "You did blame her."

He spins on her, and I cut in with, "Petra? This isn't about you."

Her eyes spark, but her cheeks color, too, even as she turns a glare on me. I meet it evenly. She knows what I mean, just as I know why she's saying this. She lost her daughter in a car accident. At the time she'd been divorced, but she'd had a good relationship with her ex . . . until the accident. Petra had been called to pick up her daughter unexpectedly after having a couple of glasses of wine. While that impairment didn't contribute to the accident — it was the other driver's fault Petra blew under the legal limit — her ex couldn't forgive her and drove her to the brink of suicide.

Now she's looking at Baptiste — whose baby was lost on her mother's watch — and she sees her ex, and I need her to back the hell down. We lock gazes, and after a moment, she nods.

"Continue," I say to Baptiste.

"I knew Sidra needed time away from me,

like she does after an argument. I wanted to give her that, but I wanted her to know I care, too. If I left her alone too long, she might think I don't want *her* around either. I got up and made her breakfast, and then I went looking for her. I discovered she hadn't been out expressing milk. She'd been emptying her bladder. I found the spot. I also found her night-torch there, extinguished, and signs of a struggle."

"Hostiles stole my wife?" Petra says.

I let her have that one, and I watch Baptiste as he snaps, "No. I understand you're blaming me, but it doesn't appear to be wild people. One person took her. One pair of tracks. They didn't leave behind anything as they did with Summer. I followed the tracks, but whoever took her knows how to cover a trail."

"Of course they do," Petra mutters.

"So first you lose your baby," Felicity says, "and then you lose your wife."

Dalton rolls his eyes my way. I know exactly what he's thinking: *Well, at least neither of us needs to play bad cop here. We have Petra and Felicity for that.*

Felicity keeps going. "And you didn't even lose them to the same people. *That* would make sense, if the hostiles kidnapped Sidra to feed the baby. But no, it was different attackers." She meets his gaze. "Or was it the same attacker? You wanted Sidra, and the only way you could have her was to run away with her. The next thing you know you're stuck with a wife and a baby —"

"Stuck?" His voice rises. "Stuck? I would happily be *stuck* with Sidra for the rest of my life. I'd happily be stuck with her and twenty children if that's what she wanted. And before you accuse me of not wanting Summer, I did. It was our decision to keep her, and I never regretted it. I want my baby and my wife back, and I'm trying to be patient here, but the longer you keep accusing me of hurting them, the longer someone is actually hurting them."

"We have Summer," I say.

"What?" He turns on me, blinking as if he's misheard.

"Summer is in Rockton, and she's safe."

He teeters, eyes shut, relief shuddering through him. Then his eyes snap open. "You took her? Someone from Rockton stole —"

"No, you dolt," Felicity says. "Why would they be here if they stole your baby? I brought them to you."

"I'm not a dolt," he says slowly, as if restraining his temper. "I had to ask. The same as you had to ask whether I hurt

Sidra, when you know how much I love her."

"And I had to ask that because I know you have experience faking deaths. Also experience behaving like utter fools, reenacting Romeo and Juliet."

He sputters for a moment before facing me and saying, evenly, "If you suspect me because of that, let me assure you that Sidra and I are not children who thought faking our deaths would be romantic. Has Felicity told you why we did that?"

"Because the settlements would have forbidden your marriage," I say.

"Yes, but we had a plan for dealing with it, one that wouldn't have left our families grieving for us. We planned to leave together, with notes to explain, and then we'd return in a few years, after we had a child so they could not separate us. Sidra wanted to ask Felicity for help. I argued, but she trusted her friend. She didn't even get a chance to explain the plan. As soon as she said she wanted to leave with me, Felicity threatened to tie her up and keep her from making such a terrible mistake. Threatened that if she ran, the whole settlement would come after us, and if something happened to me in the pursuit, well, that wasn't Felicity's fault."

I turn slowly on Felicity.

Her cheeks are bright red. "I didn't mean it like that. I was only trying to make Sidra listen to reason. I just wanted her to slow down and let me negotiate with my grandfather."

"All right," I say. "Felicity? Please join Petra in staying out of this. You've voiced your suspicions. That's enough. Baptiste? Your baby is fine. We didn't take her — we're trying to return her. I'm not sure who did take her. We found her with Ellen. And I'm very sorry to say, Ellen is dead."

Baptiste freezes, his color draining. "Dead?"

"Which is also not our doing," Dalton says. "Casey and I were out camping last week. She heard your baby crying and found her under the snow."

"Wh-what?" His eyes round. "Summer was —"

"She's fine," I say. "Ellen had her. She'd rescued her, and she was on the run, and someone killed her. She died clutching Summer to her, keeping her warm. She saved her."

"You both saved her," Petra says. "You're the one who found the baby before —" She stops, as if realizing Baptiste doesn't need that image. "Before anything happened."

"Thank you," Baptiste says. "I'm not sure how we can ever repay you, but we will. Thank you for finding her, and thank you for finding us. Ellen . . ." He slumps as the news of her death penetrates the relief at his daughter's survival. "She only wanted to help. She only *ever* wanted to help. I shouldn't have let her go after Summer. I knew it was dangerous, and we already owed her so much, and I should have said no. I was desperate, and now . . ."

"She's gone," Felicity says. "Falling apart isn't going to help you find Sidra. You're soft, Baptiste, too soft to —"

"Enough," Dalton says, the word harsh enough to make Felicity give a start. "A woman is dead, Felicity. A woman who died helping your friends, and Baptiste is allowed a moment to feel bad about that. It isn't weakness. It's called being a fucking human being."

She flinches and then her face hardens, as if she wants to snap something back. She can't, though. The only comeback would be to accuse him of equal weakness, equal sentimentality. Whatever impression Dalton's made on her, it must not be that.

After a moment, she says, "You are right. I am sorry for this woman's death. I'm just concerned about Sidra."

"As am I," Baptiste says. "I don't want to fight over who is more concerned. We both are. Now, can we try to find her? Please?"

"Could you show us the spot where she disappeared?" I ask. "Our dog can track scents."

He frowns. Again, I'm looking for signs, this time of worry, of panic. I see only confusion and then surprise and then relief.

"Your dog?" He looks at Storm. "She's a hunting dog?"

"Just for people," I say. "Residents wander into the forest and disappear. She's trained to bring them back."

"Eric's the Rockton sheriff," Petra says. "Casey is his detective. Finding things is her job. Down south, finding killers was her job."

He doesn't hesitate at that. Again, he looks relieved. "So you'll find who killed Ellen?"

Am I certain that's relief? It certainly seems like it. Dalton is watching him with equal care. He's seen the gun. He's figured it out.

Is this not the gun that shot Ellen? Or was Sidra the person holding it, and Baptiste knows nothing about that? Or did Baptiste fire it mistaking Ellen for a hostile, maybe hoping to injure and question one about Summer?

463

So many possibilities. At this point, all I can say is that my gut tells me that if Baptiste is a killer, he's an accidental one, and Lane misunderstood the situation and is covering for him.

"Was Sidra taken here?" Dalton says, startling me from my thoughts as he looks around. "Someone camped here. I'm guessing that was you."

Baptiste frowns and follows Dalton's gaze to the campsite just beyond. He shakes his head. "No, this wasn't us."

"Not you last night?" Dalton says. "Or not you at all?"

"Not us at all. We have a permanent winter site closer to the mountain, with better shelter. This is someone's temporary camp." Baptiste walks into it and looks around.

"There's evidence that animals were slaughtered," I say. "A hunting camp?"

Dalton has followed Baptiste, and they're both poking around. After a few minutes, Dalton says, "Overnight camp. They killed their dinner, and maybe a little more to-go, but that's it."

"It isn't the wild people," Baptiste says. "We haven't seen anyone else in days." He turns to us. "What if it was a lone hunter who stole Sidra? There are a few of those

464

around. There's a big man who calls himself Cypher. Sidra doesn't like him so we stay away. There's a younger man, Jacob, who we've traded with . . ."

He turns slowly to Dalton, who's bundled up, with a hat and hood, but now he takes a closer look and says, "Oh."

"Yeah, that'd be my brother."

"I . . . I've heard stories. Yes, all right. I don't mean to blame your brother for anything. I just thought, what if a man was hunting and saw Sidra . . ."

"Jacob's hunting far from here. Tyrone Cypher is in Rockton right now. But, yeah, I take your point. Some guy could have been passing through, saw Sidra, and waited for her to leave your shelter last night."

"More than one person stayed in this camp," I say. "I found multiple boot prints. One isn't much bigger than mine, which suggests a woman. That's why I thought it was your camp. A man and a woman . . ." I trail off.

"You thinking what I'm thinking?" Dalton says.

I nod.

Dalton sighs. "Fuck."

THIRTY-NINE

Who do we think camped here? The couple I accidentally set on Baptiste and Sidra's trail.

No, let's be honest. The "accident" is that I hadn't meant to endanger this young couple, but that's because I'd been thinking abstractly. I offered Cherise an irresistible reward for finding Abby's parents. I just lacked the foresight, in that moment, to see "Abby's parents" as people who might be endangered by me setting a dangerous woman on that quest.

I'd realized my mistake the moment I made the offer, which is why we'd labored to make it ironclad, in hopes of protecting Abby's mother from Cherise's ruthlessness. Even if we'd rescinded it, though, Cherise would know how valuable this information was, and she'd search for Abby's mother in hopes of a reward. The only thing we could do was close off loopholes.

It wasn't enough.

Earlier, Felicity told me I was wrong for making the offer. She might not have said much more then. She does now. I take my lumps, even as Dalton and Petra come to my defense. Baptiste says he understands why I did it, and he's grateful that I was so anxious to reunite Summer with her parents. He's cutting me slack, being kind, while I see the worry in his eyes.

In the end, all I can do is apologize, while Dalton insists that Sidra is in no actual danger.

"We were very, very clear on the stipulations of the deal," Dalton says. "We don't pay out until we see the baby's mother and confirm she hasn't been hurt. Yeah, Cherise is going to make Sidra spin us some bullshit story about how she went with Cherise voluntarily, but we know better. We'll get Sidra back, and tell Cherise where she can stick her deal."

"I would exercise more caution than that," Felicity says. "I understand the impulse. I also want to punish Cherise for what she did."

"But that's like punching a grizzly in the face," Baptiste says. "Even if the grizzly doesn't come after you, it's going to strike at the first human it sees."

Felicity nods. "She will find a way to punish Sidra and Baptiste for the loss of her reward."

The young settlers exchange a look, acknowledgment of shared ground.

"I agree," I say. "Ideally, we steal Sidra back from Cherise. If she figures it out and complains, we pay her off, as painful as that will be. And then we never, ever do business with her again."

We have two choices here. Return to where Cherise and Owen snatched Sidra or track the couple from here. Sidra and Baptiste's campsite is a kilometer away, and it seems likely that they brought Sidra back here before they broke camp. Dalton confirms that with the campfire. If they left last night, the coals would be cold by now. Also, it makes no sense to lie in wait for Sidra with all your gear on your back.

Tracking them from here makes the most sense, especially when we know they'll head for Rockton with their booty. There's no reason to do otherwise.

We split up, dividing our best trackers — Storm gets Petra and me, and Dalton takes Felicity and Baptiste. We head to the campsite first. If we had any doubt that Cherise and Owen are the couple who camped here, it disappears when Storm arrives. She's growling even before I ask her to snuffle the ground.

"When even dogs don't like you, that's a very bad sign," Petra says. I wait for her to make some comment on the fact that Storm likes *her* just fine, but Petra isn't so ham-handed. The implication dangles there, and she knows I'll see it.

I snort my response and ask Storm to follow Cherise and Owen's trail. She grumbles at that, a growling sulk that tells me she really doesn't want another encounter with the trader couple. I crouch in front of her and murmur reassurances, and she looks at me as if to say, *I hope you know what you're doing.* Then she sets out.

Our luck with using Storm as a tracking dog has been sporadic so far. Am I disappointed in that? Yes, I'll admit it. That's not her fault. While Newfoundlands are used in search-and-rescue, they aren't bloodhounds. Whatever Dalton's excuse for buying her, she really is a companion dog, and she's brilliant at that, an absolute joy in our lives. The fault may also be ours — we aren't dog trainers or trackers, and no amount of reading can fully overcome that. We've discussed sending her down south for professional training, and we might still do it. Yet she's still young, and when she can't find our quarry, it's not through lack of intelligence or commitment — it's the fault of challenging terrain.

Today, though, Storm proves that she's a perfectly fine tracker and the problem is that, too often, we've set her on the trail of people who know she'll come after them and use every trick for avoiding her. When it's someone who has no expectation of being tracked, finding them is puppy's play, and we have to hold her back from running along Cherise and Owen's trail. We get some dirty looks for that — clearly we should be able to keep up.

Finally I spot Owen, and I'm about to grab Storm's collar, realizing I lack an end-of-search signal. Another oversight on my part. Fortunately, she has no desire to get close to Owen, and she slows, glancing at me as if to say, *There he is. Can we go now?*

We cannot.

It's just Owen. He's sitting. Well, crouching actually, while performing a bodily function that Cherise obviously doesn't want to witness.

As Petra sneaks up on Owen's other side, he finishes his business, rising with his hands on his pants, pulling them up.

"Shit that stinks," a voice says, and Petra

and I go still. It's Cherise. I can't see her, but it's clearly her voice.

"Yeah, it stinks *because* it's shit," Owen says. "Yours doesn't smell like roses, babe."

"Cover it up," she says.

He grumbles that this isn't their camp — they aren't sticking around — but he knocks snow over the steaming pile as he fastens his jeans.

Petra looks at me. I gesture for Storm to stay, and then I begin to circle around to where I'll be able to see Cherise. Petra stays ducked behind a bush.

After a few steps, I spot Cherise leaning against a tree. There's no sign of Sidra, but she must be nearby. I keep circling until I'm opposite the couple, and I can see everything around them. Trees and a few low bushes. Nothing big enough to hide Sidra.

Both Owen and Cherise are armed, but the rifles are slung across their backs. I glance around for Dalton, but his group is long gone.

I step out from my hiding spot. "Hey, guys."

They both spin on me. I raise my hands. Owen reaches for his rifle, but I say, "Uh-uh. You go for yours, and I go for mine, which is a lot more accessible."

Their gazes go to my open parka, my gun right there, ready to draw.

"Storm?" I say. "Come, girl."

She bounds from her hiding place. As she does, Petra appears five paces behind the couple, but they're busy watching the dog. Petra stops there, her gun out, and waits.

"We hear you've found the baby's mom," I say.

Cherise's expression doesn't change. Her partner, however, sneaks a look her way, one that tells me what I've already suspected.

"Let's trade now," I say. "You hand her over and collect your reward."

Cherise snorts. "Since you obviously don't have the goods we were promised, we're not handing her over. We'll meet you at Rockton."

"Sure, we can all go to Rockton. Together."

"We'll meet —"

"The only reason for you to argue is if you don't have the mother."

"Yes, we don't, all right. We know who she is. We're on her trail. But we still need to talk to her."

"Talk?" I say, brows rising. "Why not just grab her and save yourself the trouble?"

"Because someone put that into the terms

472

of the damn agreement," she says, scowling at me. "Did I misinterpret something? I sure as hell understood that we need to bring her to you of her own free will. Which, yes, complicates things and . . ." She looks from my gun to Storm and launches into a string of profanity.

"Yeah, they fucked you over, babe," Owen says.

She shoots a lethal glare at him and then swings it on me. "You did, didn't you? Set me on this girl's trail and then followed, waiting until I found my prey and then swooping in like a damn scavenger. I do all the work. You take the prize and then claim you owe me nothing." She steps forward. "That was a stupid move, girl. A really, really —"

"Stop right there," Petra says as Storm growls.

They both turn to see Petra, and I wince. Cherise hadn't gone for her gun. There was no reason for Petra to reveal herself.

"Yes, I brought backup," I say. "And she's going to lower her gun right now, having realized Cherise is justifiably angry with me and not actually about to attack."

Petra's expression says she doesn't appreciate taking orders from me. She still lowers the gun.

"If I did what you think, Cherise, you'd have every right to be pissed," I say. "I did not. I'm following a separate lead directly from Rockton. I'm sure if we'd been following you for the past three days, you'd know it. Now, do you have the baby's mother?"

Cherise throws up her hands and turns in a circle, as if to say, *Do you see her?*

"If we find that you kidnapped her —"

"Oh, for fuck's sake," Cherise snaps. "That's the kind of mistake this idiot would make."

She waves at Owen, who only protests with a halfhearted "Hey." When she looks at him, he flashes a grin and a shrug and says, "Fair enough. Never claimed to be the brains of the operation. You're with me for my pretty face. Not that I'm objecting. 'Cause you really like how I look, and I reap the benefits of your appreciation."

She rolls her eyes and then turns to me. "I understand the terms of our deal. I also understand that there is no way in hell I'd get away with kidnapping that girl. She'd tattle the moment my back was turned. Also, I'd have to kick the kid's ass for ratting me out, and if you think I'd enjoy that, then you and I have a fundamental misunderstanding of one another. I wouldn't mind if I had to, but I'm not going to do it for

474

fun. I have other ways to spend my time. More productive ways."

"Like enjoying her husband's highly talented —" Owen begins.

"You done with the sales pitch?" Cherise says.

Owen's brows arch. "Sales pitch?"

"Casey doesn't want to fuck you. I know that comes as a tremendous shock, but I could write you a goddamned letter of recommendation, and it wouldn't change her mind. Now stop embarrassing yourself. The blonde seems tough enough for you. Maybe she'd like a romp."

"With him?" Petra says. "No thanks. However, if *you're* offering . . ."

Petra's trying to throw Cherise off balance, shock her. But Cherise only barks a laugh and says, "Not on the table, sugar. Not right now, anyway. I'm busy negotiating with your friend here." She turns to me. "I don't have the girl. I notice you aren't naming her. Neither am I. We're both covering our asses in case the other has mistakenly identified the target. I don't have her. I'm on her trail, though. I was given bad information on her exact whereabouts, but I spotted her this morning. Unfortunately, they were on the other side of the river, which isn't fully frozen, so I couldn't cross there and talk to them. I picked up the trail, and I thought we were getting close when my darling husband needed to take a shit."

"I had cramps."

"And now we're further delayed. Also, we're no longer the only ones tracking her. So here's my offer, Miss Casey. You can give me half the reward for finding her and setting you on the proper trail. Or we race to the finish line. But if we get to her first, I expect the full reward . . . or I *will* take her captive until I get it."

Petra balks, pointing out that we know who the target is and Cherise didn't "find" her. Yet Cherise did find out who Abby's mother is, independent of us, and unlike us, she knows where to pick up the trail. Also, as far as I'm concerned, if half the reward means Owen and Cherise fade into the forest without interfering, it's worth it. So I agree.

"You said *they,*" I say. "She wasn't alone. You saw her with someone this morning?"

"Yep, her and her husband, out looking for their little one."

Petra's gaze cuts my way, but I pretend not to see it.

"So you saw this girl . . ."

"Sidra. Yes, I saw Sidra."

"And some guy . . ."

476

"*Her* guy. Baptiste. I saw Sidra and Baptiste across the river this morning, and I'd strongly suggest that you set your pup on their trail, because that sky says snow, and their trail isn't going to last."

FORTY

Cherise shows us the trail, and I put Storm
on it. The trail is a mess, and I can't help
but wonder if we're being tricked. Whoever
walked this way is following in the tracks
left by a herd of caribou. The temperature
is rising, and it's got to be above freezing,
the sun beating down on a trail through
relatively open land, meaning not only are
the human prints almost lost among the
caribou ones, but they're all melting into
mush. And then it starts to snow, almost as
if Cherise called for the skies to open and
make it even more impossible to confirm
her story.

"Here," she says, pointing at a clear
footprint. "And before you say that's
mine . . ." She puts her own foot beside it.
Hers are about a size bigger. I don't trust
Cherise, but she plays the long game, looking into the future and setting out her pieces
for the moves that will ultimately benefit

her rather than the ones that'll fill her pocket at this moment. It's not in her interests to trick us for one reward when she might be able to parlay this transaction into a long-term relationship.

They leave, and I set Storm on that print, the only one I'm relatively sure comes from Sidra. She snuffles around a bit. Once she's confident, she starts tracking.

"He lied," Petra says. "That son of a bitch Baptiste lied. I don't know how you bought his story, Casey. I'm sorry, but that was dead obvious. First his kid is kidnapped and then his wife? Not even by the same person? I'll tell you what happened. That hostile woman — Ellen — took Abby for good reason. Those two kids abandoned the baby or they were talking about it or they were just shitty parents. Ellen took Abby and ran. They caught up and shot her, and left their own baby to die in the forest."

I glance over at her. That's all I do. Heat rises in her face, and then her jaw sets. "Yes, I find it hard to believe any parent would do that, but as a cop, you know it happens. Even more likely, it was just him. My ex was the 'maternal' one in our relationship. Maternal in the traditional, ignorant sense that women are the 'real' parents, and the guys are just sperm donors and bottomless wallets. That's how men are raised. My ex grew up sneaking his sister's dolls to play with. If his parents caught him, they took them away, terrified it meant he was gay. That's what we do to little boys, and we do the opposite to little girls who *don't* want dolls. The result is that Mom usually *is* the maternal one, the protective one. How many family annihilators are women?"

"A few," I say. "But, yes, they're overwhelmingly men. Your point being, I presume, that you think Baptiste didn't want this baby. So he tried to get rid of her, shot Ellen, and is now leading us on a wild-goose chase after a fictional kidnapper."

"You saw his gun. Does it match the murder weapon?"

"Yes."

"Yet you still think the kid's telling the truth and Cherise is lying about seeing them together this morning?"

"No, I don't think Cherise is lying."

"Mistaken, then?"

"I'm not sure."

She grumbles at that. An idea is forming in my brain. It's been there since Cherise mentioned seeing Baptiste and Sidra across the river, and my gut screamed that she was wrong. Not lying. Just mistaken.

My brain demanded — and then supplied

— an alternate explanation . . . and berated me for not asking more questions while I had Felicity and Baptiste here. Simple questions, easily answered, and yet I didn't ask, because they didn't seem germane to what was happening.

Baptiste or Felicity could tell me what I need to know. I also want to find Dalton to bounce this theory off him. He didn't hear our voices and come running while we were talking to Cherise. That bothers me, and I'm trying very hard not to freak out over it and shout for him. That would risk tipping off others in this forest. I must trust that Dalton is fine.

I could be wrong about Baptiste. If I am, then that may answer my "where are they?" question. My only consolation is that I haven't heard a shotgun blast. Which doesn't keep me from wishing we'd kept the damned weapon we'd taken from Baptiste.

After another half kilometer, I can't silence that fretting anymore. We might be hot on Sidra's trail, but we need to reunite with the others.

Petra agrees.

"I'll play signpost and mark the trail," she says. "You take the pup and go find Eric."

I set out with Storm. I've told her to find Dalton, and I'm hoping she'll catch his scent on the breeze. We walk through unbroken snow wherever possible, leaving bread crumbs back to Petra. It's less than ten minutes before Storm goes still. She sniffs the air. It's not Dalton. If it were, she'd veer that way without hesitation.

"Who is it, girl?"

Her body language is relaxed, meaning whoever it is doesn't worry her. Not Cherise and Owen then. It's a scent she recognizes, though, someone she has no strong feelings about either way. She glances at me, and there's question in that look. It suggests she's smelling another member of our party — Felicity or Baptiste — and while they aren't her target, perhaps I'm also looking for them?

"Good girl," I say. Then I tell her yes, please track the new scent. I'm not sure she'll understand my command, but she sets off at a lope.

I take out my gun. I must, in case this is Baptiste, and I am mistaken about him. We head into thick forest, and I slow Storm, only to get a look that says we're too close to the target to bother. Yet despite the thick forest, I don't see anyone.

Storm stops. She goes rigid and whines, anxiety strumming from her. I look around.

There's no one here, no place for anyone to hide.

"What is it, girl?"

I follow her gaze. Just ahead, snow has been flattened. I see prints, multiple sets. That's when I spot the blood, drops of red sunk into the snow.

I race over.

There's blood. Definite blood, recently sprayed, droplets falling into fresh snow. Under my feet, the snow isn't just trampled — it's flat. Someone fell here. A struggle on the ground, a blow, blood flying.

Two sets of prints, coming from opposite directions. One significantly smaller than the other.

Felicity's prints. I recognize the imprint of fur around the edge. The other set is male. Not Dalton's boots. That's all I can tell. His prints would be instantly distinguishable from the tread-free ones. Felicity was here. Someone attacked her.

Or she attacked someone.

If it was Felicity attacking, though, she lost. I see the male prints leaving the flattened snow of the fight . . . and dragging something with him. Dragging Felicity.

I'm following that trail when Storm whines. Not the anxiety of smelling blood, though. This is excitement. Her nose goes up, and her entire body wriggles with the joy that can only mean one thing.

"Eric?" I say. "Do you smell Eric?"

She woofs, a deep adult-Newfoundland woof, even as her massive body puppy-gyrates with excitement.

"Good girl." I glance at the trail where someone dragged Felicity away. Is leaving it to go after Dalton the right move?

"Stop right there!" a voice shouts. Baptiste's voice, ringing through the forest . . . coming from the direction Storm is looking.

From Dalton's direction.

A shotgun blast, and I'm running, running as fast as I can. I hear Dalton's voice then. Thank God I hear Dalton's voice, even if it barely pierces the blood pounding in my ears. He's saying something I can't catch, his voice calm, and Baptiste shouts at him again, telling him to get back, get back right now, get away from her.

Her?

Felicity?

Sidra?

Either way, my gut drops. I've made a mistake. An unforgivable one. Cherise said she saw Baptiste with Sidra after Sidra was supposedly kidnapped. Petra jumped to the obvious conclusion — Baptiste was lying —

484

but I'd wanted to believe otherwise. Yes, there's a selfish part of me that wants Abby's parents to be horrible people who do not deserve her, so I can keep her. But there's another part I only recognize now. The part that wants the best of all possible endings to this story by that little baby getting back to loving and capable parents. I want her to have good parents who love each other and love her and are beside themselves with panic at her disappearance.

That's the part that decided Baptiste isn't guilty. Not Baptiste and not Sidra. Neither of them killed Ellen. Neither of them got rid of their baby. Neither of them planned this fake kidnapping to get rid of us. They might be young and naive, but they are good and honest, and they deserve their little girl back. That is who I want them to be.

Then I hear Baptiste telling Dalton to "get away from her" and I realize I'm wrong.

As I work this through, I run. I don't stop running. Then I hear a woman's voice say, "Put the gun down, you son of a bitch," and I'm so caught up in my thoughts that I think it must be Sidra, talking to Dalton, and this means she is just as culpable —

No, not Sidra.

My mind replays the voice, and there is no question who I'm hearing, even before

Petra says, "Lower that damned shotgun or I put a bullet through your lying-bastard head, boy."

I see Dalton now, just ahead. Others are with him, but they're only meaningless figures until I've found Dalton and confirmed he's on his feet, apparently unharmed.

"Petra, no," Dalton says. "Everyone just hold on."

I burst through the trees. The shotgun barrel turns on me.

Petra barks, "Don't you dare!" echoed by Dalton as he pulls his own gun, swinging it on Baptiste. Then we all freeze, guns pointing everywhere, and a voice says, "Stop, everyone please, stop."

It's a girl's voice, high and tight with fear. I follow it to a stranger, rising from the ground near Dalton as she claws off a gag. A girl no bigger than me, with long black curls. She staggers in front of Dalton, and Petra snaps, "Stop right there," but Sidra ignores her.

Sidra makes it to her husband, and he nearly drops the gun in his lunge to catch her. The muzzle is down, thankfully, and Petra doesn't fire as Baptiste grabs Sidra and the shotgun slides to the ground beside them.

486

"Put the gun down," Dalton says to Petra. "Everything's fine."

"Everything is not fine," she says. "These two tricked —"

"No one tricked anyone," Dalton says. "I found Sidra. I was freeing her when Baptiste showed up, and he misinterpreted. Sidra, did I kidnap you?"

She shakes her head. "He was helping me, Baptiste."

"Did Baptiste kidnap you?" I ask.

Her eyes round. "Of course not. I . . . I don't know who did it. Someone grabbed me at the camp and put something over my eyes."

"Then how do you know it wasn't Baptiste?" Petra asks.

Sidra's eyes flash. "I do not need to see my husband to know him. It was a man. I'm sure of that. He spoke to me, but his voice was distorted. We were walking but we kept stopping, and he'd tie me up. Then he'd leave and come back. He'd left me again when this man found me and said he was from Rockton and he was with you, Baptiste."

"He is," I say. "Your husband just panicked." I turn to Baptiste. "Have you ever lent Lane your shotgun?"

His face screws up, as if he's misheard.

"Lane from the Second —"

"Yes, I know Lane," he says impatiently. "He is my friend, and yes, I have loaned him our shotgun, but I don't understand —"

"That's the gun that was used to kill Ellen." I don't know that for certain, of course, but they'll never realize that. "Someone —"

"No!" Sidra says, and she wheels, and I think she's spinning on me to deny it, but instead, she faces the forest and shouts, "Lane!"

"That . . . That's . . ." Baptiste blinks, looking lost. "Lane wouldn't . . ." He trails off, unable to finish. Then he looks at me. "This gun? This gun was used . . ."

"To kill Ellen," Sidra says, and tears glisten in her eyes as she looks at me. "That's what you said, isn't it? Ellen is dead, and Lane killed her. Killed her and came for me. Killed her and stole . . . stole . . ."

She spins to face the forest again, and when she screams "Lane!" it's a raw and horrible sound, and the force of it buckles her knees. Baptiste catches her, his face still blank with shock. I see his face, and I see hers, and the missing piece falls into place.

Motivation.

Felicity said four kids from the two settle-

488

ments hung out together. Tomas said Lane lost his best friend last year. That connection had clicked earlier. Lane knew Sidra and Baptiste, and Baptiste was his supposedly dead friend. I hadn't confirmed that because it seemed nothing more than a tragic collision of circumstance.

Lane knows Ellen. Lane also knows Baptiste and Sidra. A hostile steals their baby, and Ellen steals her back, and Lane sees her and shoots her because she's having an affair with his aunt. He has no idea she's clutching a baby under her parka. And the fact that that baby belongs to his old friends? Tragic, tragic coincidence.

That makes sense, right? And if the gun that murdered Ellen belongs to Baptiste, then that must mean Baptiste or Sidra actually shot her. The young couple have been trading their game with Lane, who's been passing it off as his own arrow-shot kills. Then, when we accuse Lane of shooting Ellen with that same gun, he realizes who actually did it and quickly spins a story to protect his friends.

That must be the answer, right?

Unless Cherise sees Sidra with a young man she presumes is Baptiste, while my gut says Baptiste *didn't* lie to us and his wife *is* missing. Who else could Cherise mistake for

489

Baptiste? Another young dark-haired man of similar build.

Lane.

Before this moment, I could only guess at why Lane kidnapped Sidra. Maybe he confessed to her, and she hadn't forgiven him. Or maybe he took her hostage as a bargaining chip against his punishment for killing Ellen.

Neither scenario had satisfied me. Now, in Sidra's scream of rage and frustration, I hear the echoes of other women, and I see the answer.

"Lane . . ." Baptiste says, looking at me as he holds Sidra, who vibrates with fury. "You think Lane . . ."

"He confessed to killing Ellen," I say. "He didn't seem to know she was holding Summer when she died."

"H-holding . . ." Sidra says.

"Summer is safe," Baptiste says quickly. "This woman — Casey — found her, and she's fine. Ellen had rescued her and she — she died holding her, but they found Summer before — before anything could . . ."

"Lane murdered Ellen." Sidra stares at me. "While she was holding my baby. He left . . . he left her . . ."

"He didn't seem to know," I say.

Her face contorts in an inhuman snarl.

490

"Oh, he knew. He knew." She turns and screams. "Lane! Show yourself, you coward! You want me so badly, come and face me!"

"Want . . ." Baptiste looks sick. "No . . . Yes, at first, yes . . . but he said he was over you. He said he was happy for us."

"He lied," Sidra spits, face contorting again. "He lied to you. Not to me, though. Never to me. It didn't matter what I said. It didn't matter what I did."

"He . . . he kept . . . ?" Baptiste sways, face green. "He kept bothering you, and you never told me."

"He was your friend, and I thought he'd get over it. He would see the truth — that it was you, and it had always been you, and I never saw him as anything but a friend. I married you. I had your baby. He would understand soon. I kept telling myself he would finally understand. And he did not."

Baptiste goes still, processing. Then his face hardens, and he strides toward the forest. "Lane! Sidra's right. Show yourself! You have something to say to me, come out here and —"

A whistle. That's all I hear. An odd whistle, and then Baptiste falls back and Sidra screams. She runs to her husband as he staggers back, an arrow in his shoulder. Sidra knocks Baptiste to the ground as another arrow whistles past. She covers his body, protecting him, as we surround them, guns out, shouting for Lane.

The forest goes silent.

Dalton motions that he's heading in. I clamp down on the urge to stop him. Instead, I motion that I'll do the same, from the other side, and he gives me the same look, the one that resists saying no, don't go. Go or stay, though, we're in equal danger from an archer in the woods.

Dalton leaves first, as I call to Storm, loud enough to distract Lane if he's watching. I'm telling Storm to stay with Petra when Sidra shouts, "Lane!"

I look to see Sidra marching toward the forest, her arms spread wide. Petra is on the ground with Baptiste, checking his shoulder injury. Baptiste stares at Sidra and then tries to rise, but Petra holds him down.

"Sidra?" I say. "Don't —"

"Lane!" she shouts. "I do not love you. You could take me captive, and I would only kill you the first chance I got. If I couldn't kill you, I would kill myself before I let you touch me. Is that clear? Do you understand? I will not be yours. I will never —"

"No!" I say. I hear her words, and I hear echoes of others, and I know what is coming, what is always coming in a situation like this . . .

I run for Sidra, but Petra is closer, and she knows the same thing I do. She's on her feet, launching herself at Sidra. That whistle sounds. That horrible whistle. Petra hits Sidra and sends her flying, and the arrow hits Petra in the chest. I'm already running at her, and I see it hit and her eyes round, mouth rounding, too, in surprise. Another arrow, this one hitting her in the shoulder, spinning her. She stumbles, and I catch her. I grab her, and her feet scuffle against the ground as she tries to stay upright.

"Cover!" I shout at Sidra and Baptiste. "Get to cover. Storm!"

Storm races to me as I half drag Petra. Baptiste says, "Here!" and I look to see him and Sidra ducking behind a deadfall off to our left. I manage to get Petra there. I glance at Baptiste, but he says, "I'm fine."

"He's not fine," Sidra says, voice quavering, "but his jacket is thick. He'll be all right."

Sidra helps me lay Petra down. Petra's fingers wrap around my arm, her face pale, eyes wide with impending shock.

"You're okay," I say. "Relax. Stay with us."

"Émilie," she says, and it takes me a moment to remember that that's her grandmother, one of the board members for

Rockton. "The . . . the hostiles . . . Your . . . your theory."

"Tell Émilie my theory about the hostiles. Got it. But you can do it yourself. Just hold on."

We don't remove the arrows, not until we get a look at how deep they're in. I undo Petra's parka. While she hasn't been as lucky as Baptiste, the arrowheads haven't gone deeper than the head. One is in her shoulder, the other just above her heart. Serious, yes. Life-threatening, though? I hope not. I really, really hope not. I can't see well enough to be sure, not without removing the arrows.

"We need to snap off the shafts," I say. "If the shafts are off, we can get her out of that jacket and —"

"Eric," Petra whispers. "Go look after Eric. And get this guy. Stop him."

I hesitate, but Sidra shoulders me aside, taking over. "She's right. We'll leave the arrows in for now. Just find your sheriff and stop Lane." She meets my gaze. "Please stop Lane."

I nod, squeeze Petra's hand, and then take off.

FORTY-ONE

From the arrow-fire, I know the direction to go. I do what we'd planned before Petra got shot — I sneak up in the other direction, presumably on Lane's opposite side. I hear Lane before I see him. He's breathing hard and fast, the sound pulling me easily through the woods, letting me approach alongside him, no danger of running smack into him. Not that I'm too worried about that. His weapon might be lethal, but he doesn't have an arrow nocked. I can see that as soon as I spot him. He's poised, bow in hand, his gaze riveted on the place where the others hide behind the deadfall.

He's waiting for movement. I don't know what he expects — someone to leap up like a jack-in-the-box? His heavy breathing tells me his adrenaline is pumping, blood pounding in his ears, rendering him deaf and blind to everything except what he wants to see.

Sidra.

He's waiting for Sidra.

He expects she'll leap up again to scream at him. Tell him that she'll never be his, and he will kill her for it. That is what men like him do. He's been raised to believe he has the right to a life partner, the right to the woman he chooses to fill that role, and if he can't have her, then by God, no one else will either. He'll kill Sidra and then himself. That is how this goes. It's how it always goes.

So Lane waits for his chance, and he doesn't hear me creep up on his left side. He hasn't seen the figure to his right either.

Dalton will have heard the commotion with Petra going down, and he'll have paused long enough to be sure we were safely under cover. Then he came here, where he'll wait to see what I do before he makes his move.

When I'm far enough behind Lane's peripheral vision, I lean out and catch Dalton's eye. He nods and motions a plan. Or I'm sure it's a plan, but we're forty feet apart in the forest, and it's not as if I see more than a few hand gestures. That's enough, though. I know what we should do, and it seems to coincide with what he's suggesting.

We both creep toward Lane from our

respective positions, staying out of visual range and on either side of him. Then, without warning, Dalton steps forward, plowing through brush, winter-dry twigs crackling. Lane wheels on Dalton . . . and that's apparently my cue to swing behind him and cut off his escape route. I dart into place just as Lane looks over his shoulder to find me there, gun pointed at him, Dalton doing the same on his other side.

"If you reach for an arrow, we fire," I say. "You can run, but this time, we're close enough to catch you."

"Also close enough to shoot you," Dalton says. "Save ourselves the trouble of chasing."

"I'm fine with shooting," I say. "In fact, I'd say it might be our best option. Our only option, really. You stole a baby. You murdered Ellen. You hoped to murder the baby with her. Now you're trying to murder your best friend and the woman you supposedly love."

"Seems to me he doesn't know the meaning of that word," Dalton drawls.

Lane's face purples. "I'm the only one who *does* know the meaning of it. Baptiste doesn't. He's no friend of mine. Friends don't do that."

"Friends don't fall in love with the girl

you like?" I say. "The girl who likes them back?"

"I *found* her," he says. "Not him. Me. I met Sidra and Felicity in the forest, hunting duck. I was their friend first, and then I brought Baptiste to meet them. I would get Sidra, and he'd get Felicity. He knew that. I found them first. So I was entitled to first pick."

"Yeah," Dalton says. "Like when you're hunting and you spot a herd of caribou. If you spot them first and bring your friend, you should get first shot, first pick of the herd. That's how it works, and if he shoots first, he's an asshole."

Lane straightens. "Yes. You understand."

"I understand if it's a herd of caribou," Dalton says. "But those were *girls*. Human beings. Not game animals. You can tell Baptiste you like Sidra, and if he's a decent friend, he won't make a play for her if there's a chance she feels the same about you. But that isn't how it went, was it?"

Lane shoots Dalton a look I can't see.

"Sidra fell for Baptiste," I say. "And he fell for her. He probably felt lousy about it, but from what I understand, you stood down. You told Baptiste it was fine . . . while you kept pursuing Sidra. She ran away with him, and you did what? Offered to help

498

them? Bring their game to the Second Settlement in trade? Felicity backed off, but you stuck close in hopes of winning Sidra. Then along came a baby, and you couldn't allow that. You took Summer. Stole her."

"I had to," he snarls. "A winter baby? How could Baptiste do that to Sidra? It proved he didn't care about her. I did what needed to be done."

"Taking their baby and giving it to the hostiles?"

His jaw sets. "I gave it to a wild woman who wanted a child. I heard Ellen mention the woman, and I knew that was the answer. I left the baby where the woman went to get water each morning, and she took her. She was *happy* to take her. Then Ellen showed up and stole her back. I'd been out hunting with Baptiste's gun. As I headed home, I heard the baby, and I heard Ellen hushing her. I found them. I told Ellen to give me the baby, but she said no. She'd been hit on the head stealing her from the hostile woman, and she was confused. She ran, and I fired, and she kept running."

"So you let her go?" I say.

He doesn't answer.

"No, you didn't," I say. "You followed enough to see her lying down. She stopped to rest. Between the head injury and the shot, she was losing blood and confused, and she'd lain down to rest, and you left her there. You left her to die in the snow. You left the baby to die with her."

"I did it for her," he snarls. "For Sidra. To save her from *him.*"

For fourteen years I have worried that someday, holding a gun in my hand, I will repeat the mistake I made with Blaine. Someone will say something, and the rage — the absolute rage I felt then — will rise again, and my gun will rise too, and I will pull the trigger.

For fourteen years, that possibility has terrified me.

And now, in this split second, it evaporates.

I feel that rage again, a blind wave of it washing over me. I see Ellen, lying in the snow, a woman who only wanted to help.

I see Ellen dead with Summer in her arms, and I think of how close that baby came to dying horribly in the snow, and all this time, I've told myself it was a mistake. It had to be, didn't it? No one would do that on purpose. Before me stands the boy who did it. On purpose. Murdered a kind and generous woman. Abandoned a baby to the elements. And for what? For a girl who never gave him a moment's encouragement.

To murder her child, destroy her life, and then try to kill her if he couldn't have her?

Lane deserves my bullet more than Blaine Saratori ever did. He may even deserve it more than Val did. But I do not pull the trigger because I can control that impulse. The situation is under control, and we are in no immediate danger, and I cannot execute Lane for his crimes. That is not my place.

I know my place. I understand it, and I will never make that mistake again.

"Lane?" I say. "You are under arrest for the murder of Ellen and the attempted murder of Summer and Sidra and Baptiste. You will appear before a joint committee of the First and Second Settlements, who will determine your punishment —"

He runs at Dalton. I still don't fire. My finger moves to the trigger, and I shout at him to stop, but I don't need to shoot. Lane is a man with a bow in his hand, the arrows still in their quiver, and he's running at a law enforcement officer with a gun.

Dalton doesn't shoot either. When Lane draws near, he kicks, his foot connecting with a crack. The young man drops to one knee, and Dalton backs up, gun still aimed.

"Shoot me," Lane says.

"I'm not —" Dalton begins.

"You're going to have to. Because I won't stop. If you let me live, I'll never stop. I'll find a way to kill Baptiste, kill that baby, and if Sidra won't come with me, then I'll kill her, too. She's mine. *Mine.* I will kill everyone who comes between me and her, and then I'll take her and —"

A figure rushes from the forest. It's a blur. That's all I see. A blur of motion, and I spin on it, my gun raised as it rushes Lane. The blur leaps on him, and only then do I see a face. A face not contorted in rage but ice-cold with it.

It's Felicity. Her hand flies up as I shout at her to get back, and as that hand rises, I see the blade in it. A blade already blood-stained, droplets flecking the snow.

The blade falls again, slamming into Lane's back, and I shout at her to stop, but I do not stop her.

I know my place, and it is not my place to stop her.

Only when she falls back, breathing hard, her hands clutching the bloody knife, does Dalton run over and pull her back. Lane falls face-first to the snow.

Felicity drops the knife and then wrenches from Dalton's grip. He lets her go. She walks over and drops to her knees beside Lane.

"You should have killed me while you had the chance," she says. "But that was always your mistake. You underestimated me. Underestimated Sidra. We made that mistake, too. We underestimated you." She leans down to his ear, her voice a hoarse whisper as she says, "Not this time. I did not underestimate you this time, Lane."

She stays there, at his side, until he breathes his last.

FORTY-TWO

There's no time to process what has happened. No time to help Felicity process it, and I know from experience that will not happen immediately. She's done what she needed to do to protect her friend. Later, the doubts and second-guessing will come, and I don't know whether she'll let me help with that, but I will if I can.

Right now, our biggest concern is Petra. She has an arrow in her chest, and we are hours from Rockton. Dalton runs ahead to bring help and motorized transport. While he's gone, we fashion a stretcher for Petra. Storm pulls it, and Sidra and I help. While Baptiste and Felicity try to do their part, both are injured — Baptiste with a minor shoulder wound and Felicity with a head injury, inflicted when Lane found her in the forest. Their job is to walk behind the sled and make sure Petra stays awake and lucid.

We've been walking for almost two hours

when I hear the whine of a snowmobile and the rumble of the ATV. Dalton cuts through brush on the snowmobile and then takes over the stretcher, guiding it through to where the ATV waits on a wider path.

Dalton sends me in the ATV with Sidra. I know why he picks her to go. He doesn't need to say it, but I know. After he sets Petra up for the ride, he stays behind with Anders to get the rest of the group to Rockton.

I drive the ATV as fast as I dare through the well-packed snow of the main trail. Sidra doesn't clutch the grab handles for dear life. She stares straight ahead, her face drawn, her mind already at our destination and what waits there.

I drive the ATV straight into town. April waits on the clinic stairs, Diana with her to help, several of the men ready to carry Petra inside. And as we pull to a halt, another figure appears from inside the clinic. Jen, holding a baby-size bundle to her chest.

Sidra is out of the ATV before it stops. She stumbles forward, tripping over her feet and nearly falling in her scramble to get to her baby. Jen descends the stairs and meets her, holding Summer out. Sidra doesn't take her. She wobbles there and then collapses to her knees, crying in relief, and Jen bends in front of her, letting Sidra take the baby

505

there, kneeling in the snow.

I turn away from the scene and help the men with Petra.

It's morning. Early morning, not yet light. I'm beside Petra's bed in the clinic. She's stable. The arrow entered above her heart, piercing less than an inch. She's lost a lot of blood, and she'll need time to recover, but she's all right, sleeping soundly as I keep watch.

I've been here all night, not leaving the clinic since I arrived.

Hiding here? Yes, I have the self-awareness to admit that. April needed me, and I wanted to be here for Petra, but it also gave me the excuse not to face the joyous parent-and-child reunion.

I slept here, in this chair. In the night, I woke to find Dalton in a chair beside me, a blanket draped over us. When I wake again at six thirty, he's already gone, and I feel the regret of that, but I feel something else, too. Relief. I'm not ready to face him. I need time to process this and grieve on my own. And as soon as that thought comes, another follows it, a realization that has my cheeks flaming and my ass out of that chair in a heartbeat.

I check Petra. Then I hurry out to see

506

Kenny walking past, and I ask him to step in and watch Petra for me.

"Actually, I was just coming for you," he says. "The kids are leaving soon, and they really want to see you first."

I hesitate, which is a shitty and selfish thing to do, and I am ashamed to admit it. I'm also snared between two sources of shame — the one that wants to flee any last moments with Summer and the one that needs to talk to Dalton.

"I should speak to Eric first," I say. "Is he around?"

"He's with the boy. Baptiste. They're talking, and Sidra wanted to bring the baby over to speak to you alone before they go."

I hesitate again, that childish impulse filling me, the impulse to lie and say I cannot see her. Nope, sorry, terribly, terribly busy. I squash it and say, "Of course. Send her over to the house, and let Eric know we're there."

"Before you go," he says. "The hot tub is ready. Where — ?"

"Later," I say. "We'll talk later."

"But it's . . ."

His voice trails off as I hurry away.

As I walk through town, I hear carols and look over to see a group of people singing. I check my watch. Yep, it's seven in the morning. What the hell are people — ? That's when I see the date on my watch.

December 21.

That's what Kenny meant. It's winter solstice. The biggest celebration of our year, and I could not feel less festive. I duck around the carolers and hurry to our house.

I'm opening our front door when Sidra appears. I hold it for her, and I smile, and I hope that smile looks every bit as genuine as she deserves. Because she *does* deserve it. This is her baby. She was, from what I can tell, a perfect mother, despite her youth. She's spent the ten days frantically trying to find her lost child. She confronted a killer to protect her family. And if there was any doubt about how much she loves Summer, it could not survive witnessing that heart-wrenching reunion scene last night.

So I smile for her, and it damned well better be a good one, or I will not forgive myself for my petty jealousy. I usher her in, and I'm about to apologize for the cold when I see that Dalton has laid the fire, in case I come back here. Thoughtful and considerate as always, which only twists the knife that reminds me I have not been the same to him these last few hours.

I start the kettle for coffee, mostly as

busywork while she settles in with the baby.

Her baby. Not mine. Never mine.

"I can't thank you enough for what you did," she says. "Even saying thank you feels like such an understatement. But I don't know what else to say."

I'm not sure how to reply to that.

It was nothing, really.

Any decent person would have done the same.

It was no trouble at all.

Platitudes, and like her, I don't want to say them. They feel empty. So I only say, "You're welcome."

Then I turn, and she rises, holding out the baby, and I know she doesn't realize what that gesture means to me, how it is a knife in my gut. She is only being kind. So I must accept that kindness and accept Summer, and sink stiffly onto the chair, holding the baby and trying not to look down at her.

Summer fusses, and I tell myself she doesn't know I'm not looking at her, her eyes can't focus enough to find mine, but my gut calls me a coward, and I look down. Our eyes meet, and her lips purse, the way they do when she's considering whether to cry, and I'm almost hoping she will.

Whoops, ha ha, guess she wants her

509

mommy. Better take her back.

Summer sucks her lips twice, as if considering. Then her nostrils flare, and it is as if she catches my scent, finally realizes it's me, and she snuggles down and my heart cracks. I feel it crack, and I feel the tears well, and I blink hard, clearing my throat.

"Have you given any thought to what Felicity offered last night?" I say. "Spending the winter with the First Settlement. I know you left because you didn't think they'd let you be with Baptiste, but you have a baby now. They won't separate your new family."

"Thank you, and yes, we're doing that. Only for the winter. We do want to be on our own. We could use help, though. Support and trade partners, and if either settlement will offer that, we'll take it."

"If you have any problems, come back here," I say. "I'm sure you'll be fine on your own once you're settled and the baby's a little older, but I'd strongly advise spending this winter in the settlement. Or here if they won't take you."

"And if they do take us . . ." She raises her eyes to mine, suddenly shy. "May we still visit?"

"Of course."

The door opens. Dalton and Baptiste enter, kicking snow off their boots. I hold

Summer out to Sidra, but she motions for Baptiste to take her, teasing him when Summer fusses at his cold touch. I watch the three of them, and yes, my heart cracks a little more, but it swells, too. They are in love, with each other and with their baby, and no child can truly hope for more.

"Did you ask her?" Baptiste says to Sidra.

Sidra shakes her head and looks at me. "We . . . we named her Summer as a joke. Not a very good joke either. But we'd like, if it's all right with you, to change that. We'd like to call her Casey."

"I . . ." I swallow. "That . . . that's very kind. It isn't necessary, though, and I think she should have her own name. Summer is good." I force a too-bright smile. "And it'd be less confusing, when you come to visit. I am honored, though. Truly honored."

"Eric thought you'd say that," Baptiste says with a smile. "So Sidra and I have a backup plan. We heard you called her Abby here, after a young woman who died. May we keep calling her that?"

I glance at Dalton. He nods.

"Yes," I say. "That would be lovely. Thank you."

"We even have a toy our Abby brought to Rockton," Dalton says. "It's butt-ugly, but it meant a lot to her, and there's no family to give it back to. That and a necklace. You're welcome to take those. You can tell her about the girl she was named after."

Sidra's face glows. "Are you sure?"

"We're sure."

"That would be wonderful. Thank you."

Sidra, Baptiste, and Abby are gone. It doesn't matter that I never met Abbygail, the joy of handing over her toy and necklace will stay with me for a long time. They will be treasured, as they deserve to be. Giving her name to this baby is even more satisfying, not only to honor the girl who first carried it, but because, in an odd way, it helps me, as if something of the baby's visit here remains with her, even as she leaves.

Dalton and Storm walk with them for a bit. While they're gone, I hurry out to tell Kenny where I want the hot tub and ask if they can set it up later while I distract Dalton. I swing by the bakery and grab two dozen holiday cookies before they open their doors to the waiting line. I hand out the first dozen to those waiting, promise I'll see them all tonight at the big bonfire celebration. Then I go home.

The moment Dalton walks into the house, I say, "I am so sorry."

"For what?" he says as he walks into the

512

living room, where I'm waiting with coffee and cookies.

"Being a complete and utter selfish bitch. I avoided you last night because I was dealing with Abby leaving. But I'm not the only one affected, and I ignored that. I made it all about me. It wasn't."

He sinks onto the sofa and tugs me down beside him. "I understood. And I think it was harder for you. You bonded with her. Me?" He tilts his head. "I'd have kept her. Happily kept her. But for me she was more of a . . ."

He purses his lips. "She was a glimpse of something else. A vision of a possibility I never really considered. Not just a baby, but a baby with you. A family that's more than you and me. After having Abby here, yeah, I can see that for us, and I think I want it. Except . . ."

He goes quiet, uncomfortably quiet, scratching at his beard.

"Go on."

He sneaks a peek my way.

"Eric? Talk. Tell me what you're thinking. If what you want isn't what I want, we'll discuss that. I'd never hold it against you."

"I like the vision I saw," he says. "If Abby needed a father, I'd be that for her. But since she doesn't, I'm just . . . I'm in no hurry. I . . ." Another glance snuck my way. "I'm not sure I'm ready to share you just yet."

"And I am thrilled to hear that, because I'm not ready to share you either. As much as I loved seeing you with Abby, part of me wants you all to myself for a little longer."

He nods. It's not the decisive nod I expect, though, and I say, "There's more, isn't there?"

"Not about this. Yeah, I'd like a kid some-day. But yeah, I want more time with just us. Seeing Sidra and Baptiste though . . ." A deep breath. "It brought back a lot of memories. They reminded me of my par-ents. Memories of them I didn't even think I still had. How they looked at each other, how they looked at Jacob. How they looked at . . ." Another scratch of his beard as he shrugs.

"How they looked at you."

He nods. "Those kids and that baby, they're a family, and I had that kind of fam-ily."

"A lot of hope," I say. "A lot of love."

His eyes glisten, and he blinks hard with a thick, "Yeah. I need to face that. Remember it. Deal with it." He looks at me. "Talk about it."

"I'm here whenever you're ready."

"I'm ready," he says. "Maybe not for a baby, but I'm ready for this."

"Then I'm ready to listen."

ABOUT THE AUTHOR

Kelley Armstrong graduated with a degree in psychology and then studied computer programming. Now, she is a full-time writer and parent, and she lives with her husband and three children in rural Ontario, Canada.

The employees of Thorndike Press hope you have enjoyed this Large Print book. All our Thorndike, Wheeler, and Kennebec Large Print titles are designed for easy reading, and all our books are made to last. Other Thorndike Press Large Print books are available at your library, through selected bookstores, or directly from us.

For information about titles, please call:
  (800) 223-1244

or visit our website at:
  gale.com/thorndike

To share your comments, please write:
  Publisher
  Thorndike Press
  10 Water St., Suite 310
  Waterville, ME 04901